The
ROSE *of*
WINSLOW
STREET

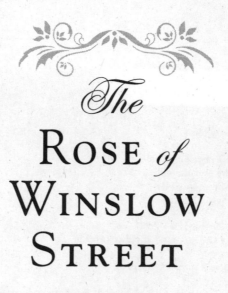

The
ROSE *of*
WINSLOW
STREET

A NOVEL

ELIZABETH CAMDEN

BETHANY HOUSE PUBLISHERS
a division of Baker Publishing Group
Minneapolis, Minnesota

© 2012 by Dorothy Mays

Published by Bethany House Publishers
11400 Hampshire Avenue South
Bloomington, Minnesota 55438
www.bethanyhouse.com

Bethany House Publishers is a division of
Baker Publishing Group, Grand Rapids, Michigan

Printed in the United States of America

Library of Congress Cataloging-in-Publication Data
Camden, Elizabeth, 1948–
        The rose of Winslow Street / Elizabeth Camden.
            p.   cm.
        ISBN 978-0-7642-0895-9 (pbk.)
        I. Title.
    PS3553.A429R67 2012
    813'.54—dc23   2011036841

This is a work of fiction. Names, characters, incidents, and dialogues are products of the author's imagination and are not to be construed as real. Any resemblance to actual events or persons, living or dead, is entirely coincidental.

Cover design by Jennifer Parker

Cover photography by Mike Habermann Photography, LLC

11 12 13 14 15 16 17   7 6 5 4 3 2 1

1

COLDEN, MASSACHUSETTS, 1879

The stately houses of Winslow Street looked utterly safe and respectable in the hot summer evening. Mikhail knew all that was about to change.

He surveyed the neighborhood through the carriage window's narrow opening. Immense sycamore trees sheltered the homes, with only the chattering of a few sparrows to break the tranquility of the evening. A trickle of perspiration slid down the side of Mikhail's face and his fist tightened around the club on his belt. Beside him, Lady Mirela remained rigid as the carriage bumped and rolled over the gently worn cobblestones. Everything about this neighborhood spoke of wealth, stability, and decorum. It hardly looked like a place for the pitched battle that was about to occur.

On the opposite bench, his two boys were playing a game of thumb-wrestling, oblivious to the turmoil roiling inside Mikhail, for he had always sheltered the children from the danger and uncertainty that was so much a part of his world. His gaze flicked to Turk. The man's bulk could barely fit inside the tight confines of the carriage. The wooden box cradled in Turk's ham-sized fists looked ridiculously delicate, but the contents of that box were too precious to be jostled with the rest of the family's belongings piled atop the lumbering carriage. The only ornamentation on the box was the elegant brass hinges that held the lid securely closed. Nothing about its plain appearance hinted at the priceless vials stored within.

The carriage slowed to a halt and Andrei looked up eagerly. "Are we here?" he asked, excitement brimming in the twelve-year-old's eyes. Did the boy's voice crack just a bit? It was the second time Mikhail had noticed that husky tone breaking through the childish voice, indicating his son was on the verge of becoming a man. Normally, Mikhail's heart would have swelled with pride at the symbol of his son's impending manhood, but not this evening.

"Yes, we are here," Mikhail said, forcing his voice to remain calm as he gazed at a stately house, looming three stories tall in the gathering darkness. An elegant wrought-iron fence surrounded the property, but there was no lock on the gate. Embellished with fancy scrolls and spindly bars, the fence was for decoration, not protection. Such a useless gate spoke volumes about the sense of security these people took for granted. His mouth thinned and years of training urged him to wrap his hand around the revolver tucked in his pocket, but he stifled the impulse. Tonight called for clear-headed courage, not brute force. He looked at Andrei. "I want you to stay in the carriage and look out for Lady Mirela. Is that clear?"

Andrei would probably rather look after a hive of bees than stay with the ominously silent woman who accompanied them, but Mikhail gave the boy no choice. "Okay," Andrei finally said.

Mikhail locked eyes with Turk, the only other person in the carriage who understood the magnitude of what they were up against this evening. "Guard the box," he said to Turk as he twisted the handle of the carriage. "I will take only Joseph with me. There is no need for too much manpower on our first approach. Tonight, we will rely on the law to get what we want. Force is our last resort," he said as he stepped down into the street.

The green, woodsy scent of hawthorn trees surrounded him as he emerged from the carriage. It was a good omen, yes? A place that smelled this fine would surely be a safe place to bring his family to live.

The carriage springs creaked and groaned as Joseph climbed down from the driver's seat. Mikhail and Turk were both large men, but Joseph was a giant. Like Mikhail, Joseph wore a coat constructed of battle-worn leather and heavy boots that were just as rugged. Beneath their coats were knives and loaded pistols, and Mikhail carried the same blunt battle stick that had served him through two wars in the Balkans.

"Let me do all the talking," Mikhail said as they strode up the path leading to the silent house. Reaching through the useless gate, he unlatched the double doors to stare at his home. It was so much more impressive than it appeared in the faded photograph he'd carried with him all these years. The grainy picture could not capture the dramatic contrast between the red bricks and the crisp white trim, nor did it show the beauty of the three stained-glass windows gracing the top story of the house. There were no lights burning behind the windows, and the long evening shadows meant it would be dark inside the house.

Mikhail's and Joseph's boots thudded on the wooden planking as they mounted the steps of the porch. Mikhail slid to a window and peered through the delicate lace draperies that did nothing to shield the interior of the house from prying eyes. He would have to fix that once the house was his, but he could not be concerned with such trivialities now. The well-being of his entire family depended upon the next few minutes, and Mikhail's eyes narrowed as he peered inside.

His breath caught, and he could not believe his good fortune. Dustcovers draped the furniture, making the pieces look like ghosts in the vacant room. The fireplace was closed off with a wooden screen, and there was no sign of life inside the home. Relief surged

7

through Mikhail as he made the sign of the cross over the front of his body.

"Slip around back and make sure no servants are home," he whispered to Joseph. Mikhail stepped away from the window, noting the spider's web stretching across the upper corner of the front doorframe. By the time Joseph returned, Mikhail was confident that the house had been vacant for some time.

"No one home," Joseph said quietly. "The house looks closed up for summer."

Mikhail removed a stiletto from his boot and began working the lock. "Then the house is ours. Go get the others."

At another time he might have been more careful with the task. He could have picked the lock, but he needed to get his family and the precious wooden box inside quickly. With a turn of his wrist he wrenched the lock from its moorings and pulled it free. A musty odor seeped from the house the moment he opened the door, but that did not stop the rush of triumph that flooded his veins as he stepped inside.

He turned to watch for the others and his heart swelled at the sight of his son helping Lady Mirela from the carriage. Mirela was not the easiest person to deal with, but his son was behaving exactly like a man should as he held his hand out to the fragile young woman descending from the carriage. His younger son was not so cautious. Lucca took a flying leap down from the carriage, tumbling to the grass on his hands and knees, but springing up with a huge grin as he was liberated from the tight confines of the carriage they had been riding in since leaving Boston. Mikhail squatted down to catch his son as Lucca came flying into his arms.

"Is this our new house?" he asked, gaping through the open front door.

"This is our *home*," Mikhail said with conviction. He set Lucca down and stood to watch Turk step carefully up the pathway, holding the wooden box as gingerly as if it were made of eggshells.

Everyone was exhausted from eleven months of travel. They had traveled over the war-torn lands of the Balkans and endured weeks of misery as they crossed the Mediterranean Sea and finally the mighty Atlantic Ocean. These last few days traveling overland should have been the easiest part of the journey, but knowledge about the pending encounter kept Mikhail on edge. Now that he had taken the house so easily, half the battle had been won.

He looked Lady Mirela directly in her eyes and winced at the anxiety lurking within them. "Never again will we be driven from our land or fear marauders in the night. I will defend this home with my life. You will be safe here."

Mirela did not respond, just stood in that listless manner of hers, her deep blue eyes looking decades older than her paltry nineteen years.

"Can we go inside?" Lucca's childish voice asked.

It would soon be dark and they needed to get moved in as fast as possible. "You and Andrei go find a bedroom for the pair of you. And one for Lady Mirela as well."

Both boys scampered inside, racing up the wooden staircase that graced the front hallway. Mikhail would give his right arm if he could siphon off just a tiny fraction of their energy into Mirela's vacant spirit, but perhaps it was still too early for her. Repairing something that had been shattered into a thousand pieces would take time, but patience was not Mikhail's strong suit. If his children needed food, he would kill a stag and drag it home. If his family was cold, he would chop down a tree for wood to warm them, but the dragon tormenting Mirela could not be conquered so easily.

Mikhail's boots clomped loudly against the parquet floors as he walked into the parlor. He pulled a sheet from a high-back chair, the whisper of fabric slicing through the quiet. Dust motes swirled in the air as he tugged another sheet from a table.

Whoever lived here had strange taste. The mismatched furniture and curious portrait above the fireplace were testament to that. The oil painting showed a thin, balding man with a fringe of wild gray hair who was staring straight out of the frame. In one hand the man held a strange contraption of disks and wheels—a gyroscope? Mikhail had heard of gyroscopes but never seen one. The wobbling disks and wheels were used for measuring momentum, but how strange to hold one in a portrait. The man's owlish eyes seemed to glow with delight as he held the gyroscope aloft and stared straight out of the portrait. Possibly the oddest picture Mikhail had ever seen.

The walls were painted a curious shade of pale green and covered with strange contraptions: an oversized compass, an assortment of maps, and something that looked like a mechanical fan.

Turk stood in the doorway, holding the small box in his mighty hands. "Turk, get that box inside and find a safe place to secure it. Stand guard over it and don't leave it for a second. Joseph and I will unload the baggage."

Three trunks, four satchels, and a single cherrywood box holding four glass vials. Aside from the house he had just claimed, these items amounted to all Mikhail had left in the world. The muscles of his shoulders bunched as he hauled a trunk from the top of the carriage. With a mighty heave he hoisted the trunk over his shoulder, shifting its weight so it sat more securely.

No, these were *not* all his worldly goods. Mikhail grinned as he trudged through the ridiculous gate, carrying his burden. The most precious things in his universe had just scampered up those steps along with Lady Mirela, who was now a part of their unconventional family. He had always liked Mirela, and now that she was under his care, he was determined to see no future tragedy would ever tarnish her luminous spirit.

As the others carried the last of the baggage inside, Mikhail stood on the porch gazing at the broadleaf trees that surrounded his house and shaded the street. The trees were some form of hawthorn, but he had never seen that precise shape of leaf. So many things were different here in America. For one thing, in Romania he would have to chop all these trees down. It was impossible to protect a house from invaders who could skulk behind a profusion of leafy foliage and wide trunks of the trees.

A movement caught his attention. The drapes in the house across the street had just moved. The fabric pulled to the side and the curious face of an elderly woman peeked out at him. Remaining motionless, Mikhail scanned the windows in the other houses up and down the street. Only the old woman behind the drapes and a man trimming a hedge two doors down were watching him. Mikhail forced himself to relax as he adopted a negligent pose and leaned against the doorframe. He smiled and nodded at the woman, as though he had every right in the world to claim this house.

Which he did. The legal documents carefully stitched into the lining of his jacket were proof of that, and soon everyone on Winslow Street would know it. Now that they were safely in America, he would ask Lady Mirela to remove the stitching so he could have the papers ready.

When Mikhail entered the house again, he wished he had not been so hasty when he destroyed the lock on the front door. That would need to be repaired in short order. He closed the door and hauled a heavy walnut table in front of the doorway to provide a barrier overnight, then followed the sound of voices to the back of the house, where Joseph and Turk were in the kitchen. The spacious room was lined with cheerful yellow tile and white enamel equipment that stood in sharp contrast to the battle-ax, club, two hunting knives, and double-barreled shotgun his men had laid on the kitchen table.

"Where is the box?" Mikhail asked.

Without a word, Turk opened a cupboard to reveal the cherry-wood box stored safely out of sight.

"We'll take turns standing guard overnight," Mikhail said. "The neighbors have already noticed we are here."

The second half of the battle would begin tomorrow, and Mikhail was under no illusions it would go as easily as the first.

⊘

Four-hundred twenty-three American dollars.

That was all he had remaining to his name after paying for use of the carriage and transportation from the port of Boston to the small town of Colden, Massachusetts. Mikhail put the money back in his billfold and slid it into a cupboard in the parlor, right beside the precious wooden box. Last night, he and his men decided to move the box to the parlor, as the risk of a fire in the kitchen was too great a hazard. The box would be safe in the parlor cupboard during the day, where it would be easy to guard, and Mikhail would take it to his bedroom each night.

Mikhail had given Joseph a few dollars to buy something to eat in the marketplace, but food was not going to be his biggest expense. He had no idea how much an American attorney would cost, but he was going to need one to secure his ownership of the house. His gaze tracked across the fine interior of the sitting room, bathed in early morning light filtering through the lace draperies. Stripped of the dustcovers, it was an extraordinary house filled with a huge array of curiosities. Whoever had been living here was going to fight to regain possession, so Mikhail could not afford to scrimp when hiring an attorney.

A clatter of footsteps sounded from the stairs, and Mikhail swept his worries aside. He lowered his voice. "Don't tell me our new house has rodents," he growled. "Who else would be up this early other than some bothersome dormouse?"

Both boys came bounding down the stairs and Lucca leapt into Mikhail's outstretched arms. At eight years old, the boy was still young enough to worship his father, and Mikhail savored every moment of Lucca's adoration. The war against the Serbs had robbed him of these years when Andrei was young, but he would never again be parted from either of his boys. He buried his smile in his son's light brown hair, the identical shade as Mikhail and Andrei.

"You know it is just me," Lucca said in Romanian.

"Yes, I do," Mikhail said slowly, carefully enunciating the English words. He had been teaching his boys the language on the tedious voyage across the sea, but he still worried Lucca might not be ready for school come September. He tilted the boy's head back so he could smile down into his face. "I love you, but you are still a bothersome mouse," he said in the same, slowly pronounced English. "I could eat you for breakfast and still be hungry."

The thud of Joseph's tread at the front door signaled his return. "I've got food," he said as he held aloft a loaf of bread and a round of cheese. Joseph ripped the bread into chunks and tossed them to the boys, who grabbed them and began tearing into them like hungry animals.

"Give me that cheese," Mikhail said. He carried it to the kitchen, but saw no proper cutting knives in plain view. He was famished and his hatchet was propped against the kitchen wall. There was a massive wooden drainboard beside the enamel sink that would serve perfectly well. Michael set the round of cheese atop it and rendered it in two perfect halves with one clean stroke of his hatchet. The boys were delighted.

Mikhail winked at them. "Do you think I can chop the rest of it into even pieces?"

"Do it, Papa! Do it!" Andrei said. A moment later he had eight perfectly split wedges of cheese. It was not until he lifted the cheese that he saw a fresh crack splitting the center of the drainboard. The force of his hatchet must have been heavier than he'd intended.

Andrei's eyes grew as round as saucers. "Are we going to get in trouble for that?"

Mikhail winced at the sight of the cracked board. The house now belonged to him, but he had no claim to the belongings and should have been more careful. Still, the damage was done and there was no undoing it. "No, boy. But from now on we will prepare our food with the proper tools."

Andrei ripped off a huge chunk of bread with his teeth. "Okay." Marie, Mikhail's late wife, would have been horrified at such manners, but fancy etiquette had never been Mikhail's strong suit. Perhaps now that Lady Mirela was living with them, they should all make an effort to become a little more civilized.

He straightened. There were many things that were going to change now that they were in America. He snapped his fingers. "Now, listen up, boys," he said in his voice that meant business. "I want you to begin calling Lady Mirela by a new name. In America, she is to be known as your aunt Mirela. Is that clear?"

Andrei furrowed his brow. "But she is not our aunt."

"She is now," Mikhail answered. He did not want to go into the complicated family history that these boys were too young to comprehend, but it was vital that the outside world perceive them as a closely knit family. "I want you to call her Aunt and forget she ever used to be known as Lady Mirela. I have already spoken with her and she agrees it is best that way. She is a part of our family now, so I think this is appropriate."

The boys seemed a little puzzled, but they would do as he directed. "And another thing," he continued. "We are Americans now, and I want to be known as Michael. It is a good name for an American."

Both children looked confused. "Mikhail is not an American name?" Andrei asked.

Michael shrugged his shoulders. "It is not as American as Michael. It is the name I wish to be known as." He tugged a lock of Andrei's hair. "Though you should still call me Papa."

"Is Lucca an American name?" his younger boy asked.

Michael thought carefully before he answered. For over a decade he had dreamed, fought, planned, and struggled to make his way to America. In all those years he had kept a picture of this house and a tattered copy of the Gettysburg Address in his billfold to remind him what he was fighting for. He had plenty of time to envision how his life would change once he finally made it to America, but his children were still bewildered by their new world. "America is a land of immigrants," he said. "You can use a Romanian name or an American name. It is very important that a man has a name he is proud of. Lucca is a good, strong name. A saint's name."

"How do you say it in American?" Lucca asked.

Michael considered the question. "I suppose the Americans would say *Luke*." He laid his hand on his boy's head and met the child's eyes. "But this is your choice, son. You can choose to go by Lucca or you can go by Luke. They are both names any man would be proud to bear."

His son stood a little taller. "I want to be Luke."

"Luke it is, then." Michael turned his focus to Andrei, who had his arms crossed over his chest.

"I'm not changing my name," he said. "My name is Andrei and I'm not changing it just because we had to come to America."

Michael noticed the edge of belligerence in the boy's tone, but he approved. This boy was no mollycoddle who would be pressured to change his ways to suit others. He was proud his son had the power of conviction and would stick to it. "If a man feels strongly about his name, he should fight for it. Luke and I have chosen new names, but I think it is right for you to be Andrei. It is your choice."

It seemed to settle the boy down a bit, but the sound of voices from outside caught his attention. "We have company," Michael said in a low voice.

Turk and Joseph both stood and walked a little closer to the weapons, but Michael held up his hand. He could see the worry in his children's eyes and did not want them to be afraid. Darting to the front room, Michael peered through the lace curtains. A bit of tension drained from him at the sight of two old men and a young man who barely looked old enough to shave standing on the front sidewalk.

He strode back to the kitchen. "It is likely just some neighbors, coming to say hello," Michael said to his sons. "Still, this is best handled by adults, so run upstairs and see if your aunt Mirela is awake." He tossed a piece of cheese to Andrei. "Give her this for breakfast and keep her abovestairs for now."

After the children were gone, Michael pulled on his leather jacket, briefly touching the slit where Mirela had unstitched the pocket to provide ready access to the legal documents. He peered through the flimsy drapes to scrutinize the trio standing on the walkway, indecision in their stances as they put their heads together to talk. They carried no weapons, and their light summer clothing made it unlikely they had anything of substance hidden beneath. Finally, the young one began moving in hesitant steps up the walkway, the two elders following behind.

"Stand guard over the box," Michael whispered as the footsteps thudded on the front porch. A knock on the door sounded a second later.

Michael adjusted the collar of his shirt before he answered the door. "Good morning," he said to the three men. The young one stood in front, and to Michael's surprise, the lad had a badge pinned to his shirt. Was the town of Colden so short on warriors they were recruiting boys to be sheriffs?

"Good morning," the young man said. "I am Sheriff Albert Barnes, and this is Mr. Stockdale, who lives across the street, and Mr. Auckland, the town librarian."

Michael nodded to all three. "I am pleased to meet you," he said in carefully enunciated English. He added no other comment, and the silence was broken only by a sparrow chattering in a nearby hawthorn tree.

The sheriff cleared his throat, his Adam's apple bobbing on his thin neck. "And you are . . . ?"

"I am Michael Dobrescu, just arrived from Romania. I am very pleased to meet you," he said simply.

All three men appeared anxious, glancing at each other, then finally back to Michael. "Forgive me, Mr. Dobrescu," the sheriff said, "but do you have Professor Sawyer's permission to use his house? We were under the impression that it would remain vacant for the summer."

Professor Sawyer. So this was the name of the man he would be battling for ownership of the house. He forced his voice and face to remain calm, for he had no disagreement with these men. "Why would I need someone's permission to use my own house?"

The young sheriff's eyes widened and he cleared his throat again. "Professor Sawyer has owned this house for years."

Mr. Stockdale, the elderly neighbor who lived across the street, stepped forward. "The professor has lived here for twenty-three years," he said. "He moved in the year after my youngest son was born."

Michael's resolve hardened. "Then he has been a trespasser in my house for twenty-three years."

Mr. Stockdale took another step closer and peered directly into Michael's face. In particular, he scrutinized the thin scar that ran from the corner of Michael's eyebrow and down the length of his face. "Are you right in the head, man? Everyone knows this house belongs to Willard Sawyer. He raised his family here. That is his portrait hanging over the mantelpiece."

So the peculiar man holding the gyroscope was the person he would do battle with. The elderly neighbor had not stopped speaking. "The professor has lived here for twenty-three years, and I have been here thirty-one years. It was February of 1848 when I moved in, the same day the Mexican-American War ended."

Michael had not expected anyone to have lived on this street for such a length of time, but that was all to the good. "If you have lived here that long, then perhaps you remember Constantine Dobrescu?"

Mr. Stockdale snorted. "Crazy old Cossack, of course I remember him. The man planted corn and potatoes in the front yard. Strangest man I ever knew. Professor Sawyer bought this house after the old Cossack died."

"That is not possible," Michael said calmly. He extracted the papers from his pocket and held them aloft. "That crazy old Cossack was my uncle and he left this property to me. These papers prove that. This house is mine."

Michael knew he sounded blunt, but his English was not good enough to express it any better. His own homeland was no longer a suitable place to live, and he had access to a perfectly good house in America. No longer would his sons or Lady Mirela live under the cloud of warfare, not if there was a safe place for them in America.

Mr. Auckland, the town's librarian, rubbed his chin. "Come to think of it, I remember this house falling to pieces after the old Cossack died. The yard went to ruin and the gutters were falling from the roof. The town had the house declared a nuisance."

Recollection bloomed on the neighbor's face. "You're right. It was a disaster. Professor Sawyer had to spend a fortune setting the place to rights again."

Michael's eyes narrowed. The fact that the professor spent a considerable sum to repair the house did not bode well. It was a complication, but one he would overcome. "The wonderful thing about America is your legal system," Michael said. "I have long admired your courts, and I believe the U.S. Constitution to be the greatest document ever written by human hands." He replaced the copy of his uncle's will in his breast pocket and laid his hand over it. "I have researched the law in America and know I am entitled to this house. I am prepared to let the courts review the evidence

18

and accept their decision. Until then, I bid you a good day," he said as he closed the door in their bewildered faces.

Michael did not move a muscle until he heard the footsteps of the three men retreat from the door and descend the steps.

Turk's voice came from behind him. "They will be back soon."

Grim resolve hardened Michael's features. "I know."

2

All apothecary shops had a distinct odor, and not a particularly good one, but Liberty Sawyer savored the scent because it meant she was buying supplies for her paints. Ready-mixed paints were an option, but there was something about grinding her own pigments and mixing them with solvent and glycerin to coax out the perfect shade of color that soothed her. Some people dreamed of buried treasure or handsome princes—Libby dreamed of watercolors.

When they arrived on St. Catherine's Island last month, she thought she had mixed enough paint to last for the summer, but in recent weeks swarms of neighborhood children had taken to following her about the island and she could not resist letting the little ones dabble in her paints. No sooner had she selected a subject to paint and set up her easel than the children began to find her. Sometimes they simply watched her, other times she gave them the brushes and encouraged them to experiment. Was there anything more dazzling than watching a child discover the beauty of the world? The summer was her best season for painting because the rest of the year was consumed with helping her father on his mechanical designs. The professor never allowed children in their house on Winslow Street for fear they might damage one of his contraptions, but on the island Libby could enjoy the children's natural exuberance as they spattered paint and created outrageous color combinations.

Libby's gaze tracked across the bottles lined up on the apothecary's shelves, her expert eye for color and texture honing in on exactly what she needed. She held one of the jars to the light and wiggled it, knowing that gum arabic had a slightly different viscosity than gum karaya.

"Libby? Liberty Sawyer?"

Libby whirled around to see elderly Mr. Alger approaching her, pleased surprise on his face. "I had not expected to see you here, but perfect . . . *perfect*!" he exclaimed. "My roses are dying and I don't know what to do."

Libby set the jar of gum arabic back on the shelf. A few years ago, Mr. Alger had admired one of Libby's paintings of the fabulous double-blooming Gallica roses she grew at her house on Winslow Street and she had supplied him with cuttings. Gallica roses were famous for their opulent display of petals, but they could be as finicky as a young girl preening for compliments. It was no surprise that Mr. Alger was having trouble with them in this beachside climate.

"What seems to be the problem?" she asked kindly. After all, she was flattered Mr. Alger had asked for cuttings from her mother's garden. She loved that rose garden so much it was hard to tear herself away each summer to go to the beach house. After her mother died, no one else shared Libby's intense interest in the world of plants, so she was thrilled when Mr. Alger asked for the cuttings.

"They have looked peaked for weeks, so I added a little more fertilizer to the soil. It didn't seem to help, and now I have tiny white insects clinging to the underside of the leaves."

Libby bit the side of her thumb, contemplating the problem. With the sandy soil on the island, roses needed a massive amount of fertilizer, but it was possible Mr. Alger had overdone it. "What did you use in your fertilizer mix?" she asked.

Then Mr. Alger did the most humiliating thing he could do to Libby. He removed a small slip of paper from his pocket, unfolded it, and handed it to her. "Here is the recipe. The apothecary recommended it, but perhaps you know something better?"

Libby stared at the page. The letters wavered and jumped before she could make any sense of them. Mr. Alger was waiting for her answer, but instead of a kindly old man, it felt like her father was looming over her, berating her in that harsh voice. Heat broke out across her body and an itchy sensation prickled beneath her dress, but Libby forced herself to concentrate on the list. She knew the likely chemicals that would appear in a fertilizer recipe, so she narrowed her eyes and stared hard, trying to recognize a single word among the flickering, jumpy letters.

At twenty-eight years old, Liberty Sawyer would rather walk down the street stark naked than admit to her illiteracy. Everyone in her hometown of Colden had been witness to her colossal failures in grammar school, but no one on St. Catherine's Island knew. Why couldn't one of those tidy apothecary jars tip over and conveniently burst into flame? Anything to divert attention from her inability to make sense of the neatly printed list in her hand. Her heartbeat thumped so hard she was certain Mr. Alger could hear it as he looked at her with expectation.

"Can I help you?" Peter Davidson, the apothecary, asked as he stepped forward. Libby breathed a sigh of relief and passed the list to him. "Mr. Alger reports that his roses are still ailing. Now they are suffering from aphids as well."

Who would have guessed that her salvation would come in the form of a balding, bespectacled apothecary? The fist squeezing her heart eased and her body resumed its normal temperature.

"I suppose you might add more phosphate to the mix," the apothecary said after studying the list. He continued to outline suggestions for the fertilizer, but had no idea what to do to discourage the aphids.

"Try a little garlic oil," Libby suggested. "Spray it on the roses on a cool morning. It will stink for a few hours, but the aphids hate it."

Mr. Alger thanked them and purchased the necessary supplies. Libby continued to walk down the shelves, ignoring the labels on the glass jars and picking out what she needed based on the item's shade, texture, and scent. She was accustomed to the adjustments her illiteracy inflicted on her and made her purchases without difficulty.

One of these days her mortifying secret would probably be discovered by the people of St. Catherine's Island, and when it happened, there would be a subtle shift in their attitude toward her. The invisible walls would be erected, the bewildered shaking of heads and whispering behind hands would begin. Such a clever girl, they would murmur. Why did she never apply herself in school? More than her next breath of air, Libby longed to be a normal woman who could have a family and children who would fling their chubby arms around her despite her flaws.

It would never happen. No doctor could promise Libby that her children would not inherit her mental defect, so it was wiser to lavish her love on the children who flocked around her in the neighborhood. Libby stepped outside into the cloudless May morning, knowing it would be a perfect day for painting. Last evening, the tide had washed ashore a fabulous specimen of driftwood she ached to paint. The twisty, craggy striations that arched across the surface of the silvery wood were a marvel of the Lord's work. How curious that sometimes objects became more beautiful as they weathered the storms and traumas of the world. What caused some wood to rot and decay into nothing, while other pieces of wood became burnished, splendid, and tougher under the relentless assault of the pounding ocean current?

Whatever the answer, Libby would celebrate the spectacular piece of driftwood by capturing its image in watercolor. If a handful of the island's children interrupted her, so be it. She would share her paints and try to teach them to see the splendor in the humble piece of driftwood.

If her artist's eye had given her nothing else, it taught her to see beauty where few others noticed it.

Michael moved from room to room, assessing the strange contents of the house and trying to learn something about Professor Willard Sawyer.

All Michael could conclude was that a crazy man had been living there. The house was stuffed with oddities. Measuring scales, telescopes, and gadgets littered the home. On a table where most people would have placed a vase of flowers, the professor had a contraption that seemed designed to automatically sharpen pencils. All those levers, flywheels, and pulleys to sharpen a pencil? But when he pulled a lever, a whir of clicking sounds triggered the machine to life and loaded up one pencil after another for sharpening.

In the middle of the formal dining room sat a bizarre pedaled contraption with cables connecting it to a fan encased behind a wire cage. Turk was fascinated and settled his huge frame into the chair to pedal the fan to life. Luke stood beside it and laughed as the cool breeze lifted his hair. The house had a personality, there was no disputing that, but the only thing that really bothered Michael was hanging in a closet in an upstairs bedroom.

A woman lived here. The wardrobe was filled with dresses and neatly arranged ladies' shoes. He felt bad about dispossessing the people who lived here, as they had taken care of the house and felt entitled to it, but it was business and it needed to be done. A man would be able to understand that. Women were far more fragile, and if there was one thing Michael could not bear, it was a woman's tears. Seeing the telltale rim of moisture pooling at the bottom of a woman's eyes was all it took to make him helpless. When a woman's voice wobbled with impending tears, all his extravagant strength and courage collapsed like a withered leaf in a gust of autumn wind. This had made living with Lady Mirela these past few months a particular challenge.

"Papa, come look!" Andrei's voice beckoned him from the home's library. He had told Andrei to search for some books that were written for children. As much as he would like to find some simple reading material for his boys to practice their English, he dreaded discovering anything that would indicate a child lived in this home. Men became fierce when protecting the security of their children, and he prayed Professor Sawyer had none. He strode to the room that was entirely covered with bookshelves.

"Look what we found under the sofa!" His boys were sprawled on the floor, and between them lay an oversized painting, a florid botanical painting unlike anything Michael had seen before.

"Is it real?" Luke asked. The silvery green petals were lush as they unfurled across the parchment, surrounding a huge saffron bloom so lifelike it looked three-dimensional. Another bud in the lower corner of the plant was still closed but on the verge of blooming. Any moment he expected those ripe petals to break away from the bud and animate the page.

"It's not real," he said, still fascinated by the painting. Unbidden, his hand reached out to touch one of the leaves. He almost expected to feel the velvety flesh of a leaf, so exquisitely had the tiny silver hairs been layered atop the mossy green density of the leaf. Some of the leaves curled away to show a delicate tracery of veins stretching across their underside.

"Can I touch it too?" Andrei asked.

Michael withdrew his hand and shook his head. "Paintings do not like to be handled, and I should not have touched it. We must be very careful with this, as whoever owns it must treasure it very much."

Although it was completely vulnerable beneath that sofa. There was no matting or frame to protect the heavy parchment. Luke twisted around and poked his head beneath the sofa. "There are more of them under here. Come look."

Michael dropped to his hands and knees and saw the stack, of which only a few were framed. Using as much care as his large hands could manage, he slid the stack out into the light of day.

"Wow," Andrei whispered as he looked at the painting on the top of the stack. A profusion of herbs sprawled forth in a riot across the page. This painting was even more fabulous than the one before. At first glance Michael thought it seemed like a tangle of green herbs, but closer inspection revealed tones of purple, silver, and blue tingeing the leaves. There were soft fleshy petals of thyme, waxy needles of rosemary, and the serrated edges of spearmint. So lifelike was the painting he almost expected the pungent scent of herbs to seep from the page.

The paintings were unsigned, but whoever the artist was, Michael knew he would like the man. The artist had more than artistic talent. It was obvious he had an affinity for the botanical world, and Michael recognized a kindred spirit. He lifted the painting of the herbs to reveal a bloom as elegantly executed as the others. Vibrant burnt-orange petals filled the page in an opulent display.

"What is that flower called?" Luke asked.

"I don't know," Michael admitted. "Many of the plants in America will be different from what we are used to back home."

"I like these pictures," Luke said. "Let's take down the picture of the scary old man and put up one of these instead."

It was not a bad idea. Michael disliked looking at Professor Sawyer every time he entered the parlor, the man's blank stare as he held the strange gyroscope a constant reminder of the family he was evicting. Michael picked up a framed painting of a spectacular amaryllis. "Let's hang this one up over the fireplace," he said. "Slide the others back under the sofa and keep your hands off them. Grubby boys and fancy parchment are not a good mix."

He lifted the picture gently, knowing that he must not damage anything in the house. He still felt bad about the drainboard he had cracked while cleaving the cheese into pieces, but it had been worth it to see the delight in his boys' eyes. He had been showing off his skill with the hatchet, which was stupid, but it felt good to be a family again. For a few hours that morning he had felt like a normal man waking up in his home and sharing a laugh with his children. He had been only twenty-four when Andrei was born, but the war meant he rarely had a chance to enjoy the simple pleasures most men probably took for granted. Now, at thirty-six, Michael would finally learn what it was like to be a normal father who did not have to fear separation from his children ever again.

He took down the portrait of Professor Sawyer and gave it to Andrei to hold.

"What are you doing?" Mirela asked from the far side of the room. She had been there all this time and no one even noticed her.

"Just swapping this picture out for a better one," he said.

"And Joseph and Turk? Where are they?" Sometimes it was hard to tell if Mirela was being bossy or if she was afraid. Or, most likely, a combination of the two. Had there ever been a woman with such a unique combination of kindness and autocratic will-power as Mirela?

"I sent them to town for supplies," he said. "I have discovered an old greenhouse in the backyard. It is in disrepair, but it can be fixed and brought back into service."

Mirela's eyes narrowed. She had the exact same shade of stormy blue eyes as Michael, but that was where the resemblance ended. Mirela's skin was like ivory and her hair a glossy black sheen she brushed a hundred strokes each night. "Michael, please don't make any more changes to this house. We can't afford it, and a green-house is a luxury."

He shook his head. "We need that greenhouse. I will be able to plant the seeds I brought from Romania. Too much of our fortune is wrapped up in those seeds to be careless with them, and the greenhouse is a godsend."

Andrei looked at him curiously. "Why can't we just plant them in the ground? Why do they need a greenhouse?"

Michael cast a wary glance out the window. It was a hot, humid day in late May, but autumn was coming and he knew the winters of New England would be harsher than anything they had known in Romania. "Our seedlings will be too young to survive the winter without a little help. A greenhouse can do that for them."

Mirela sank down onto an oversized leather chair. She looked as fragile as a porcelain doll as she was enveloped by the carved sides of the wing-back chair, but she smiled a bit as she curled her legs beneath her like a little girl. "I'm sure you'll take good care of your plants, Michael. Just like you look after all of us. I wish I could do more to help."

He swung his head in her direction, looking for any trace that she might be on the verge of breaking down. In the last few months, Mirela had finally regained a semblance of normalcy, but every day had been a struggle. On the ship across the ocean she had been forced into close proximity with hundreds of strangers, but she never once complained, even though she sometimes clenched her fists until her knuckles went white.

"You *have* helped us," Michael asserted. "Look at how quickly the boys are learning English now that you have been teaching them."

"You don't have to say that just to make me feel good," she said. It was true that Mirela had been a burden since the day she fled to his house last year, but considering the type of life she had been born to lead, her courage in following them into the unknown was extraordinary. Still, the hopeless tone in Mirela's voice was obvious, and Michael rubbed the ridge of the scar that marred his cheek, wondering what life would have been like for Mirela had she chosen to remain in Europe. He pivoted and strode to kneel down beside her chair. His voice was low but firm.

"Stop saying you are not helpful to us," he said. "You complete our family merely by existing. We would be a pack of barnyard animals if you were not here to keep us in line." She dropped her gaze as though she did not believe him, which was maddening because Mirela was the finest person he had ever known.

He grabbed her hand, imploring her to look at him. "Mirela, you were two weeks old the first time I saw you. I remember when your baby carriage was wheeled into the garden. You wore the most extravagant baby gown I've ever seen, with little pearls and lace covering every inch. The sun was shining and your tiny face was squeezed up like you were sucking a lemon, but for me, it was love at first sight. From that moment I would have stepped in front of a stampeding cavalry for you. You are the reason men fight battles and write symphonies. We *need* you, Mirela."

And for the first time in almost a year, when tears started to pool in the bottom of Mirela's eyes, they were tears of happiness. How many months had he watched Mirela wobble on the thin edge between reason and despair? If she could pull through this suffocating wall of despondency, Mirela's true spirit would emerge like a piece of white hot metal that had been tempered and strengthened by the firestorm she had endured. "You belong with us," he said with conviction. "You are my sister. We are a family, and we are *home*."

Two fat tears grew larger and spilled down Mirela's cheeks as she traced a finger down the scar on Michael's face. "I never really felt like I had a family until you took me in," she said in a fragile voice. "All of you have been so kind to me. I could not ask for a better family."

Michael swallowed hard against the tug in his throat and a suspicious sting behind his eyes. If this sentimental talk did not stop, he was going to be un-manned in front of his boys. He gave Mirela's hand a good shaking. "Tell me I am the best brother you have ever had."

She gave a watery gulp of laughter. "That is certainly true!"

"The most handsome too."

A glint of humor showed in her eyes. "Dearest Michael, I am afraid you are now pushing things."

And Michael breathed a sigh of relief. For now, Mirela was back on an even keel.

3

All the despair in the world was encapsulated in Tillie's precious little five-year-old face. Libby knelt beside the child on the floor of her brother's summer cottage and saw tears well in Tillie's huge brown eyes, her lower lip trembling with pure tragic grief. A pint-sized Joan of Arc, misunderstood and condemned by the world.

"Mama says I have to go to bed and I'm going to miss the eclipse," she sobbed.

Libby wanted to scoop the child up and kiss the tears away, but she was only Tillie's aunt, not her mother. For weeks Libby had been telling all the children on the island about tonight's rare lunar eclipse. First the edge of the moon would darken, and then the darkness would gradually overtake the moon until finally the whole moon would take on an eerie red glow. Libby invited the children of the neighborhood to meet in the backyard of her brother's cottage to watch the extraordinary event. Libby and Tillie spent the afternoon making gingersnap cookies and lemonade for the festivities. It promised to be a magical night beneath the stars as they gathered on blankets to watch the miracle of nature that was about to occur.

Only now her sister-in-law had ordered Tillie to bed. It seemed cruel for Regina to send Tillie to bed just as the eclipse was about to begin. For days Libby had prepared the children for the eclipse party and would never have included Tillie in those excited conversations if she'd known the child could not attend. Libby knew how it felt to be excluded, and she would face down a firing squad to prevent inflicting such anguish on any child.

Tillie's arms were fierce as they clung to her. "I wish you were my mommy," she sobbed into Libby's neck.

Libby's eyes widened. "Shh, baby. You have a wonderful mommy," she managed to say. "She loves you and is just trying to do her best." *And Cleopatra was just another homemaker struggling to make ends meet.* Libby hoped that white lies weren't really a sin, but didn't Regina know how long Tillie had been anticipating this evening?

Libby closed her eyes and held Tillie closer, savoring the feel of the little arms clinging to her, of the baby-fine curls against her cheek. These summers with Tillie were the best part of her year. Ever since her brother bought this cottage, she and her father had spent their summers on the island. Jasper ran the only bank in their hometown of Colden, Massachusetts, and owned a splendid house in town and one on the island to show for his hard work.

"What has my princess down in the dumps?" Jasper asked. Libby looked over Tillie's glossy curls to see her brother and Regina framed in the kitchen doorway.

"The poor dear is all aflutter about this silly eclipse," Regina said, which triggered a fresh wave of sobs from Tillie. "Only grown-ups can stay awake long enough to watch eclipses, honey," Regina said. "Look at how overtired you are already. We need to get you to bed before you make yourself sick with all this foolishness."

Jasper's dark brows lowered in annoyance. "If we send her up now, we will be listening to her shake the rafters all night. What time is the eclipse?"

Libby's quick glance out the window revealed that children from the island were already beginning to gather in the yard. Their excited chatter filled the night air as they sat on the spread-out blankets covering the rough scrub grass. One of the O'Donnell boys was making spooky sounds while the other children squealed in delight.

"It's a little early yet," Libby said. "The moon won't start to darken for another twenty minutes or so."

Jasper checked the watch that was hanging from a chain on his vest and Libby held her breath, praying he would permit Tillie to stay at least until the moon took on the red glow. "We won't have any peace if we send her to bed now," he said. "And I can't see how another hour is going to knock Tillie off her schedule for more than a day or so. Let her join the other kids."

With her cool blond beauty, Regina was like an ivory rose that remained utterly gorgeous despite a storm brewing around her. Her southern accent had a musical lilt as she turned her doe eyes to Libby. "I know you have not had the opportunity to read *Dr. Goodman's Manual on Childcare*," she said sweetly, "but this sort of overstimulation can ruin a child for days."

Libby caught the veiled barb even though it flew right past Jasper, whose mouth hardened into a thin line as he glared once again at his watch. Despite his law school training, he only had about a fifty-fifty record when it came to battles with Regina. "Libby, take Tillie outside while I talk with Regina. I'll let you know shortly what we decide."

"Good plan," Libby said as she rose to her feet, Tillie still huddled in her arms. She scooped up a tray of the gingersnaps before angling her way through the door. She deposited Tillie on the weathered planking of the porch so she could close the door to block the sound of Jasper arguing with Regina.

There was a low buzz of excitement as Libby joined the group. A few of the older children had gone off to chase fireflies, while others spotted the tray of cookies in Libby's hands and came scampering across the yard toward her.

"Miss Libby! I caught a firefly in my hand! Do you want to see it?"

She struggled to remember the boy's name. His family was summering on the island for the first time this year, but he had joined a group of the children she led on a nature walk into the scrub last weekend. She landed on the boy's name as she peered through the fingers of his cupped hands. "My heavens, Samuel! It looks like you have managed to catch two of the little critters in there. We should rename you the Wild Man of St. Catherine's Island."

At her compliment, the boy beamed and seemed to grow two inches. Tillie's spirits were restored as the little girl trotted around the perimeter of the yard, trying to imitate the older children as they raced to catch fireflies. Libby settled herself onto a blanket and Ivan the Terrible, the petulant stray cat she'd foolishly adopted five years ago, deigned to join her. Whatever loyalty and affection most people received from their pets was an alien concept to Ivan, but she could not bear to leave him to fend for himself in Colden all summer. None of the residents of Winslow Street had much affection for Ivan, and he was liable to starve if she did not take him along.

A glance at the moon revealed that the eclipse was getting closer, so she darkened the two lanterns that were on the corners of the blanket. The children noticed the dimming of the lights and came racing back to her.

"Is it time?"

"Soon," Libby said. Ivan was spooked by the gathering children and he darted into the scrub. Almost immediately, Samuel flung himself into the vacated spot beside her. "I think you are the prettiest lady on this island," the little boy said quietly.

Libby bit back a smile. *Wait until you get an eyeful of Regina!* "You are very sweet for saying so," she whispered. Libby knew most people considered her pretty, with thick chestnut hair and a willowy figure, but those physical blessings had never helped her much in life. She would trade it all for the ability to read and be a normal woman. No one ever treated her quite the same when they discovered she could not read, but children were far less judgmental. Was that why she had always adored children? She watched Tillie chase Ivan in the tall scrub grass and smiled. No, some people were designed in the womb to relate to children, and she was one of them.

She heard a thud of steps on the porch, and then Jasper joined her on the far side of the blanket. "I think I'll join you in your little shindig," he said. "It is a bit frosty inside the house right now."

Which meant that Regina was likely to be spitting nails, but at least Tillie would be allowed to see the eclipse. A glance up at the sky revealed that the earth was starting to cast its shadow on the edge of the moon. Some of the children squealed, while others jumped and pointed. Thousands of miles above them, a magnificent act of nature was taking place. So great was her thrill that Libby barely noticed the stranger who rode up to the cottage, dismounted from his horse, and hooked the reins over the hitching post. He was probably just one of the parents of the children, come to share in the excitement.

Tillie raced up to her blanket and curled against Libby's side. "Is it magic?" she asked.

Libby had tried to explain the phenomenon to the children, but honestly, she wasn't sure how to make the concept clear to a five-year-old. She hoisted the child up higher on her lap. "It's a little like magic," Libby whispered as she gazed over Tillie's head and up at the sky. What a miracle of science and nature that such an event could be predicted, but even more thrilling was the sense of belonging she felt with Tillie's weight on her lap. This evening would not be nearly so magical without the dozen children who were sharing it with her. She breathed deeply of the salty air, trying to imprint the scent and sounds of this night onto her memory.

The screen door slammed and her father staggered down the steps, a small piece of paper clutched in his hand. Professor Sawyer was seventy years old and his gait was often a little on the shaky side, but tonight it was more pronounced than normal. She set Tillie to the side and rose to meet her father.

"Papa? What's wrong?"

He looked confused. His gray hair was always a little wild, but the way he kept dragging his hand through it made it stick out at all angles. In his other hand he held the paper, which had letters printed on it, out toward her. A telegram?

"Someone has taken my house," he said blankly.

Libby glanced at the cottage behind them. "What are you talking about? We are simply having the neighborhood children over to watch the eclipse."

He dragged his hand through his hair again and waved the note in her face. "My house. My house in Colden. Someone has taken it."

Jasper came to stand behind her. "Nonsense," he said. "You own that house outright. No one can take it from you."

Now her father was waving the telegram in Jasper's face. "I am telling you, *someone has taken my house*," he said in his thin, cracking voice. Jasper snatched the paper, but it was too dark outside to read.

"Let's go inside and figure out what is going on," Jasper said as he headed indoors, Libby's father following close behind. She cast a lingering glance at the moon, now aglow with a hazy red blaze. She lingered for a moment, staring in awe as the brownish-red shade intensified before her very eyes. All the children were staring in wonder, for it was a staggering sight, but she needed to tend to her father.

By the time she arrived inside, her father and Jasper were holding the telegram before the kerosene lantern on the small kitchen table, and now Jasper looked as concerned as her father.

"What has happened?" she asked.

Jasper's dark brows dipped ominously. "It sounds as if a pack of gypsies has invaded the Colden house. They claim to be descendants of the old Cossack. What was his name?"

"Constantine Dobrescu," her father said. "He came from Romania ages ago, but he never married, never had a family. He was crazy all his life. That house was a wreck when I bought it."

Jasper tapped the telegram against the table, his expression dumbfounded. Libby wondered what kind of people had the audacity to march inside a house and declare it their own. If they were gypsies, heaven only knows what foul deeds they were committing inside the house.

"Do you have documents proving you paid for the house?" Jasper asked. "A deed?"

"Of course I do," her father said. "But all the papers are *inside* the house. The filthy thieves have probably burned the deed by now."

Libby's hand flew to her throat in alarm, but Jasper did not seem concerned. "Anything of importance will be registered at the county courthouse," he said. "All you need to do is return to Colden and have those documents pulled. It should be a simple matter to show them to the sheriff and have the squatters evicted."

She was grateful for the calm reassurance in her brother's voice. Neither she nor her father had any grasp of business, but Jasper knew what he was doing. Her father was a brilliant inventor who could rig together a mechanical cooling fan from parts lying about their storage shed, but he was helpless when it came to business affairs and relied on Jasper to look out for the family's interests.

"By heaven, if those gypsies have tampered with any of my inventions, I will have them prosecuted. I'll have them hauled up on charges and deported. Sued for every penny to their name."

Her father continued to ramble, none of it making much sense. If these people were gypsies, surely they had no money, but there was no point in trying to stop her father's tirade. He was too consumed with worry about the value of the inventions he had stored in the house to think rationally. It was clear he felt violated and cheated and heartsick. As did she.

A terrible thought came to her like a smack in the face. All of her paintings were inside that house. Those paintings were her only source of pride, the only thing that proved she had something of value to offer the world. She would not care if the Mongolian Golden Horde looted every item she owned, so long as her paintings were safe.

"We will leave for Colden tomorrow," her father said. "I will call on the sheriff and have the gypsies evicted. We must have our house back. We must salvage my designs and Libby's drawings."

She looked up. It was rare for her father to acknowledge the value of her work, although he mentioned her *drawings*, not her paintings. Libby's technical drawings were for her father's benefit. Every time he designed a new invention, she created meticulous drawings of the interior, exterior, and cutaway views to document the mechanism. Her mechanical drawings were work, but her paintings were done for love. Those paintings would be the first thing she intended to rescue from the house.

Regina stepped forward. "Surely Libby can stay here on the island," she said. "Jasper and I are planning on going to Boston to see the opera. I had hoped Libby could look after Tillie until we return on Tuesday."

Libby's head shot up. *Four days with Tillie!* Four blissful days in which she would have the freedom to be the sort of mother, or rather, the sort of *aunt* she had always wanted to be.

Her father turned his attention to her, frazzled anxiety brimming in his expression. Had her father ever needed her more than he did at this very moment? Libby knew where all the drawings were stored, all the versions of his inventions stashed away. There were precious few times in her life when her father actually needed her, and now was one of them.

"I'm sorry, Regina," she said with genuine regret. "I need to be in Colden with Father at this time."

"Naturally," Regina said a little stiffly. She was the daughter of a South Carolina congressman and had the savvy to know when she could push and when to retreat.

"Aren't you going to watch the eclipse with me?" Tillie was standing in the doorway, her voice confused. A quick glance out the window revealed the full blaze of the eclipse's glory, although it had lost its magic for Libby.

But Tillie was looking at her with love and expectation. The very soonest Libby could begin reclaiming her paintings and her home was tomorrow morning, and for tonight, there was a little girl who wanted to share an eclipse with her.

"Show me the moon, sweetheart," she said as she picked Tillie up and carried her outside.

A scream drove Michael upright in bed. The agonized wail shattered the silence of the night as Michael leapt to his feet. The house was dark, but enough moonlight streamed through the windows to reveal nothing out of place in his bedroom.

Michael nearly tore the door from its hinges as he bolted into the hallway. The screaming was coming from Mirela's room and he flung her door open, banging it on the wall. She was alone, as he was almost certain she would be. Curled into a ball in the center of the bed, she was sound asleep and screaming as if the flesh were being torn from her body.

He settled on the bed and shook her shoulders. "You are dreaming, wake up." He shook again, but she twisted away, filled her lungs, and let out a fresh round of heartrending screams.

He used his commander's voice. "Mirela, wake up. Stop this nonsense and *wake up*." It made him cringe to use such a tone with a woman, but sometimes it was the only thing that could awaken her from these night terrors.

"What is happening, Papa?" Andrei's thin voice sounded from the open doorway.

He was too busy shaking Mirela's shoulders to turn around. "It is just another nightmare. Go back to bed, son." The patter of footsteps let him know Andrei had obeyed, and he turned his full attention back to Mirela. Her face was covered in perspiration and her nightdress was damp. The night was warm, but that could not account for the heat her body was throwing off. Hadn't she been feeling better that afternoon? It had been months since she had suffered this sort of night terror and he had hoped it was a thing of the past. Was this something she was going to battle for the rest of her life?

At last she stopped fighting him and her eyes opened, still unfocused and confused. The pant of her shaky breaths filled the darkened room. "Another nightmare?" she asked him.

He nodded.

She raised a trembling hand to her forehead, brushing away the hair that had tumbled into her eyes. "Did I wake everyone up again?"

It would not surprise him if every neighbor on the street had heard her screams. Michael walked to the open window, where the weak night breeze brought the fragrance from the rose garden into the room. The moonlight illuminated the spectacular Gallica roses in various stages of bloom. His jaw tightened, but he forced his voice to remain calm. "You don't need to worry about that."

Mirela gave a heavy sigh and rolled over to face the wall. Her voice was so faint he could barely hear it. "I feel like such a failure," she said. "Every time I think I might be getting better, the memories keep coming back. I've traveled halfway around the world, and still they follow me, like dragons I can never outrun."

He shut the window, the rasp sounding harsh and final in the night. Before he left the room, he turned to face her. "This will take time, Mirela. We have always known that. If it takes a decade for you to outrun the dragons, I will be with you every step of the way."

42

He returned to his room and changed out of his nightshirt and into a pair of simple pants and boots, then bounded down the stairs. The moonlight was odd tonight, tinged with a curious reddish haze. Clearly it was some sort of eclipse, but Michael did not care. All that mattered was that there was enough light to see what needed to be done while Mirela could not witness his actions.

Michael grabbed his battle-ax before heading outside. There was nothing he could do to change the past, but he could ensure this home was as comfortable for Mirela as possible. His boots sliced through the long grass as he strode toward the rose garden, cursing himself for his carelessness. He had been so busy these past two days he had overlooked the roses growing in a rich profusion at the rear of the yard. Not until he stood at Mirela's open window and smelled their scent on the night air had he realized the danger that was growing just yards away from her.

The roses were gorgeous, the thickness of the stems indicating they were at least twenty years old. The way they twisted and climbed along the fence was as though an artist had carefully trained them for maximum display. The abundant blooms cast off a rich fragrance, a sign of the roses' perfect, vibrant health. He hefted the ax to his shoulder and took careful aim at the largest of the rosebushes. Two clean whacks and the bush was cleaved in half. With a booted foot, he kicked the vines down from where they had been trained to cling to the fence. He grit his teeth together as he attacked the next bush, funneling all his rage and despair into his swing. Over and over he hacked through the thick, woody stems that grew in abundance along the side of the fence.

The door opened behind him, and Michael saw Turk framed in the doorway. "You know what you are doing there, mate?"

He swung another mighty blow at a rosebush in full bloom. "I want these roses out of here by sunrise. Tomorrow I will cart them away and burn them someplace where Mirela will never have to tolerate them again."

Turk knew better than to question him when he was in one of these moods. The man merely nodded and went back to bed, but Michael kept slashing away, unleashing the tension trapped in his muscles against the bushes. This time tomorrow, these hated roses would be gone forever.

4

I'll kill him," Professor Sawyer said as he waved a bony finger in the young sheriff's face. "I'll march over to Winslow Street and stop at nothing until those vagabonds are either out of my house or dead."

Sheriff Alfred Barnes showed remarkable poise in the face of her father's ferocity. Libby was impressed with how the man neither flinched nor backed away from her father's aggressive stance. "Which is why you are going to wait here at your son's house while your daughter and I pay a call on Mr. Dobrescu," Sheriff Barnes said coolly. "Liberty will assess the condition of your house to ensure no damage is being done to your belongings, but I will not have a homicidal man accompany me on a professional call."

"Who said I was homicidal?" the professor demanded.

"You did, sir."

Despite his bluster, the idea of her father actually resorting to violence to reclaim their house was absurd. Her father endured years of ostracism during the Civil War due to his pacifist stance. He built contraptions to capture mice alive because he was too squeamish to use a mousetrap that would slay the little beasts. Still, Sheriff Barnes was too young to know any of that.

Despite his youth, Sheriff Barnes was conscientious about his job, as evidenced by his studying of the legal situation regarding their house. "I went to the county courthouse the same day I learned of Mr. Dobrescu's seizure of the house on Winslow Street."

Libby would have felt better if the sheriff would have referred to it as *your* house, rather than *the* house. The implication that ownership of the house was in any way precarious caused her stomach to clench. "I saw your deed from 1856 to purchase the house, but there is no clear title to the land," the sheriff said. "The final will and testament of Constantine Dobrescu is also filed at the courthouse, and it clearly left the house to his family in Romania. It is possible the sale of the house was illegal, so this is a matter for the courts to decide. Since Constantine Dobrescu's will predates your purchase, and the Dobrescus are currently in possession of the property, we will need to wait for the court to rule before I can force an eviction."

Her father's face flushed and he could barely get words out as he sputtered his outrage. "The courts could take months! Years!" he gasped.

"Judge Frey has already agreed to expedite your case," the sheriff said. "This is an unusual situation and he has sent to Boston for the necessary legal periodicals to help render his decision. He expects to hear the case within a month."

"A month!" Professor Sawyer said, scorn dripping from his voice. "Within a month those vagrants could strip the house of every matchstick. Every piece of jewelry, every article of clothing. Everything I have."

Sheriff Barnes nodded his head. "Your concern is understandable, and the judge has given you permission to remove personal items from the home for safekeeping. I will escort your daughter to the house so she can identify which items should be retrieved. Any small items, such as jewelry, she can take today. I will send men with a wagon for the larger items tomorrow."

Libby nodded, although she knew there was no jewelry to

retrieve. As the only daughter, she inherited all the jewelry when her mother died twelve years ago, but it was long since gone. Paints, canvas, and fine sable brushes were expensive. Although her father was happy to supply her with everything she needed to produce technical drawings, he had no interest in her botanical paintings. Those supplies were funded by the sale of three gold bracelets, an onyx ring, and a pearl necklace she inherited from her mother. Guilt had eaten away at her when she walked into the jeweler's shop with her mother's pearl necklace, knowing she was going to trade this tangible link to her mother in exchange for money to buy pigment and canvas. She battled the sting of tears until she laid the necklace on the black velvet pad for the jeweler's inspection, when a sense of peace descended over her. Had it been a trick of her memory that made her feel as if she could sense her mother's presence? The faint scent of her perfume? Suddenly, she knew her mother would approve of the exchange she was making. Mama was the only person in the world who understood how important painting was to Libby, and now that she was gone, there would be no one to ensure she had the paint and supplies necessary to carry on her craft. A pearl necklace could do so.

Besides, her closest connection to her mother was still blooming just steps away from her bedroom window. It was her mother's love of roses that first sparked Libby's curiosity about the botanical world. Libby's earliest memories were helping her mother work bone meal into the soil of the rose garden. Rosebushes could live for generations, and that garden would always be a precious legacy to her mother's memory.

Her father stood. "We will leave immediately."

Sheriff Barnes was resolute. For such a young man, he was completely unaffected by her father's bluster. "I will accompany your daughter to the Winslow house," he said silkily. "I will not permit hostilities in my town, and you have already threatened

Mr. Dobrescu with bodily harm. We can always return to the house if you find there is anything of value Miss Sawyer fails to identify."

It took some finagling, but her father was eventually persuaded to wait at Jasper's house. Libby sat beside the sheriff on the driver's bench as they drove to Winslow Street, and with each passing block her nerves twisted a little tighter. Even her favorite outfit did not lend her the sense of confidence it usually imparted. Her suit had a sweeping skirt made of blue Merino wool with a matching vest and a narrow black tie fastened snugly beneath a starched white collar. Jasper had teasingly called it her "man's outfit," but Libby felt remarkably confident whenever she wore it.

Although she dreaded the next few hours. How distasteful it would be to see a bunch of tramps making free with her home. It was bad enough to know they were there, but once she had seen their faces and watched them sitting on her furniture and eating from her dishes, the sight would be branded in her memory forever.

"Tell me what they are like," she asked Sheriff Barnes.

"I only spoke with Mr. Dobrescu," he replied. "I gather he is their leader."

"Then what is *he* like?"

There was a pause as the young sheriff considered her question. "He is big."

"Big?" Was that all he could think to say? Libby wanted to know if he was reasonable, if he was educated, if he had a scrap of human decency she could appeal to. "What do you mean by *big*?" she asked.

Sheriff Barnes's gaze drifted upward and he held his hand almost a foot above his own head. "Really big." Then he held his hands several inches outside his shoulders. "And wide. Not fat. But very tall and very wide. Strapping, is what my mother would call him. A great big, strapping man."

The words did nothing to comfort her. The carriage rolled to a stop and she scanned the house where she had spent most of her life, sitting quietly beneath the maple and hawthorn trees. The wrought-iron gate was cool against her sweating palms as the sheriff secured the horse to a hitching post. When the horse was secure, she took a shaky breath, opened the gate, and started walking up the slate pathway.

How strange it felt to have to knock on one's own front door. Libby mentally braced herself to confront the "big and strapping man," but when the door opened, he was tiny, barely coming up to her elbow. She had not expected children quite this young to be among the passel of vagabonds who had invaded her home. No matter how foul the deeds of this boy's parents, she would never be hateful to a child.

"Hello," she began cautiously. "What is your name?"

The child beamed with delight. "My name is Luke. I am an American!"

Even those few words revealed a heavy accent. "Very nice," she said slowly and politely. "Is your father here?"

"His name is Michael, not Mikhail," the boy stressed. "Now he is *Michael*. He is an American too. We are all Americans."

Libby glanced at Sheriff Barnes, who seemed oddly charmed by the child. She was too, not that she could afford to be charmed by a gypsy child. He had probably been trained to say these things. "My goodness, all of you are Americans. How nice," she said, for want of any other comment.

"Even Lady Mirela is an American now. We are not allowed to call her 'Lady Mirela' anymore. Now we must call her *Aunt Mirela*."

There was a heavy pounding of footsteps as another boy came bounding down the staircase. This one was older, with the same light brown hair and blue eyes as the younger boy, but he was different. This one was guarded and fierce as he hovered over the younger boy.

"Don't pay Luke any attention," he said quickly. "He doesn't speak English and doesn't know what he is saying."

"Yes I do."

"No you don't," the older one snapped back. Then there was a rapid stream of foreign words as the older boy berated the younger child in a language that was completely alien to Libby. She watched Luke's face morph from defensive to confused and then to frightened, and she had an instinctive urge to comfort the child. The boy had been so proud just moments ago, and she didn't like to see him hurt by whatever the older boy was saying in such harsh tones. She was just about to say something when a man moved into her line of sight, blocking out the view of both boys with his size.

Oh my.

Libby's mouth went dry and the bottom of her stomach lurched. He was a giant. If a medieval warrior came storming out of the pages of a history book, this is what he would look like. He was big and rugged and the way his eyes glittered above the hard planes of his face made her catch her breath. Even his clothing was odd. She had never seen pants made from leather, and was that a *hatchet* strapped to his waist?

"What have you said to my boys to upset them?" he demanded.

She took a step back. "I asked the boy his name," she said lamely.

He towered over her, his eyes boring into her as if he were preparing to whip out that hatchet to extract more information. She refused to let herself back down, not when all she did was ask the boy a simple question. The man remained firmly planted in the doorway but turned to address the two children in the same strange language she had heard before. They both scampered upstairs, and the intensity of the warrior's stare was scorching as he swiveled his attention back to her. She moved a tiny step closer to the sheriff, but the giant followed, standing only inches away from her.

"Don't talk to my children," he said in a low voice that felt threatening despite its soft volume. "Don't have any contact with them unless I am here. If you want something, everything goes through me. Is that understood?" He directed the question to Sheriff Barnes. Despite the sheriff's cool demeanor with her father, she saw him swallow and try to stand a bit straighter.

"As we notified you yesterday, Professor Sawyer has been granted the right to retrieve his personal belongings," the sheriff said. "His daughter, Miss Liberty Sawyer, will be assisting me in identifying items to be removed."

Those stormy blue eyes glowered at her, staring rudely at her smartly matching vest and tie and skimming all the way down to her tightly laced boots. "What kind of name is *Liberty*?" he asked. "It is not a proper name for a woman, it is a concept. A noun."

She didn't quite know what to say. She had always been fond of her unconventional name. "It is a perfectly good name."

"I don't like it."

His statement was blunt and completely unnecessary. "Apparently, they do not teach manners in Romania, but in Massachusetts we wait until formal introductions are complete before hurling insults and seizing houses."

The man folded his arms across his chest. "Where I am from, we do not seek out children and pump them for information. That is considered rude. Now, what is your business here?"

"I have come to retrieve my family's belongings from *our* house. I have a right to come inside and assure the safety of our belongings."

The man's eyes narrowed. "I thought I would be dealing with a man. Is there no man to handle this?" he asked Sheriff Barnes. "I do not like to conduct business with a woman."

Libby's mouth dropped open in astonishment, but the sheriff interceded before she could speak. "Miss Sawyer is the professor's designated choice to inspect the house. Don't try to force a delay by sending me back to fetch another."

Mr. Dobrescu rubbed his chin and peered at her with a perplexed look on his face. His eyes darkened like the blue of a summer sky just before a storm. He was a handsome man despite the fact that he seemed as friendly as the Spanish Inquisition. A scar marred the side of his face and his hair was in desperate need of a trim, but his eyes unnerved her. They were as hard and cold as iron.

"Don't think I will go easy on you just because you are a woman," he said. "I have a legal right to this house and I will not move my family from it."

"That is for the court to decide," the sheriff said coolly beside her. "Miss Sawyer will identify items she wishes brought from the house until the court renders its decision."

The giant nodded. "This seems fair," he said, and pulled back to hold the door open for her. "I am Michael Dobrescu, and I apologize for speaking harshly to you. But do not talk to my children or my sister when I am not here," he said and held his hand out. Libby thought he meant to shake her hand, but when she extended it, he bowed low and brought it to his lips.

She snatched her hand back. Well *that* was a European practice she was not accustomed to. She was thrown off guard and twisted her hand where his lips had touched. She stepped inside the house, and Mr. Dobrescu followed just inches behind. "I will be watching you the entire time," he warned.

"Afraid I might steal some of my own belongings?" She scanned the foyer, but it did not look as though it had been ransacked. Her father's coat was hanging where it belonged, the pencil-sharpening machine on the hallway table was unmolested, the draperies were still neatly hung. She marched inside the house to take an inventory as quickly as possible, but then froze in her tracks.

"My painting," she breathed. There, hanging above the mantel in a place of honor, was her painting of the amaryllis in full bloom. The burnt sienna petals of the flower were wholly unfurled, looking almost too heavy for the elegant stalk that supported the outrageous display of flowering blooms. She took a step forward, mesmerized by the sight of her painting hung on a wall for all to see.

"You own this picture?" the man asked.

"I *painted* that picture."

"I don't believe it," he scoffed. "You are a woman."

Libby whirled around to look at him, but he was utterly serious. "I have been painting since I was six years old. My hand and my eyes are as good as any man's."

If she'd said a donkey had painted the picture, he could not have looked more surprised. It was comical, actually, but a smile spread across the man's wide face. "My family and I have admired the paintings we have found in this house. Never would I have imagined they were done by a woman. This seems very strange to me."

Without warning, he grabbed her hand and tugged her across the room. "Come, there is something I must ask you." His huge legs strode into the study in a few strides, while she had to scurry to keep up with him. To her amazement, he dropped to his knees and slid out a stack of her botanical paintings where she had stashed them under the sofa. He peeled a few back until he found the one he was looking for.

"Here," he said with a big finger pointing to the plant. "What is the English word for this plant?"

"A squash?"

"Squash?" he echoed. "Do you know where I can find some squash in America? I find this is the only vegetable my children will eat."

Was he making fun of her? She had come to protect her belongings from a bunch of marauding gypsies, and here he was asking her where he could get vegetables for his children. It was a bit disconcerting, but she would not let him throw her off guard.

"You could ask Mr. Turner down the street if any of his summer squash is ripe yet. He has a greenhouse and it's possible he has some that is ready for harvest."

His brows lowered. "A man should not feed his children by

begging for food. Do you think these neighbors might share some shoots with me? I can grow squash."

Did he really think he would be in this house long enough to plant and cultivate summer vegetables? "I don't know," she hedged. "You will have to ask them."

Mr. Dobrescu pointed to the florid canary-yellow bloom and then the fat green vegetable that was depicted along the base of the plant. "Why did you paint the male blooms at the same time the female blooms are bearing fruit? It makes the picture very interesting, but this rarely happens in real life."

In all the years she had been painting, no one had ever asked her that particular question. Most people did not even know that squash plants had such a thing as male and female blooms, but he was entirely correct. Both blooms rarely appeared at the same time as the plant was throwing off mature vegetables, simply because the male blooms dropped off earlier in the season. "Botanical illustrators often draw a plant at both the reproductive stage and at the mature stage," she explained. "It is important to show the seeds, the bud, and the blooms. I always show the face and reverse of the leaves. One of my favorite things about painting is researching the plant before I begin. . . ."

She was rambling, and people always got bored when she started talking too much about painting. She caught herself and craned her neck to look up at Mr. Dobrescu, but he appeared completely engrossed in what she was saying.

This was ridiculous. She was there to collect her belongings, not provide this crude man with a lesson in botanical illustration. "I will take those paintings with me," she said as she reached out for the stack he had slid from beneath the sofa. Had he found the others she kept behind the bookshelf in her bedroom and in the hallway closet? Her father had always said it would be too vain to hang her own paintings, so she kept them stashed away in the nooks and crannies of the house.

Sheriff Barnes was standing in the arched doorway. "Will you carry these to the carriage for me?" she asked him. "There are others I need to collect."

"Naturally."

After passing off the paintings, she strode down the hallway to the closet where the others were stored. Mr. Dobrescu followed her. "Why do you dress like a man?" he asked.

That made her pause. She glanced down at her smart little suit, the one that always made her feel so sharp. "I don't dress like a man," she denied. "I dress in a clean and respectable manner." His comment hurt, but she would not retaliate. It would be unkind to comment on the battered leather pants he wore or the strange shirts of his children that fell almost to their knees.

"No, you definitely dress like a man," he said. "And your hair is so tightly bound . . . like you don't want anyone to see it. All of this looks very mannish to me."

She could not let him keep insulting her. Long ago she'd learned that if she did not stand up for herself, the belittling could go on endlessly. "So, you don't like my name and you don't like the way I dress or wear my hair. Mr. Dobrescu, is there anything pleasant you can say about me?"

He considered the question. Was it her imagination, or did he just sway slightly closer to her? He closed his eyes and he appeared lost in thought, as though he was struggling very hard to come up with something nice to say. At last, he raised his eyes to hers.

"I like the way your hair smells."

Her eyes widened in surprise. "My hair?" she repeated stupidly.

"Yes." He leaned forward again and breathed deeply. She took a step back, but the brute followed, sniffing at her in a vulgar display of poor comportment. "I like this scent very much," he said. "What does it come from?"

"Soap." She washed her hair with the same soap she used on the rest of her body. Libby wondered if he was making fun of her or if this was his attempt at polite conversation. If so, he was a spectacular failure.

"Could you tell me where I might purchase it?" he asked. "Too many soaps smell like roses, and my sister does not care for the scent of roses. Where did you get this soap?"

She had gotten a whole box of it from Regina, who had ordered it from France. It was obscenely expensive, and when it arrived, Regina decided she did not care for it after all and had given the whole box to Libby. "My sister-in-law purchased it. I'm not sure precisely where she got it."

"Ah. Too bad," he said.

She turned into the hallway closet and found another set of her botanical paintings safely stored on the top shelf. When she reached for them, Mr. Dobrescu stepped in front of her and pulled them down for her.

"Thank you," she murmured, wishing he would not be polite. Accepting his help felt like treason, and he was still standing oddly close to her. And the way he was leaning down . . . He was sniffing her again! She took a step backward and breathed a sigh of relief when Sheriff Barnes returned. She did not feel safe with Mr. Dobrescu's odd fascination with her hair.

"Sheriff Barnes, will you help me with these drawings?" she asked.

"Of course."

The next two shelves were filled with technical drawings she had done for her father. Most of these were from projects he had been working on several years ago: a machine for threshing hay, a design for a self-propelling fan, even a sophisticated version of an alcohol still. All of them were passed into Sheriff Barnes's waiting arms.

Although the retrieval of her paintings and technical drawings had gone smoothly, the atmosphere changed the moment she tried to go upstairs and inspect the bedrooms.

"Why must you go into the bedrooms?" Mr. Dobrescu demanded.

"Just write down what you need and I will get it for you." He walked over to her father's desk and withdrew a sheet of paper and a pencil. He held them out to her.

She felt her body heating up and glanced away. "I need to see the rooms," she said. "I can't be expected to remember everything in each room."

It was a lie. Libby's memory was flawless. She could remember the location of every stitch of clothing, where each can had been placed in the pantry, but she would eat dirt before confessing to this crude barbarian why she could not write down the items she wanted retrieved.

Sheriff Barnes came to her rescue. "She has a right to inspect the rooms," he said. "We are here to verify the condition of the house and everything inside it. This is for your own protection as well as theirs, Dobrescu. We need to go room to room."

Mr. Dobrescu looked ready to spit nails. "My sister is in the back bedroom upstairs. She is not well and I will not tolerate you invading her privacy."

"Then tell her to prepare for a brief visit. I want a visual inspection of every room in this house," Sheriff Barnes said with calm confidence. "I'm sure your sister will find this easier if you cooperate. It would be distressing for her if I had to bring in a half-dozen deputies to assist in the inspection."

Libby's gaze tracked back and forth between the two men, so starkly different. Mr. Dobrescu was a blunt, forthright man who stood more than a foot taller than the young sheriff. But Sheriff Barnes was being quite clever. He was watching and observing Mr. Dobrescu and altering his approach as he gathered more information. Mr. Dobrescu seemed unusually protective of his family, and the sheriff had chosen a clever tactic by implying the trauma that would come along with a retinue of deputies. She was grateful the sheriff was on her side.

Mr. Dobrescu locked eyes with the sheriff, looking angry enough to bite an iron bar in half. At last, he caved. "Turk! Joseph!" he barked. Two men as large as Mr. Dobrescu entered the room. Libby felt dwarfed, a field mouse amidst lumbering bison. Surely her mother's dainty imported furniture would crack under the weight of these monsters. A stream of foreign babble flew between the men. One man moved into position right in front of her, while the other went to stand in front of a cabinet in the parlor. Before he took up position, the brute picked up a shotgun and held it in his arms while he stood guard in front of the cabinet.

"There is no need for a weapon," Sheriff Barnes cautioned.

"This is my house and my rules," Mr. Dobrescu growled. "Stay here while I speak with my sister." He vaulted up the staircase three steps at a time, causing the glass in the windowpanes to rattle with each pound of his booted feet. She heard every thud as he stalked down the hallway, but the knock on the bedroom door was unexpectedly gentle. "Mirela?" he said softly, surprising Libby with the tenderness embodied in that simple word.

Libby tried not to fidget in the foyer as she was scrutinized by the two mammoth guards. How odd to feel like an invader in her own home. It made her nervous to look at the one in the parlor with the shotgun, so she turned her attention to the man standing directly in front of her, guarding the base of the stairs. He was staring at her without the least trace of embarrassment, but the scrutiny was unbearable.

"Do you speak English?" she blurted out.

"Of course." And the man's huge face broke into a smile revealing remarkably white teeth. "My name is Raghib, but everyone calls me Turk."

The man spoke beautiful English and somehow that set her at ease. "Why do they call you Turk?"

"Because I am Turkish."

She glanced at Sheriff Barnes, then back at the huge guard. "I thought you were all from Romania."

"Heaven forbid. Have you ever tasted the slop they call food in Romania?" He did not wait for an answer. "I ran into Michael during the Russo-Turkish war when I was wounded behind the lines," the giant continued. "Michael should have shot me on the spot, because we were fighting for opposite sides, but it didn't work out that way. He stitched up my gut and we have been together ever since. See?" He lifted the corner of his shirt to reveal a hairy belly with a ropy, twisting scar stretching across it.

Libby's eyes widened. She was too young to remember much about the American Civil War, but the casual way Turk tossed off the story made the grisly effects of combat shockingly vivid. Still, she was intrigued.

"Why didn't he shoot you? Isn't it treason to help the enemy?"

"I was wearing this," Turk said, holding a large silver cross hanging from a chain around his neck. "My mother raised me to follow the Lord, but sometimes it can be hard to be a Christian where I am from. I switched sides and have been with Michael ever since."

Before she could reply, Michael Dobrescu came down the steps, barely restrained fury burning in his eyes. He put his face close to hers and glared. "You may look inside Mirela's room," he said. "Do not speak to her, do not look at her. She is fragile and I will not have her upset."

Although his words told her she could look in Mirela's room, his eyes said he'd prefer she throw herself into a pit of fire and suffer a miserable death. She stood a little straighter and followed Mr. Dobrescu up the stairs. The woman was using Libby's own bedroom, so why should she feel awkward about looking inside? If anyone was the interloper, it was Mirela.

Mr. Dobrescu quietly tapped on the door before opening it. He murmured something in Romanian, then stepped aside to let Libby look into the room. The way he hovered in the doorway, blocking the opening with his arm, made it apparent she was not welcome to go inside.

From his description of his sister's fragility, Libby had expected the woman to be bedridden, but she was fully dressed and perched on the seat of the windowsill.

This girl could *not* be Michael Dobrescu's sister. Impossible. She was too tiny and delicate. With glossy black hair and flawless ivory skin, she looked like a fairy princess.

"Hello," the girl said with a smile. "Michael said you used to live here?"

Libby did not know how to answer that. The kindness in the girl's eyes made Libby doubt she intended any insult by implying this was no longer the Sawyers' house. "Yes," Libby stammered. "We are taking an inventory."

Sheriff Barnes attempted to step inside the room, but Mr. Dobrescu shifted his weight to block him. "You can see everything from where you are," he growled.

Libby remembered something curious the young boy had said after he opened the door. She looked at the dainty young woman sitting with the poise of a queen in the window seat. "Are you Lady Mirela?" she asked.

Before she had even finished the sentence, Mr. Dobrescu whirled around to face her, spreading his arms across the doorway with a mighty smack and blocking her view of the room. "I told you not to speak to her," he snapped.

Libby flinched at the ferocity in his voice. Every instinct was screaming to turn and flee, but she could not allow this man to bully her. "That is the second time I have asked someone their name and you tried to take my head off for it. I cringe in terror of what you will do if I dare ask what they had for lunch." Despite her bravado, the intensity of his stormy blue glare was disconcerting, and she felt herself wilting beneath it.

"Is there anything in that room you require?" It was not a question, it was a demand for her to finish her business and leave. He probably used that tone to intimidate serfs into quivering fear all over Eastern Europe, but rather than turn and flee, Libby stood straighter.

"I would like to meet Lady Mirela," she said calmly. With a little dip she slipped beneath his outstretched arms and stepped inside her own bedroom.

Lady Mirela was stifling laughter behind her hands. "Oh, you are very brave!" she said. Her blue eyes sparkled with wit and intelligence.

"Very brave or very fool—"

Before she could finish her sentence, the giant barged in and began forcing her backward, but then something amazing happened. The young woman raised her hand and Mr. Dobrescu immediately froze, obeying the girl's wordless command. "She seems harmless enough," Mirela said. Strange, the girl spoke only a few words, but the note of authority was apparent to everyone. Mr. Dobrescu stepped back to the doorway, almost like a footman obeying a queen.

Libby's gaze traveled over the bedding, the furniture, the surface of her bureau. Her belongings were exactly as she had left them. She pulled open the door of the wardrobe to see her clothing hanging in its proper place, without anything belonging to Lady Mirela tucked inside. There did not seem to be a single personal possession belonging to Lady Mirela in this room at all. In fact . . .

Libby swiveled around to stare at the girl. The white blouse and simple brown skirt Mirela was wearing belonged to Libby.

"I see you have made yourself at home with my clothing," she said coldly as she looked pointedly at the blouse and skirt.

"These clothes belong to you?" Lady Mirela looked crushed, and Libby felt like she had just stepped on a butterfly. "I'm so sorry," the girl stammered. "I have no clothes except the dress I fled in and it needed to be washed."

Libby gasped as two hands clamped around her waist. In a mighty heave Mr. Dobrescu hoisted her into the air and spun her around as he carried her from the room. So tightly did he clasp her, Libby could not even draw a breath.

"I told you not to speak with her," Dobrescu snapped. He kicked the bedroom door shut, then tossed Libby back on her feet. The hallway whirled and she braced her hand against the wall to regain her balance.

"How dare you," she sputtered, tugging her vest back to a decent position.

"You hold yourself out as some sort of lady," Mr. Dobrescu said. "I do not like treating women in such a disrespectful manner, but I am not sure about you, Miss Liberty Sawyer. You dress like a man and you act like an idiot."

It was the wrong word to use. "I am *not* an idiot."

"You come into a man's home and you . . . you . . ." It appeared he was struggling with the language and getting madder as he could not think of the English term. A flush darkened his face and his teeth clenched as he fought to find the right words. Finally, he landed on a term. "You *tamper* with my family in front of my very eyes? You insult my sister in our home? Yes, that makes you an idiot, Miss Sawyer."

Sheriff Barnes stepped in between them. "Pipe down, Dobrescu," he ordered. "You are to keep your hands and your opinion of Miss Sawyer to yourself. I am determined to get this inventory taken and the two of you to cooperate while we do it."

"Let me help you," Mr. Dobrescu bit out as he continued to glower at her. "Take her out to the nearest lake and throw her in to see if she floats. Except I think she might like it."

Libby narrowed her eyes. "What I would like," she said acidly, "is to have an exorcism to rid my house of a passel of gypsies."

He blanched. She expected the insult to roll off his tough exterior, but the way he recoiled at her comment was unmistakable. He drew a steadying breath and spoke in a low tone. "I accept your label of me and my men," he said slowly, "but I will not allow you to insult my children or Mirela. They are innocent, but I fear they may suffer for what I have done. Already I have seen the neighborhood children poking fun at the shirts my boys wear. I know they look strange to American eyes, but I cannot afford to buy them new clothing, and I will not allow you to cast more insults their way. This is what you do when you call them gypsies."

Libby felt her mouth go dry. Never in her life had she been cruel to a child, yet she had just lashed out and indiscriminately struck at the entire Dobrescu family. She dropped her chin, unable to continue looking at the pain in this strange man's eyes. Despite his atrocious manners and many obvious flaws, he cared for his family.

"I apologize for my comment," she said on a shaky breath. "Your sister is welcome to wear my clothes if she has none of her own. And I should not have insulted your children. I am sorry." Her hand was trembling as she adjusted her shirt, still askew from his rough handling.

Mr. Dobrescu nodded, but his face remained grim. "Very well, then. We will take an inventory of this house so you may know we have no ill will toward your belongings. Then I want you out of here."

They moved in stony silence from room to room as Libby noted which items should be sent to her brother's house for safekeeping. Mr. Dobrescu hovered behind her the entire time. Surely the Visigoths who sacked the Roman Empire were more charming than Mr. Dobrescu.

Libby breathed a sigh of relief when the door of her home closed behind her.

5

The most splendid home in the entire village of Colden, Massachusetts, belonged to Jasper and Regina Sawyer, purchased with the fruits of Jasper's tireless work at the only bank in this prosperous village. Sitting on a solid acre near the town square, the home featured a wraparound front porch and leaded-glass windows imported all the way from Italy. Regina had a wonderful garden that had been called the "Pearl of Colden," although Libby privately thought of it as the "Pearl of five gardeners, two landscape architects, and one hefty bank account." Regardless, Jasper's home was a lovely place to stay until the Dobrescus could be extracted from her house on Winslow Street.

Curled into a white wicker chair, she found the idyllic garden was a balm to her battered spirit as she recounted her disastrous morning to her father and Mr. Auckland. "All of them speak English, but they seem very different from us." Libby stared at a hummingbird flitting among the delphiniums as she tried to pin down what made Michael Dobrescu seem like he stormed out of another century. It wasn't his appearance as much as his comportment. Or lack of it.

"Their clothing was clean, but strange," she continued. "The men wore tailored coats, but they were made of leather."

"Gypsies," her father said scornfully, but Mr. Auckland was not so dismissive.

"A good leather jacket can last for generations," the old librarian said. "My grandfather fought in the Revolution, and I still have the leather coat that served him well for three years in the back country."

Mr. Dobrescu's coat looked like it had lasted through three years of target practice, but Libby held her tongue, for as usual, Mr. Auckland was helping to put things in perspective and calm her father's rattled nerves. The town's librarian had been a friend to their family for as long as Libby could remember. It was Mr. Auckland who stood beside her during those painful adolescent years when her father demanded she try harder to learn to read. Convinced that Libby was not applying herself after the teachers and tutors had failed to make headway with her, Professor Sawyer required Libby to sit in the library every day after school and stare at a book for a solid two hours.

Even after all these years, Libby loathed the sight and scent of that library, remembering the discomfort of the hard oak chair and the humiliation of sitting at the front table, where everyone in town could observe her pointless struggle. Plenty of unfortunate people lacked the proper schooling to learn how to read, but that was not Libby's problem. With a college professor for a father and countless tutors, Libby seemed to be uniquely dense. Mr. Auckland was the most patient of all her tutors, but even his lessons failed to train her mind to work properly. Conceding defeat after a year of fruitless struggle, Mr. Auckland began looking the other way while Libby sketched or paged through the art books during that daily ritual of mortification at the public library.

If her father ever knew that Mr. Auckland had permitted her that freedom, he never gave any indication of it. The old librarian had been a godsend during these tense few days since returning from the island. He sat at the garden table, casually eating from a dish of Regina's pickled walnuts and serving as a calming presence while Libby recounted her impressions of the people who had stolen their house.

"What about damage?" her father asked. "With all those children I suppose it is too much to hope the house is still in decent condition."

Libby shook her head. "The only problem I saw was to the drainboard in the kitchen. Somehow it has been cracked in half." She had noticed the ruined drainboard just before leaving, but did not want to endanger the tenuous peace she had forged with Mr. Dobrescu by asking about it.

"That drainboard was a solid three inches thick! Those children surely did it. They were probably raised in a barn and have no idea how to comport themselves indoors."

"That is where you may be wrong, Willard," Mr. Auckland said. "The old Cossack came from a very fine family in Romania. It stands to reason that his relations would be as well." Mr. Auckland had an encyclopedic memory and loved nothing more than solving a good mystery. The arrival of the Dobrescu clan had been a source of great fascination for him.

"I remember the old Cossack used to wear a fancy uniform with epaulettes and a sash across his chest," the librarian said. "It looked like the kind of thing a prince would wear for a grand ceremony, but he did not strike me as a particularly wealthy man. He used his entire yard to plant vegetables. He plowed and harvested the vegetables with his own two hands, all while wearing that silly uniform."

"Probably just a costume," her father said. "A prop from a group of traveling actors."

Libby straightened. "There is a girl among them whom they call Lady Mirela. Do you suppose it means anything?"

Mr. Auckland scratched his head. "I will have to look it up. They certainly have aristocratic titles in Romania, although the old Cossack never bragged about a title."

"Are there any books in the library that would have records of the old Cossack?" Libby asked. "Immigration records or some kind of genealogy?"

Her father rolled his eyes. "Those kinds of foreign records are not kept in a small town public library," he said sourly.

Libby's face heated with embarrassment. Despite the countless hours she had endured in that library, the books could be written in ancient Chinese for all she knew, but did her father need to shine a spotlight on the fact?

Mr. Auckland's eyes were kind. "The next time I am in Boston I can make a point of looking at some genealogical books that might keep track of European titles. If Mirela indeed has a title, it may be recorded there."

Libby perked up. "This is all rather fascinating, isn't it?" she asked, unable to keep the excitement from her tone.

"It would be far more interesting if it did not feature my house as the main attraction," her father said bitterly as he paged through the technical drawings she had brought out of their home. "Where is the grain engine?" he asked.

"It isn't there?" Libby stared at the stack.

The drafting paper crackled as her father paged through the sketches. "None of them are here. I've looked through this stack twice."

Libby tried to remember the image of the hall closet as she retrieved the technical drawings. It was when Mr. Dobrescu was getting terribly close and sniffing at her hair in that tasteless manner. She had been ill at ease and perhaps she overlooked some of the drawings.

"I will check the closet when we go with the wagon to collect the larger pieces," she said.

"I'll bet the vagabonds have stolen them," her father said. "My designs are priceless."

Libby made no comment. It was true that her father could earn a small fortune if he could ever bring himself to complete one of his designs. Nothing short of absolute perfection would be tolerated from any product Professor Willard Sawyer would show to the world, and if a design was not impeccable, he banished it to the attic and began work on another. Their home was filled to the rafters with devices and machines that were ninety-eight percent complete. Never once had he actually finished an invention and brought it to the market.

She looked over her father's shoulder as he paged through the designs. "Come to think of it," she said, "I don't see any of the drawings for your windmill in there either."

He shot her an annoyed glare. "Be sure to fetch them all next time you return to the house."

And there would need to be a next time. Her cat disappeared from Jasper's house within a few hours of returning to Colden. Ivan was one of those cats who felt superior to the human race, regarding every resident of Colden with mild contempt, but he seemed to have a preference for prowling around Winslow Street. Libby couldn't quite put her finger on why she liked Ivan so much. Was it because he was despised by most people in the town, but still maintained a puffed-up dignity? For whatever reason, she wanted that cat back, and she was pretty certain she knew where to find him. The Dobrescus may have temporary custody of her home, but she would not allow them to take her cat.

Michael used his discarded shirt to wipe the perspiration from his face and his bare chest before tossing it back on the grass. The afternoon was hot, but it was the best kind of day. His boys were with him, the sun was shining, and he was close to getting the rickety old greenhouse in working order. The glass panels had all been in good condition, and only the frames on the west side were infected with rot. Michael removed the panels, salvaged what he could, and bought lumber to replace the frames damaged beyond repair. The new frames were on a sawhorse where Luke and Andrei were painting them, a scruffy neighborhood cat curled at Luke's feet. His boys had failed to make friends in the neighborhood, but at least they had the cat for company.

Michael smiled and gave thanks to the Lord for the simple splendor of the day. No man who had been scarred by warfare and spent years away from his family would take a day like this for granted. It had been a week since he'd claimed his house, and his plans were unfolding flawlessly. He could not believe his good fortune when he first saw the rickety greenhouse in the backyard of his new house, for he had a small sack of precious seeds from Romania. The greenhouse meant he would be able to get them cultivated much sooner than he'd originally planned.

"Andrei, come help me nail this frame into place," he said. His older boy set the paintbrush down and came over to help. "I need you to climb on top of the greenhouse and nail it to the rafters from above."

Andrei's face lit with excitement at the task and he immediately scrambled up the framing like a monkey swinging from a tree.

"Can I climb up too?" Luke asked.

"Not yet, boy. The frame is not strong enough to hold the both of you. You can go up and nail the next one." Marie would have been horrified to see her boys climb that high, but that was why it was important to have a father. If the boy fell and broke a bone, it would mend and no permanent harm would be done. His boys needed to grow into strong, capable men, and that would not happen if they were never trusted with more than a paintbrush. He lifted the hammer and a handful of nails up to Andrei. "Hold the spare nails in your mouth so you have a good grasp on the first," he instructed.

Andrei knew what to do and systematically pounded the beam into place with three well-set nails. Michael was about to help

70

Andrei down when the boy looked to the far side of the yard. His mouth opened and the spare nails tumbled to the ground.

"Someone is watching us," he said in Romanian.

Michael swiveled around. Standing on the other side of the fence that bordered his yard was a man with a patch over one eye, staring at them. Michael did not move. He just lifted his hand up to help Andrei back down to the ground.

"Go back to painting the other posts," he instructed the boys before walking across the lawn.

"Hello," he greeted the man with the patch.

"Afternoon."

"My name is Michael Dobrescu and over there are my boys, Andrei and Luke. We live here now."

"So I hear." The man looked a few years older than Michael, though it was hard to tell since the patch covered a large area of his face and he had pulled his hat low over his brow. "I'm Carleton Gallagher. Lived here for about eight years."

Michael nodded. "I have lived here about eight days."

The man named Gallagher looked pointedly at the round scar in Michael's bare torso. "Looks like a rifle ball did that."

Michael touched the wound. "A matchlock musket," he corrected, then turned to show his back. "It did more damage on the way out."

When he turned back around, Gallagher was holding up his arm, revealing a stump below the wrist. "A matchlock took my left hand clean off."

"And your eye?"

"Shrapnel."

Michael nodded. He glanced around the backyard and up into the windows of the neighboring houses, but there was no one else who could see into the privacy of his yard. He unbuttoned his pants and pushed them down to expose his hip. He turned around to show Gallagher. "That is a burn from a rafter that fell on me when we were raiding an ammunition dump. I would have burned to death if Joseph had not got it off me in time."

By the time Michael buttoned his pants and turned back around, Gallagher had hoisted his leg on top of the waist-high fence. He yanked off his boot. "Snake bite from wading across the Chattahoochee River during a reconnaissance mission. Had to grab the nasty thing by its jaws to get it off me."

Michael scrubbed his hand across his face. "Snakes," he sighed. "Nothing worse than snakes. That one is going to be hard to beat," he admitted.

"What about your face?" Gallagher asked

Michael ran his thumb down the ridge of the scar running across his cheek and looked away. "That came from . . . something else."

Gallagher's one eyebrow raised in question, but when Michael did not provide more details, Gallagher simply nodded. "Fair enough."

Gallagher did not pry, and Michael liked that about the man. "Who did you fight for?" Michael asked.

"Twentieth Regiment Infantry. First Lieutenant, 1863 to 1865. You?"

Michael shrugged, wishing his answer were so easy. "First I fought alongside the Russians, then I fought against them. Then I fought the Serbs, then the Turks. Things can be complicated in Europe."

"I suppose so." Gallagher reached down to tug his boot on, which took some doing with only one hand. When at last he stood, he met Michael's gaze. "I heard you shooting off a rifle yesterday morning."

Michael nodded. "Yes. Two rabbits."

"We don't take kindly here to hunting in the backyard. It is just not done."

"I wasn't hunting. The rabbits came into the yard and we could use the food. It would be foolish to let them get away."

Gallagher shrugged. "Yeah, well, my missus didn't like it. There are kids in this neighborhood, and who knows where they will be playing."

Michael was appalled. "I am very good with a rifle and I would never shoot when a child was in range."

His comment did not seem to have any effect on Gallagher. "Like I said, my wife didn't like it. Truth be told, I don't think it is such a good idea either. So no more shooting in the backyard. Deal?"

Michael braced his hands to lean against the fence. It was true he was not accustomed to living on a street with such close neighbors. In Romania, the nearest house to him had been a ten-minute walk, which meant he had the freedom to hunt whenever he wanted. Perhaps he could teach his boys to build traps for the rabbits so he could still get some meat on the table and not frighten Mrs. Gallagher.

He glanced over the fence into the Gallaghers' yard. There were rows of well-tended tomatoes, what looked to be parsnips and radishes, and a couple of cherry trees. Along the back fence five rosebushes were lashed to a trellis.

"Please tell your wife I will shoot no more rabbits," he said definitively. He nodded to the back fence. "She must like roses?"

"They are something she can grow without killing."

Michael nodded. "This greenhouse will be ready soon. I am very good with plants and will be raising a rare variety of night-blooming jasmine. This is a very valuable flower. I brought the seeds all the way from Romania. If you like, I would be happy to remove your rosebushes and provide your wife with my jasmine."

Gallagher looked perplexed. "Why would you do that?"

"We do not like the scent of roses," he said bluntly. Michael knew it was an odd request, but he wanted those rosebushes out of there. The days were growing warmer and the windows were usually open. The scent of roses was the last thing he wanted inside his home.

"I think that would be a tough sell with the wife," Gallagher said as he touched the brim of his hat. "But thanks for not shooting any more rabbits."

6

"Be sure you get the plans for my ventilated greenhouse," her father said as he handed Libby up into the wagon. "It would not surprise me if the gypsies have seen the greenhouse in the backyard and even now are trying to sell my design."

"I'll get the plans," Libby assured him as she settled into the wagon seat beside Sheriff Barnes.

"Victory or death!" her father called after her as the wagon pulled away. She ought to be pleased he was blessing her with the ancient Spartan battle cry, but it was a bit disconcerting. Michael Dobrescu looked like he had a lot of experience with Spartan techniques of pillaging and dismemberment. Still, she had no intention of storming the house or waving a red flag in front of the Dobrescus. She was smarter than that.

When it came to physical strength, Michael Dobrescu could flick her aside as easily as a flea from his shoulder. The only way she could get the better of him was through intellect. When she last visited the house, she had flown off the handle and accomplished very little, but today she would extend an olive branch. The court would ultimately rule in her father's favor, but she needed to establish cordial relations with the Dobrescus. The court date was still a month away, which left her home vulnerable to mistreatment should she needlessly antagonize these people.

Besides, she was deeply ashamed of having called them gypsies. Words like that left scars. Slow, stupid, retarded—people had used all these words on Libby when she was the same age as the Dobrescu boys. If she had to dig the trenches and build the barricades with her own two hands, no one in Colden would call those children gypsies again.

Mr. Dobrescu was prepared for their arrival. The moment she stepped through the wrought-iron gate, the front door opened to reveal his massive form. He waited until she was in front of him before speaking.

"You have brought a list of things to remove?" he asked. His voice was guarded and reserved, but he had combed his hair and was suitably dressed, so perhaps he was trying to turn over a new leaf as well.

"Sheriff Barnes has it." While the sheriff was securing the horse, Libby retrieved a small package from her pocket. "The last time I was here, you said your sister would like the scent of this soap. I hope you will offer it to her."

A boyish grin split across the man's face, making him look utterly appealing. "Thank you!" he said in a booming voice. "It is very refreshing to find a soap without roses, which is what most perfumers seem to use." The cake of soap looked ridiculously tiny in his hand, but he held it to his nose and closed his eyes in concentration. "Vanilla with just a small bit of orange blossom," he said. Libby's eyes widened in surprise, but Mr. Dobrescu's attention was still entirely focused on the cake of soap.

"There is another scent in there. It has the tone of bergamot, but it is not." He inhaled again. "I believe it is just a small amount of the oil of amaranth. This is a most unusual combination with vanilla, but I like it."

It was impossible to dissect a fragrance simply by smell, and she was surprised he would try to show off by doing such a thing. "You peeked at the package," she said.

He glanced down at the elegant French label, illustrated with a bouquet of blooms and herbs in a simple basket. His brow furrowed and he held the soap closer to scrutinize the picture. "No, this picture is wrong. I see the vanilla plant and the flowering orange blossoms. They have not drawn the amaranth, which is not surprising because it is an ugly herb. . . . But look . . . they have drawn lavender in the bouquet, and there is no lavender in this soap. Not a bit of it—I would know."

Libby snatched the soap from his hand, staring at the drawing. He was correct in his identification of every plant depicted on the label, which she assumed were the scents distilled into the soap. She sniffed the bar, which had a bright, clean scent to it, but that was all she could really say about it.

"Are you pulling my leg?" she asked. "Can you really dissect fragrances just by a simple sniff?"

He looked befuddled. "Yes, I can tell exactly what is in almost any fragrance, but I am not pulling your leg. I have not touched your leg or any part of your body. I would not do so after the last time you were here and I treated you badly."

He was utterly serious, and Libby had to stifle a laugh as she passed the cake of soap back to him. "I apologize. *Pulling my leg* is a figure of speech, not something to be taken literally. I was asking if you are teasing me."

Understanding dawned in his eyes. "Ah. I see. Well, Miss Liberty Sawyer, you seem like the type of person I would like to tease were I free to do so, but I was not teasing you. I think you are a much better artist than the person who painted this soap label. He obviously wanted something pretty, but I think you would want something accurate. Am I right?"

She nodded. "You are right."

He waved the bar of soap aloft. "You should write to these

soap makers and tell them not to deceive their customers with false drawings. For one thing, any soap that blended the oils of lavender with orange blossoms, as this picture suggests, would be a very foul-smelling bar of soap. I will be curious to hear if they respond to you."

The last thing she wished to discuss was her ability, or inability, to strike up a correspondence with a French soap maker, so she smoothly switched the topic back to him. How fascinating to see this giant battle-scarred man discussing perfumes with the authority of a college professor. "What are you? Some kind of dealer in fragrances? An owner of a perfume shop?"

He shuddered. "Heaven forbid. It would be terrible to spend all my days inside a tiny shop. I much prefer to work outside, where I can see the sun."

It was true she could not picture Michael Dobrescu earning a living inside a shop. This man belonged on the steppes of Russia or the plains of Africa, where he could hunt mighty beasts and carry them home across his shoulders. Not that Libby was impressed by physical strength, but on some primitive level, the man standing before her was oddly fascinating. In her world of order and decorum, he was a wild, unpredictable force of nature. What would it be like to have a man like him on her side?

She needed to snap out of this nonsense. Libby straightened her collar and dragged her thoughts back to business. "The main things I will need to collect today are the rest of my father's mechanical designs. We have some traveling bags in the attic, and I would like to fill those with some clothing."

It appeared Mr. Dobrescu was also determined to be polite. "Of course, Miss Sawyer." His manner was so gracious, and the little bow so perfectly executed, it was almost as if he were a gentleman born of the aristocracy. "I will have Turk fetch the bags from the attic. Is there anything else we can help you with?"

How different he was today from the crude barbarian of a few days ago. Today he had been discussing *perfume* with her, for heaven's sake! "No, thank you," she said. "I will be able to find everything I need."

Over the next hour she went through her father's study, retrieving his tools, drawings, measuring devices, and everything of sentimental value noted on the list. Her heart squeezed when she came across the photograph taken in commemoration of Professor Sawyer's engagement to Mamie Bryant. Running her thumb along the ornate silver frame, Libby stared at the portrait of her parents, so different in temperament, age, and appearance.

Her father had been slipping into middle-aged bachelorhood when he met the young Mamie Bryant. Her mother was a shy and studious young woman, quietly dazzling the older man who'd never expected to find a wife. Stunned by his good fortune in landing Mamie, her father did whatever was necessary to appeal to his young bride. Knowing she wished to fill a house with children, he found a wonderful sprawling old house on Winslow Street in desperate need of renovation. Its dilapidated condition was the only reason he could afford the house, and the professor lavished two years of his own engineering skill and physical labor in restoring it to its showpiece condition. In the backyard, he built Mamie a greenhouse where she could indulge her love of flowering plants. Instead of a plain glass structure, the professor built his wife a spectacular gothic greenhouse, complete with white-painted arches, a gabled roof, and hand-carved spires. It was within that magical greenhouse that Libby sat at her mother's side and learned how to tend and nurture the spectacular blooms she loved so well.

Snapping out of her reverie, Libby placed the photograph in a canvas sack to take to Jasper's house. While Libby gathered belongings, Sheriff Barnes helped carry the items to the cart for her. Still, she could not find her mechanical drawings of the portable combustion engine her father was in the process of perfecting. She had sketched the engine from the front and back and had made two separate cutaway drawings of the internal views. Libby was almost certain she had left them in the drawer beside the drafting table, but she checked twice and the drawings were not there. Neither were they in the hallway closet where drawings of machines her father had abandoned were typically relegated.

She dreaded returning to Jasper's house without those drawings. Was it possible one of the Dobrescus had simply moved them? She needed to speak with Mr. Dobrescu, but did not want the sheriff there to needlessly antagonize the man. She asked the sheriff to wait in the parlor while she stepped outside in search of Mr. Dobrescu.

She found him in the front yard with his children. He was standing at full height with his arms outstretched while both boys, armed with short, blunt sticks, appeared to be trying to attack him. As soon as the smaller boy worked up the nerve to lunge forward, Mr. Dobrescu dropped to his knees and charged the boy. With a ferocious growl he tackled the boy, whose tiny body disappeared beneath a hundred pounds of pure muscle. Surely the boy's slender bones would break with such rough handling!

Her hand flew to her throat. "Oh my heavens!"

All three of them were laughing as they looked up at her. "Papa is a bear!" Luke's childlike voice came from beneath Mr. Dobrescu. "We are going to kill him!"

"Not unless you are faster on your feet, boy. You also need to make more noise on your approach. That will let the bear know you mean business."

"What on earth are you teaching them?" Libby asked.

"How to survive a bear assault," Mr. Dobrescu said as he rolled off the child and stood to his full height. "This is an important skill for all boys to master."

Libby leaned her hip against the front porch railing. "Don't tell me you have ever had to fight off a bear armed only with a stick, because I won't believe it."

His teeth flashed white in a face that was streaked with dirt and sweat. "I have never fought a bear," he acknowledged as he brushed the grass from his pants. "But it is a good thing for a man to know, yes? I would not pull your leg over this." Did he just wink at her? She must have imagined it because he went directly back to hauling the younger boy off the ground.

Libby drew her breath in surprise when the familiar shape of her cat appeared from beneath the juniper bush and sauntered toward the boy.

"Ivan!" she said excitedly. She squatted on the ground and beckoned, ridiculously glad to see her surly cat once again.

The ungrateful beast looked at her for about a second before he turned his attention back to Luke, curling around the boy's ankles in unabashed delight. Her eyes widened.

"Have you been drugging that cat?" Only a healthy dose of catnip could cause Ivan the Terrible to curl up to anyone.

"He likes me," Luke said. "Yesterday he brought me a dead frog and put it on my lap."

Well *that* sounded a little more like her infamous cat. Although, knowing Ivan, the gift of the dead frog might truly have been a gesture of affection.

"Is there something you need help with?" Mr. Dobrescu asked.

Libby turned her attention from her unfaithful cat. "Yes," she said, trying to parse her words to ask after the missing drawings without implying he had stolen them. "My father had a few designs that are not where I thought I would find them. Have you moved any of those drawings? They are all ink drawings on white paper, mostly of machinery."

Mr. Dobrescu was still breathing heavily from wrestling with his boys, but his entire attention was focused on her. Even when Luke plopped down and began tugging on his leg, the man just aimlessly stroked the boy's hair as he watched her. Finally, he spoke. "I have moved no drawings," he said. "Other than the first day when we hung your picture, we have moved none of the drawings or paintings."

"Oh." She glanced around, looking at the boys, who were lolling in the yard. A terrible thought struck her. All children loved to draw, didn't they? And if they saw paper with a nice blank side on the back, waiting to be scribbled upon. . . . Libby knew what *she* would have done with such paper when she was their age. She cleared her throat. "And your children?" she began hesitantly. She knew this man could be ferocious in defending his children, but she needed to know. "Is it possible your boys might have moved them? Or drawn in some of the blank spots?"

He cast a dark look at the boys. "Have you touched any of the drawings that are in this house?"

Both boys shook their heads. "You told us to leave them alone, Papa," Andrei said.

Mr. Dobrescu looked back at her. "It is true I told them not to touch any of the art. I do not believe they would have done so. If you would like, I will go room to room in search of these drawings for you."

He was standing in front of her, hands on his hips and looking her directly in the eyes. There was no hesitation or prevarication in his voice. She had the sense that he would be willing to dismantle the house board by board in search of the drawings if she asked him to.

Libby shook her head. "I have already searched quite thoroughly." Every drawer, cubbyhole, closet, and wardrobe had been opened. She had looked beneath every item of furniture where she sometimes stashed the larger pieces. The drawings were not there.

"What are the drawings of? If we see them, we will contact you."

"The most important drawings are of a combustion engine," Libby said. "But there are also some missing drawings of a windmill and a greenhouse. The greenhouse has a unique ventilation system on the roof."

Mr. Dobrescu's face brightened. "Like the greenhouse in the

82

backyard?" At her nod, his grin widened. "I wondered what that strange device on the roof was for. So your father designed this greenhouse himself?"

"Yes, it was quite brilliant." Some of Libby's fondest memories were in that greenhouse, but after Mama's death the greenhouse had fallen into disrepair. Two years ago Libby had suggested renovating it, but her father had no interest.

"Can you explain how this ventilation system works?" Mr. Dobrescu asked. "I could not get the metal door to open and it is getting very warm inside."

"You have been inside?" she asked in surprise.

"It was one of the first things we did," Michael said. "It took some work, but we have it back in operation."

Libby was stunned. With each passing year she had despaired as she saw the paint curl away from the beams and wood rot infect the posts. Dirt and algae spread across the glass panes until they were completely opaque. What had once been a sparkling gem where her mother reigned in a botanical paradise had morphed into a dingy, sad hulk of a memory.

"Show me!" Libby said.

Michael grinned and sprinted up the front porch steps, through the door, and back toward the kitchen. Libby scrambled to keep up as he led the way through the house and into the backyard, where her eyes filled with wonder.

It was magnificent! Gone were the rotting wood support beams. Freshly painted white panes reached upward, completing the original gothic design of the greenhouse. Glass panels sparkled in the sunlight and Libby felt as if she had just stepped back in time. She walked to the door and stepped inside.

When her mother was alive, this space was filled with flowers in gorgeous hand-thrown pots and ceramic planters. Jasmine and hyacinth had perfumed the air, and from the beams her mother had hung small stained-glass panels that had tinted the light with shades of amber and crimson. Today there were only plain wooden planting frames filled with dirt, sitting on the ground. It was a basic, homespun sight, but that did not lessen the thrill. The warm, loamy scent of freshly turned soil meant that the greenhouse was once again being used to nurture plants to life.

"If I did not see it with my own eyes, I would not believe it," Libby said. But she was elated. Just being able to walk inside a functioning greenhouse felt like an old friendship had been restored. She dropped to her knees to inspect the planting frames. "Have you already planted something?"

"Night-blooming jasmine," he said. "I brought the seeds with me from Romania."

"We have night-blooming jasmine here in America," she said. "My mother had a bush she kept in the corner of the greenhouse."

"Not like these plants," Mr. Dobrescu said. "This is a very rare strain that my father developed. I was lucky to be able to get as many seeds as I did before we had to fl . . . before we left," he said. His eyes flicked upward. "Do you know how to get the metal door on that ventilation system open? I have tried, but it seems permanently shut."

Libby smiled. Her father had calibrated the design to automatically open and close depending upon the temperature, but trying to describe the interior workings of the mechanism without showing him was difficult. "If you fetch the ladder from the storage shed, we can climb up and I will show you how it works."

He appeared surprised by the suggestion. "But you are a woman!"

"I can still climb a ladder. I've crawled atop this greenhouse many times over the years to keep the panels clear of debris."

It was comical how torn he appeared. He desperately wanted to understand how to operate the ventilation system, but he clearly disapproved of her climbing a ladder. A charming notion of gallantry, but antiquated. She looked out the greenhouse door to the older boy. "Will you fetch the ladder from the shed in the back corner?" she asked.

The boy nodded and took big loping steps toward the shed at the back of the yard. With his light brown hair and broad shoulders, he looked like a miniature version of his father. It was hard to guess the boy's age, but he now seemed older than she'd originally thought.

"Is it my imagination," she asked, "or is that boy a little larger than he was just last week?"

Mr. Dobrescu's chest swelled with pride. "Andrei grows like an oak tree shaking free of an acorn. I have seen enough food disappear down that boy's throat to feed a whole platoon of soldiers." The grin on his face was pure satisfaction.

Andrei struggled to hold the rickety shed door open with his foot while maneuvering the ladder through the opening. Several thumps and false starts caused Andrei to set the ladder down and adjust his grip. She was on the verge of offering to help, but Mr. Dobrescu's hand shot out to stop her. "Let Andrei handle this. He will figure out a way."

It seemed a little harsh when holding the door open would make the boy's task much easier, but the hand on her elbow held her firmly in place. She was about to tell him that such an action was not considered gentlemanly in America, but when she looked up, she was struck speechless by the expression in Mr. Dobrescu's face as he watched his son. It was a look of such overwhelming love she felt the strength leave her knees. Had she *ever* seen a man look at a child with such unabashed pride? Certainly not her own father. Jasper had been close to the perfect child, but not even he earned such a glowing look of approval from their father. What would it be like to have been the recipient of that sort of bighearted affection?

"I got it, Papa!" Andrei said in a voice that was as excited as it would be if he had just scaled Mount Everest. Mr. Dobrescu had been right not to let her interfere.

"Come and set the ladder over here, son." Libby moved a few steps to clear a space for the ladder, but as she looked around the area, something was not right. Something was missing. Her gaze tracked to her mother's rose garden, and she found nothing but a freshly churned pile of dirt.

Her heart lurched. The garden that had always been filled with vibrant roses was stripped bare and ugly in its blankness. She felt light-headed as she stared at the spot that had once been so beautiful, so treasured.

"Where are my mother's roses?"

Mr. Dobrescu seemed completely unconcerned as he followed her gaze to the plot of dirt. "We don't like roses," he said bluntly. "We will plant squash instead."

Had she heard correctly? Squash? Those roses had won awards all across New England. Each summer they bloomed in a riot of color and fragrance, beckoning memories of sun-filled afternoons with her mother. All that had been destroyed in order to grow *squash*?

"You had no right," she said weakly. This crude, arrogant man had already invaded her home in the most brazen way imaginable, but she was willing to obediently await the court's decision. While she played by the rules, this barbarian compounded his offense by severing the last remaining link she had to her mother. That thin, gossamer thread of joy she had shared with her mother had been ripped up by its roots and destroyed.

"This isn't your house," she said through clenched teeth.

"It is until the court rules otherwise. I do not like roses and will not have them growing on my property." His voice was implacable. Hateful.

She wanted to strike him. She wanted to find something he loved and ruin it before his very eyes. "In a few weeks the court will throw you out of this house, and you had *no right* to tear out my mother's roses. They were irreplaceable." Her throat clogged. It was silly to be mourning over some dead roses, but she felt so invaded. This man had stomped into her life and taken over everything.

"Did I do something wrong?" Andrei's young voice sounded

troubled. His father looked down and spoke rapidly to him in Romanian. Whatever he said caused the furrow on the boy's forehead to ease. He nodded and went inside the house.

Just because the man loved his children did not make him a good father. Libby looked up and struck where she knew she could do the most damage.

"What a horrible father you are," she said. "You have moved your children into this house and told them it is theirs. You have asked them to pour their hearts and energy into restoring the property, let them grow attached to this house when *you know* they will be evicted from it soon. What kind of man does that to his own children?" The poison-barb found its mark and Mr. Dobrescu's broad, handsome face blanched at her words, but anger was still roiling inside her. She looked at the blank patch of dirt. "You sow chaos and destruction wherever you go. The worst part of it is that your children will pay the price for your recklessness. While you wreak havoc, they will be left to suffer the consequences. You should be ashamed of yourself."

She turned on her heel and fled from the yard. She would have to rely on Sheriff Barnes to collect the rest of her belongings, for she was too heartsick to remain at this house.

7

Sheltered by a screen of fragrant hollyhocks and neatly trimmed yew shrubs, Jasper and Regina's garden was usually a haven for Libby, but she was still shaking from her encounter with Michael Dobrescu as she joined her father and Mr. Auckland at the garden table. It was a hot day and Libby rolled a cool glass of lemonade across her forehead.

"It is clear they are preparing to stay," she said. "They've already begun planting vegetables and some sort of jasmine he seems to think is highly prized." As the late afternoon sun lengthened the shadows, she recounted the destruction of her mother's rose garden, although the roses did not bother her father nearly as much as the missing designs. Even Mr. Auckland could not calm his increasing agitation. It was a relief when Jasper joined them at the garden table.

Her brother had gone to St. Catherine's Island to retrieve the prototype of her father's combustion engine. Jasper worked insane hours at the bank and she had felt terrible about asking him to go all the way out to the island to retrieve the engine, but everyone agreed that a complicated project might be the only way to help the professor hang on to his strained nerves. With a heavy clomp, Jasper set a canvas bag on the table. "The portable combustion engine," he said with a weary sigh as he sank onto the chair.

Libby lifted the engine gingerly from the bag to show Mr. Auck-land. "You see how small and clever it is? No one else has ever designed an internal combustion engine so light and portable."

The old librarian poked at the engine. "Very clever, Willard. If you patent it, you can make a fortune."

Libby bit her lip. Her father's refusal to patent any of his designs had been at the center of more than one pitched battle between Jasper and the professor. As she feared, Jasper immediately pounced on the opportunity. "It does not matter if the engine is not yet perfect," he said directly to his father. "Get a patent on this thing so you can protect the design. This has the potential to be very valuable, and you can barely afford to maintain your household based on what the college pays you."

Libby knew Jasper was right. Every year new technological inventions were coming to market, and her father should be protecting his designs by securing a patent. Just last year she had seen an extraordinary windmill that looked remarkably like her father's design, one of the many designs he'd abandoned when it failed to be perfect.

A shiny projection on the side of the engine caught Libby's eye. "Is that a new exhaust valve?" she asked her father. The distinct metal tube was definitely something that had not been on her drawing from earlier in the summer.

"I just added that a few weeks ago," Father said. "That valve will keep the engine cooler as it runs, meaning it will require less fuel to operate. There are many things I can still do to improve this engine before I bother with a patent," he said with a sour look at Jasper. The contemptuous way he said the word *patent* encapsulated her father's entire attitude toward his inventions. He did not work for profit or fame; he was seeking absolute perfection before he would allow anything he produced to be shown to the world. There was always something that could be made lighter, smaller, more efficient. These imperfections were a constant source of aggravation, like a grain of rice within a shoe that chafed until becoming impossible to ignore.

"I will begin a sketch of the improved design this evening," Libby said, anxious to steer the conversation back to their house on Winslow Street. "Jasper, the Dobrescus have begun modifying the house. Some for the good, some for the bad."

As she filled him in on the greenhouse and the destruction of their mother's roses, Jasper's mouth thinned with displeasure. "I'll ask the judge to order an injunction against any other modifications," Jasper said grimly. "Not that it will bring mother's roses back or wipe away the insult that has been done to our family."

Mr. Auckland straightened in his chair. "If it is any comfort to you, sentiment in the town is squarely on your side," he said. "The current gossip is that Mr. Dobrescu asked his next-door neighbor to remove her rosebushes, and Mrs. Gallagher took great offense. She planted more roses in retaliation. The Dobrescus have begun keeping chickens in their backyard and have a rooster that is bothering everyone on the street. One night a group of neighborhood children threw eggs at the house."

"Eggs!" her father sputtered. "Eggs thrown against my house!"

The old librarian held his hands up. "Mr. Dobrescu was out the next morning cleaning up, so there is no damage to the house. Just to his pride."

It should not bother her. The Dobrescus were interlopers who could not be expected to have the welcome mat rolled out for them by the neighborhood. But eggs in the middle of the night? It was not the sort of thing that made her proud.

"What kind of people are they?" her brother asked. "Chickens and roosters? And Libby's description of the planting frames in the greenhouse sounds more like agricultural cultivation rather than pleasure gardening. Are they some kind of peasants who think they can farm in the middle of a residential neighborhood?"

Mr. Auckland shook his head. "I have made some headway on

researching the family, and the more I look, the more interesting it becomes. The Dobrescu name is highly respected in Romania. The line goes back for centuries, and the family has been in control of the duchy of Vlaska since medieval times. The Duke of Vlaska controls a huge swath of the land that borders Bulgaria. It is valuable land that has been fought over for hundreds of years. Sometimes the land is taken by the Russians, sometimes by the Bulgarians. Lately it has been under fierce assault by the Ottomans. Always it has been under control of the Duke of Vlaska, who manages to negotiate with whatever invading power is ascendant."

Libby was fascinated but unable to reconcile how this mighty aristocratic family could be related to the brazen people who had invaded her home. "Do you think the old Cossack, the one who wore a fancy uniform with medals, might have been related to the duke?"

Mr. Auckland leaned back in his chair, his fingers rubbing his jaw as he contemplated the question. "The old Cossack's name was Constantine Dobrescu. It is a name that appears frequently in the duke's family, but it would be impossible to say based solely on the name."

One of the complications of Constantine Dobrescu's will was that it named his older brother, Enric Dobrescu, as heir. In the event of Enric's death, the house would descend to Enric's oldest surviving son. A curious codicil to the will explicitly stated, "My house *must* remain in Dobrescu hands. Only a man of the Dobrescu family will know what to do with this house."

Mr. Auckland confirmed that at the time of the old Cossack's death, the Duke of Vlaska had indeed been named Enric Dobrescu, and his younger brother was named Constantine Dobrescu. Still, such names were common in Romania and they could not jump to conclusions. They would need to do much better research before they could assume any affiliation between the Duke of Vlaska and Michael Dobrescu.

"Perhaps he was a servant in the duke's household," Jasper said. "He found an old copy of the will among the duke's papers, and rather than being a peasant all his life, he decided to roll the dice and claim the house for himself. If he knew the duke never intended to come to America, there was nothing to stop him."

Her father's eyes began to gleam. "His name is probably not Dobrescu at all. If I were a betting man, I would say he was a laborer in the duke's household."

"But what about Lady Mirela?" Libby asked. She stood and began pacing the garden, twisting her hands. "If you think he is a simple servant, how does she fit into this?" Michael Dobrescu seemed oddly protective of Lady Mirela, reluctant to even allow her to have contact with outsiders. Was he shielding her? Or perhaps he was hiding something. Every instinct in her body screamed that Michael Dobrescu was a plainspoken man who was incapable of deception. He seemed too blunt and crude to be related to European aristocracy, but if he was no relation to the duke's family, that meant he was an imposter. Subtlety seemed like an alien concept to Michael Dobrescu, but it was a quality any good liar needed in abundance.

"Lady Mirela is probably a two-bit actress he hired to help him carry off his scheme," her father said. "He can't fake the polish of an aristocrat, so he brought along someone who can. Simple as that."

Libby remembered something Mirela had said in that fleeting moment she had been allowed into the girl's room. The girl implied she had only one dress to her name, which undercut the notion she could be a European aristocrat.

Mr. Auckland set a new stack of documents on the table. "I went to the courthouse to see if I could glean any insight into the old Cossack," he said. "Shortly after he arrived in America, he filed a series of court petitions for a land grant. Apparently there was a convent in the mountains of Romania that had been destroyed in an earthquake. He petitioned the town to grant the holy sisters a plot of free land to reestablish their convent here in Colden. When the town turned him down, he went to the state of Massachusetts to petition for the same thing."

Her father was studying the papers that Libby assumed were the old Cossack's petition. His voice was mocking as he summarized the form. "It says here he claimed the earthquake was 'an act of God,' and that it was the sisters' 'holy destiny' to carry out their mission in America." Her father tossed the papers down on the table. "Someone ought to have explained the principle of the separation of church and state to the man."

"Keep reading," Mr. Auckland said. "Apparently the old Cossack bragged to the court that his brother often granted parcels of land to supplicants who came to him in Romania. That sort of language gives credence to the idea his brother was in fact the Duke of Vlaska." Mr. Auckland smiled and rubbed his hands together. "I think we need to learn more about the Dobrescu family than our poor local library can provide. I have some contacts at the Harvard library who may be able to help. It will take time, but if these people are related to the Duke of Vlaska, we should be able to unravel this little mystery."

"This is going to hurt, but I need you to hold still, boy."

Tears welled in Luke's eyes, but Michael could not stop to provide comfort. Three fat splinters were wedged into the side of Luke's face and they needed to be pulled before the swelling got worse and closed up around them. His fingers were sweating as he pressed the tweezers carefully below the largest splinter, grasped it, and slid it free.

Luke let his breath out in a whoosh. "One down and two to go," Mirela said as she gave Luke's hand a reassuring squeeze.

Michael was proud of how strong Mirela sounded. The moment the boys came home, bruised and bloodied from a fight with neighborhood children, she had taken charge. She secured the doors of the house, lest the troublemakers return, sent Turk for clean water, and soothed the boys while Michael frantically rummaged through the house looking for medical supplies. Andrei said three of the boys near the end of the street had been picking a fight for days. First had been the egging of their house, then came the taunts about the boys' long shirts. It was the custom in Romania for young boys to wear shirts outside of the pants, almost to the knees. The shirts were too long to tuck into their pants, so his boys had been wearing them as all the children in Romania did. *"Can I borrow your dress? I need something to wear to the ball!"* the Mulholland boy had taken to shouting at his children every time they stepped outside.

Today Andrei had had enough. He was not yet as tall as the Mulholland boy, but Michael had trained both his sons in hand-to-hand combat and Andrei was confident. Andrei toppled the Mulholland boy and was getting the better of him when the other two boys went after Luke, picking him up and throwing him face-first into a wooden fence. Luke's cries were enough to distract Andrei, and they both took a beating before they made their way home.

Michael positioned the tweezers around another splinter. "What condition were the other boys in at the end of the fight?"

"Two of them were crying," Andrei said. "I punched the little dark one in the stomach and he cried like a girl. Mulholland is a tough fighter though. I got three good punches in, but he caught me twice with a kick to the side."

Michael straightened. "You said the Mulholland boy is taller than you."

"He is."

"Then you should not have allowed him to get far enough away to land a kick. Remember, when you go against someone who is taller than you, stay close and use a quick combination of punches. It is hard for them to defend against punches coming from below."

Mirela whirled around to glare at him. "I cannot believe you are teaching these boys how to fight. Now of all times!"

Michael removed the last of the splinters from Luke's face. He did not want to argue with Mirela, but neither would he teach his children to run from a fight. He dipped a cloth in water and began wiping away the dirt that was encrusted around the scrapes on Luke's face. "Sometimes people pick fights with others because they are different. There is not much we can do about that because we *are* different and always will be. Sometimes they pick fights because they perceive you as an easy target. The best you can do in such situations is show them you are not weak, and that is what you did today, Luke. There is no shame in losing a fight. You may *never* win a fight, but if you demonstrate that you are not the sort to run away, you make it too difficult for them to want to bother with you. Eventually, they will give up." He turned and looked directly at Mirela. "I wish it was not this way, but that is the situation for these boys."

Exhaustion pulled him down onto a seat. For the second day in a row, he had walked over fifteen miles in desperate search of a particular type of tree he needed if his business was going to survive. In Romania, he knew the terrain well enough he could have gone out and found what he needed in short order, but America was an alien landscape. He needed to find an area where the soil was moist and sandy but had plenty of sunshine. Guessing where to find such conditions was exhausting, but he could not afford to stop looking. As soon as Luke was feeling better, he would go out and search again.

"Am I going to need stitches?" Luke asked.

Michael tried not to smile. Two years ago Turk had given Andrei a row of six tiny stitches when a scythe had cut into his leg. Ever since, Luke had desperately wanted some for himself. "A doctor is coming by the house later today to see Aunt Mirela. We will ask him to look at your face and decide."

Luke looked at Mirela. "Why are you getting to see a doctor? You weren't in a fight."

Mirela's face flushed a bit. "I haven't been feeling so well," she said softly. "I hoped it would get better now that we aren't on a ship anymore, but I still feel bad."

"What hurts?"

Michael gathered up the medical supplies and returned them to the box. "No more questions, Luke. You should never ask a lady why she wants to see a doctor. It is not gentlemanly."

Silence hung in the air, but he felt no need to elaborate. There was little he had been able to offer Mirela since she'd moved in with him, but at least he could protect her privacy. He retrieved his wallet from its hiding place in the parlor, counting out the dwindling supply of bills inside. He handed one to Mirela.

"I hope this will be enough to cover the doctor's fee. If it is not, tell him we will have some eggs soon. Or Turk can go hunting if the doctor would like some meat."

Mirela nodded but could not meet his eyes. "I understand," she said. There was a time when she would have worn enough jewels around her throat to pay a doctor's salary for an entire year. No matter how poorly her life had turned out, Mirela never complained, never asked for more than he could afford to provide for her.

The thought of Luke being thrown against a fence made him feel sick. He needed to earn more money. Quickly. Then he could buy his children proper clothes and make sure Mirela got whatever care she needed to finally heal.

And pay his attorney. Three times he had met with Mr. Crane to prepare for the looming court case, and each meeting ate further into his dwindling savings. Mr. Crane swore Michael's legal position was strong, but they could not afford to scrimp in preparing to defend Uncle Constantine's will in court, and it was getting expensive.

He looked over to the cabinet where his four precious vials were stored. They would be useless unless he could get the correct sort of resin to serve as a fixative. He knew exactly which sorts of trees would serve his purpose, but the contents of his vials would go bad unless he found the trees soon. Until he found them, he would not rest.

Michael fed a bit of kerosene to the wick, casting a greater rim of illumination around the geologic map spread across Professor Sawyer's desk. He'd found the map of Massachusetts beneath a stack of old atlases on the bottom shelf of a bookcase. Each swirling band of color indicated a different layer of geologic strata. If he could determine which color indicated sandstone, he could make an educated guess about where a grove of red juniper trees might be located.

Michael muttered a curse under his breath, wishing he had gone to class more during the one splendid year he had been able to attend college. He had enrolled in botany and chemistry classes, but they'd held little allure to a young man who had just arrived from the Romanian countryside to the glittering city of Paris. What had his father been thinking? Sending a man with Michael's weaknesses to Paris was like sending an alcoholic to be educated in a winery.

Michael rubbed his eyes and focused again on the map. Did the light green shades indicate limestone or sandstone? Or was it granite? Because if it was granite, there would be no red juniper trees for miles.

There was a heavy pounding on the stairs, and the study door flew open without a knock. Turk filled the opening, breathing heavily. "Lady Mirela is not in her room," he said. "I am worried about her. You know how she can get."

"Mirela has been in good spirits today," Michael said. "Perhaps she went for a walk?" She'd had a clean bill of health from the doctor earlier in the day and that seemed to put her mind at ease. At dinner, she'd laughed at Joseph's stories and insisted on helping the boys clean up after dinner. Before going up to her room to retire, she'd laid her hand against his cheek and thanked him for being the best brother in the world.

"I'll go see," Turk said. "You should check the rest of the house. It is not like her to go for a walk without telling anyone."

Michael stood so fast his chair tipped over. It was true. Mirela could be strong when safely protected behind the walls of her own home, but was timid when it came to venturing out on her own. And why had he blithely accepted her vague statement that the doctor gave her a clean bill of health?

"I'll search the house, you take the streets," Michael said.

Turk was out the door before he had even finished the sentence, and Michael went from room to room, flinging open doors and calling her name. When he found nothing, he bounded upstairs and did the same on the second floor, pausing only in Mirela's bedroom to look for any sign of where she might have gone. The bed had not been slept in, but neatly folded on the dresser was a stack of the boys' shirts. And a note.

```
I cut and hemmed the shirts for the boys. I wish I
could have done more for all of you. Love, Mirela.
```

The windows were open, allowing the warm summer air to waft inside the room. The scent of roses from the neighboring house carried on the breeze, and his jaw clenched as he tossed the note down.

He banged on Joseph's door. "Mirela is missing," he said. "Get dressed and search the attic. I'll search the yard."

Dread filled his throat, and his sense of foreboding grew even stronger when he realized that Mirela's open window had caused her to smell those roses.

The door banged as he strode out into the backyard. "Mirela?"

His voice echoed on the night air. He checked the yard, the newly planted gardens. He scanned the chicken coop and behind the shed.

Then he went to the greenhouse, the thin light from the moon revealing the horror within. "No," he breathed. He tugged at the door, but she had locked it from inside. He rattled the door. "Mirela, can you hear me!" he shouted as he banged on the door.

She was curled on her side, motionless on the ground. Could she still be alive with that much blood lost? Her dress was soaked with it and her skin looked like parchment.

He did not stop to think, he merely acted. With a forward lunge he plunged his shoulder against the glass, smashing it into a thousand shards. Pain sliced through his arm, but he ignored it as he kicked the flimsy support posts to the ground. Glass crunched beneath his boots as he sped to her side.

Her skin was clammy, but tears fogged his eyes when he saw a little blood weakly pulse from the cuts on her wrists. She was still alive. "Stay with me, baby sister," he murmured. "This is just one more battle we need to win. Stay with me."

He whipped off his shirt and tore it in two, using the fabric to bind her wrists. His own blood was running down his arm where shards of glass were still wedged in his skin, but he ignored the pain as he twisted the fabric tighter. It was not possible that Mirela would die here, not after everything she had triumphed over to get this far.

She was light in his arms, her face waxy and motionless in the moonlight. He carried her up the stairs, vaulting up them two at a time before laying her gently on her bed and shouting for Joseph to summon a doctor.

Tears rolled down his face at the sight of the perfectly hemmed shirts for his boys. He covered his eyes with his palms. "Why, Mirela?" he whispered. "Don't you know we all depend on you? Every one of us."

But she lay as still and lovely as a porcelain doll.

The room was silent except for the sound of the doctor's pencil scratching across the paper as he wrote instructions for Mirela's care. Michael sat motionless in the study, but his mind reeled. He'd thought Mirela's demons were all in her head. He'd thought that with time and care she would emerge from this hibernation that devoured her spirit to live a normal and whole life.

He'd been wrong. Mirela had syphilis.

The doctor had given her the terrible diagnosis that afternoon. Michael cursed himself for failing to even consider such a tragedy from happening after the brutal ordeal Mirela had endured. He was numb as the doctor outlined what they should expect. Mirela must never marry and never have children. The doctor's accounts of babies born to women with syphilis were chilling. They could be born blind, covered in sores and crying incessantly from pain until they finally screamed themselves to sleep. Mirela had always longed for children, but now motherhood was another dream that had been torn from her life. With proper care, she might live five years or fifty years, but she would battle this disease for the rest of her life. There were treatments that could stave off the escalation of the disease, but they were painful and costly.

"I'll find the money," Michael said.

The doctor shook his head. "She is not yet at the stage to begin the treatments. In the meantime, here is a diet she should follow to restore her blood. She should also drink a full glass of water every hour for the next several days. She must not be left alone, as she may try to re-injure herself if given the opportunity."

Michael turned his pain-filled eyes to the doctor. "She seemed so happy this evening. She laughed at dinner and smiled as she helped the boys clean the kitchen."

"It is not unusual for people who have resolved to end their life to feel this sort of peace," the doctor said. "They see an escape route and believe an end to their torment is near."

Joseph would stand guard over Mirela for the rest of the night. Tomorrow he would send Andrei to purchase the items on Dr. Kennescott's list for Mirela's new diet. Because of Mirela's kindness, Andrei would be able to walk into town with a shirt that looked just like what all the other American boys wore.

After the doctor left, Michael looked up the darkened staircase. A little light filtered from the open door of Mirela's room, but a sense of utter hopelessness settled like a millstone on Michael. For almost a year he had been forced to witness Mirela wither beneath soul-destroying despair and he had been *worthless* in stemming the tide.

But there was one thing he could do.

Dawn was still a few hours away, but this task could be handled now. With grim resolve he strode to the back of the house to get his battle-ax, then pushed through the kitchen door into the backyard. His bandaged arm throbbed with pain, but he ignored it as he vaulted the fence into his neighbor's yard. With grim resolve he strode forward, planted his boots, and began hacking away at the rosebushes that grew against his neighbor's trellis. With every blow he was striking out at the men who had violated his sister. Leaves rustled and the stems gave an ugly rasp as he tugged them free from the roots and threw them aside. Never again would their scent drift through Mirela's window and arouse memories that were best left in the past.

It took less than five minutes. There would be repercussions, but he did not care.

8

It was a warm afternoon, but a faint breeze ruffled the sycamore leaves that shaded the front lawn of Jasper and Regina's home. Libby sat on the front steps, watching Regina align herself over the croquet ball, a mallet held between her dainty hands as she planned her next move. Regina never played a game she did not intend to win, and she scrutinized the playing field with the intensity of a general scoping out a battlefield.

There were three players that afternoon: Libby, Regina, and Mrs. Sally Gallagher, her next-door neighbor from the house on Winslow Street. When she and her father first moved into Jasper's house, Libby thought it would be no more than a day or two before the sheriff could right the wrong that had been done to them. Days had stretched into weeks, and their visit was now nearing the one-month mark.

"Careful that you don't strike my ball," Sally Gallagher said. "That is a northern ball and not likely to welcome a southern assault." Sally's wit was as charming as a mosquito bite, but Regina still summoned a gracious smile at the quip.

Libby wondered if such comments hurt. Regina hailed from one of the most prominent families in South Carolina. Before the war her father had been a congressman and owned a tobacco plantation that spanned dozens of miles. As a child Regina played with silver tea sets and dressed her dolls in silk gowns imported from Paris. When she was twelve, the Civil War came to South Carolina, and that way of life was lost forever. The family fortune was gone, her father driven from political office, and a girl who once lived in a rose-tinted fairy tale came crashing down to a world of tilling the soil for potatoes and making soap from hog fat.

Regina's family pinned their hopes on their clever daughter. After years of meticulous budgeting, Regina's parents saved enough money to send their only child to college. Her college application had been submitted using only the initials of her first name, and she had been accepted into the same law school class as Jasper Sawyer. When the college discovered her deception, they were outraged and denied her enrollment, but not before she met and charmed Jasper. After their marriage, Regina settled in enemy territory. Libby had to admire the way Regina clung to the soft lilt of her southern accent. A less confident woman would have masked it after moving to New England, but Regina wielded her accent like the sea sirens of Greek mythology used their voices to lure sailors to their doom. Her delicate, melodic tone was so alluring that men positively melted at the sound of Regina Sawyer's voice.

"Now, Sally," Regina said with a smile, "can I help it if you failed to anticipate upcoming moves?" Regina gave her ball a solid strike, sending it bouncing off both Libby's and Sally Gallagher's balls. A masterstroke. It would be impossible to catch up with her now.

"Well, I seem to be losing on all fronts today," Mrs. Gallagher said. "At least I should get some satisfaction if Carleton goes to the courthouse and files that lawsuit like I told him to."

Libby looked up. "What lawsuit?"

"We are filing a lawsuit against that barbarian who has moved into your house," Mrs. Gallagher said with righteous indignation. "Two weeks ago he showed up in the middle of the night and destroyed every rosebush on our property. Can you imagine the nerve? A man like that simply must be stopped."

Libby had already heard about the Gallaghers' destroyed roses, as it was impossible to go to the market and *not* hear about the latest scandal. Libby stepped onto the lawn to take her turn. She was distracted and her ball rolled ineffectively into a wicket, coming to a complete stop and costing Libby a point. Michael Dobrescu was simply so *odd*. He was brash and crude, but why couldn't she stop thinking about him? She wondered what he would look like if he got a decent haircut. She wondered how he got the scar on the side of his face. More than anything, she wondered what sort of woman appealed to him. An ultrafeminine woman like Regina, or a more down-to-earth woman? Would he be a caring and gallant husband, or the sort who ordered his wife around like a vassal?

Not that it mattered. Michael Dobrescu was completely off-limits to her and always would be. She looked up at Mrs. Gallagher. "Did he give any explanation for ruining your roses? Did he even own up to the deed?"

"Oh yes, he came over the very next day and apologized to Carleton, although they were *my* roses and I'm the one with whom he should have spoken. He said some sort of claptrap about his sister being ill and an aversion to the scent of roses. Then she should keep her window shut, that is what I say." Mrs. Gallagher moved into position and fired off a healthy shot that moved her ball through the sixth wicket and earned her a point.

Regina casually strolled about the lawn, scrutinizing the evolving position of the croquet balls. "Do you suppose the sick sister is the 'Lady Mirela' you mentioned?" Regina asked.

"She must be. She is the only woman in the house, and she did seem a bit frail when I saw her."

"She is a good deal more frail now," Mrs. Gallagher said. "Doctor Kennescott has been over to the house almost every day." Mrs.

Gallagher looked both ways, then spoke in an exaggerated whisper. "Rumor has it she tried to commit *suicide*. Can you believe it?"

The breath left Libby's body in a rush. She sank down onto the steps of the front porch, wondering what kind of agony that girl must have felt to take such a drastic measure. "What happened?"

"They say she slashed her wrists in the greenhouse," Mrs. Gallagher said in a conspiratorial tone. "From my bedroom window I looked down into the yard, and sure enough, a big panel of the greenhouse glass was smashed in and I saw bloodstains on the ground. Shocking." Mrs. Gallagher walked back to her ball and tapped it further along the course. "Your turn," she said to Regina, but Libby's mind was still reeling.

Libby could only imagine how this would devastate Mr. Dobrescu. She felt dizzy and overheated. She waved her hand in front of her face to cool herself, but it did little good. Mrs. Gallagher came to sit beside her on the step.

"You must not let this distress you," she said. "Those people are not like us, and it won't be long before the court will make them leave. You should rest assured that everyone in the neighborhood is squarely on your side," she said firmly. "None of the grocers in Colden will sell food to them, so they must go into Bridgewater to buy their supplies. All the parents on Winslow Street have forbidden their children to play with the Dobrescu boys, which is just as well because those boys are incorrigible, picking fights with all the children on the block. Why, the Lancaster boy had a cracked rib because one of the Dobrescu boys kicked him in his side. Kicked him! Hardly the sort of people we want on our street. I can't wait to see the back of them."

Libby was well aware of the hostile sentiment in town toward the Dobrescus. When Mr. Dobrescu walked his boys into church last week, no one sat beside them in the pew. After the service, when others were congregated on the lawn outside the church to chat and catch up on gossip, ladies pulled their skirts aside as the Dobrescus walked past.

"Is Miss Mirela faring better?" Libby asked. "Is she likely to make a full recovery?"

It was Mrs. Gallagher's turn at croquet and she rose to her feet. "I have no idea. No one I know has dared to set foot on the property, lest those two wicked children attack."

Of course no one had paid a visit. The Dobrescus were pariahs in this town, and it was unlikely anyone had come to help them in this time of terrible need. They had eggs thrown at their house, were the target of at least two lawsuits, and now they could not even walk into the town square to buy a loaf of bread. The Dobrescus were her enemy, and now everyone in Colden had taken up her cause and was rallying behind her family to oust them from her home.

Never, never would she approve of what Michael Dobrescu had done to her family, but this could not go on. Jesus told His followers to love their enemies. Pray for their enemies.

Libby stood and straightened her shoulders. She could not love the Dobrescus, but she could take them a loaf of bread and a quart of milk. Perhaps she was the least likely person in the entire town to extend a hand of kindness to the Dobrescus, but she was going to do it.

9

This must be what it feels like to be a traitor. Libby swallowed hard as she walked up the slate pathway to the front door of what used to be her home. Mr. Stockdale stopped trimming his bushes to stare at her, the two Masterson children quit playing kickball, and on the front porch next door, Mrs. Gallagher's rocking chair froze mid-rock. All were staring at her as she walked up the pathway, a large covered basket over her arm.

Her errand of mercy was not as private as she had hoped, but she kept her gaze fastened on the front door. She knocked and awaited an answer, feeling the stares of her neighbors boring into her back. Even the squirrel perched on a nearby rock stopped its feverish gnawing of an acorn to watch her. Wasn't there some law against aiding and abetting the enemy? They used to shoot people for that during the War.

There was no answer to her knock. A combination of early morning heat and anxiety caused a little trickle of sweat to creep down the small of her back. Libby knocked again, wondering if she would be forced to leave the basket on the front step when the fabric covering a window wavered. Had it been her imagination? But it moved again and this time the cautious face of one of the young boys stared straight at her. A moment later the front door opened a sliver, only enough to reveal one troubled eye.

"What do you want?"

The boy could stand a bit of guidance on etiquette, but he was not Libby's concern today. "I came to visit with your family," she said cautiously. "I understand Miss Mirela has been ill. I brought some bread and a little bit of blackberry jam." She brought a lot more than that. Given the size of the three huge men who lived there, plus the appetite of an adolescent boy, she had packed her basket with ham, cheese, apples, tea, and a quart of milk.

The door opened a bit wider, letting Andrei look her straight in the face. "Last time you came, you got mad about the roses." The accusation in his voice was plain, but all Libby could see was the cut on the boy's lip and an ugly bruise darkening the corner of one eye. She did not know if this boy was being bullied or if he had been the instigator, but she did remember what it was like to feel like an outsider at his age. She softened her tone.

"Yes, I did," Libby said. "But I am not angry today, and I think your family might welcome a visit. Is your father home?"

"He is sick. You can't see him." The boy was putting up a good show of bravado, but it was impossible to miss the panic in his voice. He was afraid.

"Oh dear," Libby said. "Things must be very bad inside, am I right?"

The boy glared at her, mistrust warring with indecision on his face. He also glanced more than once at the basket she carried. If the child was hungry, she was not about to stand on the front porch arguing with him. With a firm hand, she grasped the side of the door and pushed her way inside.

"I have milk and it is best to get it into a cool place as soon as possible, right?" So focused was she on winning Andrei's cooperation, she did not hear the danger coming from above.

"What do you want?" a voice lashed out. She whirled around to see Michael Dobrescu looming at the top of the staircase. Her hand flew to her throat and she gasped. *Is this the same man?* His bloodshot eyes were bright with fever and the way he was leaning against the upstairs wall made him look like a tree about to topple over in a good stiff wind. One arm was cradled in a sling and he used the other hand to prop himself against the railing as he descended the stairs. He winced with each painful step.

Libby clutched the handles of the basket. "I heard that Miss Mirela was feeling poorly. I brought some food." But it was more than a bit of food she wanted to offer this family, especially now that she knew even the Dobrescu patriarch had taken ill. The Dobrescus were strangers in a foreign land that had not welcomed them, but they were still part of the human family. They had brought most of the trouble down upon themselves with their blunt and aggressive actions, but they were still people who bled when they were cut, hungered when there was no food. When their children were ridiculed, the pain rippled through the entire family. She wanted to assure them they were not alone and someday soon the darkening clouds would lift. The people of Colden had not done a very good job at that, but perhaps she was the best person to do so.

It took Mr. Dobrescu a full minute to lower himself down the stairs. When he arrived a fine sheen of perspiration covered his skin and she heard a rattle in his lungs with each breath.

"What happened to you?" she asked softly.

What a relief to see a bit of humor glimmer in his eyes. "Just a stupid flesh wound," he said. "Didn't get it cleaned up in time and it is infected. I will live."

But the way he was swaying on his feet made Libby not so sure. She set the basket down and grasped him by his good arm and propelled him toward the parlor. "*Men,*" she muttered under her breath. "Somehow, I think you would say that even if you had both limbs hacked off." It was surprisingly easy to steer him toward the parlor and coax him to sit. He slumped against the padded back of the settee and spread his legs out, his enormous frame filling most of the space. She noticed that Andrei remained in the front hall and had opened her basket, rummaging through it like a hungry jackal.

She placed her hand on Michael's forehead and was nearly scorched by the raging fever.

"You are liable to burn this house down if we can't get your temperature under control. Have you seen a doctor about this?"

"Turk stitched me up."

"Did he clean the wound? With soap and water?"

Mr. Dobrescu turned to look at her. "Soap? What is that? I don't think we have this new-fangled *soap* in Romania." For a moment she was taken aback, and then she noticed the telltale lifting of the corner of his mouth. He must not be too deathly ill if he could joke with her. Her comment did sound terribly condescending, but he spared her the embarrassment of a reply by gesturing to her with his one good hand. "Come sit beside me."

There was barely any space left on the settee, but she found enough room to perch on the edge. The moment she was settled he wrapped his big hand around her wrist, pulling it to his nose. He closed his eyes and breathed deeply from the back of her hand. "This is a different scent you wore than the last time you were here."

Libby's jaw dropped. What kind of man went pawing after a woman the moment she came within arm's length? Regina had bought a bottle of fancy lotion she'd quickly tired of and given to Libby. The silkiness of the scented lotion was pure luxury, and Libby had taken delight in using it every morning that week. She ought to jerk her hand away, but the expression on Mr. Dobrescu's face was so intriguing, like a wine connoisseur sampling a fine vintage of cabernet. She was mesmerized by how tiny and fragile her hand felt when encased in his work-roughened palm.

His tension drained away and a smile floated on his perfectly sculpted lips. "Neroli blossom with a bit of white lily and jasmine," Mr. Dobrescu said. "Very nice."

He was wrong. The lotion was scented with orange blossoms,

but she did not want to be petty and correct him. Still, it was oddly charming to watch this hulking brute try to dissect the various scents in her lotion.

Andrei came scurrying into the room carrying the jar of jam. He spoke to his father in Romanian, clutching the jar to his chest and fidgeting in excitement, but Michael held up his hand. "Say it in English."

First Andrei glanced at her, then to Michael, his brow furrowed and lips compressed in thought. Finally he held the jar out toward her. "I do not know the English word for *this*."

"Blackberry jam," she supplied.

Andrei looked back to his father. "Can I have blackberry jam on the bread?"

Mr. Dobrescu nodded. "First you must thank Miss Sawyer for her kindness."

Andrei did so, then tore off to the kitchen, summoning his younger brother to join him. That jam was going to vanish before nightfall. She smiled at the sound of kitchen drawers opening and slamming, punctuated with the excited chatter of Romanian voices as the boys indulged in what was apparently a treat for them. But when she glanced back at Michael, he looked exhausted and troubled.

"It was very thoughtful of you to bring the bread and jam," he said. "By chance did you bring any spinach?" She blinked, not quite certain she had heard him correctly, but he repeated the question.

"No. I did not bring any spinach."

He nodded. "I see."

An awkward silence stretched between them. It was such a strange request that Libby knew there must be a reason for it. "Would you like me to bring you some spinach? I can stop by Olaf Gustafson's vegetable stand on the way home."

Michael shifted on the sofa, looking as uncomfortable as a sinner in a church pew. "Normally I would not ask such a thing, but my sister requires a special diet. And not all of the shopkeepers in this town welcome our business."

None of the shops in town welcomed their business, if rumor was correct. "I see," Libby said. Why should she feel guilty for what her neighbors were doing? Their actions were a show of loyalty and support, and she should feel no shame about it. Nevertheless, she doubted the local shopkeepers would deny an ailing woman the nourishment necessary to restore her health.

"I heard that your sister tried to harm herself," she said softly. "Is it true?"

There was no flinch in his eyes, only sad acceptance. "It is true." He looked as though he had aged ten years at the simple statement. Furrows formed along the side of his mouth and the skin around his eyes crinkled in concern. "She has been struggling for a while now, but things have gone worse for her in recent days," he said. "I wish there was a way for me to come to her rescue, to fix what is broken inside her . . . but I find this is impossible for me to do."

He reached into a small drawer in the sofa table. "The doctor gave me a list of food Mirela should eat for the next few weeks. She lost a great deal of blood and it is difficult for her body to manufacture more unless she is fed properly. I have been sending Joseph into neighboring towns to purchase what she needs, but it has been difficult. Milk and spinach do not last long in this heat, and we must go every day." He dropped his gaze. "I have been too sick to help."

He spoke the words in a low voice that radiated with shame. Libby sensed that if this man was hungry, he would rather pull up and chew on the floorboards before stooping to ask for help, but when the needs of his family came into play, he would do whatever was necessary to get them fed.

"I will be happy to go to the market for you," she said. "Tell me what you need and I will fetch it immediately."

The droop of his shoulders and the bob of his Adam's apple

let her know how much this was costing him. "Here is the list." Michael extended the page to her, and she had no choice but to take it. It was much longer than mere milk and spinach. It was a long list, but all of the words were utterly incomprehensible to Libby. She let her gaze travel up and down the page, pretending she was perfectly capable of understanding the words written in spindly, wavering script.

She bit her lip. Would she ever become accustomed to the embarrassment of not being able to read? It did not matter how keen her memory, how quick her grasp of mechanical details—any five-year-old child could read, while she was an utter failure. Still, she had become adept in masking her shortcoming over the years.

She looked up at Mr. Dobrescu. "Can you read English?" she asked.

"Yes."

She pushed the piece of paper back into his hands. "Show me." All she needed was to hear the list read a single time and it would be burned into her memory.

Mr. Dobrescu was peering at her through those disturbing eyes. Normally they were a deep stormy blue, but today they were so bloodshot they seemed almost purple. He tapped the list against his knee. "Is this some kind of test?"

She did not flinch. "Yes. It is a test to see if you can read English. Tell me what the list says."

He pierced her with another of those probing stares, making her feel like a child whose hand was caught in the cookie jar. So long did he scrutinize her that Libby thought she might have to resort to another tactic to learn what was on the list, but finally, he picked up the list and began reading. "Spinach, potatoes, fresh parsley, milk . . ." He continued reading while Libby committed every item on the list to memory.

When he finished reading, Libby turned to look at him. "There are ten items on that list, but you only read nine," she said.

"I did not include eggs," Mr. Dobrescu said. "We have chickens in the yard so there is no need to purchase eggs. Did I pass your test?"

She took the note from him and folded it carefully before putting it in her pocket. "Excellent, Mr. Dobrescu. Your command of English is quite impressive for someone . . ." She stopped herself before saying something terrible. *For someone so uneducated*, she had been about to say. Why was she assuming he was uneducated? He and his men were ham-fisted brutes who seemed more comfortable in a barnyard than a drawing room, but he spoke at least two languages and could read and write, two things Libby could not master despite years of torture sitting in a schoolroom.

Fortunately, Mr. Dobrescu had not caught her near slip. "Then let us try teaching you a bit of Romanian," he said. "You have been mispronouncing our name very badly. The emphasis is on the first syllable. *Dobrescu*," he enunciated for her.

The way he pronounced his name made it sound entirely different. Musical, even. Libby tried to imitate him, but it still sounded wrong. He said his name again, and this time Libby noticed the way he rolled over the R sound. It was a difficult thing for her to master, since her tongue simply did not want to cooperate. Or was this a movement she should be making in the back of her throat?

When Libby tried for a third time, a smattering of giggles came from behind her. She turned to see both boys standing in the corner, their faces smeared with jam and laughing at her attempts to pronounce their name.

"Perhaps I will do better if you say it for me, Luke."

The child's smile was huge as he shouted his name for her, but Libby still could not roll the trill in the middle of their name. Both boys came rushing forward, eager to provide advice on how to master the correct pronunciation, but it was a combination of rhythm and trill that was simply very difficult for her American mouth to master.

116

"Why don't you call me Michael," Mr. Dobrescu said. "You will damage your throat if you keep mangling our name."

It was terribly improper to call an unrelated man by his first name, especially one with whom her family had such a contentious relationship. But perhaps that was all to the good. If she and the Dobrescus could learn to see each other as honorable people, perhaps the looming court decision would not be so ugly.

"All right, Michael."

The children were suffering from cabin fever, so Libby took them with her to the market. Besides, what better way to show the shopkeepers of Colden that she wished this embargo against doing business with the Dobrescu family to end?

The sidewalks of Colden had been laid down decades ago, and roots of the mighty elm and silver maples had spread out to lift and buckle the path. The roots were annoying, but the trees provided a wonderful green-tinted shade on their walk to the market. It felt so natural, the way Luke's hand was clasped in her own. A typical mother would probably take a moment like this for granted, but Libby savored every second of having a young child look up to her like she was a fairy godmother, taking him on an unexpected outing. A smile spread across her face and she clasped Luke's hand a little tighter.

However, only a fool could miss Andrei's guarded look as he scanned both sides of the street on their journey. Was it because he'd had a bumpy ride these first few weeks in Colden, or had he always been the suspicious type? If the Dobrescus were gypsies, as her father contended, the children would have been accustomed from infancy to be mistrustful of others and on the lookout for trouble.

Michael Dobrescu stood guard over his children like a grizzly bear protecting its young, and never would she have a better chance to glean a little insight into their life in Romania than at this very moment. Luke's hand was trusting within her own, but she felt no shame as she began peppering the children with questions.

"What was a typical day like in Romania?" she asked.

Both children looked confused at her question. It was very impressive how quickly they were learning English, but perhaps she needed to be more blunt if she was going to get any insight. "Did you live in a town like Colden? Or a big city like Boston?" When they did not supply an answer, she kept probing. "Or did you move a lot? Traveled from town to town?"

"No," Luke said. He did not elaborate, so Libby tried again.

"Did you live in the country? Where there are not many people but lots of farms?"

Luke nodded vigorously. "Yes. Our house was a farm."

It made sense. Michael seemed like a rough-hewn sort of person who belonged outdoors swinging a scythe or driving a plow behind a team of oxen.

"What kind of farm did you have?" She directed the question to Andrei, whose command of English was better than Luke's rudimentary vocabulary. "Did you have animals? Like cows and chickens, or did your grow plants?" She was not certain he would know what the word *plant* meant, so she stopped and grasped some of the fronds of wild grass that grew alongside the pathway. "Plants like this? Or corn? Or wheat?"

"Plants," Andrei said. "But not like this."

"Perfume!" Luke blurted out. "Papa grows the best perfume in the world."

Libby turned an amused glance to Luke, who was skipping and tugging her hand in his excitement to move faster. She must not forget how difficult it was to learn a foreign language, and even if he got some words wrong, she could still probe for more information. "Perfume, you say!" Libby said with a forced laugh. "I can't imagine what a perfume farm looks like. Can you describe it to me?"

Luke spun away from her grasp and held his hands out as wide as he could stretch them. "Roses. Roses everywhere." He stopped and struggled to find the words, shaking his hands in frustration. The poor child was trying so hard to communicate, but did not have the command of the language to do so. Finally, Luke turned to Andrei and spoke in a quick stream of Romanian. Andrei provided the translation.

"He says that even if you stand on the roof of our house, all you would see is roses. Everywhere you look, there are roses."

Her steps stilled. What kind of farm would have nothing but flowers? Surely the boy was exaggerating. Maybe their mother liked roses and Michael Dobrescu had indulged her with a lavish rose garden. After all, Libby's own father had gone to great lengths to build a greenhouse that would please his wife, so she knew men were prone to doing such things for a woman they adored.

Why should that hurt? Whatever relationship Michael Dobrescu had with his late wife was none of her business. The woman had given him two fine sons, and based on the care Michael lavished on his sister, it was likely he would have been equally protective of his wife. What would it be like to be the object of that sort of adoration? Any man who planted acres of roses to please his wife must carry quite a torch for her. He was unlikely to be the sort who would flirt with an illiterate spinster.

Olaf Gustafson's vegetable stand was the first place they needed to stop. Libby had been to school with Olaf, where he was famous for his willingness to eat poison ivy on a dare. Now Olaf was married with two small children. Six days a week he manned the vegetable stand, and on the seventh he went to church with his wife and children. If he still ate poison ivy on a dare, Libby had not heard of it.

Luke's hand was still clasped within her own as they approached the stand, but she reached out to snag Andrei's hand too. Andrei apparently thought himself too old to be seen in such a juvenile position, but Libby tightened her grasp and pulled him closer.

119

"Have you any fresh spinach today?" she asked, maintaining her grip on the struggling Andrei.

"Plenty," Olaf said. He looked with curiosity at the two children. It was not unusual for Libby to have a passel of neighborhood children following her about town, but these two were clearly strangers to Olaf. Rather than waiting for the inevitable question, Libby took the initiative.

"I've brought the Dobrescu children with me. They will be a great help carrying all these things home, right, Luke?"

"Dobrescu?" The disbelief in Olaf's eyes was as if she had said she had the children of Genghis Khan in tow. Olaf looked with confusion from the children to Libby. He scratched his head and shifted his weight from side to side. Finally, he looked her in the eye.

"Um, Libby? Do you know who these kids are?"

It was true that Libby had never won any prizes for academic brilliance in school, but did Olaf really think her this dim? She smacked her forehead with the palm of her hand. "Oh heavens, I must have a stupid spot the size of Brazil. Do you think these scamps are related to that man in my father's house?"

Olaf winced in sympathy as he nodded. "I'm afraid so."

She clasped her hands and leaned forward with an urgent whisper. "Help me, Olaf, what should I do?"

He gave a helpless little shrug. "I think you are going to have to make the best of it."

She allowed the tension to drain from her face. "I suppose so. How about you give me those bunches of spinach two for the price of one. I need something to perk me up from this disaster."

To her amazement, Olaf did not quibble.

It took less than an hour to make the rounds at the vegetable stand, the bakery, and the dairy. After Libby collected the items for Mirela, she decided to stop by the pharmacy to buy a few

120

peppermint sticks for the children, and at the milliner's shop simply to look at the new hats. At each stop she made a point of introducing the Dobrescu boys. Andrei was a quick study, and after the first incident at Olaf's vegetable stand he had figured out precisely what she was doing and began cooperating with her. She hoped he was not laying it on too thick with the way he smiled up at her and pretended to hang on her every word, but at least it was having the desired effect on the shopkeepers.

As she suspected, Michael Dobrescu was waiting for them, watching out the front window with the eyes of a hawk. He flung the front door open as soon as she came within sight of the house. "The townspeople gave you no trouble?" Worry loomed in his troubled expression.

"There was a group with pitchforks and flaming torches, but I battled them off," she said. It took a moment for Michael to process her humor, but his look of relief was palpable. She pressed the basket into his hands. "I had no trouble," she said softly.

The blazing smile of gratitude that lit his face almost melted her bones. If she had thought Michael Dobrescu's strength had been dangerous, it paled in comparison to his gratitude. She was helpless to resist as he opened the door wide and invited her inside.

10

The rumor mills in Colden moved faster than a summer storm, and her father was waiting for her when she returned to her brother's house. "Arthur Stockdale tells us that you went to the house and spent over two hours inside," her father said. "Two hours! And I hear you were traipsing about town with the Dobrescu children, filling your basket like you were shopping for Christmas." The hair on her father's head was even more wild than usual, indicating he had been dragging his hands through it, which he did whenever he was plagued by a perplexing issue. "I am giving you the benefit of the doubt and am assuming you were there in order to gather information for the coming court case. Or perhaps searching for the missing mechanical drawings."

Libby set the empty basket down on the kitchen counter and nodded a polite greeting to Mr. Auckland, who was sitting at the kitchen table before a stack of old books. The memory of Andrei's delight as he slathered jam over the freshly baked bread was worth any criticism hurled her way. "I dropped off some food," she said. "I also went into town to get a few other items. Both Mr. Dobrescu and his sister are ill, and the local merchants are refusing to do business with them. They have to walk almost five miles just to purchase something to eat."

"All to the good," her father said. "Neighbors should stick up for one another, and that is exactly what the people of Colden are doing. You are undermining their heartfelt efforts, and I trust it will not happen again. Now, sit down and listen to what Mr. Auckland has learned about the old Cossack."

Mr. Auckland laid his hand across a heavy book with an ornately embossed leather cover. "I just got back from Boston, where I've been prowling through the library at Harvard," he said. "I asked for everything they had about the 9th Duke of Vlaska. I wanted to learn if there was a legitimate connection between the duke and the old Cossack, or if their identical names were just a coincidence. We found the Duke of Vlaska's obituary from August of 1870 in the *New York Times*. The obituary mentions a brother, Constantine Dobrescu, who emigrated to America and settled in Colden, Massachusetts. So the old Cossack was in fact the younger brother of the Duke of Vlaska."

Her father clapped his hands together and leapt from his seat. "Did you hear that?" He practically danced around the room. "Don't you understand what this means?"

Libby just stared. "No. I don't see how this helps our case at all."

"Libby, *think*!" her father implored. "You have witnessed that this person who calls himself Michael Dobrescu is a crude boar with no manners. His children are wild animals and his henchmen are likely hired off the docks. Is this a man you believe could be the son of a duke? Offspring from near royalty?"

Mr. Auckland opened the ornately bound book, using a silk ribbon marker to guide him to a particular page. "This book chronicles modern European aristocratic families." He turned the book so Libby could see a page where a large photograph had been tipped into the book and pasted beside the text. "That is a photograph of the 9th Duke of Vlaska and his wife," he said. "Can you see any resemblance to the man you know as Michael Dobrescu?"

She scrutinized the photograph. A severe man in a military

uniform looked directly at the camera. A sash was draped diago-
nally across his uniform, and a gold chain as thick as her wrist
hung around his neck. One hand rested on the hilt of a jeweled
sword, while the other he held stiffly forth to support his wife's
hand. So proud and forbidding, the man looked like he could be
the emperor of the universe.

Libby leaned closer to the photograph, scanning the structure of
the Duke's face, the blade of his nose, the shape of his eyebrows,
none of which resembled Michael Dobrescu. The duke's hair was
oiled and scraped completely back from his wide forehead, revealing
a distinctive peak in an otherwise straight hairline. There was no
resemblance between Michael and the duke whatsoever.

Her attention shifted to the duchess. She looked equally rigid,
a small woman poured into a satin sheath encrusted with pearls
and dripping with jewels. She wore a ceremonial sash identical to
her husband's, with a small tiara nestled amidst a fringe of tight
curls. Her compact stature barely reached the duke's shoulder,
and it was impossible to believe that this petite woman could be
Michael Dobrescu's mother.

"I don't see any resemblance at all," she said. "Neither one of
them looks like Michael Dobrescu."

Her father pulled the book toward him. "That's right!" he
gloated. "The man in our house is an imposter. If he was the duke's
oldest son, he would be living in a palace in Romania."

Everything her father said made sense. If the old Cossack had
been an ordinary soldier from Romania, it stood to reason that
his nephew could be a simple soldier or a farmer like Michael Dobrescu. That was the scenario her father feared. Learning that the
old Cossack was an aristocrat, the younger brother of a duke, made
it far less likely that Michael had a legitimate claim to the house.
After all, why would the oldest son of a duke be so eager to leave
behind a title and come all the way to America to seize her house?

Her father continued. "Somehow the man calling himself

Michael Dobrescu saw a copy of the old Cossack's will and is trying to pull off the impersonation of the century. He is a lump of coal pretending to be a diamond. He won't succeed."

She thought of the acres of roses. Wouldn't an aristocratic household have ready access to flowers? Perhaps Michael was responsible for raising the fresh flowers that filled the rooms of the ducal palace.

"But how can we prove it?" Libby asked. "I can't imagine a court will be convinced he is an imposter just because he does not share a resemblance with the old duke."

Mr. Auckland leaned forward in his chair. "It will be easy enough to prove who he is *not*. The oldest son of Enric Dobrescu would be the 10th Duke of Vlaska, and that is the person named in the old Cossack's will. It should be easy enough to get a picture of the current duke. Or at least find out what happened to him. I gather the region has been swept up in a number of wars for several years, and those things can sometimes be rough on reigning aristocrats. All we need to do is track down information about the current duke so we can prove Michael Dobrescu is a fraud."

The mysterious girl they called Lady Mirela had attempted suicide. Was it possible she was a member of the duke's family? And she fled her home, taking loyal servants with her? If she was a member of the duke's household, it would be reasonable to assume she had heard tales of an eccentric uncle who had emigrated to America long ago and left a house to the duke, which no one bothered to claim. If she wanted to escape from Romania, be it from the war or conflict with her parents or any one of the hundreds of reasons a young woman might run away from home, the unclaimed house in America would be a perfect place to flee. Was it possible that Lady Mirela was the mastermind behind the entire plot to take over the house?

When she voiced her suspicions to her father, he agreed. "If Lady Mirela is the duke's daughter, she would need help claiming the house," he said. "The will specifies the house is to go to the next *male* Dobrescu. It doesn't matter if she is the daughter of the duke or not. She is precluded from inheriting the house."

Libby narrowed her eyes and tried to remember exactly what she observed those few moments she was in the same room as Lady Mirela. Her manner and bearing were aristocratic. When Michael first tried to drag Libby from the room, Mirela held up her hand and Michael had immediately halted, as if he was deferring to her. Could Michael merely be a figurehead, while Lady Mirela was steering the ship?

They needed more information, and they needed it quickly. "The court date is just over a week away," Libby said. "Will you be able to find what you need before then?"

The old librarian looked at her father. "Are you up for a train ride to Washington, Willard? There was nothing about the new Duke of Vlaska at the Harvard Library, but I expect we will find more current information at the Library of Congress."

"I'll go. If it is the last thing I do on this planet, I will drive those gypsies from my house. Filthy liars. Thieves too."

Perhaps they were liars and thieves. She did not know them well enough to vouch for their honesty, but she did know they had qualities of great love and perseverance within that family. "I'm not certain what kind of people they are," Libby said, "but I think what the townspeople are doing is wrong. I don't think the Dobrescus should be shunned, especially not when they are battling terrible sickness and despair in the house. They don't deserve that."

Her father sank into a kitchen chair, looking as weak as if she had punched him in the stomach. "*They* don't deserve this? *They* don't deserve what has happened to them?" he said, suddenly looking every one of his seventy years. "I am an old man. My entire life has been devoted to work. In the last forty-five years, I have taught thousands of students in exchange for a modest salary and the chance to tinker with my inventions. After years of saving, I scrimped together enough money to buy a house where my wife could be proud to raise her children. I spent years repairing that house with my own two hands." Her father's voice started to wobble, but he would not stop speaking. "I have worked for everything, *everything* I have. I never cheated anyone or asked for something I was not entitled to. And one day, when my back was turned, a group of foreign vagabonds slid into my home and declared it theirs."

He banged his fist on the table, rattling the cups and saucers. "What if the court says they are right? They have done *nothing* to earn that house. The old Cossack scribbled something on a piece of paper decades ago and that is supposed to wipe away all I worked for? All the years I worked and toiled and saved to buy that house?" To her horror, her father's eyes filled with tears. "Did none of my labor exist?" he asked in a thin voice. "I am an old man with pain in my joints. I have less and less energy to keep teaching hundreds of students every year, but I am the one who has been thrown out onto the street."

He was openly weeping. When he set his hands on the table, they were shaking with palsy and his face was carved with lines of exhaustion. "I can't lose my house. I don't have enough time to start over again," he said on a ragged breath. "I know it is not Christian of me, but I am thankful my neighbors are supporting me. It is comforting to know they see the injustice of what has happened and are using whatever small power they have to lend me support . . . because for the last four weeks, I have had no power at all."

The tears subsided, but he leaned his forehead on his hand and stared at the floor. Libby rose to her feet and moved to stand behind her father's chair. She wrapped her arms around his shoulders and hugged him. "Please don't make yourself sick over this," she whispered. "I don't know how, but I am certain all of this will unfold in a way that will get you back into your house. It will only take a little time."

One of her father's hands covered her own and squeezed it. "You are a good girl, Libby. I have often been disappointed in you, but that does not mean I do not appreciate your finer qualities."

A smile tugged at the corner of her lips. Her father's compliments were as fleeting and rare as a hummingbird in the depths of winter, but she must accept these little gems whenever they occurred. His next words made her pause.

"I don't want you going back to that house. The Dobrescus are dangerous people and you are to keep away from them. If you love me, if you are *loyal* to me, you will stay away from them."

Libby squeezed his shoulders, but carefully gave no reply.

The Dobrescus may have been dangerous people, but never had Libby seen two boys appreciate a jar of jam as fiercely as Andrei and Luke. Whatever chicanery she suspected of Michael or Lady Mirela, Libby was determined to see that those boys would enjoy the simple pleasure of another jar of jam. Besides, Libby pounced on any excuse she had to spend time with her niece, Tillie, and it was a perfect day to pick blackberries to make another batch of jam.

Regina looked as coolly beautiful as ever, a broad-brimmed straw hat framing her face as she carried the basket into which Libby and Tillie deposited the berries. Ever since she was a child, Libby had been coming to this stretch of road leading away from town, where the blackberry brambles were dense and thriving. She reached through the scratchy leaves to pluck out the ripest berries.

"Careful not to touch my dress, honey," Regina purred as Tillie emerged from the bushes with a handful of sticky berries clutched in her palm. "That dark juice on your fingers will stain and never come off." Regina was resplendent in a milky-white gown with tiers of fabric flouncing from her waist. Carefully holding her skirts away from the bushes, Regina refrained from the berry picking, but watched as Libby showed Tillie how to spot the ripest berries, the glossy fat ones that had turned fully black.

"I wish you could have seen Mirela," Libby said. "Something about her demeanor made it seem like she did not fit in with the rest of the family. I would give anything to know your take on the situation. Somehow I think she may be the most dangerous person in that house."

If Lady Mirela was a fraud as her father suspected, Regina would be able to discover it. Regina had been trained since birth in the right turn of phrase, posture, comportment. Everything from the proper tying of a hair ribbon to the correct way to rise from a chair was second nature to Regina, and she would know how to spot an imposter. It was possible that her father and Mr. Auckland would succeed in proving Michael was not the duke's son, but what if that was all a clever diversion? What if the real danger was from Lady Mirela?

She was surprised by Regina's response. "If she is the daughter of a duke and was forced to hire servants to impersonate a male heir, I rather admire her. Doesn't it strike you as shamefully unfair that the old Cossack's will specified the oldest *male* heir? Why shouldn't Lady Mirela rewrite the rules so that she can establish a life for herself in America?"

Libby's hand stilled. Only the droning of a few insects filled the silence as she pondered the question. Libby had never had any grand ambition for herself, but Regina had firsthand experience with being excluded from a dream simply because she was a woman. Regina's wickedly sharp mind would have made her an excellent attorney. What must it be like to have a desperate craving for something one was forbidden to pursue?

"I would like to know more about this Lady Mirela. Perhaps I could accompany you to deliver the jam," Regina offered. "I love a good mystery."

Libby shook her head. "They keep her so tightly guarded I don't think there is any way you could meet her."

"Perhaps that ought to tell you something. If she is an imposter, they may not think she can be trusted to stick to the story."

"Or she may truly be ill. If you could have seen the expression on Michael's face when he talked about what she had done . . ." The hollow look of despair on Michael's face was haunting.

"So he is *Michael*, is he?" Regina strolled forward, a cat that had just spotted a juicy partridge. "Did you know you blush when you mention Michael Dobrescu?"

Libby refused to rise to the bait. She reached a little higher into the bush to pluck some sun-drenched berries from the top of the bramble. She handed one down to Tillie. "Try eating this one, honey. The berries that get the most sun are always the sweetest."

Tillie popped the berry into her juice-stained mouth and her eyes widened in surprise. "This one *is* better!" she agreed. Libby nudged the girl to the opposite side of the bush, where the full strength of the western sun had sweetened the berries.

"Mrs. Gallagher says he is a handsome man, in a rugged sort of way," Regina continued. "And I suppose he must be lonely, if he is a widower. Although now that he has someone to make his children blackberry jam . . ."

Regina was perfectly charming as she dangled the sentence ripe with innuendo, but Libby had plenty of experience in sidestepping her sister-in-law's verbal swordplay. She maintained a calm expression as she dumped a few more berries into Regina's basket.

"Each time I deliver food to that house, they fling the door wide open and invite me in. And I have learned more during those visits than Father has in his endless hours of fruitless speculation around Jasper's kitchen table." She stretched to reach higher in the bush, but the dappled sunlight breaking though the tangle of leaves made it difficult to see.

Regina followed, helpfully holding forth the basket. "I think it is kind of charming, your friendship with Mr. Dobrescu. You've never really had a serious suitor, have you?"

Truly, it must have been difficult for Regina to have kept those claws sheathed all morning. Libby plucked a few more berries from the tall branches. "No one will have me, Regina," she said good-naturedly. She turned around and flashed her sister-in-law a wink and a smile as she deposited the berries in the basket. "My illiterate stupidity, of course." Regina had a bad habit of dancing around Libby's shortcoming, but if Libby beat her to the punch it was amazing how quickly Regina backpedaled.

"I am simply suggesting that you could exploit this little friendship," Regina said. "The man seems to have a modicum of trust in you, and perhaps you could probe for more. Find out what skills he has. What he lacks. I think your time in the house would be far more productive spent on those kinds of questions rather than hunting down those silly old drawings you did for Professor Sawyer."

"Those drawings mean a great deal to my father."

"Well, in all likelihood they are gone forever," Regina said. "Dobrescu probably burned them for kindling; you can't put that sort of thing past a gypsy." Regina popped a blackberry into her mouth, careful to lick the dark stain from the tips of her fingers before turning a smile on Libby.

"I wish you would not call them *gypsies*," Libby said. "Those sorts of words leave scars."

Regina raised her brows in innocence. "Why of course!" she agreed. "And I want you to know that if you have a fancy for Mr. Dobrescu, I will support you one hundred percent! I think it would be sweet for you to find someone of your own, and perhaps the two of you will be very well suited."

Libby maintained the tight smile on her face and watched Tillie trudge forward with another handful of berries for the basket. "I think we have enough blackberries now, sweetie," Libby said. "Do you want to help me make the jam? I'll let you lick the spoon when we are finished." Tillie's eyes lit up and she jumped with abandon.

"Can I, Mama? Please, please, please?"

Regina reached down to stroke a curl away from the girl's forehead. "Of course you can, sugarplum. We need a nice large batch of jam for Libby to use as ammunition, don't we?"

11

The next day, while her father and Mr. Auckland set out to look for answers at the Library of Congress, Libby went back to the house on Winslow Street, carrying a basket with blackberry jam and seeking answers of her own. Her father's admonition to stay away from the Dobrescus was still ringing in her ears, releasing nervous butterflies in her belly. She had always been an obedient daughter, and disobeying a direct order made her feel like she should be put up against a wall, blindfolded, and shot at dawn. Still, she was convinced this was the right thing to do. Before walking to the house, she had stopped at the bakery and purchased two loaves of bread, as well as some cheese and two quarts of milk.

She walked up the stairs of the front porch and raised her hand to knock on the front door, but paused when she heard voices inside the house.

Eavesdropping was such a terrible habit, and she ought to have been ashamed, but Libby did not feel the least bit guilty as she angled a little closer to the door and held her breath, trying to decipher the words. They would probably be speaking in Romanian, and it was unlikely she would learn anything really juicy, so she shouldn't feel guilty, right?

It was one of the children speaking, enunciating words slowly

135

and carefully in English. Her brows rose in surprise as she recognized the words.

"'. . . and dedicated to the proposition that all men are created equal. Now we are engaged in a great civil war, testing whether that nation, or any nation so conceived, can long endure. . . .'"

The Gettysburg Address? Like any girl born and raised in New England, the words were engraved in Libby's heart, but she was surprised they would hold any interest for people from Romania. In halting, heavily accented English, the young voice continued to speak the words that resonated so profoundly in American history. The young voice struggled over some of the trickier words, but Michael patiently repeated the correct pronunciation and made both children say it properly. The boy continued to recite the Gettysburg Address, and it would be wrong to interrupt when it was obvious how hard the child was working. She waited until he recited the final profound statement.

"'. . . and that government of the people, by the people, for the people, shall not perish from the earth.'"

"Well done, Andrei!" Michael's voice boomed. "Your turn, Luke."

Now was her chance. She knocked and heard an immediate scurry of little feet rushing to the door. When they flung open the door, she was relieved by the sight of two healthy and bright-eyed boys.

Libby smiled. "I thought you might like some company."

Andrei eyed her basket. "Did you bring more jam?"

"Andrei, that is not polite. Invite our guest inside." Michael sounded better, even if she could not yet see him. After stepping inside and closing the door, she spotted him resting on the couch, his arm still in a sling but the bright flags of red gone from his cheeks.

"Your color certainly looks better," she said.

"Papa's fever is gone," Luke said as he tugged on her skirt. "Do you know the Gettysburg Address?" The way he mangled the word

Gettysburg was simply precious. She could not resist running her fingers through the boy's hair and smiling.

"Of course. It is a great speech."

"I wanted them to memorize the Declaration of Independence, but it is too long," Michael said. "We have been preparing for the Fourth of July, and it is important for these boys to know about the greatness of this country."

Luke pulled on her skirt again. "Joseph bought a turkey. We are fattening him up in the backyard. And we are growing pumpkins for pie. We will have the best celebration ever."

Libby met Michael's eyes across the room. "Isn't it a bit early to start planning for Thanksgiving?"

Michael straightened and looked confused. "I saw a picture in a book of the American holiday celebration. It showed lots of people dressed in black clothes with turkeys and pumpkins. I thought this is what we are to do on the Fourth of July. Is this wrong?"

If he had not sounded so earnest, Libby might have laughed, but she could see this was of the utmost importance to Michael. "I'm not sure there are any particular foods you should have on the Fourth of July. Everyone has turkey and pumpkin pie on Thanksgiving, but that does not happen until November."

Michael gestured for her to sit in the leather wing-back chair opposite him. "It is a good thing you have come to tell us these things. I wish to celebrate these holidays correctly."

She curled into the chair and watched the children tear through the contents of her basket. "Have you been able to get what you need from the local shopkeepers?" she asked, holding her breath.

"I went to the market with Turk," Andrei said. "We went to the same places you took us on Wednesday, and no one gave us any trouble." That did not stop him from plowing through the contents of her basket like a child on Christmas morning. When Luke landed on the box of chocolates wrapped in shiny gold foil, his eyes grew round and he opened his mouth wide, speechless with delight.

When she glanced up to see Michael's reaction to Luke's happiness, she was stunned to see his eyes fastened on her. No man had ever looked at her with that sort of heat in his eyes. Her heart sped up and she skittered her focus away, landing on a faded scrap of newspaper on the coffee table. The paper was wilted and yellowed with age, with a number of creases pressed into the document, as though it had been carefully folded and preserved for many years. She could not read the document, but the strange squiggles and markings above the letters did not look like the English language. She looked up at Michael with a question in her eyes.

"It is the Gettysburg Address . . . written in Romanian," he said simply.

Her brows lifted in surprise. "I am surprised it is of any interest in Romania."

Michael lifted the scrap of paper and folded it as carefully as if it were a holy relic. "In 1875 our newspapers printed the Gettysburg Address to mark the ten-year anniversary of the end of the American Civil War. At that time, Romania had been controlled by the Ottomans for centuries. No sooner had the Turks been thrown out of the country than the Russians tried to take control. What is the difference of paying tribute to a sultan or to a czar? I wanted to be part of a country that was governed by and for the people. So yes, America is of great interest to the Romanians. I knew if I survived the wars, I would figure out a way to bring my family here."

Libby shifted in her seat, wondering if this man was the son of a duke or a servant in league with a clever young lady. Michael's face appeared to be wide and open with no subterfuge lurking behind those dark blue eyes, but nothing he said could wipe out the stark fact that he had barged into her house like a thief in the night. How did that bold act of aggression correlate to the rule of law? "I don't think there is anything in the Gettysburg Address that condones trickery to commandeer another person's property."

Michael's face settled into hard lines. He raised his head and

138

thrust his jaw out. "We are two families who have a disagreement. We both have strong claims to the same piece of property, but rather than argue with guns, we have a court system that is governed by a set of rules. Do you know how lucky we are to have a place where everyone is treated equally? Do you know how *rare* that is in this world?"

Libby did not feel lucky. She felt awful about what had been done to her father, and what was going to happen to the Dobrescus when they were evicted. They had little money and no friends in this country. What would happen to them when the court ruled in her father's favor?

She turned her attention to the boys, eager for anything to wipe away the troublesome thoughts. Luke and Andrei had found her box of jacks that Tillie played with, only the boys were using the pieces to build some sort of tower. "Do you know how to play jacks?" she asked them. When it was clear they did not, Libby joined them on the floor and showed them how to bounce the rubber ball and try to scoop up the pieces.

The boys learned quickly and she delighted watching them scamper to collect the pieces. All the while she felt the heat of Michael Dobrescu's gaze upon her as she played with his children. She had very little experience with men, but there was no mistaking the look of sheer masculine desire in his eyes.

And she quietly savored every moment of it.

"Michael won't like it."

Turk's voice was adamant, but Mirela knew what she wanted and was good at getting things when she set her mind to it. "Then don't tell him. But I am going up in the attic, and since you are determined to be my watchdog, you are coming with me."

Mirela issued the order with more confidence than she felt. How could one sound confident when shame pulsed through her body with each beat of her heart? When she tried to circumvent God's will by committing the sin of suicide, it was an act of stunning cowardice unworthy of the Dobrescu name. It was hard to even look Michael in the face. Of all the people living in this house, he had sacrificed the most to make this journey with her. Now she would help him by uncovering the mystery she knew was hidden somewhere in this house.

Besides, her wrists were still too sore to lift anything heavier than a loaf of bread and she needed Turk's strength to properly search the attic. Uncle Constantine's will had summoned them to this house for a reason, and the attic was the only place she had yet to explore. Had he left a message hidden somewhere in this house? Some clue as to why he left Romania so abruptly? Almost three decades after his death, there seemed to be no trace of Constantine left in this strange house. No old Romanian documents, none of his old military medals or uniforms, nothing to indicate that an eccentric man from a rural European village once lived there.

The attic was the only portion of the house no one had explored, and Mirela was certain there must be something up there. Why else would she be plagued with this nagging sensation that Constantine intended them to do something important with this house? There had been a curious line in her uncle's will, *"Only a man of the Dobrescu family will know what to do with this house."* Her uncle was speaking to them through that document, urging them to do something important, and Mirela needed to discover what it was.

Turk grumbled the entire way up the narrow staircase leading to the dusty confines of the attic. It was sweltering up there, and Turk swiped the perspiration from his face with a handkerchief, then offered it to her.

"No thank you," she said delicately. Never let it be said that Turk was not a gentleman beneath all that muscle. Despite the sunny afternoon, it was dim beneath the steeply sloped roofline, with only tinted light seeping through the three stained-glass windows. The attic was crammed with stacks of books, old trunks, and pieces of partially finished machinery that had been abandoned beneath the rafters. There was little room to walk as Mirela twisted to navigate through the towers of old boxes.

"What is it we are looking for?" Turk asked, his nose twitching in the stale air.

"I don't know," she responded. "Anything that seems like it might have come from Romania, or once belonged to Constantine Dobrescu."

"Why do you suppose the people in this country keep calling him the old Cossack?" Turk asked. "Don't they know the difference between a Russian and a Romanian?"

Mirela shrugged. "There are so many Russians in Romania these days, I suppose it does not make any difference."

Despite the amount of material to be sorted through, they moved quickly, as it was easy to see Professor Sawyer's stamp of ownership everywhere. She knew almost nothing about Constantine Dobrescu, other than he was raised to be a rose farmer, wanted to join the Church, but family responsibility funneled him into military service. Then, without warning and without explanation, he packed his bags and left for America, never to return.

What a strange sense of connection she felt for the uncle she had never met. Like Constantine, Mirela had been forced to wander from city to city, country to country, all in search of what? Surely God had a purpose for her, or He would not have sent Michael into her life time and again to rescue her. What did He intend for her to do with her life? After the tragedy that happened in the rose fields, Mirela still believed she could recover and be blessed with children someday. When the doctor told her otherwise, the dream she had been clinging to these past sixteen months was snuffed out and she was overwhelmed by crashing waves of despair.

Why did God keep slamming doors in her face? Blow, after blow, after blow. Each time she survived another storm and tried to build a new life, she was slammed back down. Surely there must be a reason. Surely there was something important she must do with her life or she would have died long ago. She sensed that whatever power had driven her uncle to America was now compelling her as well. She would not stop searching this house until she found it.

After two hours, Mirela's clothing was soaked with perspiration and she was trembling with exhaustion. She had yet to find anything belonging to Constantine Dobrescu, but could not bring herself to stop looking. On the few occasions they stumbled across something that warranted closer inspection, Mirela held it before the tinted light coming through the stained-glass windows to try to decipher it. There had to be *something* in this house from Constantine. She could sense it.

She leaned her head against the window, smiling at the irony of the profusion of roses that decorated the stained glass. She wished the window depicted anything besides roses, but at least the glass carried no fragrance. How ironic that they looked exactly like the type of roses grown on the Duke of Vlaska's estate.

She stiffened and a tingling sensation raced across her skin. They were *exactly* the same roses grown by the duke. The artist had captured the unusual vermilion shade of the blooms and extravagantly dense petals. "Turk, look at these windows," she said with a trembling whisper. The first window showed a field of roses set against a clear blue sky of early morning. The middle window was far more disturbing. A simple crucifix was set into the space between two mountains, and it was surrounded by falling rocks, flames, and torrents of rushing waters, the sky filled with storm clouds and despair. The final window was once again serene. It depicted rugged green mountains set against the last moments of a fading sunset. Again, a small crucifix was set into the mountainside.

Turk stared intently at the windows. She could tell he recognized the Duke of Vlaska's roses. "What do they mean?" he asked.

"I have no idea." The only window she truly understood was

142

the first one, showing the rose fields that appeared to be the Duke of Vlaska's estate. She even recognized the distinctive chain of mountains on the horizon of the first window. The last window had an odd sort of serenity, but a sense of melancholy as the fading sunset struggled to cast light over the lush green mountainside.

"Maybe they depict Constantine's life," Turk speculated. "His early years growing roses in Romania, then a time of war. Is the last window here in New England?"

It would make sense for him to have a setting sun if this window depicted the final years of his life. But the mountains did not look like those she had seen in Massachusetts. They looked more like the Carpathian Mountains of Romania.

"I don't know," she said, but she was oddly attracted to the center window, with the strange rocks appearing to fall from the mountains toward the cross. "I remember hearing of a convent that was destroyed by an earthquake. Before he left Romania, Constantine was very concerned for the surviving nuns. Perhaps this is the artist's way of depicting an earthquake."

Turk nodded. "We must ask Michael what he thinks."

Mirela nodded. Michael had sacrificed more than any of them to bring her to America, and he had a right to know what she had learned.

12

Michael sat sprawled on the garden bench, his shirt unbut-toned so the sun could reach as much of his skin as possible. His body was still mending and basking in the sun's healing rays soothed his spirit. Ever since he was a child, Michael longed to be outside, where he could throw himself into working the land and enjoy the warmth of the sun on his skin. From this position in the garden, he could also listen to the voices of his children drift through the open kitchen window as they spoke with Libby Sawyer.

She had come several times this week, and he savored her visits. When Libby was around there was laughter and sunshine. Sometimes they sat in the garden and talked for hours about everything from plants to history to the correct way to score a game of croquet. Other days she played with the children, for which he was grateful. His boys still had not made friends in the neighborhood, and they thrived on her attention like plants starved for sunshine.

Libby and the boys were inside, but did she realize he was only a few feet away and could hear everything she said through the open window? Luke was prattling about the grumpy cat he was convinced was his new friend. "He takes my socks and hides them up in the tree. Only my socks, no one else's socks," Luke said proudly. "It is a game he wants only to play with me."

"I suppose it might be a game," Libby said, although Michael could hear the skepticism in her voice. He wished Luke was not so lonely that he sought out friendship with a surly animal that menaced the entire neighborhood.

"So did you have any pets in Romania?" Libby probed. "A dog? A cat? If you lived on a farm, perhaps you had something bigger, like a pony?"

Here it comes, Michael thought. He was surprised it had taken her this long to begin snooping into their life in Romania. He cocked his ear to hear better.

"We had cats," Luke said. "They were good for catching the . . . the little animals. You know, the *little* animals."

"Mice?" Libby asked.

"Are mice the little animals that eat your food in the middle of the night?"

Her laughter was like cool water falling over rocks in a stream. "Yes, that is what mice do. What other animals did you have on this farm of yours?"

"Chickens." There was a long pause, as Luke either struggled with his English, or perhaps he was done speaking. They kept very few animals on the farm, so there was not much Luke could offer in reply to the question, but clearly Libby was searching for any scrap of information she could grasp in that wickedly sharp brain of hers.

"So your father sold chickens? Or was it eggs?"

"No. Papa sold roses." Michael felt a smile curve his mouth. He could almost see the confusion on Libby's face as she tried to figure *that* one out.

"My goodness. I can't imagine what a rose farm must look like."

"It was huge," Andrei said. "Papa knows all about roses and flowers. He has the best nose in all of Europe. People came from all over the world to ask him to smell things."

Once again, it sounded like Libby was speechless. There was

a time when Michael would have swelled with pride to hear his boys boast about his skills. It was true about his nose. Even blindfolded, Michael could tell the difference between a white rose and a red rose. He could smell jasmine essence and determine by scent alone if the oil had been extracted through a distillation process or the more elegant enfleurage technique of melting the oil from the petals. So keenly attuned was his sense of smell that he could predict which combination of oils and resins would yield a scent with a pleasing bouquet.

Those days were over. For a single glorious year in Paris he had reveled in the world's greatest perfumeries. The celebrated perfume houses sought him out, eager to acquire his phenomenal talents, but Michael had not seriously considered any of their offers. If the wars had not intruded, he would be living amidst the thousands of acres of rose fields and cultivating the rare strain of night-blooming jasmine his father had developed. A single ounce of that precious jasmine oil was worth over a hundred American dollars, and he had sixty-four ounces. Of course, it wouldn't be nearly as valuable if he was unable to find the proper tree to harvest the resin necessary as a scent fixative. If he sold it in its raw state, it would be worth much less than one hundred dollars an ounce, since it was the resin that fixed the scent into a bouquet of exquisite beauty that could linger on the skin for hours.

His precious jasmine essence would not last much longer. Without the resin, his perfume would fade into the ether after only a few minutes on the skin. Michael estimated he had less than three months to either find the correct resin and save the jasmine essence or sell it to a perfumer who could salvage it.

Libby continued to pepper the children with questions. Did he grow anything besides roses? How was it possible for a farm to have nothing but flowers? And people paid him for this?

He cocked his head again. How interesting that she asked no questions that would help her in the court case. It would have been easy for her to ask the name of his father or even if they knew the Duke of Vlaska, but she asked none of this. Instead, she seemed completely engrossed in what sort of work Michael did with flowers. Given her fascination for the botanical world, perhaps it was only natural.

He froze. If there was anyone in this town who could help him find the trees he needed, she was sitting not ten feet away.

Would she help him again? Already this woman, who should be his enemy, had been so generous with her time and her kindness. He would rather endure a public flogging than impinge on her generosity again, but he had no choice. Libby Sawyer was one of the few people in this town who would even speak with him, let alone extend herself to help.

He stood. It was time to show off for his boys and start persuading Libby to get him what he needed. She always smelled delightful, and today was no exception.

She startled when he came in the back door. There was a momentary flush of guilt staining her cheeks, as if she was embarrassed to be caught pumping his children for information, but he flashed a smile to set her at ease. He clasped her fingers, drew them to his face, and kissed the back of her hand.

"Neroli oil, with a bit of white lily," he said definitively. "The same scent you were wearing when you visited us last week."

She looked at him with skepticism and withdrew her hand. "The picture on the label shows oranges," she said.

"Did the label show the orange fruit or a white blossom?"

"The fruit."

"Then the label is wrong. Neroli is the name for orange blossoms, a very strong floral scent, and it is what you are wearing. It is an entirely different scent from the oil extracted from the orange peel, which is a citrus scent. I once found a perfume that blended the oil from the orange peel with the essence from the orange blossom. It was a noble idea, but too powerful. I do not believe this perfume sold well."

Libby's stare was as piercing as a panther evaluating its prey. "Are you making fun of me?" she asked cautiously. "Somehow you look like you would be more comfortable storming a fortress than discussing flower blossoms."

He found his way to one of the kitchen stools and gently lowered himself onto it, never taking his eyes from her. "If my life had turned out the way I intended, I would have done nothing other than walk in my fields of blooms and discuss perfume," he said truthfully. Instead of the glory of basking in his sun-drenched fields, he had to fight men he had no grievance with, surrounded by the sweat and stench and agony of wars he wanted no part of. "Truly, there are few things I enjoy more than discussing flowers and the scent they create."

Understanding dawned in her face. "That is what you did in Romania? Grew roses for perfume?"

"Yes, but I grew other flowers as well. Jasmine, hyacinth. Sometimes we grew iris, but those were tricky."

She nodded. "I found the same thing. When I dug one up and brought it home to paint, it wilted within the hour. I had to paint it in the wild. It took me three afternoons and I was nearly eaten alive by mosquitoes."

He grinned. "I would like to see your painting of the iris, if you still have it."

"Of course I have it." She was as eager as a child as she scampered to retrieve the painting, but there was nothing childlike about her womanly form as she darted up the staircase. Liberty Sawyer was as tempting as any woman he had ever seen. Was it because she loved the same things as he, or was it the tempting curve of her figure poured into that dress? Both were very appealing, but he would need to be careful to keep these feelings tightly under wraps. His quest was too important to be sidelined by these inconvenient feelings that plagued him every time Libby came within twenty yards of him.

On the other hand, this irrational attraction might serve a purpose. His eyes narrowed as he watched her descend the stairs, her arms filled with paintings and a heart-stopping smile on her face. It would be dangerous to begin waging a battle for the house outside of the courtroom, but a clever one. Perhaps the easiest path to this house was smiling at him with her arms full of paintings.

⁂

Libby loved talking about plants with Michael. Her paintings looked ridiculously fragile in his oversized hands as he sat beside her on the sofa, but he always had such fascinating questions for her. He pointed to a stem of a Cucurbita vine that was turning upward.

"The way this stem is curving, why have you painted it this way?"

"That shows that this is a plant that is hungry for sunlight," she said. "You will often see those vines reaching out to find a patch of sunlight. It is in their nature to do so."

The grin he gave her was boyish. "I understand this need for the sun. I always feel better when the sun is bright as well." He set the painting down. "In your trips into the field to study plants, have you ever seen red juniper trees?"

"Red juniper? The tree with the little blue berries?"

"Those berries are actually seedpods, but yes, I think you understand what I am looking for. They usually grow in sandy soil, and many times farmers plant them along the edges of their crop to serve as a windbreak. At least they do in Europe. I need to find a supply of these trees so I can tap them for resin. It will not hurt the tree, but I need resin to formulate my perfume. I would be willing to pay the farmer to allow me to do this."

She was stunned when he suddenly pushed off the sofa and knelt on one knee before her. "Libby, you have no cause to help me," he said in an earnest voice. "I have been nothing but trouble to you and your family, but does that mean we are destined to be enemies in all things? Because I think you are a woman of great quality. I watch you march into town armed with nothing but the strength of your compassion for a family in need. You are smart and courageous, and I find this very attractive."

The gentle roughness of his voice made Libby catch her breath. No man had ever spoken to her in such terms, but Michael knew nothing of her terrible illiteracy or the years of taunting she had endured as a child. *"Libby Libby, ain't that quick; Libby Libby, dumb as a stick!"* She felt like a fraud as he praised her. Libby was the girl who was ridiculed in the schoolyard and her air of confidence was only a mask, but was it wrong to savor his praise? Never could she imagine Michael Dobrescu on his knees before *anyone*, yet here he knelt, with admiration glowing in his eyes.

"If you could help me find the red juniper tree," he said, "I will be able to blend a magnificent perfume. Some would consider it a foolish thing to want to produce such an extravagant luxury." His gaze tracked to her painting of the amaryllis that still held a place of honor above the mantelpiece. "But I believe you have an appreciation for things that enrich our life with beauty. With your knowledge of the natural world and my skill with perfume, perhaps you and I can look beyond the enmity and build something of great value."

He turned his gaze back to her. It was true she was the closest thing he had to a friend in America, and he needed her help like a dying man in the desert needed a drink of water. It was a heady sensation, but her father's warnings rang in her ears. The logical piece of her brain told her Michael Dobrescu could be manipulating her, pandering to her insecurities in order to extract the information he needed from her. While she became drunk on the sensation of feeling needed and admired, she endangered her relationship with her father merely by associating with the Dobrescus.

But never before had she been needed like this. Michael Dobrescu, with all his awesome strength and ferocious will to succeed, was looking at her with yearning in his eyes. The pride she felt when he first recognized the quality of her paintings paled in comparison to this exhilarating sensation of being needed. Respected. She had every reason in the world to deny him, but there was no question in her mind what she would do.

"What time shall I meet you?"

Regina was pleased that Libby had agreed to go on an outing with Michael Dobrescu. They lingered in the garden for an evening cup of tea and Regina provided advice for extracting the maximum amount of information from Michael. "Away from the house and those children, his guard will be down," Regina said. "Plus, you are doing him a tremendous favor, so he may be more inclined to chat if he thinks it is the only way you will help him. What a perfect opportunity for you to slide in and do a little digging."

Libby watched as Regina dangled a long, thin stream of honey into her cup of tea. When the last of the honey stretched and broke away, Regina dipped her spoon and began stirring. It seemed so calculating, but Libby knew her sister-in-law was correct. It was not as though she was going to trick the man. All she wanted was to know the truth about his family, and she could not trust any of the Dobrescus to tell it to her. That meant she needed to pounce on whatever tidbits he dropped.

"It still feels underhanded," she murmured, taking a sip of her own tea.

Regina shrugged her shoulders. "Nonsense. Herman Banks at the county courthouse told his wife that Mr. Dobrescu paid a visit just yesterday. He asked to see how much your father paid for the house back in 1856. Then he asked to see the tax assessments over the last twenty years. It sounds to me as if the man is preparing to stage an aggressive assault in court next week to undermine your father's ownership of the house. You would be foolish not to turn over every stone as well."

"I don't understand," Libby confessed. "What does that have to do with the legitimacy of the old Cossack's will?"

Regina set her teacup down. "Your father paid the city a grand total of two hundred dollars for that house. Can you imagine? Two hundred dollars! The house had been vacant for years and it was a fire hazard and a public nuisance. The city wanted it off their hands and your father got the house for a song."

"I had no idea. . . ." It certainly made her father's claim more tenuous. A fresh wave of anxiety swamped her. How could it be possible for a family to emerge from nowhere to dispossess them of their house? And yet it seemed to be happening. "I know my father poured a fortune into renovating the house," Libby said. "It was a ruin when he bought it and he could barely afford all the renovations. That sort of investment must be worth something, don't you think?"

Regina shrugged. "Here is the real problem your father has," she said as she leaned forward. "If the old Cossack's family had not been properly served notice about the pending sale, they have a legitimate cause to dispute ownership."

"But they *were!*" Libby protested. "Michael has a copy of the will that he carries with him everywhere he goes."

Regina gave a sad shake of her head. "The will is different from a notice of sale. The law required the city to give proper notice to the Dobrescu heirs of the pending sale of the house. They never did. After Mr. Dobrescu left, Herman Banks practically turned that courthouse upside-down looking for any evidence of notification, but it is not there."

Regina took a sip of her tea. "So you see, my dear," she said in that purring southern voice, "I certainly hope you can make the most of your scavenging through the wilderness with Mr. Dobrescu. You need to find something to prove that the man is an imposter, because otherwise, he is almost certainly going to win the lawsuit."

13

It was a misty morning, with vapor still hanging in the air as they passed the cranberry bogs that dotted the countryside like patchwork quilts to the west of the village. Libby remembered Regina's advice from the evening before. *Speak of inconsequential things,* she had said. *Don't broach anything of substance until his guard is down.*

Libby borrowed Jasper's horse and wagon to travel toward the western ridge, where she suspected the soil would support the type of red junipers Michael was looking for. She was almost certain she had seen a cluster of the trees along the top of the ridge, where the wagon could not take them. They parked the wagon, tied the horse to a fence bordering the O'Malleys' cranberry field, then climbed the steep slope on foot. Michael led the way, with Libby struggling to keep up as he pushed higher up the embankment, stepping over fallen logs and through the heavy undergrowth of ferns.

As much as she tried to concentrate on gleaning insight into Michael's history, she kept getting distracted. *Quit looking at the man's shoulders*, she thought for the third time since leaving the wagon. It did not matter how appealing the width of them or how they set off his finely tapered waist. Neither would she keep dwelling on the way the tiny crinkles fanned out from his eyes when he smiled at her. If she accomplished nothing else today, Libby was determined to rid herself of this foolish notion that Michael Dobrescu might be interested in her as a woman. Even if he was, the very notion ought to appall her. Either this man had a legitimate claim to her house and was on the verge of disinheriting her, or he was a liar, a fraud, and an imposter intent on swindling her family. She must cease these bizarre thoughts about the man. Snuff them out like a candle flame. The only interest she had was predatory. As Regina suggested, Libby must seek out and glean as much information about his past as possible.

But as they tromped through the green-tinted world beneath the sycamore and hickory trees, her resolve was constantly tested. There was no path and the undergrowth was thick as they pushed their way to the top of the ridge. Always, Michael was careful to hold a stray branch so it would not strike her as she followed him up the embankment. She was insane to keep dwelling on how good it felt to walk within the sphere of his protection.

"Soon you will see a patch of sunlight ahead," she said. "The ground will get very rocky and I think this is where we will find the juniper trees." She had brought her canvas and supplies here to paint in the sunlit grassland at the top of the ridge many times. The bounty of the American wilderness stretched for miles in every direction, and she felt at peace up there.

Libby pulled her skirts to the side as she searched for footing along this steep section of the hillside. An occasional maple root provided a bit of traction in the damp soil as she pushed farther up. "I see it," Michael said.

Patches of sunlight broke through the screen of leaves and Libby smiled in relief as they trudged into the grassy clearing at the top of the ridge. She gestured to the far side of the meadow to the cluster of juniper trees.

"Are those the type of trees you have been looking for?"

She did not even need to point, for Michael had already spotted them and his eyes narrowed as he scrutinized them. "I'm not sure," he murmured as he set off across the field with his long-legged stride, devouring yards of land with each step. Libby had to hoist her skirts and scurry to keep up with him, ambling along in his wake. By the time she crossed the field and arrived at the stand of juniper trees, Michael was examining the coarse, densely packed cluster of the leaves, so narrow they looked like pine needles. He twisted a cluster of the leaves, pinching and rolling them between his fingers, then bringing them to his nose to sniff. Libby held her breath as she scanned his face, looking for the slightest sign that she had succeeded in finding the tree he so desperately needed. For years she had been filling her brain with arcane, useless knowledge about plant life, and if that knowledge could *finally* be put to some useful purpose . . .

"No, this is not a red juniper tree," he said. "This is a white juniper, a cousin to the red juniper, but its resin carries a faint hint of fragrance. It will not work for my purposes. I need an odorless resin."

Her lungs deflated and she dropped her gaze. Libby hoped her disappointment did not show on her face, but she kept her voice steady as she asked Michael to describe precisely how the red juniper differed from the white juniper. Perhaps she could still succeed in locating the tree on the outcropping.

"The seedpods of the red juniper will develop a blue tint late in the season, but these will always stay brown."

Libby bit her lip. The moment he said "blue tint," she knew precisely what he was describing, so she must have seen the tree. Only a brainless fool would confuse a red juniper with a white juniper. She started gnawing on the side of her thumbnail as she racked her brain for where she had seen those blue-tinted seedpods.

The weight of his hand on her shoulder startled her, as did the look of amused concern on his face as he smiled down on her. "Do not be so discouraged," he said. "We will find the right tree eventually, and I am grateful you have been so kind to bring me this far."

She had to look away, for she was not the least bit kind. She felt devious for agreeing to Regina's plan to ferret out information from him, and stupid for not knowing the difference between a red juniper and a white juniper. She could not give up and head home yet. "I often come up to this glade, but I've never explored the other side of the ridge. Perhaps it would be worth pushing a little farther?"

Michael nodded. "I would like that."

As they ambled through the tangle of knee-high grasses, Libby sneaked a peek at him from the corner of her eye. "How is it you learned so much about plants?" she asked, hoping she did not sound like she was prying into his life. Surely discussing plant life was an innocent question on a day such as today.

"My family has worked the land for generations," he said in his open, unabashed manner. "These things were bred into me before I could even talk. As I grew older, I worked the land and learned everything I could from the experts who had accumulated a lifetime of wisdom from working the fields. I went to college for a few classes, but I learned very little there."

Her jaw dropped. "*You* went to college?" she gasped.

"You say this as though I had flown to the moon." Again, he said it in that amused, congenial manner, even though he had every right to be offended by her unspeakably rude tone.

A wave of heat flushed her cheeks. "I'm surprised you could have fit into one of the desks. That is all." She was pleased she was able to say it with a straight face, especially since he roared with laughter. "Where did you go to college?"

She held her breath, wondering if he would answer her. "I went to the University of Paris," he said casually. "I was supposed to study chemistry and botany, but there were far too many temptations in Paris for me to stay cooped up in a classroom."

158

She raised an eyebrow. "I suppose those Parisian temptations are rather world famous."

His grin was unabashed. "Indeed they are! There is a wonderful street called the *Rue de Grenelle* that is home to the world's greatest perfumers. The street is filled with great artisan shops, and at night there are so many lights twinkling from the cafés it is as if the street glows. But the best are the perfume shops. People come from all over the world to blend and sell their perfume in Paris. Of course, perfumers are a paranoid people, always afraid you will steal their secrets." He looked down at her and winked. "Which is why I still feel a bit guilty for eavesdropping on one of them as he spoke to his apprentice and learned that the resin of the red juniper is the perfect fixative for perfume."

Her jaw dropped. "Eavesdropping? I would have thought you were too big to hide around a corner and eavesdrop!"

"I was standing right beside them. They simply did not know I understood Turkish."

Her eyes widened in surprise. "Do you speak French as well?" she asked.

"Mais bien sûr," he said easily.

The "simple peasant" from Romania was anything but simple. English, Turkish, and now French? Her heart sank. Her father's best shot at regaining their house was to prove Michael Dobrescu an imposter, with no blood relationship to the old Cossack or the Duke of Vlaska. Perhaps if he was a servant within the duke's household he would have picked up some foreign languages. But would a duke send a servant all the way to France for an education?

He would if the servant possessed a nose as brilliant as Michael's. If the duke grew roses for the perfume industry, he may have wished to begin blending it on his own estate. What better way to do so than to send one of his servants to France, where he could learn the intricacies of the industry? She needed to keep asking questions, but carefully. *Keep your probing general*, Regina had advised her.

"How did you learn Turkish?" she asked. "It seems an odd language to learn."

"Not if you live in a country ruled by the Ottoman Empire," he said with a good-natured grin. He proceeded to tell her more about the history of his country, but they quickly moved on to comparing the horticulture between Romania and New England. His accent was musical and she was entranced by the fascinating insights he so freely shared with her.

After coming back down the hillside, they drove Jasper's cart to a copse of trees that clung to a rocky stream where she found some wild irises for him, which pleased him immensely. They kept up a constant search for the elusive red juniper, but their failure to locate the tree did not seem to discourage Michael. He just kept asking her questions about the climate and plants and growing conditions in America.

The heat built rapidly, causing thunderheads to form in the late afternoon. "I don't like the look of those clouds," Michael said with a glance at the dense clouds. The two of them were more than ten miles from town, and Libby supposed it only made sense to cut the day short and return home.

She hated to see this magical day end. That morning she'd believed Michael was probably a servant in the duke's household, but now she was more confused than ever. Her father was due back from Washington tomorrow, but she feared he was only going to learn who Michael was *not*—not the son and heir of the Duke of Vlaska. Finding out who Michael *was* would be much more difficult, and Libby had been able to glean very little.

What about Michael's wife? He had never spoken about her and Libby was becoming increasingly curious. If she could learn something about his wife, it would shed insight into his life in Romania. She bit her lip, shamed that she would probe into such a delicate subject to further her own ends, but she needed to know who this man was.

"What was your wife like?" she asked impulsively.

"Marie?" Michael asked.

She shifted on the hard seat of the wagon and tamped down her guilty conscience. "That was her name? Marie?" At his nod, she voiced the question again. "What was she like?"

He mulled over the question before answering. "She was a good wife. A good mother." The clomping of the horse's hooves against the dusty road was the only sound to fill the awkward silence. Michael glanced over at her. "Is that what you wanted to know?"

The logical part of her brain wanted to know if Marie was an aristocrat or a woman as earthy and hardworking as Michael. The irrational part wanted to know what Marie looked like! Was she prettier than Libby? Had she had an easy laugh or was she the type of woman who was withdrawn and serious? Did she share Michael's love of plants? "When did she die?" she finally asked.

"Four years ago. It was one of the few times in those years when a truce allowed me to be home for the planting season. I was allowed to be a normal family man, and during the days I taught my boys the skills I had learned from my own father. In the evenings we ate together as a family on the terrace overlooking the rose fields. Marie always loved the roses. One morning she was helping me work bone meal into the soil when she stepped on the edge of a hoe and it cut through the leather on her shoe. The wound became very bad." Michael paused and his face darkened. "I do not know the English word for the disease, but it made her whole body become stiff with seizures. She died not long afterward."

It sounded like tetanus to her. Libby had heard of the ailment that came from putrefied cuts and caused the body to undergo spasms so powerful it became impossible to breathe. It was terrifying how a woman healthy enough to be helping her husband in the fields could take a wrong step and perish a few days later.

"I'm sorry, Michael," she said. "Those words sound so inadequate and I wish there was something better I could say."

He seemed nonchalant. "It was four years ago, and I do not dwell on it anymore. I am sorry she is not here to help teach Andrei and Luke because she was a good mother. Still, I see her in my boys. Marie was a big and strong woman. A real farmer's wife. Our boys will grow to be just as strong."

As always, when Michael spoke of his children he seemed to be bursting with pride, but his comments confirmed what Libby was coming to believe about Michael Dobrescu. He was no aristocrat. He spoke of learning the farming trade from his father. The old photograph of the Duke of Vlaska showed an imposing man draped in medals, not at all the sort of man who worked a farm. Nor would the wife of a duke's son labor like a common field hand. Hauling fertilizer and cutting it into the soil was backbreaking work, and it sounded as though such a chore was commonplace for Marie.

A fat drop of rain struck her hand. The wind was picking up, carrying the scent of newly mown hay and the promise of a summer rainstorm. They were still four miles from town, but a glance at the sky made Libby skeptical they would make it even another mile before the deluge began.

Michal flicked the reins and the horse moved into a canter. "Do you know anyplace to seek shelter?" he asked.

A few more cool drops of rain splashed onto her skin. The chill of the raindrops did not bode well. Cold rain meant it would likely be a powerful thunderstorm. "There is an old threshing barn on the far side of the orchard," she said. As they rounded the bend she could see the ominous dark clouds on the horizon and hoped Jasper's horse was not the kind to be spooked. The rain was liable to catch them before they reached the barn.

She cast a worried glance at Michael, but a grin had split his face wide open. "You look like a frightened mouse. A little rain will feel good in this heat."

Normally Libby would be cataloguing the reasons she loathed being caught in the rain. Her dress could be damaged and the cart mired in mud, not to mention the risk of pneumonia, but somehow she knew that even if the worst happened, Michael would extricate them from whatever difficulties arose. Even as the rain gathered momentum, he appeared to savor the sensation of the cool drops striking his face and the wind blowing in his hair.

Libby spotted the badly overgrown path leading through an abandoned apple orchard to the barn. Michael turned the horse, steering the wagon over the ruts and grooves that had been worn into the soil in earlier generations. The barn loomed only an acre off the road, but even from this distance Libby could see daylight filtering though the cracks in the weathered planking. When they pulled up to the barn, she could see that the hinges of the over-sized door had long since rusted through, leaving it propped at an angle to cover the opening. It was impossible to swing it open, but Libby's eyes widened as Michael squatted down to work one hand beneath the door and another along the side. With a mighty heave and the sound of ancient wood creaking in protest, he pushed his legs straight and hoisted the door out of the way to place it against the side of the barn.

With rain rolling through the dust on his face and a grin that could melt a sheet of arctic ice, Michael turned to welcome her inside the barn. Libby darted inside to escape the downpour that was imminent, while Michael grasped the reins of the horse and drew him through the oversized opening, cart and all.

The barn was spacious and musty with nothing but a little old straw covering a dirt floor. Michael got the horse inside just as the sky opened and released the cooling rain it had been harboring for hours. With big, well-built hands he stroked the coat of the horse, rubbing him down and patting him affectionately. Even the way Michael looked after the horse made Libby's heart ache.

She had failed on all fronts today. She was still inexplicably besotted with the most inappropriate man in all of America, and she had learned nothing useful about Michael Dobrescu. Libby had taken

Regina's advice to ask a series of sidestepping questions, but all they had done was reveal more contradictions. Perhaps it would be best to follow her own instincts and confront the problem directly.

The sound of raindrops pelting the ancient boards of the roof echoed through the barn. Libby stared at the downpour falling from the sky and formulated exactly what she wanted to know. She drew a steady breath, turned to face him, and asked. "When did you first learn about the old Cossack's will? And why did it take you so long to come here?"

His hands stopped stroking the horse. He froze for a moment, but she caught the look of fierce concentration that lit his eyes as he averted his face. "I was fighting a war. I could not leave without being branded a coward." His hands went back to stroking the horse, but he did not meet her gaze.

She crossed in front of the doorway and to the other side of the horse, where she could have a direct view of his face. "Who is your father?"

"The Duke of Vlaska." There was no hesitation in his voice, just a simple statement of fact.

"I thought he was dead," Libby said. "Are you suggesting you are the current Duke of Vlaska?"

This time he looked directly at her, although in the dimness of the barn all she could see was a face carved in shadows and a curious glint in his eyes. "Succession in Romania works the same as in the other European countries. The oldest son is the Duke's heir."

"And are you his oldest son?"

"I am."

"Then why are you here? Don't you have a palace somewhere you can claim as your own?" She kept her head high and the bitterness from her voice, but knew she was treading on dangerous territory. Michael kept stroking the horse, his gaze never leaving her face. Finally, he stepped around the horse and casually sauntered to within a few inches of her. She was tempted to withdraw deeper into the shadows of the barn, but she would not let him see her flinch. Not even when he lifted his hand and tipped her chin up to see her better in the gloom.

"I find I no longer care for the scent of roses," he said. "And there are roses all around the duke's estate."

She jerked her chin away, the destruction of her mother's rose garden brought fresh to her mind. "You expect me to believe that? You seem to be quite adept at annihilating roses you do not like."

He stared at her for a long moment before turning away to tend to the horse. The jangling of metal buckles filled the silence as he loosened the harness. "I do not wish to argue with you over this," he said tightly. "The decision to uproot my family and travel halfway around the world was not made lightly. It was no longer possible for us to continue living in Romania, so I came here." There was an edge to his voice and grim resolution in his eyes.

She remembered something Mr. Auckland had said about how war could be hard on aristocratic families. Was it possible the dukedom had been a casualty of the war? If a chunk of Romanian territory had been ceded to the Turks or the Russians, perhaps the duchy of Vlaska no longer existed. If his home had been swallowed into another nation, the duke's family would have been driven from the land.

A cold fist of fear clenched her belly. If Michael was in fact the son of the duke, and if he had nothing to go back to in Romania, there was no power on earth that would stop him from taking possession of the last remaining property to his name. Men with few options fought hard.

She walked to the open doorway of the barn, watching the sheets of rain pouring from the sky. She had no idea how much longer she was going to be trapped with Michael Dobrescu, but she wanted to get away. She wanted to forget she had ever met the big, blunt, and oddly charming man who loved the scent of perfume. She did not want to see him and his family driven from the only safe harbor

165

they had left in the world, but neither could she let her father be thrown onto the street. Everyone in this town knew it was Professor Sawyer's home, and surely no judge from Colden, Massachusetts, would condone their eviction from it.

The strength drained away from her limbs, and she leaned against the side of the barn opening. Was it only a few minutes ago she had laughed when Michael picked up the massive door and heaved it to the side? Now all she felt was despair as the mist from the late afternoon storm penetrated her clothing and weighed down her spirits.

"I wish I could have found the red juniper for you," she said softly. It seemed such an insignificant gift to offer, but finding the tree was important to Michael and the only thing she could do for him.

A rustle of fabric and the tread of his boots signaled that he had come to stand behind her, so close she could smell the scent of leather and sweat and man. "I wish I could build a castle for you," he said simply.

He settled his hands on her shoulders, their weight and warmth soothing. She closed her eyes and leaned back against him, knowing he would not push her away. Her head rested alongside the strong column of his neck, and never had she felt so oddly comforted as his strength radiated into her. She felt every breath of air he pulled into his lungs, his big chest expanding and contracting as she leaned against him. It was the most intimate moment of her life.

It was possibly also the saddest, because Libby could not ignore the fact that the court case that would drive a wedge between them forever was only two days away.

The sun was setting behind a blaze of red and purple clouds when Michael drove the cart back to Jasper's house. The journey was silent except for the rhythmic clopping of hooves against the cobblestone street. An occasional gust of wind sent droplets spattering off the heavily leafed trees, but Libby already felt grubby and damp. And she knew her day was about to get worse when she saw who was waiting for her on the front porch of Jasper's house.

Her father's steely glare blasted her as Michael reined the horse to a stop in front of the house. She had not expected his return until tomorrow, but what her father discovered in Washington must have brought him home early. Jasper was sitting casually on a rocking chair, but her father shot to his feet, a book clenched in his hand so tightly his knuckles turned white. Libby wanted to wilt and dissolve as she sat beside her father's sworn enemy. She cringed, knowing the fragile bond she had forged with her father over these last few weeks had just been shattered.

"You'd better leave," she whispered to Michael. "Take the horse to the carriage house and get out of here as quickly as possible."

"No. I shall escort you to the door," he said calmly.

Obviously, Michael had never seen her father in a rage. Not that Willard Sawyer ever became violent, but the sheer force of his anger could be a blistering thing. The rage would only last for an hour or two. He would catalog her shortcomings as a daughter and as a woman, listing the burdens she had brought into his life, the embarrassment of her mental deficiencies, his charity in supporting her. After his rage had run its course there would be days of stony silence, his anger simmering just beneath the surface.

"I'm not in any danger from my father, but you should go. Just go," she said.

Michael pulled the breaking lever and sprang down from the seat. Libby tried to scramble down, but the hem of her dress became snagged in the wheel axle and her urgent tugs did nothing to free it. In an instant Michael was by her side, leaning across her and pulling the trapped muslin free. Libby's eyes widened in horror as his two hands encompassed her waist and she was bodily lifted from the cart and set on the cobblestone street as gently as if she were made of porcelain.

"Get your hands off my daughter."

She startled at the venom in her father's voice and scurried toward the house, but she was no match for Michael's long-legged stride as he caught up with her at the base of the porch. Didn't he realize that he was making the situation worse?

Michael looked her father directly in the eye. "Mr. Sawyer—"

"*Professor Sawyer.*"

"Professor Sawyer," Michael amended. "Your daughter has been very gracious. Her knowledge of the plants in the area is astounding."

"Her *foolishness* is astounding! And I ought to have you arrested . . . taking liberties with a mental deficient too stupid to know your motives."

Libby flinched at the fury in her father's voice and heat gathered in her cheeks. Michael's brows lowered and he moved to stand between her and the professor. "My English is not perfect and I do not understand what you just called your daughter, but I understand the tone," Michael said calmly. "You have cause to resent me, but Libby does not deserve to be the target of your anger. I will not leave her in a house where she may be treated harshly."

Her father's mouth compressed into a hard line, and even Libby was startled when he drew his arm back and hurled his book at Michael's head. The cover of the book splayed open and the pages went flying in the breeze. Michael knocked the book away as if it were no more bothersome than a flea. Never had she seen her father become physical in any way. Her father fought with words that cut, not fists, and certainly not by throwing things.

Libby tried to step around Michael, but he shifted to block her progress. "I will find a safer place for Libby to spend the night until your temper has cooled. No woman should be subjected to a man who is under the rule of anger."

Libby wanted the ground to open up so she could sink beneath the soft, warm cocoon of the earth and be spared her father's blistering response. But he surprised her. Rather than retaliate, her father drew himself a little taller, and from the four-foot height of the porch, he was able to look down his nose at Michael Dobrescu.

"Under the rule of anger?" he scoffed. "I am no barbarian who storms into houses and grabs what he wants. I am a man of civility. Throughout my entire life I have embraced the wisdom of a solid education and a refined culture. These things may seem alien to you, but they are prized in America."

Michael said nothing, but he flicked a glance to the book splayed upon the grass, then back to the professor.

The silence lengthened. Libby still felt like shriveling from mortification, but Michael stood with the confidence of a man who had nothing to fear. Finally Jasper stepped around her father and walked down the front steps. "Libby, there is a dinner plate in the warming oven for you." He looked at Michael. "I would like to offer you dinner as well, but I think it best not to pour fuel on simmering flames."

Michael nodded his head. "I understand."

"Libby has always been safe in my house, and today is no exception," Jasper said. "No harm will come to her under my roof."

Michael turned his gaze to her, question in his eyes. Instinctively, she knew Michael was willing to protect her from whatever physical or emotional danger might harm her. She wished he had not witnessed her father chastise her like a disobedient dog, but all her father's sound and fury amounted to very little. He would never physically harm her, and she had long ago built up a concrete shell to protect against the sting of his words.

"My father's anger will blow over soon," she said quietly. "And you should go back to your children."

Michael took a step closer to her. He was as dirty and grubby as she, but a warm strength radiated from his face as he looked down at her. How was it possible for a man to be so big and imposing, and yet seem so gentle? When he cupped the side of her face with his hand, she gazed up at him without flinching. The caress of his thumb against her cheekbone was so tender she had to brace herself from turning her face closer into his palm.

"Please know that whatever happens in the courtroom, I care for you, Libby." The words were so gently spoken she could hardly hear them, but still they sliced straight through to her soul.

She felt like a piece of her was leaving with Michael as he walked alone down the street.

14

By the time of the court hearing, Libby was still in disgrace and her father had forbidden her from sitting with him at the litigant's table, only a few feet away from Judge Frey. She sat instead beside Regina in the front row of the gallery, where she had a bird's-eye perspective of the packed courtroom below. Everyone in Colden had come to the hearing, anxious to see Professor Sawyer regain lawful possession of his house. Almost like in a wedding, the benches behind her father filled with his supporters from the neighborhood, while the rows behind Michael Dobrescu's table were empty. As the appointed hour drew near, the townspeople became less discriminating, and soon every seat in the courtroom was taken. When the standing room along the walls was filled, spectators clustered outside the windows, which had been opened to provide a bit of relief from the heat.

At her father's table were his lawyer, Mr. Auckland, and a gentleman Libby had never seen before. She was certain he was a stranger to Colden, for she would have remembered anyone who dressed so exquisitely. The young man's cravat was wickedly dashing, but not something worn in a village like Colden. Her father was smiling as he traded quips with his lawyer and the strange newcomer. Whatever her father learned in Washington must have been good news, because yesterday she had heard him laughing with the old librarian late into the night.

Of course, whatever he learned had not been shared with Libby. "You are liable to go blather it to the gypsies," he had snapped at her. "You can learn about what sort of man you have been cavorting with in court alongside the rest of the townspeople."

Dozens of times people approached her father's table to shake his hand and clap him on the back. It could not have been a more stark contrast to Michael Dobrescu's table, where he sat with only a single lawyer. Wearing the same battered leather jacket he always wore, Michael looked utterly alone and friendless. She knew her father was going to win this case, and her stomach clenched at the thought of what was going to happen to Michael and those children.

Judge Frey walked into the courtroom and everyone stood, a hush settling over the assembly as the showdown was about to commence. He took his seat behind the raised desk, adjusted his robes, and banged his gavel. Libby's legs felt like rubber and she was grateful when the judge motioned for the crowd to sit.

"We have a difficult case to settle," Judge Frey said. "The last will and testament of Constantine Dobrescu was properly filed in this court and sent to his heirs in Romania, but the sale of the house on Winslow Street was not properly executed. The Dobrescu heirs therefore have the right to contest Professor Sawyer's title to the house."

Her father's lawyer, Mr. Colberg, rose to his feet. "Your Honor, rather than discussing the complicated legal intricacies, we would like to present evidence that the man claiming to be the Dobrescu heir is an imposter. We have amassed indisputable evidence."

The judge's eyes grew round. "*Indisputable*, you claim?"

"I have written evidence, photographic proof, and a living witness who can testify that this man is a fraud."

Excited chatter rose from the spectators in the courtroom, and the judge banged his gavel. "Your motion is out of order, but I will allow you five minutes to present your evidence. If you can prove this man is an imposter, there is no need to proceed with this hearing."

"Excellent." From beneath the table, Mr. Colberg lifted the fat book with the ornate leather binding that Libby had seen earlier. Opening to a specific page, he laid it before the judge. "This book chronicles modern European aristocratic families, and you are looking at a portrait of the 9th Duke of Vlaska, the older brother of the old Cossack." He brought forth another photograph from the file on his table. "And here is a photograph of the current Duke of Vlaska. As you can see from the inscription, this photograph was taken in March of 1871 upon the young man's elevation to the title. As is the custom, the photograph and the announcement of a new duke was sent to all the capitals in Europe and to Washington, D.C., where it was on file at the Library of Congress. The man wearing the ermine robe is Enric Dobrescu, the 10th Duke of Vlaska. He is standing alongside his wife, Sophie. The youngsters in the photograph are the duke's children. The man in this courtroom is clearly an imposter."

Libby's gaze flew to Michael. The flexing of the muscle in his jaw was the only sign of his tension. Libby reached out to clasp Regina's hand as she watched the judge scrutinize the picture. Three times the judge stared at Michael, then back at the photograph, his brows lowering in concentration. Finally, he set the photograph down and addressed Michael.

"The appearance and demeanor of the man in this photograph are entirely different from the man I see sitting before me." He held aloft the picture so Michael could see it. Everyone in the courtroom leaned forward, but it was impossible to see much of anything from a distance. The judge raised an eyebrow. "Are you claiming to be the man in this picture?"

"I am claiming to be the oldest son of the 9th Duke of Vlaska," Michael said calmly.

Her father's lawyer stepped forward. "Your honor, I have a

witness here who can testify that this man is an imposter. Dominic Sterescu is a Romanian citizen who is currently serving as an agent for American companies exporting goods to eastern Europe. He attended college alongside the current Duke of Vlaska, and he is prepared to testify that he has never seen the man in this courtroom. Mr. Sterescu?"

The elegant young man Libby noted earlier rose to his feet, adjusting the fit of his satin waistcoat. Mr. Sterescu nodded to the judge, then turned to face Michael. After a moment he turned back to the judge. "I shared an apartment with Enric Dobrescu, the current Duke of Vlaska, when we were both students at the University of Bonn," he said in an accent that was identical to Michael's musical cadence. "For two years we lived together and I consider him a great friend. Never have I laid eyes on the man who is in this courtroom."

Michael spoke a rapid stream of Romanian, startling the crowd and causing Mr. Sterescu to turn to face him. When Mr. Sterescu responded in the same language, the judge banged the gavel.

"Only English will be spoken here," he warned. "Mr. Dobrescu, whatever questions or statements you wish to make to the witness must be in English."

Michael rose to his feet, towering over the witness, but his demeanor remained calm and self-assured. "Have you ever visited the Duke of Vlaska at his home in Gardisau?" he asked.

Mr. Sterescu shook his head. "I have never had the privilege."

"Then you know little of the duke's family?" Michael asked.

"I have met his wife, Sophie. I never met his children." He nodded to the photograph that was still on the judge's raised podium. "They certainly appear attractive, as I knew Enric's children would be."

Michael nodded. "Those are all the questions I have," he said, and took his seat again.

Libby almost fell off her chair. Surely he could not leave the conversation at that! She glanced at Regina, but she seemed as bewildered as she. The judge looked annoyed as he directed another question at Michael.

"Mr. Dobrescu, if you have some validation as to your identity as the 10th Duke of Vlaska, I need to hear it immediately. Otherwise I am prepared to rule in Professor Sawyer's favor."

Libby held her breath and the courtroom went silent. "I am the oldest son of the 9th Duke of Vlaska," Michael said. "My uncle's will specified his house was to go to the duke's oldest son. I am the duke's illegitimate son, and I was recognized as such by my father."

A murmur raced through the courtroom. To admit to illegitimacy was shocking, but Michael made his pronouncement proudly and without hesitation. Libby blinked. She knew what it was to carry a shameful secret, and she envied Michael's ability to speak his truth with no trace of embarrassment.

The judge looked distinctly uncomfortable. "Courts generally only recognize legitimate children for purposes of inheritance. Unless a will makes specific reference to include illegitimate offspring, I believe your brother is the legitimate heir."

Mr. Dobrescu's lawyer, who had been silent up until then, finally rose. "Your honor, at the time of Constantine Dobrescu's death, the current duke was not yet born. On the day the old Cossack died, the *only* child of the 9th Duke of Vlaska was Michael Dobrescu, who is sitting here in this courtroom today. Michael was eight years old at the time of his uncle's death. His younger brother would not be born for another three years. Michael Dobrescu can be the only heir."

Her father shot from his seat, his hand vibrating in rage as he pointed across the courtroom. "He could be anybody's by-blow. We have no idea who this man is."

"I have proof," Michael said in a firm voice.

Libby felt the air leave her body in a rush. As much as she wanted her father to win the case, she had loathed the possibility that Michael could be an imposter. His being the illegitimate son of the duke could be a perfect explanation for his curious mix of sophistication and rough-hewn demeanor. A weight of anxiety settled around her as she watched Michael step forward to present his evidence to the judge, certain that he was telling the truth. He laid a document before the judge.

"This is the registration of my birth at the family's chapel in Gardisau. My father granted permission for me to share the Dobrescu name. This is the signature of my mother, and this is the signature of the 9th Duke of Vlaska. The word below his signature, *tată*, is Romanian for 'father.' I am sure Mr. Sterescu can testify to that."

At the behest of the judge, Dominic Sterescu came forward and confirmed that the document was an official church record of a birth, with the 9th duke's signature above the line for father. Not that any of this was persuasive to her father or his lawyer.

"Your Honor, that document does not prove this man is Michael Dobrescu," her father's lawyer said. "We suspect this man's entire family to be a den of thieves and gypsies. They have not comported themselves like civilized people. Items have gone missing from the Sawyer household. This man may be an imposter who worked on the Vlaska estate and stole that birth certificate."

Michael was still standing beside the judge's table. He picked up the photograph of the current duke and laid it beside the book containing the picture of the man he claimed to be his father. "These men both have a distinctive peak in their hairline," he said. He brushed his own hair straight back from his face. "I have the same marking. As do my sons. All the people of the Dobrescu family have this distinctive trait. You see from the picture that even the children of my brother have this same hairline."

Libby stilled while she watched the judge examine the photographs. She remembered the time she studied the 9th duke's portrait and noticed that pronounced tiny peak in an otherwise straight hairline. It was unusual, but hardly proof of paternity.

The judge agreed with her. "Mr. Dobrescu, I cannot award a house based on such a quirk. We have laws and rules for these things, not supposition." The judge dragged his hands through his hair in frustration and flipped about the documents accumulating on his desk. Then he stilled. He picked up the photograph of the current duke and his family.

"Who is this girl?"

Libby saw Michael's shoulders tense. "That is the duke's sister, Lady Mirela Dobrescu. She is also my half sister."

"Is she the girl who is here in town with you?"

"She is."

A flurry of excited voices filled the courtroom and the judge leaned back in his chair in satisfaction. "Then someone go fetch her and we can solve this little mystery right away."

If the girl in the photograph of the current duke's family was prepared to vouch for Michael's identity, it would be almost impossible to refute her testimony. Libby swung her head to look at her father, whose face was flushed in anger as he spoke in urgent tones to his lawyer.

But Michael shocked everyone. He shook his head. "I will not permit my sister to be questioned," he said in a firm tone. "She is not well, and I will not have her paraded in this courtroom. I forbid it."

Her father shot to his feet. "She is probably some gypsy he picked up on his travels. Otherwise, why can't she show herself so we can judge for ourselves?"

Rather than respond to her father's outburst, Michael swiveled and looked upward, directly at Libby, sitting in the front row of the gallery. "Miss Sawyer can testify to the identity of my sister."

Her eyes widened. She had not realized he knew she was sitting there, but his intense blue gaze was locked on her, as was every other eye in the courtroom. The weight of all those stares was so heavy she felt as though she could barely draw a breath. Judge Frey looked up at her.

"Have you met the woman he claims is his sister?"

It was only for a moment, but Mirela's delicate frame and porcelain beauty were etched in her memory. "I have," she said.

"Then come down and examine this photograph," the judge ordered.

Her father was standing and looking up at her—not in anger, but in panic. His eyes were haunted and his Adam's apple bobbed while he twisted his bony fingers in anxiety. He was afraid. More than anything she longed to race downstairs and comfort him. No matter how bumpy their relationship, he did not deserve what was happening to him.

People shifted in their seats to let her pass down the narrow row. On trembling knees she walked down the staircase and then up the center aisle of the courtroom. Michael stood in front of the bar, his face drawn with concern as he watched her. Did he understand what he was asking of her? Identifying the girl in the picture seemed such a harmless thing to do, but he was asking her to drive the stake through her father's case.

When she reached the front of the room, the judge turned the photograph so she could see. The young man at the center of the portrait looked a little like Michael, with the same sculpted planes of his face and line of his nose, but he was of slighter build. Her focus shifted to the young girl in the portrait. The photograph must have been taken several years ago, because Mirela looked to be only thirteen or fourteen years old, but she had the same delicate beauty and gentle eyes. Hundreds of tiny pearls were sewn into the fabric of her dress and a small tiara rested on her head.

"Yes, this is the girl I saw living in my house."

"You are certain?" Judge Frey was looking at her with sympathy in his eyes. After all, if her father lost this case, she would be homeless as well.

"I am certain," she whispered. She looked at the other people in the young duke's family. The splendid clothing they wore displayed more wealth than Libby's father would earn in a lifetime. Michael Dobrescu was no peasant. He was the closest thing to royalty this town had ever seen. Even the elaborate certificate that recorded his birth was on embossed paper affixed with a satin ribbon. The duke's bold scrawl of a signature filled most of the lower half of the document. Then Libby's eyes widened.

In the space where Michael's mother should have signed her name, there was a small X. It was the universal sign of illiteracy, one she knew all too well. Libby could sign her name—her father had successfully drilled that much into her head—but the simple X Michael's mother had written made her intensely curious. And sympathetic to the woman.

The judge announced that he was satisfied with Michael's identity, and he proceeded to move to the substance of the case.

When Libby returned to her seat, Regina leaned over to whisper in her ear. "I hope your father's lawyer is smart enough to ask for a delay, as their entire case hinged on proving Mr. Dobrescu an imposter. The fool seems to want to plow ahead even though his other arguments are weak."

As the hours passed, Regina's assessment proved accurate. Mind-numbing talk about property titles, due process, and statutory law dragged on for hours. Much of the audience dwindled away when it became apparent there would be no quick victory for the Sawyers. Time and again the law appeared to be on the Dobrescu side. Despite the professor's long tenure in the house, he never had clear title to purchase it. Even to Libby's unschooled eyes, it appeared Judge Frey was looking to throw any benefit of the doubt toward her father, but his lawyer was inadequately prepared.

Through bleary eyes, the judge looked at her father's lawyer. "Mr. Colberg, can you cite any case law that would allow the title of a house to revert back to the state in the event an heir never files a claim on said property?"

"I have not yet investigated that issue, but I'm certain such case law exists."

Libby could practically hear Regina roll her eyes. "That is the foundation of the entire case, and the fool didn't bother to look it up," Regina muttered.

"My father hired him because he has been the college's attorney for three decades and he could get a reduced fee," Libby whispered.

The judge banged his gavel. "I am going to postpone the hearing until more research can be conducted. I am sympathetic to Professor Sawyer's concerns regarding the mechanical drawings that have gone missing from his house. Given these are directly related to his livelihood, I am giving the professor or his representative several hours of access to the house to thoroughly search the premises for his property. Sheriff Barnes will accompany you, and I suggest that the Dobrescus vacate the house while the search is being conducted. I gather there was some unpleasantness the last time Miss Sawyer searched the house."

A flush heated Libby's face at the memory of being hoisted out of her bedroom by Michael Dobrescu. He manhandled her as though she weighed no more than a loaf of bread. She tried to summon the sense of outrage she'd felt that day, but how strange that all she could feel was affection. How typically Michael, to barge forth and defend his family with whatever tools he had at his disposal. Act first, think later. Lady Mirela was lucky to have such a champion on her side.

For Libby had no one.

Michael felt like a leper.

As spectators left the courtroom, their steely glares burned him. When he left the courthouse, people drew away from him, turning their backs and pulling their skirts aside. Even Libby appeared shaken and reluctant to speak with him as she pushed through the crowds toward her father.

It did not matter. Among the dozens of people leaving the court-room, there was only one person he needed to see. Dominic Sterescu was a stranger to him, but a dangerous stranger. Across the court-yard, the young man was only a few steps away from boarding a carriage and leaving town. If Sterescu got away before he could be neutralized, Michael's hard-fought victory in smuggling Mirela out of Romania would be jeopardized.

Michael shouldered through the crowds, jostling a man off the path and almost causing another to stumble down the steps of the courthouse. He quickened his step to bound across the yard and toward the street. Dominic Sterescu had already opened the door of the carriage and was about to step inside. "Sterescu!" he shouted in his command voice. "Wait! Don't go."

The young man paused and looked over his shoulder. With re-luctance, he lowered his foot and turned to face Michael. "Mr. Dobrescu," he said with a brief nod. "I'm sorry if my testimony put you in a difficult position, but my first loyalty must be to the duke."

Sterescu spoke in Romanian and Michael answered in the same language. "I have no argument with you," he said as he extended his hand. After a moment of hesitation, the younger man shook his hand, but when he sought to withdraw it, Michael's grip tightened and refused to let go.

"I have no argument with you," Michael repeated in a low voice, "but I know who you are, and I know why you were expelled from the University of Bonn. I do not believe your new employers in America would be pleased to know the Romanian agent they have hired has been disgraced and branded as a cheater in the circles of Europe."

A flash of anger lit Sterescu's eyes, but Michael maintained his iron grasp on the man's hand. "I repeat, I have no argument with you. But if you tell my brother that I am in America, or that any of my family is here, I will blanket every American newspaper with advertisements that announce your shameful past at the university."

Michael stared hard into Dominic Sterescu's troubled eyes. Sterescu's disgrace when he was caught cheating on a philosophy exam was eight years ago, but that sort of stain lingered on a man's reputation. A stupid mistake made by an eighteen-year-old should not carry a life sentence of shame, but that was what Sterescu faced if Michael carried out his threat.

"Both of us are seeking a new start here," Michael said slowly and carefully. Winning clear title to the house on Winslow Street would be a minor victory compared with the real prize he had won for Mirela, and it would be jeopardized without this young man's cooperation. "I have no desire to cause you harm, and will keep your secret as long as you keep mine. My brother," he said slowly and clearly, "is *never* to learn we are here."

A tightening of the young man's hand and a firm return of the handshake gave Michael hope. "Mr. Dobrescu, as far as I am concerned, I never saw you today, and I never intend to see you again." This time when Sterescu tried to withdraw his hand, Michael permitted it. "I would rather submit my body to a living autopsy than return to Romania. I look forward to a long and happy life in America, and I wish the same for you." He turned and mounted the steps to the carriage. "What Enric doesn't know won't hurt him."

Michael rubbed a thumb along the thinly ridged scar as he watched the carriage roll down the street, remembering the rage that burned in his half brother's eyes the day he brought the riding crop slashing down against Michael's face. Michael prayed Sterescu was wise enough never to carry tales back to the Duke of Vlaska.

His jaw tightened as he pondered his dilemma. From the moment his brother was born, that child had been showered with gifts, land, titles, and power, and yet still Enric seethed with jealousy over the love their father had so freely bestowed upon his illegitimate son. Enric had managed to control evidence of his resentment while their father was alive, but once the old duke was dead, there was very little to contain the simmering envy that burned inside him.

Even if Michael won clear and undisputed title to the house on Winslow Street, it would be years before he could be certain Enric's power could not reach them there. Mirela's actions in the greenhouse put them in a more precarious position than ever, for if Enric ever learned of that suicide attempt . . .

Michael forced the thought away. In a perfect world, he and Mirela would have assumed new names in America that would have insured their anonymity, but his need to secure title to his uncle's house precluded the use of false names. Always there was the danger that Enric might someday learn where he had fled with Mirela, and Michael could only pray that Mirela was fully healed before that day came.

15

The boughs of the pine branches were rocking in the stiff autumn breeze, the tiny seedpods nestled deeply among the needles. A dusting of early snow gave a pale cast to the tiny berries, which would soon feed birds.

Libby snapped awake from the dream, memories of the red juniper tree still vivid in her mind. She knew *exactly* where they were. The trees were down in the DeRooy valley, named after the old Dutch settler who had first tried to set up a trapping company there. She saw the cluster of red juniper trees when she was searching for the wild echinacea that sometimes grew in the valley. The trees were growing all along the western bank of the steeply sloped valley wall. There must have been dozens of them.

She sat up in bed, wishing she could tell Michael about the red juniper trees. It had been two days since the court case, two days since she had learned Michael was no imposter out to swindle them. The niggling fear that Michael might be a fraud had kept Libby's wayward fantasies in line, but now they had broken free and were running rampant through her every waking thought. The sight of Michael wrestling with his children in the yard, Michael following her around the house to smell her hair, the strength of his shoulders as he picked up a barn door to haul it out of the way.

He wasn't a fraud, he was exactly what he presented himself to be. A bold, hearty man who adored his family and plowed through any obstacle to care for them. She sprang out of bed and yanked on her clothes, anxious to find Michael and tell him about the red juniper trees.

Unfortunately, Regina had other plans. "I have the most fabulous news," she said as she snapped a white tablecloth over the table in the backyard garden. "I've invited guests to a luncheon and I need your help." She sent Libby a wink. "I think you and your father are going to be very pleased."

There was no avoiding it. The entire household was buzzing with curiosity about Regina's surprise, and Libby would need to wait at least until after the meal to escape notice and visit the Dobrescus.

They set out a platter of cold ham, bowls of chilled cinnamon apples and cucumber salad, a plum cake, and a basket of poppy seed muffins. Next to a pitcher of water, a bottle of champagne rested in a crystal bucket of ice. There were two extra places at the table, but Regina stoically refused to reveal the identity of the guests.

Libby cut some flowers from the garden to make a centerpiece. Twice she rearranged the flowers in the vase of water, each time wondering what Michael would think of the arrangement. She knew if he were there, he would not comment on their appearance, rather he would be interested in the combination of scents. Amidst a handful of fern leaves she had inserted a few sprays of indigo salvia mixed in with sweet alyssum. Both were nice, but the fragrance was subtle. The real power of the bouquet was in the single stalk of an oriental lily in the center of the vase. Was it a good choice for the salvia and sweet alyssum? Or too overpowering? She didn't know if it was a suitable match with the salvia, but she was certain Michael would have an opinion.

There my mind goes again, she thought. She could not even set the table without thinking of the man. The kitchen window slid open with a rasp and her father leaned his head out the window.

"Regina's visitors are here," he said. "They are coming straight back."

Libby cast one last look at the table and could not resist a final tweak to the angle of the lily in the centerpiece. She turned to greet the visitors as Regina led them around the house on the garden path, followed by Jasper and Tillie. The two men were of similar height, both middle-aged, both with neatly groomed and oiled dark hair. Even their small, clipped mustaches were identical. Libby raised her brows. Twins?

"And this is Libby Sawyer, the professor's maiden daughter," Regina said in her exquisite southern accent as she strolled into the garden.

At least she did not say *spinster*, Libby thought as she stepped forward to greet the men. "Libby, this is Mr. Mark Radcliff and Mr. Raymond Radcliff. The Radcliffs are well known as the very best estate attorneys in all of New England. Better yet, they have experience with international wills and estates. They have agreed to take on your father's case."

"How very kind of you," Libby murmured, but her mind was racing. The men were elegantly attired, with fine silk weskits and each of them sporting a watch hanging from heavy gold chains. When Libby looked at her father, she saw him shifting in anxiety and knew exactly what he was thinking. Attorneys like this would cost a fortune.

Regina was already pouring drinks and inviting the guests to sit. Mr. Auckland had been invited as well. Regina spooned some cinnamon apples onto a plate as she chatted with the attorneys.

Her father had yet to sit. He cleared his throat and touched Regina's elbow. "Regina, if I might ask for your assistance inside the kitchen?" he asked quietly. "It will only take a moment."

Libby rose from her chair. "I'll go as well," she said. Once inside the house, she could see her father struggling to find the words, but Libby was not so diplomatic.

"Those men must cost a fortune," she said in a harsh whisper.

"Not to worry, dearest. I have already covered their fee."

Her father's eyes nearly bulged from his head. "Jasper doesn't make that sort of income. Those men could put us both in the poorhouse."

Regina patted her father on the arm. "Nonsense. You remember those little green earrings I received for my tenth birthday? I always told Jasper they were merely green glass, because I just assumed they were. What sort of parent gives a ten-year-old real emeralds?" She shrugged her shoulders as a gorgeous blush tinted her ivory cheeks. "Well, it was before the war and my Mama always did like fine things. Turns out those earrings were the genuine article, and I traded them in for a little pin money to fund the Radcliffs' fee. So everything is taken care of, and soon you will have your house back. I am certain of it."

Her father sank into a chair and Libby's hand flew to her throat. Regina had always been nonchalant about allowing Libby to enjoy her cast-off clothing and perfume, but never had her generosity included something as grand as emerald earrings. The only time Libby could recall seeing them was when Regina wore a tailored riding habit identical in shade to the earrings. Still, she was shocked. Her father seemed equally confounded. "Regina, those earrings must be very precious to you."

Regina leaned down to embrace her father-in-law, still collapsed into his seat. "Nonsense, Willard. We are all family now and I am determined to see that you get your house back. That college attorney you were using was no match for the case you are up against and the Radcliffs are the very best. Positively *lethal* in the courtroom, I am told." She whirled away in a flounce of perfumed voile and laughing good spirits, while Libby stood in dazed disbelief.

Her father lowered his head, rubbing his forehead in agitation. "I don't know what to say," he finally stammered.

Libby drew a steadying breath. The gift was substantial, but it would not have seemed so strange had it come from Jasper. It was likely that her father would lose the house if they could not reverse the avalanche of evidence that had emerged to weigh against them. Those two attorneys sitting in the garden might be the only chance her father had of holding on to his home.

Libby knelt down to look at her father directly. "The earrings are already gone and the fee has been paid," she said quietly as she took his hand. "I think you should accept the gift, and we will figure out a way to repay Regina's kindness later. After we are back in our home."

The strength in her father's fingers as he squeezed her hand was reassuring. She could forgive his surliness over the past few weeks. What man would not be thrown off-kilter after what Michael Dobrescu had done to him?

When they rejoined the luncheon, the rest of the occupants at the table had already begun to eat. Libby pulled Tillie onto her lap while they dined and the Radcliff brothers entertained them with stories of their trips to Venice. Libby had never traveled outside of Massachusetts and she was eager to hear about Europe, but her father was impatient to get down to business.

"The judge granted me permission to search the house for my mechanical drawings," he said, creating an abrupt break in the conversation. "All day yesterday I inspected that house with a fine-toothed comb, but the drawings aren't there. The gypsies have taken them. I want to know what my options are."

The laughter and conversation sputtered to a halt. Only the drone of a few insects flitting about the delphiniums filled the air. Finally, the lawyer closest to her father set his glass down.

"Mrs. Sawyer mentioned your concerns about the missing drawings," he said. "We can make a motion regarding the contents of the house, but this is a separate and distinct issue from the title to the house."

THE ROSE OF WINSLOW STREET

Regina waved her fan in front of her face. "Personally, I think they probably used them for kindling. Gypsies are prone to doing that sort of thing."

"What's a gypsy?" Tillie asked.

Libby stroked a curl from the girl's forehead. "It is not a very nice word," she said gently, shooting Regina a dark look over Tillie's head.

"I want to annihilate that man," her father growled. "He has taken my house. He has taken my drawings. I swear by all that is holy he is trying to take my daughter." At Libby's gasp, her father whirled to fix her with an angry glare. "Yes, my daughter! That man has more tricks up his sleeve than a traveling magician. Don't think he is fascinated by your charms, Libby. The man only wants to take whatever is mine."

The summer heat suddenly escalated and Libby fought the temptation to stand and flee the table. "Now, Willard," Mr. Auckland said. "Libby is a fine and sensible girl any man would be proud to have."

Regina rose and topped off the professor's glass. "It is too nice a day to be worried about that nasty Mr. Dobrescu," she said in her infinitely sweet voice. "The Radcliffs are going to take care of him in short order and all this unpleasantness will be behind us, right?"

Her father only grunted, but Mr. Raymond Radcliff sensed her father's unquenchable need to strategize against the Dobrescus and proceeded to outline his plan of attack.

Libby's gaze traveled around the lush greenery of Regina's splendid garden. No matter how lovely the garden, how clear the summer day, it was impossible to be in her father's presence without the corrosive taint of his bitterness seeping out to spoil the mood. He had cause to be aggrieved, but did that mean they could not enjoy the beauty of the day? Their plates were filled with food, their bodies were healthy and warmed by the summer sun. They had friends, family, and now the assistance of the best attorneys.

190

Couldn't he find a few minutes to enjoy what blessings he had, rather than enumerating what was lost?

She watched a bumblebee gorge itself on a delphinium in full bloom, which was much more fascinating than the tense legal jargon surrounding her. There were always people in this world who counted their grievances, rather than giving thanks for their blessings. There was a time when Libby had done the same. From the age of five, when her appalling inability to read first became apparent, until the day Mr. Auckland rescued her in the library and gave her permission to quit trying, Libby had subjected herself to daily castigations of her shortcomings. She had learned to break herself of the habit.

After all, Father is always on hand to remind me of them, she thought as she suppressed a wry smile.

16

The next morning, Libby made certain she would be able to sneak out of the house without scrutiny. It was the Fourth of July and she had already told her father she planned on escaping into the country for a little painting. She was famous for disappearing from the house in the early hours to paint using the morning sun, and no one would think it strange when she disappeared for several hours. Before leaving, she grabbed her canvas bag of art supplies, plus a few treats for the Dobrescu children from the kitchen.

She simply had to tell Michael about the location of the red juniper trees. In the twenty-four hours since she remembered where they could be found, she'd thought of little else besides her need to get the information to him, which was causing guilt to gnaw at her. She still remembered the way her father wept at the prospect of losing his house. Was there anything worse than seeing an old man cry? She ought to fear Michael rather than indulge her fascination with him.

Libby headed to the old Congregational churchyard in search of a subject. The ivy growing along the ancient limestone walls of the cemetery would be an excellent study. No doubt a dull subject to some, but Libby was fascinated by the ability of the ivy shoots to find a crevice in the weathered stone and latch on to spread across the surface of the rocks.

Ivy was an easy subject for her. Much more challenging was the worn, pitted surface of the limestone. Libby pressed her fingers into the cool surface of the grainy rock, feeling its pores and the uneven weathering of the stone. Capturing it in watercolor would be a challenge, but one she was eager to attempt. How could ivy get nutrients from stone? Perhaps Michael would know.

She shook her head, frustrated she could not go even an hour without thinking about the man. Her father's comment about Michael's interest in her as a means to get the house had hurt, doubly so because she knew it might be true.

Two hours later, her painting was complete. She could not leave the churchyard until it dried, so she lay in the grass and watched the white patches of clouds twist and turn across the azure sky above. Some might find it strange to relax in a graveyard, but Libby always found the spot where generations of her ancestors were laid to rest to be an oddly comforting place. What would those descendants from the *Mayflower* think of her odd fascination with Michael Dobrescu? Their stalwart Puritan heritage saturated every drop of blood in her body, but she was tempted to cast it all aside and fling her arms around Michael Dobrescu and dance like a wanton by the light of the fire. Some of her Puritan ancestors would probably be horrified, but weren't the Puritans the original rebels? They led a revolution in England, then plowed forward to America in search of their perfect "City on a Hill." Somehow she was certain more than a few of them would nod in approval at her choice.

The spreading branches of an old elm tree blocked one corner of her vision, but the occasional sparrow flitting through the leaves amused her. If Ivan were there, those sparrows would be prey. Still, she missed the weight of Ivan on her chest and longed for the simple comfort of her pesky cat.

Was she destined to go through life with only the comfort of her cat and the sound of songbirds to keep her company? She enjoyed playing with other people's children, but those children inevitably went back to their own homes, leaving Libby alone with her cat. Michael Dobrescu already had children. If she married Michael—

She sat up abruptly, so fast it took a moment for her head to stop spinning. Michael Dobrescu liked the way her hair smelled but had never given her any other concrete proof he was attracted to her. Deciding she'd done more than enough thinking for the moment, she lifted her painting of ivy and held it up before the sun, looking for damp patches on the paper. Seeing none, she rolled it into a cylinder, secured it with a ribbon, and set off for the house on Winslow Street.

Libby darted beneath low-hanging branches so she could approach the house from behind. If she walked down Winslow Street, her father would hear about the visit within the hour, so she kept behind the screen of trees that ran along the length of the backyards on Winslow Street.

She heard them before she saw them. Childish squeals mixed with bold adult laughter. Peeking over the back fence, Libby was appalled to see the two boys riding on top of Michael and Turk's shoulders. The boys were grappling with each other as the men moved back and forth across the yard.

Michael was not wearing a shirt. He had both arms raised to brace Andrei, who was sitting on his shoulders. Michael's tanned skin glistened with perspiration and his muscles flexed as he shifted to balance the boy. Andrei's arms were longer, so he was doing a better job at reaching out to nudge Luke, but she could tell Michael was trying to compensate by sidestepping and angling away to make things more even for Luke. What a man! She covered her mouth to prevent the laughter from spilling out, but both boys swiveled to stare at her, their blue eyes wide with surprise.

"It is the jam lady!" Andrei said.

When Michael spotted her, he sank to one knee and lowered his head so Andrei could jump off his shoulders. Turk did the same and both boys came racing toward the back fence, but Libby had a hard time dragging her focus away from Michael. She had never seen a grown man without a shirt, but his broad shoulders and muscular physique made a magnificent sight. After a brief nod to her, Michael turned away and grabbed his shirt. With his back to her, he swiped the fabric across his damp skin, then shrugged into the shirt. It was impossible for her to tear her eyes from the rippling of muscle that played across his back as he performed the simple act.

Luke crawled up the fence to grin at her. "Did you bring us more jam?"

She smiled at the eight-year-old imp who was bracing his forearms across the top of the fence. "What makes you think I brought you jam?"

"You love us and you miss us?"

That much was true! She fought and won the battle to keep the grin off her face. "I love and miss my cat, but I don't bring him jam."

Michael was still buttoning his shirt as he approached her. She had not seen him since the day in the courtroom and had not spoken to him since he dropped her off at Jasper's after the oddly tender moment in the barn. His expression was guarded as he scanned her face, but Libby could not hold back her smile. She was anxious to tell him where they could find the red juniper trees, but she didn't want to blurt it out in front of everyone. Somehow the moment seemed too special for that.

"I came to make sure you were celebrating the Fourth of July properly." She scanned the yard, noting the table covered with fruit and a pitcher of lemonade. There was also some kind of squat bread, probably a Romanian delicacy, but at least there was no sign of turkey or pumpkin pie. "Can I join you?" she asked impulsively.

196

"Andrei, go open the fence door," Michael said. Before the words were out of his mouth, the boy had gone tearing across the yard to the gate. Michael walked on the other side of the fence as Libby headed toward the gate, and they didn't break eye contact as they strolled the length of the yard. When she reached the gate and turned to enter the yard, Michael stood directly in front of her, blocking her path. There was unease in his blue eyes.

"I was not sure we would still be on speaking terms," he said quietly.

They shouldn't be. She ought to hate and despise the threat he represented, and yet, when she looked up into his handsome, honest face, all Libby felt was relief. He was not a liar, a thief, or an imposter; he was merely a man who had a legal disagreement with her father. The way his hand clasped the top of the fence and his weight shifted from side to side betrayed his anxiety. He was nervous about her reaction to him. Why should that be endearing to her? He certainly *ought* to feel guilty over what he was doing to her family, and yet all Libby wanted to do was set the man at ease.

She angled her head up so she could see him better. "Am I supposed to call you something fancy? Lord Dobrescu or something?"

A snort of laughter greeted her question. "Michael is fine. Baseborn children rarely have titles, and I am no exception."

Michael stepped back to hold the gate wide and she joined the family. The children swarmed around her canvas bag and she made a great show of rummaging through her brushes and paints before pretending surprise when she found a jar of strawberry jam. Andrei snatched the jar and held it over his head.

"We can put this on the birthday cake. It will make it not so terrible."

Libby looked up. "Whose birthday is it?"

"Mirela is twenty years old today," Michael said. "Instead of being born on a saint's birthday, Mirela was born on Independence Day." He turned his head so he could look at Mirela sitting beneath

197

the pear tree and sent her a gentle smile. "Surely this means you were fated since birth to someday end up in America, don't you think?"

Libby glanced at Lady Mirela. Once again, she was wearing one of Libby's old gowns, but all Libby noticed were the bandages encircling both of Mirela's wrists. Was the girl still suicidal? Libby felt bad about insulting her the first time she saw Mirela, but surely that couldn't have played a role in the girl's drastic actions, could it?

Mirela beamed up into Michael's face as though she worshiped the man. "Yes, surely it was fate," she said with a bright smile.

Libby walked the few paces so she could stand before Mirela. "We have never formally met," she said. The brief incident in her bedroom when Michael had carried her from the room hardly qualified, but Libby found herself fascinated by this delicate young woman. Now that she knew Lady Mirela was in fact the daughter of a duke, she had no idea how she was supposed to greet her. Should she curtsy? For pity's sake, though, this was America and titles were not supposed to matter. Besides, it would be hard to befriend a woman with a title, and there was no doubt Mirela needed one. The Dobrescus were pariahs in the neighborhood, and Libby doubted that Mirela had a single friend in America.

Libby sank down beside her. "I am Libby Sawyer and I hope that we might learn to be friends."

Mirela's china blue eyes widened. "You are very generous." Her gaze flicked to the boys, who were spreading the strawberry jam across the squat cake. "I know you have brought my family food when no one else in the village would have anything to do with us. I would consider it a great privilege to be friends with such a person." Then the girl laughed. "I would be happy to offer you a piece of birthday cake, but I am not confident it is fit for consumption. Turk and I made it, but neither of us is skilled in the kitchen."

Andrei was sawing at the cake with a knife, but the cake appeared to be as tough as a piece of steak. Even the rasping sound of the blade dragging through the cake sounded ominous.

198

Joseph stepped forward. "I have a bottle of wine," he said. "The cake will taste better if we have a glass or two before we eat it."

"I'll get the corkscrew," Turk said.

Five minutes later, the adults were seated around the tree-shaded table with a glass of golden chardonnay. Even at the round table, Libby was amazed at the way Mirela seemed to be the natural leader. It was not merely because the men deferred to her—it was her quiet dignity that seemed to command respect among the loud, boisterous crew. The moment she suggested a toast, everyone immediately stilled to listen to her.

"To our first Independence Day in America," she said as she met the eyes of the people around the table. "I pray we can make our new life in America something worthwhile, something we will never regret. If I live to be one hundred, I will never be able to find the words to thank you all for my freedom. I would not be alive today without each of you." Her gaze traveled around the table. "Joseph, Turk, and especially you, Michael. You are my heroes."

For a moment, Libby felt like she had stepped back in time and was witnessing a medieval lady pay homage to her knights. All three men looked at Mirela as if they idolized her, and the radiance that shone from Mirela's face seemed almost mythical. Libby had always assumed that Michael was the leader of the family, but now she knew that Mirela was the focal point of this odd group of people.

Then Michael stood and held the bottle of wine high. "To Uncle Constantine," he said officiously. Only a few inches of wine remained in the bottle, but Libby's eyes widened as Michael proceeded to pour it all onto the grass.

Mirela leaned closer. "It is a Romanian custom to pour wine onto the ground for our deceased friends," she explained. "I think our uncle would be pleased that we remembered him on this day."

"I think your uncle would want us to uncork another bottle," Joseph said with a grin. When Michael went to fetch another bottle of wine, Libby looked about her, memorizing the sound of the boys'

199

laughter, the scent of freshly turned earth. She did not know how much longer she would be able to sustain these unlikely friendships, but she would treasure these memories. In the years to come, she knew she would often revisit this day.

⁓

The cake was awful, but after two glasses of wine and a splendid hour of sunlit laughter, no one seemed to mind its leathery texture.

"You must use either yeast or baking soda if the batter is to rise," Libby said.

Understanding dawned in Mirela's eyes. "I saw the ingredient, but since it only called for a tablespoon I thought it was not so important. Next time I will know better!"

There were so many questions Libby longed to ask Mirela, but all were far too intrusive to ask a virtual stranger. The photograph of Mirela with the duke showed a young woman dressed in silks and dripping with pearls and diamonds. What could have caused her to turn her back on such a luxurious life to flee to an uncertain future in America? And, unlike the rest of her family, Mirela arrived with only the clothes on her back. Libby had seen trunks of clothing and supplies that belonged to the men, but Mirela seemed to have nothing of her own. Was it because there was nothing else she wanted? Was her life so terrible she literally wanted nothing to remind her of Romania?

Mirela sat in the grass and leaned against the trunk of the pear tree with Ivan lounging in her lap. The lazy cat soaked up Mirela's attention as she stroked his fur, but Libby could not help but look at the thin strips of gauze encircling the girl's wrists.

Mirela caught Libby's stare before she could glance away. Mirela's fingers stilled on Ivan's fur. "Does everyone in the town know what I tried to do?" she asked.

Her question was direct, and it would serve no good to lie to the girl. "I'm afraid so," Libby said softly. She wanted to ask why

Mirela had done it, what had caused her to believe her life was so horrible she could not endure even another day. Instead, she reached out to touch the back of Mirela's hand. "How are you feeling these days? Is there anything I can do to help you?"

Like a shot, Michael strode across the lawn in three tremendous strides and flung himself down on the grass beside them. The cat startled and scampered away, but Michael was brusque as he stretched out on his back, plopped his head in Mirela's lap, and looked up at his sister. "You don't have to answer any questions you don't want to," he said bluntly.

Libby startled a bit at the implication she was prying, but Mirela was saying something to Michael in Romanian. A moment later she looked at Libby with apology in her eyes. "Forgive me," she said. "I was telling Michael he does not need to be so terribly protective of me anymore. I learned a few weeks ago that my life will not turn out as I had hoped. It has been difficult for me to accept, but I am learning to be at peace with it." Despite her words, Mirela's face was troubled.

Libby looked at the simple cotton dress Mirela wore. It was one of Libby's old gowns that still had some paint smears on the skirt from a brief period when she'd dabbled in oil painting. It must feel odd to go from living in a palace and wearing silk to living in a house on Winslow Street and wearing secondhand clothing. Was this what Mirela was referring to when she suggested her life was not turning out as planned? Or was there something darker in Mirela's past?

Michael stayed sprawled on the lawn, but he rolled his head so he could look at her. "Now that you know we are not gypsies or vagabonds, surely you must have some questions."

She had plenty, but most of them were still terribly intrusive. Still, he had invited her question and perhaps she would never have a better opportunity than this very moment. "So you two are brother and sister . . ." she began cautiously.

"Half brother," Mirela corrected.

What was the proper protocol to ask about a duke's mistress in front of his legitimate daughter? And yet Mirela seemed to idolize Michael, so surely she could not be too sensitive about the topic.

"Who was your mother?" she asked Michael cautiously.

Michael did not seem to be the least bit offended as he rolled away from Mirela and propped his head on his elbow to see Libby better. "My mother's family kept goats on land owned by my father, the duke. Her job was to milk the goats, and over time she learned to make goat cheese. People came from miles away to buy that cheese. My father, who was single at the time, saw her and struck up a . . . well, a friendship, I suppose you could say." He swiveled his eyes to look at Mirela and grinned. "No one wishes to know what their parents did behind the haystack, and I am no different in this." Mirela covered her mouth to smother laughter and blushed. She even blushed gorgeously.

Michael turned his attention back to Libby. "In any event, they carried on for a number of years, and I came along during that time. My father acknowledged me and made sure I wanted for nothing. Of course, there was no talk of marriage. A duke does not marry the daughter of a goat farmer." Michael rolled to a sitting position. Libby clasped her hands together in an effort to avoid the temptation to reach out and brush the strands of grass from the back of his shirt.

A shout from across the yard interrupted her thought. A stream of Romanian chatter came from both boys as they gestured toward Mirela. She laughed and scampered off to join them.

Michael looked at her. "My boys wish Mirela to judge their handstands. This is one of the few areas in which Luke surpasses Andrei, and he is anxious to show her." Michael plucked a strand of grass and began idly chewing on it. "Anyway, my father eventually married the duchess," he continued. "She was the youngest daughter of a German prince and gave birth to first Enric and then

Mirela. By then my father had become a Christian, and I do not believe he was ever unfaithful to the duchess. His fascination with my mother had cooled, but he made sure I was provided for and received an excellent education. At heart, my father was a botanist and loved working in his rose and jasmine fields. I shared that passion and he taught me most of what I know about growing flowers for the perfume industry. He was a good man, Libby."

The way he said it revealed a touch of defensiveness, as though it was very important for her not to think unfavorably of his father.

Still, it seemed odd to her that the stern-faced man in the portrait, the man who looked like he could be emperor of the universe, could have fallen for the daughter of a goat farmer. What sort of woman was Michael's mother?

"When I saw your birth certificate in the courtroom," she began cautiously, "I noticed that your father signed it with a big lordly signature that took up half the page. But your mother signed with an X."

There was a long silence as Michael stared at her. "That is correct," he finally said.

She swallowed, knowing there was no graceful way to ask her next question, but she desperately wanted to know. "Could your mother read and write?"

He turned away from her and plucked another blade of grass, rolling it between his big fingers as he stared at his sons demonstrating their handstands for Mirela. "Would you think less of her if she could not?"

Libby dropped her chin. She thought less of *herself* for her inability to read, but oddly, she did not feel the same for the goat farmer's daughter. Such a girl probably had no chance to attend school, which was a very different story from a girl who had the help of tutors, teachers, and even the town librarian. "No," Libby said honestly. "I suppose there may be any number of reasons someone may not learn to read."

203

Michael nodded. "There was a school in the village, but it was several miles from where my mother lived. Also, I don't think my grandfather could spare her. She was his only child and there was much work to be done, so my mother never went to school." He dropped the blade of grass and turned to her, and his next question shocked her.

"Can you read?" he asked.

She caught her breath and her eyes flew to his. "Why do you ask that?"

"It is none of my business, but today I noticed when Mirela showed you the cake recipe and asked what she did wrong, you did not even glance at it. And I remember you would not read the list of food items I needed at the market, but asked me to read them to you. I often read such things for my mother, and always she had a very good memory of everything I said to her. I noticed you have this same quality."

He was looking at her with curiosity, but not judgment. She looked away and straightened her skirts. "Of course I can read," she said. Because she could pick out a few words if she was given enough time to process the information, it was not precisely a lie, but she couldn't tell him the full truth. She could not bear to see his warm admiration wither into pity or scorn.

She straightened. There was only one thing on the planet that would truly impress this man, and she had the power to deliver it. "How would you like to see a stand of red juniper trees?"

His face transformed. Hope surged into his eyes as he leaned toward her. "You have remembered where they are?"

"I know exactly where they are. They are down in the DeRooy valley. I can take you to them today, if you'd like."

Michael sprang to his feet, then she gasped when he swung her up into his arms and whirled her in a circle. Her feet went flying out behind her and she clung to his neck as the yard spun around her. Michael kept spinning her in a circle as peals of laughter sounded from his strong throat. She was breathless by the time her feet landed on the ground, her head still whirling so badly she dared not let go of him lest she fall. Both Luke and Andrei had come running.

"Can I go for a ride too, Papa?" Luke asked, crowding in front of her to get a handhold on Michael.

"Yes, you can go for a ride, Luke." Michael squatted and wrapped his big hands around Luke's hips, then tossed the boy high into the air. Luke squealed with delight, and soon Andrei was clamoring for a ride as well. When Libby's head ceased spinning, she saw that Mirela had drawn near, curiosity brimming in her eyes.

"Michael is excited over some trees I found for him," Libby said modestly, but Mirela grabbed her arm.

"You found him the red juniper tree?" she asked.

Libby startled. "Does the whole family know about his search?"

"Oh heavens, yes!" Excitement brimmed from Mirela's eyes. "We can't sell our perfume unless we can get some resin. Michael's jasmine oil is in danger of going bad if he can't get that resin very soon."

"I see," she said. She didn't, but it hardly seemed to matter. Michael was clapping Turk and Joseph on the back, and then he turned back to her.

"When can we go?"

"It is about an hour's walk," Libby said. She glanced at the sun, already starting to edge toward the west. "It is a little late today, but I can meet you tomorrow."

"Yes. Tomorrow!" Michael said.

Then she realized it would be difficult to sneak out of the house so surreptitiously again. "Meet me at the abandoned barn on Storybrook Lane," she said. "From there it is another forty minutes or so down into the valley."

They agreed on a time and Libby sat down beside Turk and Joseph to watch Michael wrestle with the boys. Had ever a man adored his children more than Michael? It was yet another facet of his personality that drew her to him.

Her father had been correct in his assessment that Michael Dobrescu was a dangerous man, for she was becoming hopelessly ensnared in his web.

17

Libby's father and Mr. Auckland were drinking lemonade on the front porch of Jasper's house when she returned. Spiked lemonade, given their jovial mood.

"Have you had a good day, Libby?" her father asked in rare good humor as she mounted the front steps.

Spending the day with a group of Romanian immigrants celebrating their first Independence Day had resulted in the most delightful day of her life, but she merely smiled. "I did a bit of scouting about for new specimens to paint." Which was not a complete lie, since the ivy clinging to the cemetery walls was rolled into her canvas sack.

With a casual flick of his toe, her father tilted a porch chair toward her and gestured for her to sit. "My daughter, the brilliant artist," he said with a wide smile and no trace of scorn. "As soon as we are back home, we must display a few of your paintings. They are sheer poetry of watercolor and artistry."

Now I know he has been drinking, Libby thought. Never had her father suggested that any of her paintings were worthy of display, but he lauded her work for several moments before pressing a glass of lemonade into her hands and raised a toast.

"To American independence, good friends, and excellent

lawyers," he said with a hearty laugh. To Libby's surprise, the lemonade was not spiked. The sweet, cool liquid was refreshing as she swallowed and relaxed back into her chair.

Actually, her father had been in much better spirits for days now. He had resumed work on the portable combustion engine and even asked Libby to draw a cutaway diagram of the new fuel circuit. Last night, when Tillie spilled a glass of juice on the professor's notes, Libby was prepared to sweep Tillie to the safety of her room, but her father had simply laughed. "Not to worry," he said as he smiled down at Tillie. "I've got it all up here," he said as he tapped the side of his forehead.

"Jeremiah, what do you say we send for Jasper and Regina and start a game of croquet?" her father asked Mr. Auckland. "Even with Regina's miraculous skills, I have a feeling I am on a lucky streak and today may be our day to finally beat them."

Mr. Auckland shook his head. "Perhaps Libby can be your teammate. My wife will have my head if I don't get back soon."

Her father's gaze swiveled to her. "What do you say, Liberty-bell? Are you game?" It had been years since her father had used that affectionate nickname, and it cut through her defenses like a hot knife through butter. Besides, she loved a good game of croquet.

"I'm game," she said.

Never would she forget the look of blessed relief on Michael's face when he first gazed upon the cluster of red juniper trees clinging to the side of the valley slope. "Thank you," he murmured reverently. And then he surprised her when he made the sign of a cross and knelt down on one knee. He lowered his head and spoke quietly in Romanian. After a few moments, he stood and looked at her.

"I thank you as well, but I needed to thank the Lord. I must never take these blessings for granted." She was oddly touched that he felt comfortable enough in her presence to utter a prayer. Michael was still staring at the trees like a man struck dumb in wonder, and he reached out to clasp Libby's hand in his warm, solid grip. When she returned his squeeze, it was as though they were connected in an enchanted moment. "You have no idea what this means to me and my family," he said in a voice that was shaking with emotion.

It was true, she didn't. He had said something about needing the resin to make perfume, but that hardly seemed to warrant this sort of dazed wonderment.

"Do you know who owns this land?" he asked as he made his way down the steep side of the bank to get closer to the trees.

Libby hoisted her skirts as she followed him down the embankment. "I don't think anyone owns it. It is too steep for farming or grazing."

Michael reached through the dense screen of pine needles and rubbed his fingers into some sap leaking from the trunk of the tree. He straightened and brought his fingers to his nose, and if possible, his smile grew even broader.

"No scent," he said. "You want to smell?"

Libby really didn't care, but the eagerness with which he extended those sticky fingers to her made it impossible to resist. She leaned in a little closer and held his wrist as she drew her fingers to her nose. "I can't smell anything."

"Of course not," Michael said with pride. "These are fine red junipers, so the sap has no scent. Tomorrow I will find out for sure who owns this land and how I can tap these trees. As soon as I have the resin, I can begin blending perfume."

She followed in his footsteps as he climbed back up the steep side of the valley. Was there ever a bigger contradiction than Michael Dobrescu? The man looked like Hercules, but all it took to make him positively giddy was to begin discussing perfume. He was thrilled to explain the difference between top note and middle note compounds. "Did you know that smell is the only sense that is fully developed at birth?" Michael asked her as they crossed Mr.

Richter's cranberry field. He was full of these odd bits of trivia. The scented oil of the iris plant was harvested from the root, not the flower; rose oil came only from the petals, but the entire lavender plant could be used to make oil.

"Marie's favorite scent was lavender," Michael said. "It was hard for us to compete with the French in lavender, but she was determined to try. Her first harvest was a disaster. It had almost no scent, but she kept cutting more chalk into the soil, and by her third year . . . well! That lavender would put even the Frenchies to shame!" Michael stopped so abruptly she almost slammed into him, but he did not notice. He closed his eyes and a little half smile played about his mouth. "It had a sweeter scent than most lavender, with just a hint of grass beneath the floral scent. Even when it was dried, that gentle hint of green came through and made it unique. Marie did well with that lavender."

There was that niggling bit of jealousy, roused every time she thought of the woman who had shared Michael's life and borne him two fine children. Apparently, she also appealed to his sense of smell by producing the world's best lavender. The path to most men's hearts was through their stomachs, but not Michael Dobrescu. Marie had figured out the way to charm him through his nose.

Always when he spoke of Marie, he said her name with fondness. And why shouldn't he? He had married the woman, so surely he must have cared for her. Probably loved her. Libby started walking again and was relieved when Michael roused himself from his reveries to follow her.

"Was she pretty?" The question popped out of Libby's mouth before she could call it back.

Michael swiveled his head to look at her, but he did not break his stride. Only the sound of their boots slicing through the underbrush cut the silence, although she could see a hint of a smile on his mouth. Finally, he spoke.

"Let me just say that if Marie and I had had a daughter, it would

210

have been better for the girl to look like me." Libby's eyes widened in surprise. Michael was a handsome man, but heaven help any girl who looked like him.

Michael laughed at her expression. "You must understand. My father picked Marie for me to wed. She was the daughter of a very rich shipping merchant, but had trouble finding a husband despite her father's money. My father wanted the shipping connections, and Marie's father wanted access to the duke's influence. My father and I rode to Bucharest so I could meet her."

Libby kept her gaze trained on Michael as she walked beside him through the knee-high cranberry bushes. The idea of an arranged marriage seemed so antiquated, but Michael spoke of it as though it were commonplace.

"I am embarrassed to admit that the first time I saw Marie, I was disappointed. I had already resolved that I would consent to the match because it made excellent sense, but when I saw Marie . . . well, I could understand why the men of Bucharest were not pounding down the door to get to her," he said with a good-natured smile. "Her father allowed me to take Marie for a walk in his garden so we could get to know each other, and it did not take long to recognize her appeal. She was a big, strong woman with a heart to match. I knew within the hour that we would get along just fine. Other men dismissed Marie because of her looks, but I was lucky. Over time, I came to see her beauty because she was such a good woman," he said simply.

Now Libby was embarrassed at the rush of relief she had felt when she learned Marie was homely. For Michael to think so highly of a woman, she must have been very admirable.

Michael pointed to a slab of granite that angled up from the ground to form a natural ledge. "Let us sit and have a bit of a rest," he said in a solemn tone. Never before in all their tromping through the wilderness had he needed to stop for a rest, nor had she been in need of one. But he seemed serious, and curiosity led her to the

211

granite slab. It was too tall for her to sit on, but Michael's hands effortlessly spanned her waist and lifted her into place. With one hand braced against the rock, Michael turned to peer out across the length of the cranberry field. The low, bushy vines were in full flower, carpeting the field with pink blossoms that would soon begin forming tight little berries. The same breeze raking across the rippling cranberry bushes ruffled Michael's hair, and she had to clasp her hands together to stop from impulsively reaching up to comb through the long strands.

"Well, Libby, I have been thinking about our problem," he finally said. "My boys enjoy your visits, and ever since I met you I have trouble getting the thought of your smile out of my head."

Her eyes widened and her mouth went dry. He looked distinctly uncomfortable as he stared across the field, but he wasn't finished speaking and Libby would not stop him for all the gold in the world. "I have always thought you very pretty. A man would be blind not to think so, but when you smile! Well, your smile fills half of your face, and it makes the other half beautiful."

Libby was struck speechless. Had he been suffering from the same irrational infatuation she had been battling these past six weeks? A sense of joy started to bloom inside and she beamed a smile directly at him.

"Don't show it to me!" he said with a nervous laugh and turned away from her. "Your smile will distract me, and this is serious business I wish to discuss." He shifted his weight and stared off into the distance again. "You have a love of the outdoors and for plants, just as I have. You get along well with my children and it is obvious to anyone that you would be an excellent mother. I think we would be a good match. Perhaps you would consider marrying me?"

And finally he turned around to face her. If she'd not been sitting on the rock she would have collapsed into a puddle of jelly at his feet. His handsome face was drawn and serious as he looked at her, and the thought of being able to live within the shelter of this man's protection for the rest of her days was beyond her dreams. She wanted to fling herself into his arms. She wanted to shout to everyone in Colden that this audacious man whose heart was as wide and deep as the Atlantic Ocean wanted to make her his wife.

Instead, she bit her lip and thought rationally. Her hands were trembling and she clasped them together so he would not notice. "It is not because of the house, is it?" He looked confused, as if he didn't understand her question.

"The lawsuit over the house," she clarified. "You aren't marrying me just to get to my house, are you?" She bit back the nervous laughter that threatened to spill over, feeling embarrassed to even ask such a question, but she needed his reassurance about this.

"Well, yes," he said. "If we got married, it would solve a lot of problems, don't you think?"

She felt like he had slapped her. With a shove she leapt down from the rock, whirling away to hide the crushing disappointment in her face. What an *idiot* she was! She clenched her teeth and felt the blood pounding in her ears as she strode through the field. Michael came up behind her, but she did not pause.

"Libby, this is a very logical thing for us."

She didn't want logic, she wanted to be adored. Cherished. For once in her life she wanted to believe a man would be willing to cross a raging sea on her behalf, slay a dragon, marry her even if she did not come with a house attached.

"I think you should stop talking now," she said between clenched teeth.

"Why would I stop talking? You have not agreed to the plan, and I think it is a good one. A logical one—"

She stopped, turned to face him, and spoke in a lethally calm voice. "If you say the word *logical* one more time, I am liable to burst into flame."

He laid his big hands on her shoulders, making her feel ridiculously petite, which was another reason to resent him. She was beginning to like the way his strength made her feel feminine and protected, which was utter rot. "I can see that I have offended you, but I do not know why. You had better spell this out for me, Libby."

She would cut her tongue off before telling him that she wanted to be courted, to be valued for something beyond the planks and tiles of a house. It was pathetic to imagine this son of a duke would be interested in an illiterate spinster, but her pride would not let it show. She forced the muscles of her face to relax, cooled the fire in her eyes. "Tell me," she said with false calm. "What exactly did Marie's father give your family in exchange for taking her off his hands?"

Michael rubbed his jaw while he studied her through troubled eyes. "We received two hundred cubic feet of cargo space on all of his ships. Plus, he let us use his warehouse free of charge."

She pasted a tight smile on her face. "Ah . . . the warehouse space. I could see how that would sweeten the deal."

Michael nodded. "Well, yes. Otherwise we would need to rent storage space near the port, and that is very expensive. So it was a good deal for us."

"How fortunate for you." She turned and began walking toward the main road. Was she really going to have to walk alongside this man for another two miles before she could get home? She would give her eyeteeth if she could scrub this entire day from her memory. She had been harboring pitiful daydreams about Michael almost since the hour she met him, so perhaps it was just as well she was subjected to this conversation so she could kill the fantasies once and for all.

"I can see that I have been clumsy with my marriage proposal, and this has offended you, but I think I did what was necessary. I told you I find you attractive, which is true. I pointed out the legal advantages in regard to the house, which is another bonus. I did everything Turk said I should do, and yet somehow I have spoiled this."

She did not think it possible, but each time Michael opened his mouth, he set off another bombshell to make her feel worse. She narrowed her eyes. "You discussed this with Turk?"

He nodded and for the first time had the grace to look uncomfortable. "Well, yes. I feared the customs might be different in America, so I went to him for advice."

"You sought out a mercenary soldier from Turkey for advice on courting an American woman?"

"It was either Turk or Joseph, and Turk has a way with women. In Europe, they practically fling themselves at him. It is very amusing to watch." He dragged a hand through his hair in frustration and sent her a sheepish grin that normally would have made her weak in the knees, but all it did today was make her heart ache. "Why don't you tell me about how these things should be done in America, and I will fix what I have done wrong, yes?"

She closed her eyes, because if she kept looking at him she was either going to laugh or cry, but she was not certain which. She drew a ragged breath and forced her voice to be calm. "I want to pretend this conversation never happened. I don't want to exchange a single word with you, because honestly, if you keep talking, you will figure out a way to make everything worse. So let's start walking, and whatever you do, stay silent. Pretend we are behind the lines in enemy territory and you dare not speak a single word lest sudden death pour down from the skies. Please."

Without waiting for a response, she turned and set a brisk pace toward Colden. She heard a skeptical grumble from Michael, but the clomping of his footsteps let her know he was following. "I have never been behind enemy lines with a woman. This is something I would never do, but I will play along with your request."

"Thank you." She turned and resumed a brisk pace, anxious to stay ahead so she would not have to look at him.

They only managed to take about twenty steps before his voice sounded from behind her. "I think you should know, the way you

215

are stomping can be heard from a mile away. Those enemy soldiers could be upon us at any moment."

His voice was serious, but she knew if she turned around she would see humor glittering in his eyes, which was why she kept her eyes fastened on the sight of Colden in the distance. She froze and crossed her arms over her chest, staring stonily straight ahead. His footsteps halted just behind her.

"Tell me," she asked icily. "Have you ever been trapped in a corner where there was absolutely no hope for you because you had botched every possible route of escape?"

"Something tells me this is where I am right now."

Her eyes narrowed, but she still refused to turn around and look at him. "Maybe you should ask Turk, just to be sure." She began walking again, desperate to get out of his orbit. She needed to be alone before she could start nursing her wounded pride.

When they came to the fork in the road at the Vanderbergs' cranberry field, she refused to step another foot with Michael in tow. "You can follow that road down a mile, and it will join up with the south end of Winslow Street. I'll take the old Cheney road back to my brother's house."

Mercifully, he did not argue with her.

18

He should have known Libby Sawyer wouldn't agree to marry him so easily. Michael plucked a strand of saw grass from the side of the road and chewed it as he strode down the dusty lane toward Winslow Street. He was sorry for whatever he had said that offended her, but he wasn't discouraged. Good things were worth fighting for, and Libby Sawyer was at the top of the list of things he wanted to fight for. He had known for weeks that a marriage to Libby would be the logical solution to his problem, but there were plenty of other reasons he wished to marry her. He adored Mirela and the children, and his camaraderie with Turk and Joseph added a robust element of friendship to his life, but none of that stopped him from becoming lonely. He wanted a *woman* by his side. Libby was smart and funny and attractive. When she smiled at him, he wanted to lift a thousand-pound boulder to impress her. Whenever he had a triumph, he wanted Libby to be there to share it with him.

After the day she joined them for the Fourth of July celebration, Michael was certain that Libby was the woman he needed to complete his family. Already she had a power over him that was frightening in its intensity. Libby was the partner he had been missing, and he would've been a fool to wait any longer before proposing. And it was more than his physical desire for Libby. He wanted to make her laugh. He wanted to watch her eyes sparkle when he spoke about the pollination behavior of flowering bulbs. Women seemed to like fancy words about love and poetry, but such things did not come easily to him. His feelings for Libby were strong, like the turbulent pull of an ocean tide, but he was clumsy with putting such things into words.

There would be plenty of time to figure out how to soothe Libby and win her back, especially since he believed she wanted to be won. He tossed the strand of grass aside and reached down for another, gnawing on the fibrous stalk as he walked.

He slowed his steps, suddenly attuned to the quietness of the afternoon. Normally, a day in the country was alive with sounds: the rustling of leaves, the drone of insects. Those sounds were there, but they seemed very distant to him. He felt a clench in his belly.

Something was wrong. He had not survived all these years by ignoring this sensation.

He tossed the stalk of grass aside and quickened his pace, knowing he was needed at home. The face of Dominic Sterescu slammed into his brain. Had the man contacted Enric after all? It was now possible to send a telegraph message across the ocean, and even now the wheels of Mirela's destruction could be set in motion. He clenched his teeth and kept plowing forward, devouring yards with each stride. Surely Enric could not be coming after them, not this quickly. Perhaps this uneasy sensation was because one of the boys had taken a tumble. Or Mirela had taken a turn for the worse again.

When he rounded the bend where a thick tangle of blackberry brambles grew, he could see almost a full mile down the road. And near the end of that road was a wagon with two huge men at the driving bench.

Something was wrong. Turk and Joseph were supposed to be at the house with Mirela, not riding around in the countryside in some borrowed wagon. He launched forward, his lungs filling with air and the muscles in his legs straining with the effort to run faster as he tore down the narrow country lane. He shouted after the wagon, yelling so loudly his voice grew hoarse, but finally Joseph swiveled around and saw him. A moment later the wagon slowed to a halt as Turk drew on the reins of the horse.

Michael kept running, his alarm growing when he saw Mirela on the driver's seat beside Turk and the heads of his boys emerging from the rear of the wagon. Joseph sprang down and came striding toward him.

"What is going on?" he demanded, noting the grim set of Joseph's jaw.

"The sheriff came by the house this morning with an army of men. They brought eviction papers."

Michael narrowed his eyes, his hands curling into fists. "For what cause?" he demanded.

"The judge says the professor gets to retain possession of the house until a formal ruling on ownership of the house is released. They threatened us with deportation unless we abided by his order."

A cold fist squeezed his heart as he looked past Joseph to his family huddling in the wagon. He had promised them stability, but once again they were uprooted and tossed into the whirlwind. His hands clenched into fists. "You allowed this to happen?" he asked quietly. "You put up no fight?"

"Turk and I were willing, but Mirela was not. She was adamant. She insisted there was to be no violence, and you know how bossy she can be."

Running away went against every instinct in his blood. He cursed that he had not been there to prevent Mirela's catastrophic decision. It was always easier to defend a possession than take it back, and Mirela's order had put them in a dangerous position. "Where are you headed?" he asked Joseph.

"There is no money for a hotel and I don't know anyone who would welcome us," Joseph said. "You described an abandoned barn to the west of the village where you took shelter from a rainstorm. I figured it would do."

Michael nodded, but his mind cringed at the thought of Mirela sleeping in the dirt. She had endured far worse conditions, but never when she was under his care. "It will do for tonight," he said grimly as he began walking toward the cart.

Plans to get back into the house were already taking shape in his head, forming and clicking into place even as he strategized ways to comfort his traumatized family. He could see from the way Luke was holding his stomach and Andrei's sullen expression that they were not doing well.

He forced a glint of humor into his eyes. "Thought to take off without your old man, did you?" It was not particularly humorous, but the worst thing he could do was permit himself to display the rage seething inside him. If the easing of the tension around Luke's mouth was any indication, it was working. He ruffled Luke's hair as he walked past the wagon and braced himself to deal with Mirela.

But when he came up beside her, Mirela was surprisingly calm. She managed a sad smile and laid her hand on his arm. "We will be all right, Michael," she said softly, but with conviction.

Perhaps Mirela did not understand how hard it was to regain a position after being ousted from it. Mirela was wrong to abandon the house. The townspeople of Colden were too soft and spineless to mount a physical challenge against them, but he would not berate Mirela in front of the others. What did she know of military strategy? When he extended his hand to her, she took it, and he guided her down from the wagon. "We will be back in a moment," he said to Turk as he led Mirela toward the screen of blackberry brambles.

"I know your intentions were good," Michael said when they were far enough away that the children would not hear. "But I am going to work with Joseph and Turk to devise a strategy to get

back into the house. Tonight. The faster we move, the more likely
we are to catch them unawares."

Mirela lifted her chin. "No."

The calmly spoken refusal took him aback. He set his hands on
her shoulders and spoke slowly but forcefully. "Yes, Mirela, we will."

"No you won't."

He waited for her to elaborate, but the droning of bees in the
blackberry brambles was the only sound to break the silence. A
trickle of perspiration slipped down his face as he glared down at
her. "Mirela, you aren't being logical."

"I won't condone the use of force," she said. "The way we took
the house was *wrong*. I was in too much of a daze that night to
understand exactly what was going on, but not anymore. I insist
we abide by the ruling of the court."

He dropped his hands from her shoulders and stalked a few
feet away. When Mirela used that autocratic tone, he knew she
meant business, but he wasn't going to stand for it today. "I won't
permit my family to be homeless when I have the ability to provide
for them," he snapped out in anger. "You cannot ask this of me."

"What of Professor Sawyer's family?" she asked, and he flinched
when Libby's image flashed before him. "You have always been
relentless in protecting and providing for your family, but it is
wrong to do so at the expense of others. Every person in this
town is one of God's children, and that includes Professor Sawyer. Does he not deserve an equal measure of your respect and
compassion? Were it not for a quirk of fate, could not any one of
the strangers in this town be your brother? Your father? Your son
or daughter or wife?"

The words stung and he looked away, but Mirela grabbed his
chin and forced him to look back at her. "Michael, I love you, but
you have trampled on decent people who stood in your way. You
have justified your actions by relying on man's law over God's law.
And you know better than that."

Her words vibrated with urgency. The heat of the summer pounded down on him and he was tired, angry, thirsty, and worse still . . . he knew Mirela was right. A better man would be able to tell her so, but the slow burn of rage at the sight of his family hurled into the street made his throat clamp up around any conciliatory words he might utter. He turned his back on her and stalked to the wagon, bracing his hands on the dry, cracked boards as he looked at his children. Once again, fear and uncertainty lurked in their faces. He forced the corners of his mouth to turn up into a smile he hoped they would believe was genuine.

"Tonight we will sleep in a barn," he said. "In the course of history, most soldiers have taken shelter in barns, so after this night you will be part of a long line of heroes. Right? Turk and Joseph can back me up on this."

Andrei looked skeptical, but at least Luke seemed willing to play along. Joseph returned to his position in the driver's seat and the wagon resumed rolling down the road. As Michael walked alongside the wagon, the danger of their situation crashed down upon him. They had no friends, no money, and no shelter.

Libby sensed something was different before she even stepped foot onto Jasper's property. A visitor's carriage and horse were tied to the hitching post, all windows of the house were wide open, and the sound of her father's laughter carried on the evening breeze. The moment she stepped inside she saw Jasper and one of the identical twin lawyers Regina had hired. Was he Mark Radcliff or his brother, Raymond? She did not have time to ask, because her father came rushing toward her.

"Pack your bags, Liberty-bell! The gypsies have been evicted from our home!"

"What?" she gasped, her brain unable to process this shocking turn of events.

222

"That's right . . . the judge has signed an order evicting those vagabonds from our home. We can move back into our house this very evening!"

She turned to Mr. Radcliff, too stunned to even formulate a question.

"It is true," he said simply. "Judge Frey has shifted the burden to the Dobrescus to prove they were never served notice on the sale of the house. This makes it far less likely they will win their lawsuit. That being the case, the judge said possession of the house reverts to your father until the court issues its final ruling." The lawyer executed a jaunty little bow. "You are free to move back into your home this very evening."

"But . . . what has happened to the Dobrescus?"

"Gone!" her father said with delight, but Mr. Radcliff was a little more dignified.

"Sheriff Barnes took care of business this morning," he said. "We waited until Mr. Dobrescu was out of the house, which we had reason to suspect would occur today, and the eviction was carried out immediately. The sheriff brought plenty of men to insure the eviction went smoothly."

Libby felt sick. "But where have they gone?"

The lawyer shrugged. "I'm sure the sheriff's men took them wherever they wished to go. They have use of the town's wagon until they can find a new situation. So long as he does not barge into another unoccupied house, I'm certain we will all be happy!" He chuckled at his own joke and her father succumbed to peals of laughter. Libby simply stared in disbelief. While she had been tromping through the woods, Lady Mirela was being thrown out onto the street. And those two boys. They had nowhere to go and no one in this town was likely to lift a finger to help them.

She needed to get back to the house on Winslow Street immediately. Perhaps the neighbors could shed light on where the Dobrescus had gone. Libby whirled around and clattered up the stairs. The faster she could stash her belongings into a bag, the sooner they could set off for Winslow Street.

By the time Libby arrived home, the sun was setting and the gloom of night was overtaking the town. In the dwindling light, Libby ran from house to house on Winslow Street, pounding on the doors and asking if anyone had knowledge of where the Dobrescus had gone. No one could tell her anything until she came to Judith Barclay's house at the end of the street.

"I went blackberry picking and saw them heading down Story-brook Lane," the woman said as she bounced a toddler on her hip. "They looked well enough to me, except the younger boy was crying."

At the thought of Luke's tears, Libby's mouth thinned. But at least she had a good idea of where they were headed. The old threshing barn she and Michael had taken shelter in was just off Storybrook Lane.

"Thank you," Libby said before turning back to her own home. Walking up the familiar slate path and beneath the wide-spreading branches of the maple trees should have been comforting, but everything felt surreal. Inside the parlor there was no trace of the Dobrescus. No laughter from Luke, no ravenous Andrei forever on the prowl for something to eat. Most obvious, Michael Dobrescu was gone, and the house lacked something without his brusque, booming presence to fill the ordinary rooms. Instead, a dense crowd of well-wishers from the neighborhood was streaming into her home, bringing bottles of wine and homemade cranberry bread.

The sting of Michael's ham-fisted marriage proposal was a distant memory. Now all she wanted to do was run out into the night and be sure he and his family were safe. Her father's laughter grated as he clapped Jasper on the back and she winced at the scent of the cheese and wine passed around by her neighbors. All she could think about was a family huddled outside in the darkness.

19

Libby set out in the morning before the sun had fully risen, carrying a basket stuffed with as much food as she could find. There was little in the house save what the neighbors had brought the previous evening. She took the half loaf of cranberry bread, a large wedge of cheese, and two flasks of wine. It wasn't the best nutrition for the children, but it was something and the market was not yet open for business.

A vague feeling of guilt swirled up inside her, combining with the damp heat of the morning to make her feel sick. She had played no role in what had happened to the Dobrescus yesterday, but Libby still felt complicit in the rough manner in which they had been treated by the town.

A blister rubbed her heel raw and the basket was cutting grooves into the sweaty palm of her hand, but she kept up the brisk pace. If the Dobrescus were not at the abandoned threshing barn, she would need to borrow a horse and start a more extensive search. As she approached the apple orchard, Libby had to balance the basket awkwardly against her hip as she hoisted herself up the embankment and into the orchard. Relief flooded through her when she saw the wagon beside the barn, a horse casually grazing on the overgrown grass.

She dropped the basket and ran toward the barn. "Michael? Michael, are you there?" she asked breathlessly.

The broken barn door was propped against the opening, but it tilted outward as one of Michael's massive men poked his head out to look at her. She froze at the sight of the rifle clasped in Turk's hand.

"It's just me," she said, holding her hands up in a placating fashion. "I mean you no harm."

"Are you alone?" he asked bluntly.

Before she could answer, Libby was surprised to see Lady Mirela duck beneath Turk's arm and slip into the field. "Libby," she asked softly, "why have you come?" The clothes Mirela had slept in were grubby and strands of her silky black hair had sprung free of the haphazard bun.

"I want to help," she said simply. "And I brought a little food. There isn't much, but enough for a decent breakfast, I think."

Mirela looked exhausted, but she managed a smile and her eyes softened. "You have always been so kind to us. It is ironic, don't you think?"

Libby dropped her gaze. She was no hero. In truth, if she didn't have an unseemly fascination with Michael Dobrescu, she probably would never have gone out of her way to befriend this family in the first place. It was Michael's huge, generous spirit that had broken through her hostility and forced her to regard these interlopers as decent people. Walking a few paces, she retrieved the basket from where she had dropped it, then cleared her throat.

"Is Michael here?" she asked.

"He and Joseph have gone into town in search of more substantial lodgings," Mirela said as she beckoned Libby inside. It was dim inside the barn despite the morning sun that glimmered through the cracks in the weathered old boards. Luke and Andrei were sitting on the dirt floor, propped up against the side of the barn, watching her through suspicious eyes. A pile of apple cores gave evidence to what they had been eating. The boys accepted her gift of food, but there was no lightening of their spirits as they ate in silence. Who could blame them for being sullen? The barn was musty and filthy, and it was clear all of them had slept on the ground with only rolled-up clothing to serve as pillows. Three trunks, a few satchels, and some assorted weapons were all the belongings the family possessed, clustered into a corner of the barn.

And one very fancy box containing four vials of jasmine essence. It was unlikely Michael would have time for tapping juniper trees for resin, and each day that passed, the essence was a little closer to going bad.

After the hastily consumed breakfast, Libby and Mirela stepped outside for a walk in the apple orchard. Libby knew Michael was too deeply committed to this country to leave, but it seemed cruel to drag someone like Mirela into a life of such chaotic uncertainty. "Is it possible for you to return to Romania?" she asked gently. "I can understand why Michael wishes to remain, but it seems that you have sacrificed a great deal to come here. Somehow, you seem like the kind of person who should be living in a palace and waiting for some handsome aristocrat to sweep you away."

A sparrow twittered in the branches above them and they had walked several steps before Mirela replied. "No, I will never go back. I will be able to heal in America, but I don't think that can happen in Romania."

Libby glanced at Mirela's wrists. The bandages were gone and the scars had sealed over, leaving a series of angry red lines on Mirela's ivory skin. What kind of torment would drive a young, vibrant woman to take such an action? The polite thing would be to avert her gaze and pretend not to notice the scars, but Mirela had no friends in America. Or at least no female friends who might be able to understand her troubles better than the hulking warriors with whom she lived.

Libby stopped walking and turned to face Mirela. "What

happened?" she asked softly. She glanced at Mirela's wrists. "You don't have to tell me, but if there is anything I can do to help you cope with what torments you, I would like to know."

The faint smile that curved Mirela's mouth was infinitely sad. "I am afraid that medical science has already said there is no hope for me. Perhaps I will live five years, perhaps I will live fifty years . . . but I will do so as a single woman. I was told I must never marry or have children."

The stark words sounded so cruel and final. What sort of terrible condition would condemn Mirela to such a fate? "Was there someone you wished to marry? Back in Romania?" she asked. It was easy to believe that Mirela's gentle beauty would have had suitors lining up around her father's ducal palace. Then again, a woman in Mirela's position might not be free to choose the man of her heart if she was destined for a political alliance. If even Michael had submitted to an arranged marriage to benefit the family, surely a prize like Mirela would have been a pawn in the aristocratic alliances that ruled Europe.

"Not really," Mirela said simply. "It is no secret what happened to me in Romania, for there were many witnesses when my brother came to rescue me."

Libby was confused by the strange statement. "Michael?"

"No, my brother Enric. The duke. I found myself in a terrible situation, but Enric rallied some soldiers and was able to save me." Mirela turned and began walking down the grassy aisle between the apple trees. Libby scurried to catch up with her.

"It happened more than a year ago," Mirela said. "The war with the Ottomans had been raging for months, but the fighting had never come close to Vlaska, so I felt safe. Enric had gone to the coast to negotiate the shipment of more armaments to the Serbs. Michael had been living in Serbia for more than a year, leading troops in the skirmishes against the Ottomans. You must understand, I lived in a palace, not a castle. It was a beautiful mansion, with wide glass windows and sweeping balconies. It was not designed for defense. So when a regiment of the Ottomans came storming through, there was not much we could do to defend ourselves."

Libby felt her blood run cold, fearing where this story was going to lead. Mirela spoke calmly, as though it had happened long ago and to a different person. "They came as the sun was setting. I heard a·crash of glass shattering and men yelling in a language I did not understand. Our servants screamed and ran for cover. It did not seem that the Turks were interested in killing us; they were simply looting whatever they could stuff into their bags. They were tossing silver, paintings, whatever they could grab onto the rugs and rolling them up to carry away. I tried to run for cover, but one of them spotted the necklace I wore. He tore it from my neck, the pearls rolling everywhere. I can still hear the sound of those pearls bouncing and rolling across the marble floor."

Mirela's voice stayed calm, but her footsteps had quickened. No woman should be forced to recount the horrors of something like this, and she laid a hand on Mirela's arm. "Mirela, you don't need to tell me this."

But the unnaturally calm voice continued as though Mirela had not heard her. "The man who tore my necklace scrambled to collect the pearls, but another soldier noticed the silk of my dress, and his eyes narrowed with anger. They did not assault any of our servants, but I was a target. Their rage, their anger was all focused on me because I belonged to one of the aristocratic families that was leading the rebellion against Ottoman rule in Romania.

"They carried me out into the rose fields. The soldier flung me on the ground, and then one man after another crawled on top of me. It went on for hours. Sometimes I passed out, but I remember coming to when I was thrown over the back of a horse and carried farther away from the house. It was still dark, but I knew we were on Vlaska property because I could smell the roses all around me. There it continued. All the next day, and into the next night as well. The sun was rising on the third day when something alerted the men and they scrambled for their horses and fled. My brother Enric had been summoned from the coast. He gathered soldiers and they found me."

For the first time, Libby could hear the pain as Mirela's voice wobbled over the words. "Enric was crying as he picked me up from the ground. I had never seen a grown man cry before, and it broke through the shell I had built around myself. I started to cry too, and we sat there in the dirt, holding each other as the tears flowed. The other soldiers Enric brought saw everything. It is no secret in Romania what happened to the Duke of Vlaska's sister."

A gnarled trunk of a fallen apple tree lay on the ground, and Mirela stopped walking to lower herself onto the log. Libby sat beside her, overwhelmed by the horror of what she had just heard and at a loss for words. But Mirela's story was not finished, and she continued in that blank tone so curiously devoid of emotion.

"In the days that followed, I was numb. Aside from the looting, the house was not damaged and we were able to move back in. Enric hired soldiers to guard the house lest the Ottomans returned. I pretended nothing had happened. Each morning I would rise, bathe, and dress. I took control of the household and oversaw the servants. At mealtimes I dined alongside my family and made simple conversation. I went through all the motions of a normal life, but it was as though I was sleepwalking.

"The morning when I broke began like any other. My maid styled my hair and I wore a new dress made of light blue silk. I went downstairs for breakfast and saw a huge bouquet of roses that had been placed on the table. The smell was overpowering. It filled the room and sent me hurtling back to that night. It was a filthy, rancid feeling. The scent crawled over my skin and seeped into my clothes and hair. I vomited on the floor and started screaming. I tore at my dress and my hair to rip the disgusting stench off my body. Enric was horrified. He summoned the servants and they tried to stop me from clawing my own body to pieces, but their hands sent me into greater panic. I screamed until my throat was too raw to make sound, but that did not stop the hysterics. For days I could not bear to be touched or even looked at.

"I believe Enric thought he was acting in my best interest. Day and night, he stood guard over me, terrified I would try to hurt myself. But Enric could not help me, nor could any of the doctors he summoned to treat me. One of the doctors told Enric of a sanitarium in Bucharest that treated hysterical women. Enric was told it was the only hope for me."

Mirela bowed her head and her eyes drifted closed, as though she could not bear to look at Libby. "When I became hysterical at the sanitarium, they put me in ice water baths until I stopped fighting them. Then they kept me in a darkened room, with no sound, no windows, and no stimulation. Do you know what it is like to be utterly alone, day after day? I started to shut down and go numb. It was easier to submit to the treatment rather than face the ice water baths and the restraints. I had been broken by the rape, but the sanitarium shattered me. I cannot think of those days without the terror coming back."

"You don't need to speak of it," Libby said. "I can understand why you don't want to go back to Romania."

Mirela reached out to clasp Libby's hand. "But you must understand, Michael saved me. When he learned what happened to me, he came to Bucharest and got me out of that awful place. The first thing I heard was his voice cutting through the dark silence. I will never forget the sound, like the roar of an enraged bear coming from downstairs. Then the door of my room banged open and I saw him, silhouetted by the light streaming from behind. I felt like an angel had descended into purgatory to rescue me. Within five minutes, I had been taken out of that terrible place.

"When Enric heard what Michael had done, he was furious. The doctors had assured Enric I was getting better because I was no longer hysterical. Enric has always been jealous of Michael, and he was convinced Michael took me from the sanitarium merely as a power play against him. He came storming over to Michael's house. Never had I seen a man so brave as Michael as he faced Enric's rage. He did not move or flinch, even when Enric brought his riding crop down against Michael's face. The blood was running down his face, but Michael stood like a slab of granite in front of me, insisting that I be allowed to remain in Vlaska.

"Everyone could see I was able to be calm, so Enric let me stay. For a while. I moved back into the ducal palace, but I knew the sight of me reminded Enric of his failure to protect me, of his humiliation in weeping before his men. A week after I returned, I asked a servant to shut the windows so I would not have to smell the roses from the fields. When Enric learned of my request, plans were made to send me back to the sanitarium. I panicked and fled to Michael's house. I had always known he intended to sail for America one day, but when Michael learned of Enric's plans, he said we must all leave immediately. He said I would never be safe in Romania as long as Enric was my legal guardian. We left that very night and came here."

Mirela continued to outline what Michael had lost by leaving Romania so abruptly. He had a fine country house with hundreds of acres of good agricultural land. With no time to liquidate his assets, he abandoned his estate and took nothing but the small amount of jasmine essence he had already distilled from the harvest. Even here in America, Michael could make no move to sell his estate for fear that the proceedings would lead Enric to their new home in Colden. If ever Libby needed proof that Michael Dobrescu was a champion, it was in his selfless act of spiriting Mirela out of Romania.

Mirela turned her wrists up, the red slashes obscene in the bright light of morning. "If Enric learns I attempted suicide, he would see me locked up in that sanitarium for the rest of my life." A wry smile turned up the corners of Mirela's mouth. "So you can see, I do not mind the inconvenience of sleeping in a barn."

And then Mirela stood, drawing a deep breath and letting her gaze roam over the abandoned apple orchard. She seemed to draw strength from the very sight of the bucolic landscape. "I was selfish and cowardly when I tried to subvert God's plan for me that night in the greenhouse. I am beginning to understand there may be a reason for my suffering. I know what it is to be frightened and alone, and lose all sense of hope. Experiencing these things has taught me about compassion. Perhaps I am meant to use this insight for some higher purpose. I still don't know precisely what I am meant to do with my life, but I believe God has a plan for me. And that knowledge has given me great comfort."

As she spoke, Libby saw Mirela's resolve strengthen. There was a fierce beauty in the woman as she looked out into the field and breathed deeply of the apple-scented air. "There is *something* here I am meant to do," Mirela said, a note of aching wistfulness in her tone. "I believe I was destined to come to America and that house on Winslow Street. I feel as though my uncle Constantine has beckoned me here, but I still don't understand what it is he wants me to do."

Mirela paused, then turned to look at Libby. There was no challenge in the younger woman's face, only a look of gentle concern. "I have always felt bad about the way Michael took the house so abruptly, but you must understand, Libby . . . I intend to fight for that house. I am a patient woman and am prepared to wait for the court to rule, and to do so in the spirit of God's law. It is my hope that we do not become enemies in this process, but I truly believe the house belongs to Michael."

Her words were firm. How strange it felt to have a challenge delivered so bluntly, but with such grace. Libby's father would react with a barrage of angry words; Regina would coyly offer soothing expressions while secretly plotting her own line of attack. Libby knew in her heart the only just settlement for the house would be for her father to retain ownership, but that did not mean she would demonize Mirela.

She met Mirela's gaze directly. "I am sorry about what happened to your family yesterday and will do whatever I can to make you comfortable. But I hope you will not hold it against me if I do everything in my power to make sure my father retains ownership of the house."

Mirela's smile was resigned. "Libby, I would expect no less of you."

20

Libby spent the day with the Dobrescus, picking apples and helping them cart water from the nearby stream. Time and again she peered down the dusty path to search for Michael's return, but there was no sign of him. By late afternoon the sky had darkened with storm clouds and she could not afford to linger any longer. Libby left the barn and made the long walk back to Winslow Street.

She darted inside the house just as the raindrops began to fall and was surprised to see Jasper in the study with her father. "Did you bring Tillie with you?" she asked hopefully.

Jasper dragged his hand through his hair. "She is at home with Regina. I just came over to talk some sense into Father before he loses his mind."

"I am not deaf, Jasper," her father said in a sour tone. He was sorting through stacks of paper like Rumpelstiltskin searching for a needle in a haystack. "I simply want justice, and I am determined to get it."

"What is going on?" Libby asked, noting Jasper's rigid stance and her father's agitation. It was unusual for her father to be at odds with Jasper, the perfect child who excelled at everything. On the rare occasions Jasper tore himself away from the bank for a visit, her father usually rolled out the red carpet and killed the fatted calf.

"Father wants to bring criminal charges against Michael Do-brescu for stealing the mechanical drawings."

Libby's head swiveled to her father. "Do you have any proof Michael took them?" The drawings were a potential gold mine should anyone ever capitalize on them, but Michael had little interest in any business aside from his perfume.

"I have proof the drawings are valuable," her father said. "I have proof they are missing. And we all know who the only interloper in this house has been. I think this is enough to put before a judge and a jury. I would relish the sight of Michael Dobrescu at the mercy of a Colden jury."

The sound of rain kicking up outside added to the undercurrent of tension that seized the room. Jasper paced nervously across the floor. "I can't let you do this, Father."

"Why not? I am convinced the man is guilty, and he should be punished for it."

Jasper braced a hand against the window frame, staring moodily out at the pouring rain. The way his shoulders sagged made him look so defeated—sapped of energy and drained of hope. When he turned to look at his father, his face was bleak. "I took the drawings," he said.

Libby gasped, and her father looked like he had been shot. "What are you saying, boy?" her father demanded.

Jasper pushed away from the window frame to stand in front of Father's desk. "You have never filed a patent on *anything*. For decades these inventions have been lying around the house because you can't bring yourself to declare them finished. I filled out the proper paperwork and sent the drawings to Washington to get patents on your designs. I did it to protect you."

The rage was liable to start at any moment. Until her father's inventions were utterly perfect he was unwilling to let them see the light of day, but what Jasper did made sense. After all, on more than one occasion Libby had seen technology that looked chillingly similar to her father's designs. Jasper's actions would protect her father should others produce a similar invention. Just last year she had seen an entire set of windmills that looked remarkably like what her father had designed. If she had not known her father had banished the windmill plans to the attic years ago, she would have thought they were her father's design.

The strength left her legs and Libby dropped onto the sofa. While her father and Jasper raged at each other, Libby closed her eyes, summoning up the image of those windmills. There had been three of them, clustered alongside an intracoastal waterway, their sails turning slowly in the breeze. The neck-bearing pin in the center of the sail was precisely what her father had designed. She had sketched that pin according to her father's meticulous description, both from the outside and the inside cutaway drawings. She knew exactly what it looked like, and they had been on those windmills. It was hard to even breathe. It took an effort to drag in a lungful of air and raise her head.

"I saw the windmills, Jasper," she said quietly.

Her brother swiveled to look at her. "What windmills?"

"Father's windmills have been licensed and are operating on a piece of land just outside Plymouth. I saw them."

Jasper's eyes narrowed. "I never licensed them for use, Libby," he said dismissively before turning back to her father. "All I did was fill out the paperwork on your behalf. I didn't want other inventors to beat you to the punch if they came up with similar designs."

Her father, trying to digest the information, fiddled with a pencil as he stared hard at Jasper. But all Libby could see was the heavy gold watch chain hanging from Jasper's vest. It was the sort of chain a robber baron could afford, not a small-town banker.

Other things started to make sense. The exquisite clothes Regina wore, her emerald earrings, the summer cottage on the island. These things had been purchased by the fruits of her father's labor.

"You licensed the windmill design," she said through clenched teeth. "How else could Regina have emeralds the size of robins' eggs swinging from her ears?"

Both men turned to glare at her and Jasper's eyes smoldered in resentment. "She was given those earrings by her parents," he said angrily.

Libby shot to her feet. "She bought them at the same time she bought an emerald-green riding suit. I never saw or heard about those earrings until she bought that outfit, and then she wore them all the time. How many other licenses to Father's work have you sold?"

"That's enough!" Jasper roared. "All I did was take action to protect him. And protect *you* as well, since you are unlikely ever to get married and will be a burden on our father for the rest of his life."

She tried not to flinch, but the words scorched. "Thank you so much, Jasper," she said in a trembling voice. "Although I'm sure Father would have appreciated a royalty check from your ill-gotten gains."

"Are you accusing Jasper of stealing from me?" her father demanded. A roll of thunder sounded from outside, underscoring the ugliness of the accusation.

"I don't know a kinder word for what he did," she finally said.

Her father stood, bracing himself with one hand on his desk and using the other to point a trembling finger at Jasper. "That boy has never disappointed me," he said. "From the day he was old enough to speak, Jasper has made me proud with his intelligence, his industry. He is a child any man would be proud to call his own, and I won't have you insulting his integrity. You are barely fit to wipe his boots."

She flinched. Not that she was deluded about where she ranked in her father's esteem, but the contempt seeping from his words had never sounded so scornful. Jasper was a thief and a liar but remained unsullied in her father's eyes.

238

"Look at the watch chain he is wearing! Look at the house he lives in! *Father, think.* Jasper used your designs to get where he is. If he had only told us what he intended, it would not be so terrible, but to operate behind your back . . . Do you think he *ever* would have confessed to obtaining those patents had we not gone looking for the drawings?"

"Get out of this house," her father snapped. "I have allowed you to continue living with me all these years because you are my flesh and blood, but I will not allow you to besmirch my son's name. If I am forced to choose between you and Jasper, I choose Jasper. I want you out of here."

Jasper took a step forward. "Father, really—"

Her father held up his hand, stifling any further comment. "This is my house and my decision. I will reconsider my relationship with Libby when she withdraws her vile accusations. Do you choose to do so, Libby?"

Her father's face was a mask of anger, with no trace of love or disappointment, just hard, twisted antagonism. All she wanted to do was escape it.

"No. I won't withdraw it." She looked to the window, where the rain was pouring down in sheets. Somewhere out there the Dobrescu family was taking shelter in a leaky old barn. She would rather share space in their barn than live with a father who despised her.

It felt surreal as she walked to the hook beside the front door and removed her cloak. Jasper came to stand beside her.

"Don't be insane, Libby. You know his anger will blow over in a few hours."

Perhaps that had been Jasper's experience, but Libby knew her father could keep this kind of bitterness simmering for weeks. Besides, all she wanted to do was find Michael. She wanted to fling herself against that wide chest and feel his arms close around her, protecting her from all the pettiness and hurt in the world. She stepped around Jasper and opened the door.

Cool air and the spatter of rain against the slate path surrounded her the moment she stepped outside. No one tried to stop her as she walked into the rain. There was plenty of time before the sun would set, and if she hurried, she could reach the barn on Storybrook Lane within an hour.

She quickened her steps, feeling the cool rain slide down her face. In less than an hour she would have Michael Dobrescu's strong shoulder to lean against.

21

Rain streamed through the cracks in the barn's dilapidated roof, turning the dirt floor into a muddy mess, but they had blankets to sit on and enough sheltered spaces in the barn to stay dry. The boys were in the corner playing with a toad they had captured, while Michael, his men, and Mirela huddled around the single kerosene lantern he'd bought in town that afternoon.

"The jasmine oil will bring around two thousand American dollars if I sell it now," he said, refusing to let his mind dwell on the additional thousands of dollars it would bring if he had the resin. Acquiring the resin and using it to make the perfume looked increasingly unlikely. It would take weeks to harvest and refine the red juniper resin, then find the laboratory space to lease for blending the perfume. Michael needed to secure a home for his family now. He could wait no longer. If he was on his own, he would endure any deprivation necessary to make the fullest use of the precious oil, but he could not afford to do so when his family was vulnerable.

"I saw a farm for sale this morning," he said. "There is a cabin on the land and I can learn how to grow corn or wheat." Work as an ordinary farmer was a noble profession. It was not what he dreamed of, nor would it make use of his skills, but when his children were hungry and afraid, only the most selfish of men would put them at risk to pursue something as frivolous as perfume.

"Will two thousand dollars purchase a farm?" Joseph asked skeptically.

Michael had no idea. "If not, we can make arrangements with a bank. I am willing to lease the land. Whatever it takes to get us into a safe home."

Mirela laid her hand on his arm. "If you sold your house and land in Romania, you would have a small fortune." By the light of the flickering lantern, the pain in her soft blue eyes was heartrending. She switched to French so the children would not understand what she said. "It was my fault you had to leave in such a hurry. The boys should not suffer because you needed to help me."

Michael shook his head. "Don't even think it." If he tried to sell his estate while he was still in Colden, it would create a paper trail Enric could follow straight to Mirela. Michael's only hope of selling his estate without the risk of leading Enric to Colden would require a return to Romania. Leaving his family or uprooting his children yet again to drag them back to Romania was not an option.

"I am strong now," Mirela said in a voice that sounded like the old Mirela. "If you wish to return to Romania to sell your estate, I will be fine here. My path is not yet clear to me, but never again will I interfere with His will for me. You need never fear that I will hurt myself again. This I swear to you."

He covered her hand with his own. "When you speak in that tone, it reminds me of Father."

She smiled. "A high compliment."

"I meant it as such. But there will be no more talk of my return to Romania. We will figure out a way—"

Turk held up his hand. "Someone is coming," he whispered.

Michael snuffed out the flame. He signaled to the boys to be quiet, then waited for his eyes to adjust to the darkness. Joseph pressed a rifle into his hand. He moved carefully toward the door, his boots sliding only a little in the mud. The rain pelting on the old wooden roof sounded louder in the sudden silence, but the person outside was making no effort to be quiet.

"Michael? Are you in there?" It was Libby, her voice sounding thin and tired. "You can put down whatever battle-ax you've got at the ready; it's only me."

He tossed the rifle to Joseph and grasped the door leaning against the barn to push it aside. A curse escaped his lips when he saw her, soaked to the skin and squinting to keep the rain from streaming into her eyes. A quick glance around revealed she was alone.

"Get inside," he said grimly. Whatever had pushed Libby into a driving rainstorm could not be good. He nodded to Turk to re-light the lantern. The rasp of flint was followed by the glow of a flame, and he gasped at the shattered expression on her face. Her hair hung in sopping locks, her clothing soaked and plastered to her skin, but it was her reddened eyes that startled him. She had been crying, and Libby was not the sort to break down over trifles.

"What happened?"

She sniffled and swiped at her nose. "I had a falling-out with my father."

His eyes widened in disbelief. "And he allowed you to leave the house? In the middle of a storm?" Libby startled at the outrage in his voice, so he took a breath and tried to moderate his tone. "Surely he tried to persuade you to stay until things could be talked out more calmly."

Her broken little laugh was filled with sorrow. "I don't think he really cared all that much."

His hands trembled as he laid them on her shoulders. What sort of father would not fight for his own child? Libby tried to appear so tough to the world, but beneath that sturdy exterior, she had a tender center that was vulnerable to every slight and insult hurled at her. He pulled her against him, ignoring the sodden clothing. She was freezing! A curse escaped his lips and he hoped the heat from his body would seep into her clammy skin to provide some warmth.

"Mirela, you have some dry clothing, yes?" Mirela was already pulling a skirt and blouse from the bags they had packed.

"Turk, grab that blanket so Libby can dry herself. And the rest of you turn your backs. Mirela will help Libby change into something dry." But at his words, Libby's arms tightened around him and she buried her face deeper into his chest, clinging to him like a lifeline in a raging sea. She was not crying. He would feel the shudders if she were, but she was still too upset to let him go. He rocked her gently, murmuring into her ear. "It will be all right," he soothed. "We will fix whatever it is that has hurt you."

He folded his arms tighter around her. The last time he had seen Libby she was snapping mad over his clumsy marriage proposal, but thank the Lord she seemed to have gotten over that, because he wanted to be the one she leaned on in times of trouble. "We must get you into dry clothing," he murmured. "You will make yourself sick if you stay in these wet clothes."

He felt her nod against his chest, but it was still several more moments before she pulled away and turned to Mirela for help. Both boys were staring at Libby in amazement, surely as baffled as he that any father would allow a woman to flee into such hazardous conditions. With a pat on Luke's shoulder, he nudged his son to the other side of the barn. "Turn your backs, boys. Mirela will help Libby."

The boys and his men complied, listening to the wet fabric as she peeled it off her skin and the spatter of water as they wrung out the cloth. He felt sick to his stomach, because he was certain he was responsible for whatever had sparked the fallout with her father.

❦

The wool blanket was harsh against her bare skin, but Libby welcomed the brisk rubbing as it heated her clammy body. It was awkward to be naked in front of another woman, but Mirela kept her eyes averted as she handed Libby dry clothing. Even more awkward was the presence of the three hulking giants on the far side of the barn, but she knew Michael would massacre anyone who dared sneak a glance. When she was dry and decently clothed, she sat beside Michael on one of the three trunks that surrounded the single kerosene lantern and told them the events of the evening.

"Jasper needed the drawings to obtain the patents," she said. "He was able to copy all my father's notes, but the drawings were the one thing Jasper could not do on his own. We never would have noticed the theft if you had not arrived from Romania."

Michael's hand tightened around hers. "Then why is your father angry with you and not your brother?"

What a complicated question that was! How could she explain twenty-eight years of frustration to a man like Michael? The days, weeks, years when her father forced her to stare at the McGuffey's readers, ordering her to memorize the text. The endless drills that always ended in tears and yelling. Her father would never settle for less than absolute perfection, and among all her father's endeavors and creations, Jasper was the only thing he had ever produced that was perfect.

"Jasper swore he never licensed any of the patents," she said simply. "My father will go to his grave believing whatever Jasper says."

Unless Jasper could be proven wrong. Libby straightened at the thought. There were three windmills clustered alongside a wide stretch of marsh just south of Plymouth. Nestled among the windmills was a house where the owner lived. It would be easy enough to ask where he obtained the technology for the unique windmills. If she could see the document licensing the windmills, she would know for certain if Jasper was lying.

Except she could not read.

"Will you take me to Plymouth?" she asked Michael impulsively.

He looked as stunned as if she asked him to accompany her to the moon, but the urgency to get to Plymouth had just become the most important thing in her world. "I need to see those windmills and the papers that licensed the technology. It is the only way to prove to my father they are his designs."

Michael raised a hand and gestured around the barn. "Look at where my family is living! I don't have a decent roof over their heads, my children are sleeping in mud, and you want me to take you to Plymouth?" The disbelief dripping from his voice might have dissuaded a less determined person, but not Libby.

"There is no reason for you to continue living here," she said rapidly. "Mr. Auckland will take you in. Now that his children are grown he has three empty bedrooms, and he's always been sympathetic to your cause. If I can get your family into his house, will you go with me to Plymouth?"

Michael stood and stalked to the opposite side of the barn, dragging a hand through his hair as he paced. "This does not make sense to me, Libby. Why don't you write to the patent office in Washington and inquire if the technology was sold?"

"That will take weeks, and I don't think I can wait another day before I know." And she needed Michael with her to read the paperwork regarding the windmills. She had flat-out lied to him regarding her ability to read and she needed to confess it. Strange, that lie was now more embarrassing than her illiteracy. She bit the corner of her thumbnail, wishing she could roll back the clock and retract the stupid boast that she could read. Reluctantly, she raised her head and locked her eyes with his. She would confess her shame in front of the entire family, for all of them were affected by this request.

"Michael, I lied to you the day I told you I can read." The tightening of his features was the only sign he had heard her, but the others around the lantern appeared stunned. She ignored their reactions, only focusing on Michael and how he would digest this shameful aspect of her character. He was motionless as he stared at her. "I don't know why I was never able to learn, but it was not from want of effort. My brain simply won't recognize letters and hold them still on a page long enough for me to understand what the words say. I would trade all the stars in the sky if only I could learn to read, but I should not have lied to you about it. For that I am so sorry."

The rain had trickled to a stop, making the silence in the barn even more pronounced. So acute was her embarrassment she was tempted to flee back outside.

"I can read," Luke boasted.

"Be quiet, Luke," Michael said harshly. He turned away from her and walked toward the front of the barn, staring bleakly out the narrow gap where the door leaned against the opening. If he would only turn so she could see his face, she might know what was going on in his mind. She held her breath, wondering if she had just destroyed the respect of the only man she had ever loved.

"So I suppose this is why you need me to come with you to Plymouth. To read those documents for you." His voice was expressionless and he did not turn around when he spoke.

"Yes," she said softly.

Michael braced his hand against the side of the barn as he stared into the night. The breadth of his shoulders and the muscular column of his neck were testaments to his strength, and Libby desperately longed to lean on him and follow wherever he led. What did it matter if he only wanted her for the house? All she wanted was Michael.

Finally, he turned to her, weary resignation in his face. "Libby, I believe I am the cause of your troubles. Your relationship with your father has been bad ever since I arrived, and I do not think this news about Jasper would have been so destructive had I not already put you on thin ice. If you can find safe lodgings for my family, I will try to repair the damage I have done by taking you to Plymouth."

He slowly crossed the barn to squat down in front of her, never once looking away. His callused palm was warm around her icy fingers. "You must never lie to me," he said softly. "Whatever your story, be it good or bad, I will accept. I am not your father, who will storm and rage at you when disappointed." And the warmth in his eyes made her believe every word he spoke was true.

"You are perfectly and beautifully made," Michael continued. "You are exactly as God intended for you to be, and I love you precisely as you are."

Her vision grew watery as her heart expanded inside her chest. Not since her mother had died had anyone said they loved her, but Michael said it with no embarrassment and loud enough for his entire family to hear. His face was gentle as he smiled at her, and never had she felt such a profound sense of belonging.

"I love you too, Michael."

Those big arms encircled her in a bear hug. From the corner of the barn she could hear Luke and Andrei groaning. Michael must have heard it too, because his sides were shaking with laughter. And here, in this muddy barn with a leaky roof and no furniture, Libby felt as though she had finally found a home.

22

She was correct about Mr. Auckland's willingness to provide shelter for Michael's family. When they appeared on his doorstep, the old librarian's wife had been horrified at the sight of the muddy visitors, but welcomed them inside anyway. Turk said he would haul water for laundry and Joseph would do any heavy lifting the elderly couple wished in exchange for room and board. The boys appeared content as they downed warm molasses cookies at Mrs. Auckland's kitchen table, but Libby saw the tension radiating through Michael's tall frame the entire time he carried the family belongings into the Auckland home.

Now, riding in the train toward Plymouth, Libby could see he was still tense and distracted. It felt strange to be riding in such close proximity to a man. Michael held her hand on his lap, idly tracing the outline of her thumbnail as he stared at the endless fields of ripening ryegrass rolling past their window, the steady chug of train engines filling the silence. This level of familiarity was probably not the wisest thing for two unmarried people traveling together, but she could practically hear Michael grinding his teeth in anxiety over leaving his family. If holding her hand gave him a small measure of comfort, she would let him do so.

Besides, if she could earn her way back into her father's good graces by proving she was right about Jasper, all this nonsense over the house could be settled in short order. The house was plenty big enough for the Dobrescu family should she and Michael marry. Hadn't he suggested precisely the same thing just a few days ago when he asked her to marry him? She realized she could no longer be offended by Michael's clumsy proposal. Someone polished and sophisticated like Jasper would have known how to phrase an offer of marriage with great finesse. Not Michael. He was a raw, blunt man who spoke exactly what was on his mind. The corners of her mouth curled and she clasped his fingers a little tighter. She was coming to love Michael's eager, two-fisted manner of reaching out for exactly what he wanted.

Given her vehement reaction to his first botched proposal, he was unlikely to bring up the subject of sharing the house again unless prompted.

She glanced up at him. How precisely did a girl go about telling a man she wanted him to propose to her again? Heat flooded her cheeks and she cleared her throat.

"It did not go so well the last time you tried to discuss a logical resolution about sharing the house," she began cautiously.

He stiffened. "I told Mirela about my offer of marriage to you," he said as cautiously as though he were poking a hornet's nest. "Mirela understands why you were angry and said I am a block-head. I think perhaps when it comes to women, she is correct."

Libby suppressed a smile. "I think Mirela is a brilliant woman and you should pay more attention to her."

The tension went out of his spine and he smiled down at her. Would she ever grow accustomed to the beauty of his eyes when they sparkled with laughter? Michael picked up her hand and kissed the back of it. Then, ever so softly, he bit the tip of her index finger before releasing her hand. "I have already learned this, Libby," he said warmly.

Libby rubbed the spot on her finger that was still alive with sensation. She did not realize such a tiny act could send a thrill throughout her entire body, but she needed to keep a steady head. "Well, you don't have to worry that I will explode again," she began. "Although if Shakespeare tried to pen a more dreadful proposal than yours, even he would be stumped."

"I have bested the great Shakespeare?" He winked at her. "This is quite an accomplishment. Do you think Shakespeare would tell me to try again?"

The clatter of the train rolling over the tracks and the gentle jostling of the railway car seemed so utterly normal, but this was about to become the most important conversation of Libby's entire life. Her hands curled around the rough leather covering the bench, her fingers suddenly icy. "Nothing ventured, nothing gained," she said in a calm tone. "Besides, you were right that getting married and sharing the house would be a . . . well, a *logical* thing for us. A solution to our problem."

Michael sobered and he reached over to pry her hand away from the bench and envelop it in his large palm. How *safe* she felt with this strong man beside her. "My desire to marry you is not based on logic," he said. "I love you, Libby. I should have told you that day in the cranberry field, but as we have already discussed, I am not always good with words."

Her heart was pounding so hard it could probably be heard in the next railcar. "You are doing fine, Michael." Hope was gathering momentum inside of her, but his next words sent her crashing back to earth.

"I once thought marriage would be a solution to our problem, but now I realize it is not. I am sorry, but I can never allow my boys to live under the same roof as your father." Her breath left in a rush. Michael's words were gently spoken, but they were like a fist to her chest.

"I have seen how he treats his own daughter and do not believe he will treat my children any better," Michael said. He kept talking, but she couldn't hear him. All she heard was the clattering of the train and the rush of blood in her ears. The beautiful dream she had been building was falling apart, but she had to sit on this awful bench and pretend everything was fine. "I see," she whispered.

She withdrew her hand, but Michael snatched it back just as quickly. "I still want to marry you," he insisted. "I love you and will marry you even though there is no house attached to you." He tilted her chin so she was forced to look at him. Tiny crinkles fanned out from his troubled blue eyes, and never had she seen such concern in a man's face. "Do you believe me, Libby?"

She bit her lip. Hadn't she wanted proof that he cared for her and not the house? She had it, but rather than elation, she could not shake a sense of impending sorrow. Loving her father's enemy was no solution to any of their problems. She had *nothing* to offer him. All she would be was yet another burden as he struggled to support his family.

She managed a sad smile. "I don't even come with any shipping connections or free warehouse space."

There was no change in Michael's expression. "I have tasted your blackberry jam. This seems like a fair dowry I would be willing to accept."

She tried to smile, but it was too hard. Aside from her talents in the kitchen, all Libby would bring to this marriage would be some paint-stained clothing and a canvas sack full of art supplies. Michael's eyes darkened. "Libby, you will need to make a choice soon. I still intend to fight for that house on Winslow Street. It belongs to me and when I win it, I will not permit your father to continue living there. Do you understand this?"

She stiffened and slid a little farther away on the bench. "That seems a little cold, don't you think?"

He nodded. "Perhaps, but there is no way the house can be shared between our two families. I cannot permit your father to treat my

252

children as harshly as he treats his own daughter. Never. I will burn the house to the ground before I let that happen."

She clenched her teeth, dazed by this abrupt turn of events. Why did men have to be so difficult? Her father was grouchy and impatient, but she had survived perfectly well in his household. And if Michael wasn't so single-minded, he would see there should be room for compromise. It was only because *men* were involved that there was a problem. Women would sit down over a pot of tea and talk their way toward a solution, figure out a way to coexist within the same household. Michael was waiting for her to respond, but she was too angry. She crossed her arms and glared out the window at the passing fields.

Hadn't Michael's fierce sense of protectiveness been one of the things that appealed to her? She could hardly blame him for defending his children.

"You must make a choice, Libby. I can make you no promises of a fine house or an easy life. I can only pledge that as my wife you will never doubt that I love you and that I will protect you with the last ounce of my strength."

It seemed petty to keep her arms crossed. For the second time, Michael was offering to make her his wife, and she was in a snit again! But why, *why* couldn't he budge just a little? All Michael saw was the bad side of her father. He knew nothing of when Libby was a child and her father held her on his lap and let her sob her heart out after bullies had tormented her. Or the wonderful days she and her father spent working side-by-side on his inventions. Her father was an awkward and lonely man. He would never be able to show the same sort of bighearted affection that came so naturally to Michael, but Libby had no doubt her father loved her.

If the court ruled in Michael's favor and he won the house, it would be a profound injustice. Her father had *earned* that house. As a child, Libby witnessed him coming home, exhausted from teaching, only to pick up his tools and start working on the house.

For years she heard that hammer pounding away long after the sun had gone down. He poured his sweat and labor into that house, and what had Michael done to earn it? Opened an envelope in Romania and then waited twenty-seven years to make an appearance?

Ignoring her snit, Michael reached over to clasp her hand, holding it possessively. She spoke no words, but returned his squeeze. Perhaps this cloudless, perfect afternoon would be their last day together as allies. The house on Winslow Street was becoming a curse, and she could see no way forward for them. She leaned against his side, and he responded by lowering his cheek to rest against the top of her head. She didn't want to think of the house or her father or what dark clouds lay on the horizon. She only wanted to savor this moment with a magnificent man who, for the moment, seemed to be in love with her.

Their feet crunched atop the rough oyster-shell path that led to the windmills. Libby had seen these windmills when she traveled to Plymouth to attend the marriage of a friend a year ago. They could be seen from miles away, their broad sails slowly turning in the steady breeze coming off the estuary. It was an oddly serene sight, although Libby's hand was trembling inside Michael's confident grasp as he walked beside her.

Why had she never anticipated how much noise a windmill made? The sails were constructed of tightly stretched fabric that snapped in the stiff breeze rolling off the salt marsh. The groans of the rotating axles sounded like lazy animals, and the sound of the steady grind of the millstones pulverizing grain into flour came from behind the clapboard walls of the mill. A stone house, looking prosperous with its wraparound porch and fresh white paint, was nestled beneath a cluster of windblown oak trees. Surely it was where the owner of these windmills lived.

"Do you think they are your father's design?" Michael asked.

Libby felt dwarfed by the mighty windmills as she walked among them, listening to the steady chop and grind of the millstones. She shielded her eyes from the breeze, swiping at tendrils of hair that whipped about her face as she looked up into the rotating sails. "The sail axle is the same. Father's design has a distinctive wind shaft that protrudes from the center, just like these. I would have to get inside the windmill to examine the internal mechanism to see if it is exactly the same."

She circled around the back of the windmills to examine them from behind. So far, everything she saw was a duplicate of what she had drawn for her father. "Let's see if the miller is home so we can ask," Michael said. It was perfectly sensible, but Libby felt hypnotized as she stared at the immense sails turning in the breeze. Was it really possible these magnificent machines could be the product of her father's design? If they were, she had helped make them possible. She caught her breath as a flood of pride rushed through her. Could it be possible she had played a part in the creation of such magnificence? What an odd combination of serenity and power these machines had.

"Yes, we ought," she finally said. She could not tear her gaze away from the windmills as Michael held her hand and practically dragged her to the miller's home. While he knocked, she turned toward the salt marsh so she could admire the windmills.

Michael delivered another round of thudding knocks, then called out their presence. "No one is here," he said.

Libby walked down the path toward the closest windmill. "No matter. I think I can get inside and learn what I need to know." Each windmill had a door at its base wide enough to push a wagon inside for delivering grain. A flimsy board was pushed through a bracket, but Libby easily lifted it aside. It was even louder when she stepped inside the windmill.

And there it was. The exact same grain hopper that automatically fed the millstones with a steady stream of kernels. How many times had she sketched it as her father tinkered with the design? She craned her neck to look up into the tower. The cantilevered wind shaft was her father's most distinctive innovation, but it was near the top of the windmill.

"I need to get up there," Libby said, already stepping toward the rungs that were built into the side of the structure.

"Let me go," Michael said. "You are not dressed for climbing ladders."

Libby ignored him and grasped a rung above her head. His hand was like a manacle around her wrist.

"It is not seemly for a woman to climb ladders," he said. "Tell me what to look for and I will go."

"Michael, now is not the time for a lecture on proper womanly behavior." Ignoring decorum, she gathered her skirts up and draped them over her arm. "I need to see the shaft for myself. It is the only way I will know for certain if it is exactly what I sketched for my father."

Michael's face clouded with concern as he studied the spur wheels, shafts, and countershafts that reached up into the interior of the space. This was an alien technology to him and she knew there was no way he could communicate precisely what he was seeing.

"It will only take a moment," Libby said as she lifted herself up the first rung. She hoisted herself up quickly, moving into warmer air as she neared the top. The higher she climbed, the more narrow the space as the walls drew closer to the machinery. All to the good, as it would make it easier to inspect the wind shaft.

When she reached the top, she clung to the top rung of the ladder with one hand while she turned to study the shaft, so close she could touch it if she was foolish enough to let her fingers come near the rotating blades of metal. She studied the break lever, the winding gear, and the distinctive cantilevered wind shaft. It was exactly the same as her father's design.

Jasper had lied.

256

She should feel vindicated, shouldn't she? Here was proof that her brother was a liar and a thief and could no longer maintain an unblemished reputation in her father's eyes, but all Libby felt was sad. As she stood there, listening to the steady grind of her father's magnificent machine, she wondered if she should even tell him what Jasper had done. What good would it do to destroy the one perfect thing her father valued in this life?

"Is it your father's design?" Michael's voice called up into the clerestory of the windmill.

"Yes," she whispered. She realized he would not be able to hear over the clattering of the machinery. "Yes, it is," she called out louder. There was no point remaining up there in the sweltering heat at the heart of her brother's betrayal, so she turned to face the ladder and begin her descent.

A rasp drew her attention. She looked at the gear behind her and gasped in horror. The hem of her skirt, caught in the metal teeth of the rotating wheel, started dragging her toward the machine. She tugged at the fabric, but it did not pull free of the slowly turning wheel. She tugged so hard her fingernails tore against the fabric, but the teeth continued to pull her skirt further into the gears.

"Michael!" she screamed. "Michael, come quickly!"

The fabric of her skirt was pulled taut, with no more left to give before she would be pulled off this ladder and into those relentless grinding teeth. Could she get out of this dress in time? Not with the way it was fastened all the way up her back. It was impossible to tear her eyes away from the sight of that wheel, but Michael was coming. The wall was shaking as he bounded up the ladder.

"Hurry," she shouted as she tried in vain to pull her dress free, the metal gears pulling her closer and closer. She might as well have tried to hold back the tide. Michael scrambled as high as he could until his shoulder brushed against her thigh. His eyes narrowed as he assessed the situation. Without a word, he reached toward the wheel and grabbed a handful of fabric. The veins on the back of his hand bulged and his knuckles turned white as he pulled. His arm trembled under the force of his pull, but only a few inches of cotton pulled free. The wheel kept turning and dragging Libby farther away from the wall.

"Turn around and hold the ladder with both hands," he said. But Libby was spellbound by the sight of the gears dragging more and more fabric into their teeth. *"Do it,"* Michael ordered. She would have to trust him. She let go of her skirt and turned around to cling to the ladder with both hands. The muscles in her arms were weakening under the strain of fighting against the wheel.

Beneath her thigh, the muscles in Michael's shoulder bunched and strained. He groaned through tightly clenched teeth as he struggled to wrench the fabric free. She prayed for God to help Michael, to send just another ounce of strength into those mighty muscles. She heard the tearing of fabric, and with blessed relief the tension dragging at her dress lessened, then ceased entirely.

She was free.

She was free, but she was shaking so badly she could not trust herself to speak. A glance down at Michael showed him to be heaving in gulps of air, trails of sweat trickling down his face. The mundane clatter of the machinery and blowing of the wind filled the tower, indifferent to the epic battle for her very life that had just taken place.

"Th-thank you," she managed to stammer.

"You are welcome, Libby." He sounded as winded and shaken as she. A ragged laugh broke through his lips. "I am truly an idiot. I should have bargained with a marriage proposal before freeing you."

She leaned her forehead against the rung of the ladder, still shaking too much to trust herself. "No g-gentleman would push a lady in such circumstances," she said through chattering teeth.

"I am not a gentleman. I am a warrior, and we use whatever advantage we can get." He gave her an affectionate slap on her rump. "What of it, Libby? I think you owe me a little something after this."

She could hear the smile in his voice. If she had the energy, she would tell him she owed him everything and that there was nothing she would not give to him. She wanted to give him her heart, her devotion, and every one of her tomorrows. She wanted to give his sons a mother. If it belonged to her, she even wanted to give him that stupid house.

A wave of exhaustion overcame her and she sagged against the ladder. Michael felt it and braced a hand against her back to prop her up. "Careful," he warned. "This sometimes happens after a battle. Following great stress, a body can lose all its strength. We need to get you down quickly."

All the way down the ladder, Michael guided her and talked in soothing tones while she tried to force energy into her depleted muscles. When her feet hit the straw-covered ground, she used the remainder of her strength to turn into Michael's arms and let him hold her.

Libby's fingers entwined with Michael's as the two of them walked back to the train station. From the moment her feet had landed on solid ground, they had not let go of each other. First he held her, murmuring soothing words into her hair while tremors racked her body. When she felt the need to give thanks to God, Michael held her as she knelt in the straw and said silent words of thanks. Never had she prayed like this in front of another, and it felt oddly intimate as Michael fell to his knees beside her and said a prayer along with her. As they walked back to the train station, the torn hem of her dress trailed in the dust, but Libby did not care. She was alive and walking beside the man she loved. She had no idea how they would resolve the conflicts that lay between them, but they would find a way. She had found her man and could not let him go.

As they walked, Libby turned her face toward the estuary, savoring the brackish smell on the breeze as it rolled across the water. Normally, she did not care for the briny smell of a marsh, but at this moment it meant she was alive, and she breathed deeply, wanting to encapsulate this moment in her memory forever.

She could not doubt that Michael truly cared for her. No one could fake the look of terror in his eyes as he came bounding up that ladder. He wanted to marry her, even though she was at odds with her father and might never come into possession of the house on Winslow Street.

"Someone is coming," he said.

Ahead of them, a man in a cart was prodding a pair of draft horses down the country lane toward them. His wagon was loaded down with sacks of grain. "I wonder if this is the man who owns the windmills," she said.

As the wagon drew closer, Michael lifted his hand to flag the man down. The clopping of hooves slowed, then stopped. "My pardon, " Michael said. "Are you the miller who owns those fine windmills down the road?"

The man straightened with pride. "That I am," he said in a thick New England accent.

"My friend and I have come from Colden to admire these windmills," Michael said. "I had heard they were very distinctive and wished to see them for myself."

The man knocked his straw hat back to study Michael, probably afraid of a possible competitor for the county's milling work. "It is a new design. Brand new," he said laconically.

"Would you tell us where you obtained the design?" Michael asked. "We are from Colden and will pose no threat to your business this far north."

The man's demeanor relaxed a bit and he nodded. "Hop on board."

The miller's name was Caleb Standish and on the short ride

back he explained how he built his first windmill four years ago. He explained how the cantilevered wind shaft meant it was easy to adjust the mill for whatever he needed to process. Mostly he milled corn, wheat, and barley, but he used one as a fulling mill and one for crushing oil seeds. After seeing to his horses, Mr. Standish invited them inside his home to show them the paperwork for the mills.

"Here is the basic design," he said, bringing forth a document that looked exactly like one of Libby's cutaway sketches. "It is different from most windmills, so you might need to hire an engineer the first time you build one. I can recommend a fine man from Boston."

The miller continued to explain the internal workings to Michael, but Libby's focus darted to other papers on his desk. She couldn't read any of them but would recognize the name Sawyer if it appeared somewhere on the paperwork.

Finally, Michael asked the question she had been dying to hear. "Who do I contact about licensing this technology?"

Mr. Standish gave a brusque laugh. "That is the curious thing. It is a woman who sells it. Let me see if I can find her name." Libby's heart skipped a beat and she shot a glance at Michael. She had expected that Jasper would have kept his cards close to his chest, but perhaps he had hired someone to take the patent to market. The miller pulled out another drawer and began riffling through papers, but Libby was worried. Unless Jasper's name appeared somewhere in those papers, it would be difficult to accuse him of outright theft of the technology.

"Mrs. Regina Sawyer," the miller said, thrusting a paper in front of Michael. "She's the one who signed off on the license. These new windmills are expensive, but they have paid me back many times over. I suggest you get in touch with this Sawyer woman for a license."

Libby sank into a chair. Why would Jasper drag his wife into this? Her mind reeled, but Michael was thanking the miller for his help and preparing to leave. Libby felt like a sleepwalker as she nodded to the miller and followed Michael out the door.

✵

Michael's boots thudded on the wooden planking of the train station platform. They still had ten minutes before the arrival of the train that would take them back to Colden and the tangled mess of Libby's family.

Libby was shaken, Michael could tell that much by her silence on the walk back to the train station. Normally she was such a chatterbox, but she was as tight-lipped as a crocus that closed its petals at night and refused to open again until dawn. At least she let him hold her hand, but he knew she was riddled with anxiety. Her relationship with her sister-in-law was bound to take a turn for the worse, which meant Libby would have even less of a family to lean on. Where could she go if her father continued to banish her, and her brother and his wife were thieves? He wished he could wipe the anxiety from her face as quickly as he'd pulled her skirts from the gears.

Michael was used to doing battle. If the mission was to haul Mirela out of an insane asylum, he barged in and did it. If it was harvesting a hundred pounds of rose oil before the end of the season, he labored in the fields until the job was finished. But how did one give a woman confidence in herself? The people in Libby's family had always belittled her, and Michael had not helped matters when he suggested the house was his motive in offering marriage. Still, he would learn from his mistakes. Libby needed to know she was his treasure and he would do anything for her. For today, that meant helping her deal with the thorny mess of her family.

He needed more privacy than this bustling train station platform could provide. Michael guided Libby to the far side of the platform and down a flight of stairs leading to the ground, where a path curved around a vendor selling meat pies and descended toward the bay. A stand of old sycamore trees partially sheltered a bench from prying eyes.

He guided Libby to the bench, sat down, then tugged her forward to sit across his lap. "Michael!" she gasped.

"Hush. No one can see us." He liked the feel of her on his lap, but she swallowed and glanced about.

"It's unseemly," she said in a halfhearted protest. That didn't stop her from draping her arms around his shoulders.

He bounced his knee, bumping her into the air and settling her more comfortably onto his lap. "It is a bit, isn't it?" He set his hands on her hips and liked everything about the way she fit against his body. "Come," he urged. "Tell me why you are still upset."

She looked at him as if he were a simpleton. "I need to tell my father what Regina and Jasper have done, but I don't know how."

His brows rose in confusion. "What do you mean? You go to him and tell him what you saw in Plymouth." It was typical for a woman to make things more complicated than necessary, but he would help her put this in perspective.

"It isn't quite that clear-cut."

"Of course it is," he said. "I know you do not want to hurt your father's feelings, but what happened is a hurtful thing. You cannot soften it by thinking up fancy words. Speak to him in a straightforward manner."

She rolled her eyes. "You were not in the room the last time I spoke to him in a straightforward manner. I ended up in the middle of a rainstorm."

Michael did not hesitate. "Then I will be with you when you deliver this information. No man should be allowed to bully a woman because she comes with news he does not wish to hear. The only reason he has done so in the past is because he believed he could get away with it. That ends today." He grasped her chin, tilted her face toward him, and kissed her deeply. She was wearing no perfume today, but her skin carried a faint scent that reminded him of apples. It could be because they had been living in an apple orchard, but Michael knew it was simply the way her skin naturally smelled.

When he withdrew, he smiled at the attractive flush that darkened her cheeks and made her eyes sparkle. "If you had looked at me like that the first time I saw you," he murmured, "I would have flung you over my shoulder and carried you off to the nearest church. No man can have a woman look at him like that and not want to marry her."

Libby's smile lit her entire face, but he couldn't let himself get carried away. The coming drama with her family loomed over her head, and he would help her solve it. "It will be late before we get home tonight," he said. "What will your family be doing tomorrow?"

"I suppose my father will go to Jasper's house for Saturday luncheon. Regina always sets out quite a feast."

Michael nodded. "Then tomorrow we will call on them and discuss the matter with everyone there."

The chugging of an engine in the distance heralded the arrival of their train. Michael pulled her closer, savoring these last few moments. It felt good and right to have this woman in his arms. He breathed deeply, praying they would find a way to build a life together.

23

Libby twisted her hands in trepidation after knocking on Jasper's elegant front door. She clenched her teeth, now understanding how he could afford the splendid house. Perhaps Jasper would not reign quite so supreme in her father's eyes when the truth was revealed. Would it make her father love her any more? She had never been his favorite, but at least she had never stolen from him.

All Libby could think of was the confrontation about to occur, but leave it to Michael to become distracted by the way things smelled. Walking up the front path he had stopped first to smell the hydrangeas and then the elderberry bush. Framing the door were two urns filled with rosemary shrubs that held him utterly mesmerized. He leaned over and pinched off a leaf, held it to his nose, and inhaled deeply.

"There is a hint of pine mixed in with a soft, woody undertone. Very unusual."

"Please," she muttered, not exactly sure what she was praying for, but wishing Michael would drop that rosemary sprig before Regina saw it and accused him of thievery. She braced herself for a confrontation, but when the door opened, it was little Tillie, clutching a handful of dandelions and grinning with delight.

"Aunt Libby!" she said as she threw her arms around Libby's

skirts with all the strength in her little body. Was anything so won-derful as the wholehearted embrace of a child? Libby's eyes drifted closed, the sudden realization that a rift with Jasper and Regina could jeopardize her ability to see Tillie. She bent low to sweep the girl up into her arms, savoring Tillie's musical laughter at being raised high in the air.

"We were not sure if you would be joining us," Regina said, her voice cool as she glided into the front parlor. Libby stiffened at the sight. Regina was wearing a fabulous dress of canary yellow with a satin bodice and a low princess-cut neckline. She looked as fresh and innocent as a spring morning, but Libby knew it was an illusion. Regina's eyes widened in surprise as Michael stepped into the foyer behind her.

"And look," Regina said. "You have brought your . . . brought the Romanian. It is a pleasure to finally meet you, Mr. Dobrescu." Regina batted her lashes and gave Michael a coy little tap on his shoulder with her fan. "Gracious, it looks as though Libby has been keeping a little secret."

The irony of the phrase was too much for Libby to stomach. "I came to discuss some business with Father. Although you probably need to hear it, since it involves you as well."

"My goodness. I hope it doesn't have anything to do with that patent nonsense. You *know* Jasper was only acting in your father's best interest. Willard really ought to thank him."

Libby set Tillie down, then reached for Michael's hand. His firm squeeze gave her courage as she drew a deep breath and walked toward the back of the house. Jasper and her father were under the awning on the back patio, drinking lemonade and reading the newspaper.

"Look who has come to join us," Regina said with a tight bright-ness. "Libby has made a new friend. Willard, would you like to dine with Mr. Dobrescu, or shall I ask him to leave?"

Both her father and Jasper shot to their feet. "What is *he* doing here?" her father demanded.

266

Michael shifted uneasily on his feet. "Perhaps the child should go inside for a few minutes."

Libby was embarrassed she had not thought of protecting Tillie from the conflict that would likely break out. Regina snapped her fingers.

"Tillie, go practice on the piano for a few minutes. The grown-ups need to talk."

Tillie still clutched her handful of dandelions as she toddled toward the house. "Okay," she said in an obedient tone. Libby's heart turned over. If the family fractured as a result of this news, it was possible Regina would not allow her to keep seeing Tillie. Should she forget about the windmills? Try to go on as though she were not aware her father was being swindled by his own son?

But Father had a right to know. Her decision made, Libby took a deep breath and steeled herself. She kept her gaze riveted on Jasper as she spoke the words on trembling breath. "Michael and I went to Plymouth yesterday. We saw the windmills and I know they are built on Father's design. I spoke to Mr. Standish. He told us everything."

Jasper did not move a muscle. He kept staring at her with mild bewilderment in his face.

"We saw the papers," Libby said. "Mr. Standish even gave us instructions on how to get in touch with Regina to obtain the license. I know everything."

Jasper finally spoke. "I have no idea what you are talking about."

"I do," Regina said coolly from behind her.

All eyes swiveled to Regina, who strolled forward and lifted the pitcher of lemonade from the table. Without skipping a beat, she began filling the glasses with exquisite grace.

"I licensed the patents," she said without a hint of shame. "They were just gathering dust down there in Washington and it seemed a shame to let all of Willard's hard work go to waste." Her father stared at Regina in confusion, but Jasper looked stunned. His face lost all color and his chest crumpled inward as though he had lost the ability to draw a breath.

"Don't look so surprised," Regina said to Jasper. "You always said your father was sitting on a fortune if he would get over his perfectionism and bring those inventions to market. I just helped him along." She took a sip of lemonade and winced at the sour tang. Spooning a little more sugar into the glass, she continued speaking as she stirred. "It is not as though I *stole* the money," she said. "It is all staying within the family and I'm sure your father won't begrudge the money I have spent providing Tillie with a decent home."

Libby's pulse was racing, the heat pounding down and making her dizzy, but Regina remained serene. Only a person secure in the knowledge they did nothing wrong could appear so blissfully unruffled. Was it possible Regina had no trace of a conscience whatsoever? "When were you going to tell us," Libby demanded. "Would you ever have told Father? Or were you going to wait until you had enough money to buy another summer house?"

Regina's face went hard. "I think that's quite enough, Libby. I fully intended to share some of the proceeds when the time was right. That was how I was able to pay for those lawyers, and there is plenty more where that came from. It is *family* money," she insisted.

Jasper stood, stumbling a bit as he rose to his feet. "Father, I had no idea. I'll return the money."

But for the first time in his life, her father ignored Jasper as he braced both hands on the table to push himself to his feet. The trembling in his arms was so severe he knocked over the pitcher of lemonade, the crystal shattering on the tile below. One hand clutched his stomach, as though he was about to be ill. The other shook violently as he reached out for balance, stumbling away from Jasper and the rest of the family.

"Father, sit down," Jasper said. "You'll make yourself ill."

"Don't speak to me." His voice was as faint and raspy as a

withered autumn leaf. "Don't ever speak to me again." On shaking legs he shuffled toward the gate in the garden fence, looking like a blind man staggering about in the dark.

This is my fault, Libby thought. She wanted to knock Jasper off the pedestal her father had put him on, and she had succeeded. Never had she taken less satisfaction in being proven right than at this very moment. She lurched toward her father.

"Let me take you home," she said. To her surprise, her father let her take his arm and guide him through the gate. Michael followed behind. She hoped Michael's presence would not provoke an outburst from her father, but he seemed oblivious to everything going on around him, stumbling over a garden rake and heedless of the napkin he still clutched in his hand.

Father was lost in a daze as Michael drove the wagon home to Winslow Street. Libby was accustomed to seeing her father angry and hostile, but this lost, broken behavior was new. The prospect of exposing his inventions to the critical eyes of the world had always terrified her father. Libby was certain his anguish was not about the money Regina had siphoned away; it was the mortification of knowing his imperfect inventions were no longer something he could keep private.

When they arrived home, she helped her father step down from the wagon and walk up the slate pathway. She took the key from his hand to open the front door. Before entering the house, he looked her in the eye for the first time since Regina's revelation.

"Do you think Jasper knew what she was doing?" he asked in a pained whisper.

The look of shock on Jasper's face had been real. Regina had the cunning to orchestrate the scheme and cover her tracks, but how could Jasper have been ignorant of the money that was flowing in and out of Regina's hands? Jasper worked an exhausting schedule, so perhaps he truly was ignorant of Regina's activities.

"I don't think he knew," Libby said quietly. The relief in her father's eyes was palpable. Rarely did he give her opinion much credence, but this afternoon he seemed anxious to latch on to any piece of exonerating information. The trembling in his hands eased and he stood a little straighter.

"That girl was never good enough for Jasper," he said darkly. "My son would have never betrayed me unless *she* had driven him to it." He turned to step inside the house, then stiffened. "You may enter the house, but that man is not welcome here."

Libby glanced back at Michael, but his face was neutral, as though her father's words carried no more power than arrows glancing off a stone wall.

"It is all right if you wish to stay with your father," Michael said.

She hesitated, one foot inside the house, the other beside Michael on the porch. The words he spoke on the train came back to her. He said she would need to make a choice, and soon. Her focus flitted to the spreading branches of the beloved silver maple tree she had climbed as a child. Captured in watercolors as a young woman. Just last spring, she had helped Father prune it while he sang a rousing rendition of "Beautiful Dreamer." That had been a good day, one of the best. Staying with her father in this house was the *safe* choice.

"Libby?" her father asked. "Are you coming inside?" His expression reminded her of Tillie when she was on the verge of breaking into tears. How terribly weak he had grown over these last few months. He swallowed hard and twisted his hands, but managed a cautious smile. "Liberty-bell? It is time to come inside."

It was hard to listen to him plead. Her father was a lonely man, and she would always harbor an instinctive love for him. But in her heart a new loyalty was beginning to grow and take root. If her future lay with Michael, she could not stand idly by while her father shunned him.

"I am going for a short walk with Michael," she said quietly. The fleeting look of panic on her father's face was masked before she could even be sure it had been there. "I will return soon to check on you."

Her father straightened his vest. "No need," he said stiffly. "I am not an invalid." He closed the door quietly.

She wished he had slammed it. When her father was surly and mean it was easier to throw up her defenses. This broken, needy man was much more difficult to turn away from.

Libby seemed oblivious to the curious gawking of her neighbors, but Michael felt the stares drilling into his skin like a weevil boring through the flesh of a plant. He followed Libby across the street to a garden bench in Mr. Stockdale's front yard. She said old Mr. Stockdale welcomed visitors and she had no qualms about taking advantage of the bench. The last thing he wanted was to be parted from Libby, but he eyed the bench reluctantly. "You think it would be okay?" he asked. "I already have a reputation in this town for barging in where I am not wanted."

Libby patted the empty space beside her. "Let the neighbors see that we are friends. Perhaps it is the best way to ease their hostility. And my father will never become accustomed to the sight of us together if I keep meeting you behind his back."

Sitting directly across the street from her father's house, they were as blatant as two crows on a field of snow.

He sat, folded her slim hand inside his own, and gazed at the house across the street. For six weeks it had been his home, so vastly different from the rural estate he'd lived on in Romania, but a wonderful old house nevertheless. He surveyed the neatly trimmed boxwood hedges and the stately lines of the roof. It would have been a good solid home in which to raise a family.

And then he spotted it: the secret Uncle Constantine had hidden in plain sight. The secret Mirela was so certain had been beckoning to her all along.

Michael's jaw dropped open and his eyes grew round in disbelief. How could he have lived in that house all this time and
missed something so obvious? Every instinct in his body urged him
to vault across the street, barge through that silly wrought-iron
fence, and burst into the house to seize what Uncle Constantine
had saved for them.

The pieces of the puzzle were coming together. *"Only a man
of the Dobrescu family will know what to do with this house."* It
had seemed an odd sentence for his uncle to include in his will, but
now Michael knew it was not chauvinism—it was a hint! Uncle
Constantine had been following the tradition set forth by generations of Dobrescu men when he chose that hiding place.

He needed to play this carefully. "Libby, how many fireplaces
are in your house?" he asked in a shaking whisper.

"Three," she said. "The one in the parlor, the one in the kitchen,
and the one in the back bedroom. Why?"

Michael stared at the roof of the house, wondering if he should
tell her. Doing so would be reckless, but this was the woman with
whom he planned to build a life. If she was not trustworthy, it would
be best for him to find out now. He closed his eyes, considering his
decision one final time. His heart was racing and he knew he was
about to take the biggest gamble of his life. He would trust Libby
with the discovery he had just made.

"Then why are there four chimneys?" he asked, even though he
knew the answer.

Libby looked taken aback. "What do you mean? There are only
three."

"You only see three *chimneystacks,* but see how the one on the
west side of the house widens at the base? It was built that way
to accommodate two fireplaces on the ground floor. There must
be a fireplace in your father's library that has been covered over
with bookshelves."

For generations, the men of the Dobrescu family had secreted their valuables in a chimney for safekeeping in times of war. The ducal palace had nine chimneystacks. Invaders never thought to match the number of chimneys with the fireplaces inside a home. A fireplace that was boarded up and sealed over made an ideal place to hide valuables. In this case, his uncle had built bookshelves across the fireplace.

Michael knew he was on the scent of something big. He was not even born when Constantine Dobrescu set sail for America, so he had no idea what his uncle might have stashed in that chimney, but the old Cossack wanted it to be found. Whatever was hidden behind those bookshelves was of immense value to his uncle.

"The bookshelves were in the house when your family moved in, correct?"

Libby nodded. "Yes. I remember being intimidated by those massive shelves, but Father loved them. Why would your uncle cover up a fireplace?"

"Because he hid something of great value inside."

Her eyes grew wide. "What is it?" she asked eagerly.

"I have no idea."

If Libby's father won the house in court, Michael would never discover what was hidden in that chimney. Although the professor had scored a temporary victory in shifting the burden of proof to Michael to show he had never been properly served in Romania, Michael knew this victory would not last. His lawyer had already found a mountain of case law to contradict the Colden judge, and this was a ruling that would be overturned in a higher court.

The battle for the house could drag on for years. And Michael could not wait that long to discover what his uncle intended for them to find.

He stood and began pacing circles around the garden bench, thinking how best to handle this. No one knew why Constantine Dobrescu had immigrated to America. Some speculated it was a failed love affair, but most thought it was a dispute between

Constantine and Michael's father. The old duke told Michael this was not so, despite the fact that his younger brother had been bitter when he was required to become an officer in the army instead of joining the Church. Constantine had done his duty and was on good terms with his older brother. Why then, did he immigrate with no explanation? And what had he hidden up that chimney?

"I need to find my lawyer. There is something in that chimney, and I need to know what it is."

Libby cast him a doubtful expression. "I don't think my father is going to let you waltz into that house to rip out his bookshelves."

"No, but I think he might be willing to strike a bargain."

There was a pause while Libby digested the information. "Tell me you aren't thinking what I think you are . . ."

Could he do it? Could he offer the professor clear title to the house in exchange for whatever was stashed inside that chimney? It was quite possible there was nothing up there. Or merely some old military medals or photographs an eccentric old man thought valuable. But it could be something of tremendous value—jewels or gold or antiques that could be used to purchase a house for his family.

When he told Libby of his proposal, she was skeptical. "Why would my father agree to the deal if these fancy new lawyers are probably going to win the case anyway?"

"He might win before a Colden judge, but I am confident a higher court will be more impartial, and I *will* appeal a ruling that favors your father. If your father lets me remove my uncle's belongings, of which he was never aware in the first place, it is a no-lose situation for him."

"I expect my father will go on a treasure hunt the moment he hears of your proposal."

Michael rubbed his jaw as he considered the risk. "Possibly. I'll have my lawyer include a clause that my offer will expire within one hour of delivery. He won't have time to find anything. Whatever my uncle hid in that chimney belongs to the Dobrescu family. You know that, Libby."

"Yes, of course." She bit her lip while she mulled over the situation. "My father has always preferred safety over a gamble. If you make him this offer, I think he will probably accept."

Michael looked back at the house, cursing his blindness once again. If only he had noticed the missing fireplace when he still had possession of the house, he would already know what his uncle thought so important he needed to hide it from the world. Now there was only one way to be certain he would have access to that chimney.

And that was to strike a bargain with the professor.

Mirela was adamant. "I must know what is in that chimney," she said. "I have long sensed our uncle wanted us to come here, and the answer to what I have been searching for is in that chimney."

They had been discussing Michael's unconventional bargain for the contents of the boarded-up chimney for over an hour. He, his men, Mirela, and Libby were sitting on a blanket beneath the shade of a hundred-year-old oak tree in Jeremiah Auckland's backyard. How naturally Libby fit into their group. Not many women would be comfortable sitting on the ground like this, but with a cascade of pink skirts spread around her and the sun casting amber glints from her chestnut hair, she looked as lovely as a bloom from one of her paintings.

"I think it is insanity," Turk said. "You have a fighting chance for winning the house outright, and I've never known you to run away from a fight. There is *no proof* your family was ever served notice that the house was about to be sold."

Everything Turk said was true, but it would take a brave judge to make such an unpopular ruling, and lately it seemed Judge Frey had been favoring Libby's father. Michael was almost certain he would need to appeal the case to a higher court, which would cost more time and money.

"After all the appeals are said and done I will probably win, but how many years will it take to discover what Uncle Constantine thought so important?" Michael said. "I think we should strike a deal with the professor. The contents of the chimney in exchange for clear title to the house."

Turk was still skeptical. "Whatever is in that chimney has been there for at least twenty-seven years," he said. "It could be ruined by water. Eaten by rats."

"Or there could be nothing at all," Michael said grimly. But not knowing would torment him until the end of his days. He turned his troubled eyes to Mirela, the only one of their group who looked serene as she sat in the dappled sunlight, carelessly stroking the fur of that lazy cat resting in her lap. Could she truly be as calm as she appeared? He scrutinized her face, looking for the faintest sign of trepidation or anxiety, but her confidence was unshakable.

"Uncle Constantine wanted us to find the contents of that chimney," Mirela said. "The rest of that house is just bricks and tile and boards. I would trade it all for whatever is in that chimney."

Her words fueled his resolve. This gamble could be the biggest mistake of his life, but he had to take it. "Then it is decided. I will speak to my lawyer first thing on Monday morning."

24

I t amazed Libby how quickly the legal process moved when all parties were in agreement. On Sunday evening, Libby stopped by the house to tell her father to expect an offer from Michael on Monday morning regarding a compromise. She advised him to have his lawyers present and to be prepared to make a decision quickly. As anticipated, her father needled her incessantly to tell him what would be on the table.

"It's some sort of trick, isn't it?" he asked. "Why would he demand my answer with only an hour to make my decision? He has something up his sleeve."

Libby did her best to reassure him. "Father, you have the best lawyers in the entire country on your side. The offer will be so clear-cut even Tillie could understand it. I pray you will accept it, for I truly believe it is in your best interest."

Not *our* best interest. In all likelihood, Libby would never spend another night beneath the roof of the house. Her loyalty was with Michael, and her future would be with the Dobrescus. A smile tipped the corner of her mouth. If ever she doubted that she was wanted for herself rather than her house, Michael had killed those doubts with his willingness to embark on this deal.

But on Monday morning, the confidence that had been flowing through her veins evaporated. The study of the Winslow Street house was packed with lawyers, the Dobrescus, and friends her father had summoned to help him make his decision. The terms of the deal were stark in their simplicity. Professor Sawyer would allow the Dobrescus to dismantle a single wall in the house and remove the contents. If he did not agree, the professor would need to take his chances in court. Libby's gaze tracked to the bookshelf. She had lived here her entire life and never suspected that behind those shelves lay a decades-old mystery.

For the past hour Michael had looked tense and grim. His usual self-confidence was gone as he ceaselessly clenched and unclenched his fists, a nervous habit she had never witnessed in him before. His anxiety was contagious, and Libby found it difficult to even draw a full breath of air.

With one minute left in his allotted hour, her father consented to the deal. She was jostled to the side as men started dragging chairs around the desk, spreading the legal documents in tidy stacks. Michael's face darkened even further, and Libby feared she was about to witness the man she loved lose the only thing of value left to his name, all in exchange for a pipe dream.

A gentle hand rested on the small of her back. Of the fifteen people crowded into the room, Mirela was the only one who appeared calm. "It is going to be all right, Libby," she said in a low voice, as comforting as a warm ray of sunlight.

The papers were signed.

Michael rose to his feet and every eye in the room swiveled to him. "The wall we need to open is directly behind you," he said, gesturing to the bookshelves. A murmur of surprise ran through the crowd, and the professor grumbled about the burden of clearing the shelves, but the document he had just signed was unequivocal. Any wall Michael wished to dismantle could be done so immediately with witnesses from both parties.

For the next ten minutes, the squeak of nails being pulled from the shelves and the pounding of sledgehammers filled the room. After the shelves were down, Turk and Joseph wielded a pair of sledgehammers against the thick wall of plaster. Chalky dust swirled in the air, but all of the observers stayed close, watching as each chunk of plaster collapsed to the floor.

Michael shucked his jacket and joined his men, eager to release the tension pulling his muscles as tightly as the strings on a violin. Signing those papers had been the right thing to do, but it would not make his fate any easier should there be nothing but a pile of ashes inside that chimney. The boys would be fine. Children could adapt to anything, but what of Mirela and Libby? How could he ask a woman to marry him if he had nothing but the contents of a wagon to offer her? He swung the sledgehammer in a wide arc so hard a three-foot section of plaster shattered to the ground, revealing a row of dusty red bricks behind. A gasp from the crowd indicated surprise, but it was exactly what Michael had expected to see.

"It is an old fireplace," he said brusquely, picking up a crowbar to pry off the boards covering the opening of the fireplace. The acrid odor of old smoke tinged the air, and a murmur of anticipation hummed through the onlookers. He could see Libby's worried face from the corner of his eye, but he could not bear to look at her. He nodded to Andrei. "Fetch the lantern. It won't be long now."

Michael knocked away the flimsy boards covering the fireplace opening. In less than sixty seconds, the gaping black hole was wide open. Andrei pushed the lantern forward, and the assembled crowd gasped at what was revealed.

An assortment of small wooden chests filled the open space. Most were no larger than breadboxes stacked on top of each other. Michael's heart thudded, his breath coming fast and hard. Using the cuff of his shirt, he swiped the perspiration from his face and swallowed hard. Whatever was encased within those boxes would direct the course of his future. He knelt down, and with the care of a surgeon, removed the top box from where it had been hidden from the light of day for three decades.

The box was so light he feared it might be empty. A thick coating of dust covered the top, and he brushed it aside lest it contaminate whatever was inside. Kneeling in the clumps of dust and old plaster, he opened the lid.

It was filled with papers. Letters, mostly. With shaking fingers, Michael lifted the top envelope, noting the delicate, spindly handwriting that was certainly a woman's. The letter was addressed to his uncle Constantine there at the house on Winslow Street. A quick look at the rest of the cask revealed more of the same, all written by the same woman's hand. He opened the letter, noting the Romanian script, but too anxious to make sense of the tightly written lines.

Mirela knelt beside him, picking up one of the letters as her curious eyes scanned the text.

His heart thudded as he turned back to the fireplace. What if the boxes contained nothing more than old letters? He lifted the next box, this one almost as light as the first. He tried not to let disappointment show on his face when all that was revealed was scrolls of papers, tied with ribbons. There were a few old leather books at the bottom of the box. He slid the ribbon from one of the scrolls and spread out the fragile paper.

He stared at the writing, trying to make sense of it. It was written in no language he knew. Turk was kneeling in the rubble beside him, and Michael showed him the letter.

"Do you know this language?"

Turk spoke a smattering of southern European languages, and he stared hard at the text, but finally shook his head. "I can make no sense of this writing."

A crowd had gathered behind Turk to look at the document. One of Professor Sawyer's identical twin lawyers peered through a monocle at the scroll. "It is in Latin," he said.

280

"Do you know what it says?" Michael asked.

The delicate page was passed to the lawyer, who studied it closely. "My years studying Latin are ones I have tried to forget, but perhaps I can decipher a few words."

Michael was too impatient to wait and lifted out one of the dilapidated books at the bottom of the box. The fragile leather was like desiccated autumn leaves. His fingers were trembling as he opened the cover. This time the words were not entirely alien to him. He stared at the bold handwriting, some Romanian words catching his eye, but the spelling and syntax were strange. Mirela leaned over his shoulder, scrutinizing the text.

"It looks like some very old form of our language," she said, her trembling hands reaching out to take the fragile book from him.

The next box contained more of the ancient bound volumes, written in the same bold hand as the book he'd just examined. He pushed the box toward Mirela, who was engrossed in the volume. Mirela might find them fascinating, but Michael was growing increasingly anxious. Only two more boxes remained. He pulled one forward, noting the substantial weight of the box and praying it had something of value besides old books and letters. This box was by far the largest of the group, big and deep enough to hold a horse's saddle and still have room to spare.

Inside the chest was a stack of rough-hewn candlesticks that were almost three feet tall. Joseph picked one up and used the corner of his shirt to buff some of the tarnish away. After a bit of spit and polish, a trace of color emerged through the blackened surface.

"It looks like brass," Joseph said, and Michael tried not to let the disappointment show. He saw six candlesticks stacked inside, along with some plates and cups, all of them made of brass. In a cloth bag resting at the bottom of the chest was a crucifix. Like the candlesticks, it was made from cheap brass and stained with decades of tarnish. The roughly hewn brass crucifix had a simple beauty to it, arousing an instinctive sense of reverence in him. Michael set the crucifix down gently beside the candlesticks, ashamed of the crushing sense of disappointment that was making it hard to breathe. There was only one box remaining.

The final box was smaller and lighter than the previous one, though still as long as his arm. It was the only ornate box in the group, made of lacquered mahogany and inlaid with ivory. Michael sensed he was holding something of great value in his hands. If the sudden hush that fell over the onlookers was any judge, they sensed it as well. A little gold clasp held the box closed, but it easily gave way and Michael opened the lid.

The fabric inside was a splendid green satin embroidered with gold threads in an exquisite display of flowers and vines. His hands shook as he lifted it from the box. It weighed no more than a cloud. Suspecting the fabric protected something of great value, Michael rose and carried the parcel to the desk, where the light from the window could illuminate the treasure. The crowd parted before him as he carried the green satin bundle, then gathered in a circle around the desk as he prepared to unwrap the mystery inside.

He unfolded the layers of priceless satin to reveal another layer of fabric, but it was yards of stained, cheap linen that was disintegrating in places. He lifted the fragile linen aside, but there was nothing underneath.

His eyes widened. He turned the linen over, but still there was nothing. It was fashioned like a woman's dress, but its coarse texture and rudimentary cut indicated it was the dress of a peasant. He scanned the green satin and the linen, looking for something small and valuable that must have been wrapped in the old dress.

Had he just traded a magnificent house for some moldy old letters and cheap candlesticks? Waves of disappointment began crashing down on him when a ragged breath broke the silence, and he fixed his eyes on Mirela, who was staring at the cheap linen dress as though she were looking at a miracle.

282

"I understand," she said on a shaky breath. "I understand *every-thing.*"

Tears began spilling down her cheeks, but her face was lit with a blinding smile. One of the professor's twin lawyers handed her a handkerchief and she took it gratefully. As she wiped her cheeks, her skin seemed to glow from within and she began to laugh. When she finally caught her breath, she turned to Professor Sawyer.

"Sir, did you ever receive any communication from an old Romanian woman?" she asked. "I believe her name was Alma Codreanue, but she would have called herself Mother Alma."

All eyes turned on Professor Sawyer, who rubbed his jaw as he thought. "I've never received any letter from Romania, that is for sure. But come to think of it . . ." He closed his eyes in thought. "There was an old woman who came here once, looking for your uncle. That must have been about twenty years ago and he was long dead. Jasper had scarlet fever, so I didn't have any time for strange visitors. She barely spoke English and I couldn't make sense of what she was trying to say, but she seemed to think the old Cossack had left something for her. This place was a moldy, moth-eaten mess by the time I bought the house, so I took everything out and had it burned. I told her there was nothing here for her. That was the first and last time I ever set sight on anyone from Romania until you people showed up."

Mirela looked drained as she sank into a chair, but her eyes still held that curious glow and her voice radiated with confidence. "Michael, I know why our uncle came to America. And I *finally* understand why I was meant to come as well." She nodded to the stack of worthless casks strewn before the fireplace. "The letters say these are the relics of the Convent of Saint Katerina. This was the convent our uncle was so desperate to save after it was ruined by an earthquake, the convent he memorialized in the stained-glass windows upstairs. Uncle Constantine brought the relics here for safekeeping until the nuns could follow. The old books are the diaries of Saint Katerina, written in the twelfth century." Mirela's trembling hand covered her heart as she caught her breath, still ragged in her excitement. "No wonder Uncle Constantine was so anxious to protect these treasures. The diaries are written in Saint Katerina's own hand. I don't know why the sisters took so long to arrive and claim their treasures, but our uncle died before they could make it here."

Her face was still wet with tears, but Mirela was utterly magnificent in her joy. She rose to her feet with the strength of a crusading queen and met his gaze. "I believe I am meant to look for the sisters and bring them their treasures," she said. "If I have to travel a thousand miles, walk through storms of fire or ice . . . I will not stop searching this land until I find the holy sisters. And then I will live among them for as long as God wishes me to remain on this side of heaven."

The breath left Michael's body in a rush and Mirela's image blurred before his eyes. She had found her calling in life, and her suffering in Romania had served to lead her to this exact spot.

All along Michael had naïvely thought it was his determination to immigrate to America that had brought them to Colden. Now he knew this had been Mirela's journey, and he was merely guiding her to where she needed to be. He felt no shame as a fat tear rolled down his face in front of Libby and all his neighbors, for he had done precisely as God had intended for him to do, and never had he felt so honored. He had just gambled away the last bit of property he owned, and with the exception of a little bit of jasmine oil, he was penniless. But his way was clear to him. If Mirela needed him to guide her to the wilds of the Arctic or the distant shores of the Orient, he would fulfill this mission.

25

Libby felt like part of a wonderful adventure as she sat around the Aucklands' kitchen table with the documents from the chimney laid out before the group. Mr. Auckland had gone to prowl through the stacks of the library to see if he could learn the whereabouts of Mother Alma's convent. He said the library owned a hefty directory of religious orders that might help him locate the holy sisters. While they awaited his return, Libby and the Dobrescus gathered in the kitchen to look more carefully through the contents of the chimney. Luke and Andrei sat on the floor polishing decades of tarnish from the brass candlesticks. Libby sat curled beside Michael as they listened to Mirela read the letters and begin piecing the story together. Turk, Joseph, and Mrs. Auckland rounded out the group, fascinated by the story as they listened to Mirela.

"The sisters needed to await permission from the Holy Father before they could leave Romania," Mirela said. "After their original convent was destroyed in the earthquake, they moved to a carriage house at the base of the mountain until better lodgings could be found. The house was in a valley plagued by floods, and Uncle Constantine feared for the security of their relics, so he took them to America. Over and over in the letters, Mother Alma apologizes for taking so long, but first there were problems getting permission, then with accumulating enough money and finding sisters who were willing to make the journey."

In the dim recesses of Libby's mind, she remembered Mother Alma's visit to their house on Winslow Street, for it had been she who first answered the door. She was only seven or eight when the old lady came knocking, wearing peculiar clothing and speaking in an accent so thick it was hard to understand her. Libby had been alarmed by the strange woman and ran to fetch her father.

Now she felt terrible for the way she had fled from the old lady. Perhaps it was normal for a child to be afraid of anyone who was different, but she wondered what would have happened if her father had been a little more patient with Mother Alma's broken English.

"Do you really think the sisters are still here in America?" Libby asked. "Might they have returned to Romania?"

Mirela shook her head. "I feel in my heart that they are here. The letters written between Mother Alma and my uncle speak of their conviction that they should come to America. I do not believe they would have left after so many years of struggle to get here."

The thudding of footsteps on the front porch heralded the return of Mr. Auckland from the library. He nudged the door open with his shoulder, as his arms were weighed down with books. He was winded by the time he found an empty spot on the table to set the books down.

"They are in Kentucky!" he said breathlessly. "I found mention of them in a directory of religious orders. They founded the convent in 1859, and their numbers have been growing ever since."

"Where is Kentucky?" Mirela asked, but Libby was appalled. Compared to Massachusetts, Kentucky was a backwater. And so far away! But if Mirela was determined to settle there, she must hold her tongue.

"I think it is a fair distance from here," Libby hedged.

Mrs. Auckland went to fetch a map, while her husband paged through the books he'd brought back from the library. "They belong to an order that is committed to a life of poverty and service," he said. "The linen dress you found today was said to have belonged to their founder, Saint Katerina, who died in the twelfth century. She was from a wealthy and noble family, but she turned her back on that to devote her life to God."

Mrs. Auckland returned with an atlas to show the family where Kentucky was in relation to Massachusetts. Michael left Libby's side to study the map and pin down the location of the tiny village where the convent was located.

It was chilly without Michael's reassuring arm surrounding her. A twinge of anxiety took root in Libby's mind as Michael located the remote mountain pass. It looked terribly isolated to her.

"Well then," Michael said, "we have quite a journey ahead of us."

Her heart sank. Libby followed Michael's finger as it traced a path across Connecticut, through New York City, across New Jersey and then through Pennsylvania and West Virginia before finally reaching Kentucky. Michael would be leaving her, and she did not know if he would ever return.

"You will take me then?" Mirela asked, hope shining in her eyes.

Michael's smile was broad. "I have already brought you halfway around the world. What kind of man would abandon the adventure this close to the goal?"

This close! It looked to be more than a thousand miles between Colden and Kentucky. When Mirela flung her arms around Michael it was impossible to miss how he beamed with elation. All Libby felt was dread at the pending separation, but Michael was already gearing up for the next chapter of his grand quest.

"When can we leave?" Mirela asked.

Michael ruffled her hair. "Given that we are homeless and there is nothing to hold us here, we might as well begin immediately."

Libby blanched. There was nothing to hold Michael and his family in Colden any longer. Luke and Andrei were jumping with excitement at the prospect of a treasure hunt, Mirela was brimming

287

with euphoria, and Joseph was already gathering up their belongings. And Michael was not even looking at Libby as he grinned down at Mirela. There was no chance he would ever regain possession of the Winslow house, and now he was moving on to Kentucky without her.

An urgent pounding on the door interrupted the celebration. Before Mrs. Auckland could even make her way across the kitchen, the door burst open and Arthur Stockdale, Libby's elderly neighbor from across the street, came rushing into the house. Libby shot to her feet. Mr. Stockdale was out of breath and looking directly at her.

"Come quickly," he said. "Something is wrong with your father. He is outside swinging a sledgehammer against that chimney that was opened up this afternoon. He has gone insane and no one can talk any sense into him."

Libby's breath froze. This sounded like more than her father's random frustrations. Never, in all of her father's rages, had he ever resorted to any type of violence. She sprang to her feet and reached for her cloak.

"I will come with you," Michael said.

More than anything, she longed for the comfort of Michael's solid presence at her side, but she shook her head. "The sight of you will inflame him more." The weight of what lay before her came crashing down. Her father's brilliant mind had been deteriorating for some time. She had seen the signs, but it was easier to attribute it to his normal grouchiness worsening with age. Was it possible that the stress of the court case over the house, and now Jasper's betrayal, had finally broken her father's mind? All she knew for certain was that if her father caught sight of Michael, it was liable to make the situation worse.

Her limbs were heavy as she moved through the house, collecting her clothing and stuffing it into her satchel. She needed to hurry, but she dreaded what she would find when she returned home. Had it only been three days that she and the Dobrescus had been enjoying the generous hospitality of the Aucklands? It had been the happiest three days of her life. After being a part of this warm group of people, she had realized they added a richness to her life she had not known was lacking. She found it impossible to look at any of the Dobrescus as she moved through the house, gathering her paltry belongings.

Before she could leave, Michael stepped in front of her. "I will come see you tonight," he said. "Watch for me outside your window and meet me when you can. Your father need not know of my presence."

She bit her lip. If Michael was going to leave Colden, it would be easier to walk away now, where it would be impossible to break down and beg or cry in front of so many witnesses. She could not be certain she would be so stoic otherwise. She pushed toward the door, but Michael blocked her exit. "Promise me you will meet me tonight," he said with a low note of urgency. "I love you and can't let this come between us. Not now, when we are about to be separated."

So he would be leaving. Libby could not trust herself to speak. With the barest nod of her head, she turned and left.

The sun had slipped below the horizon and light was dwindling as Libby arrived back home. A group of neighbors stood in the yard, forming a semicircle a safe distance from the sledgehammer her father was swinging against the exterior of the fireplace. Libby winced when she saw his thin cotton shirt, completely soaked in perspiration as he struggled to heft the sledgehammer and slam it against the bricks of the chimney. His breath was punctuated with sobs, but his focus was riveted on the spot where he had managed to chip a hole in the side of the chimney.

The neighbors parted for her as she rushed forward. "Father, this is dangerous," she said as she got as close as she dared.

His breathing was so labored she feared he was on the verge of a heart attack. "Don't try to stop me," he said on a ragged breath. "This chimney is contaminated, and it needs to be destroyed."

"That is what he has been saying all evening," Mrs. Stockdale said. "There is no talking him out of it."

Libby looked at the wide base of the chimney. He was attacking it on the portion that housed the fireplace in the study. In her father's twisted reasoning, he probably believed the hidden contents of the chimney were yet another invasion of his home, polluting it beyond repair. He had never been reasonable about the Dobrescus, and she would not waste time trying to convince him that an empty chimney was no threat to the sanctity of his home. Logic was useless, but perhaps she could appeal to his engineering skills.

"Where is the demolition plan?" she asked calmly.

The sledgehammer landed with a thump on the lawn, her father leaning over and bracing himself on its wooden handle as he dragged air into his lungs. He turned a curious eye to look at her. "Plan?"

She glanced up at the tall column of bricks, stretching up along all three stories of the house. "You do have a demolition plan, don't you?"

He followed her gaze up the length of the chimneystack. He swiped a hand across his sweating brow, then swiveled his attention back to Libby. "No, I haven't done that yet."

She took a step forward and stood beside him as she looked critically at the width of the chimney base. "Unless you have a plan, the fireplace in the back bedroom will be damaged and unsafe."

Her father shook his head. "I don't care. This entire chimney is coming down, and I won't rest until it is finished."

"I agree with you," she said calmly, ignoring the mutterings of surprise from the assembled group. There would be no talking her father out of this, but if he brought the chimneystack down with his haphazard assault, it would be dangerous to anyone in the vicinity, and maybe even render the house unstable. "I think the task can be done much more efficiently if we put a demolition plan together. I will help you."

Her father wobbled on his feet, and she grabbed his arms. A handful of neighbors stepped closer to help, but their presence seemed to make him more agitated.

"Make all those people go away," her father whispered in a shattered voice.

He was sinking to the ground, the strength in his body leaving him. Libby guided him down onto the soft grass.

"Are you all right?" she asked. "Can you get enough air?"

Her father nodded, but she covered the center of his chest with the flat of her hand, assessing the rapid but steady beating of his heart. He brushed her hand away and sent her a weak smile in the fading light. "I'm fine, Libby. Your idea for a demolition plan is a good one, but I can't think while all those people are watching us."

Libby sent a glance of appeal to her neighbors. Concern mingled with pity on most of their faces, but a few of the older children were snickering. She took three large strides to Mr. Stockdale and spoke in a low voice. "Can you make everyone leave, but keep an eye on us from your front window? I will signal if I need help."

Mr. Stockdale nodded and began shepherding the neighbors away. She returned to sit beside her father in the grass. His muscles were trembling with exhaustion and he stared weakly at the patch of grass between his bent legs. She waited until the neighbors drifted away, all the while listening to her father's labored breathing. It took a few moments, but he finally managed to catch his breath. While his body may have returned to normalcy, his brain was still racing.

"We will begin working on a demolition plan tonight," he said. "You can sketch the layout of the house, and I'll make the plan. It is going to create a mess on the first floor."

She nodded cautiously. "All right."

"I should be ready to begin work demolishing the chimney by tomorrow. Wednesday at the latest."

"I will see about hiring someone to help us with the heavy labor."

"No," her father said. "I want to do the work myself. I *need* to do the work." He used the sleeve of his shirt to wipe the perspiration from his brow. No sooner had he dabbed his forehead than sweat started beading up again, but when he looked at Libby, his eyes were sane. They were burning with anguish, but the madness had vanished.

"I know I sound crazy," he said. "I have been driven nearly mad by anger and bitterness, but I will work through this, Libby. My home has been violated. The inventions I never wanted released have been sent into the world, where I had no say in how they were built or deployed. Every one of those designs has inadequacies, and those flaws are now laid bare to the world. I know Jasper and that woman think I was foolish to have withheld the patents, but it was my right to do so. My right to continue working on the designs until I was satisfied with them. They robbed me of that chance. And while everyone in this town thinks the treasures hidden in that chimney make for a thrilling bit of mystery, I feel like I have been sharing my house with the enemy for twenty-three years. I *know* how irrational that sounds, but I cannot stop the thoughts and I need to pull that chimney down. If I can do that, with my own sweat and labor, it will be like purifying my house."

As odd as her father's feelings sounded, the manner in which he expressed them was perfectly logical. "I am not stupid," he continued. "I see how you look at the Romanian and I know you have hopes to marry him. But before he ever steps foot back into my house, I am going to pull that chimney down and take control back. And then I will *invite* the man in. I will be able to accept Michael Dobrescu as a member of my family once I am back in control of my house." His eyes were lucid and his voice was calm. The tension drained from Libby's muscles and a glimmer of hope lit her mind.

Her father needed her help to get back on his feet. She struggled to pull him upright, and he seemed every one of his seventy years as he shuffled into the house on trembling legs. He was still shaky and upset, but she did not fear he would do any further harm to the house or himself. She nodded across the street, where she could see Mr. Stockdale silhouetted in his window. At her sign, he returned her nod, and she saw him and his wife retreat back into their home.

She was alone with her father. Everyone on the street had returned to their homes, where soft lights cast warm illumination behind their windows. Mothers were preparing supper while the laughter of children drifted from open windows. All of those women who had gathered in a semicircle around her father had gone home to husbands they could lean on, children they could nurture.

Her life was about to revert back to the way it had always been. She would help her father with his designs and pray his sanity remained. Perhaps her relationship with Regina would thaw enough so she would be allowed to play with Tillie on occasion, but if not, she had her surly cat, Ivan, for companionship. And other people's children she could enjoy watching grow and come of age.

But after spending the most enchanted summer of her life with the big, boisterous Dobrescu clan, she felt more solitary than ever. The trip to Kentucky would take at least a month, and maybe Michael would return for her, maybe he would not. If his sister was destined to live with the nuns, perhaps he would decide to stay.

Michael had come to Colden for a house, and now that he had no hope of ever attaining it, there was nothing left for Michael Dobrescu.

Michael felt the waves of insecurity radiating from Libby with every step they took in the moonless night. His brow lowered as he listened to her recount her father's breakdown.

"He thinks that getting rid of the chimney will heal his sense of violation," she said. "I don't know if it will or not, but he would have kept smashing away at the chimney until he killed himself if someone had not intervened."

Michael's heart sank. "There is no way you can come with us to Kentucky then?" He had studied the maps and knew that his journey would take longer than he'd originally assumed. There were no trains that cut through the remote mountain pass where the nuns lived. It would take weeks to walk over the rugged terrain on foot, leading a wagon weighed down with the chests of relics to be delivered to the holy sisters. Now that he understood how long it would take to travel to Kentucky, he feared leaving Libby for such a lengthy journey. But he was compelled to go. It was more than just a matter of returning some old books and a scrap of linen. Mirela was convinced the Lord had directed her path to America, and for some reason they did not yet fully understand, she was going to serve a very important purpose here and it was his responsibility to guide her passage.

But it felt wrong to leave Libby. She had already become entwined in the fabric of his family, and it was not right to leave her behind when she was riddled with despair. "If we were to get married immediately," he said, "would you consider coming with us?"

It seemed the perfect solution to Michael, but Libby appeared stunned by the suggestion. "I can't . . ." She glanced back at the house, then scanned the neighborhood. "I can't leave so abruptly. My father needs me." The panic faded from her face, to be replaced by an emotion Michael could not understand. Shame? Despair? Whatever it was, it caused Libby to twist her hands and pull away. She wandered over to stand beside an old silver maple tree, leaning against the trunk and turning away from him. She spoke so softly he could barely hear her words. "Michael, I don't think you want to marry me. I can't read, and our children may have the same affliction."

294

How desperately he wished he could show her just a tiny corner of his heart to prove what she meant to him, but his English was not good enough to express the bone-deep contentment he felt when he was with her. He moved to the opposite side of the tree trunk so he could see her face. She stared at the ground and he had to tilt her chin up in order to speak to her. "I will rejoice for any children you and I have together, and I don't care if they can read or not. The worth of a child is measured by their strength of character, not academic gifts."

Libby nodded, but her jaw was clenched. It would be criminal for him to leave her when she was this despondent. "It was not from want of effort that you never learned to read, and to belittle yourself over your inability is to somehow question God's creation. Libby, you are made precisely as God wished you to be." He folded her into his embrace, feeling her thin frame tremble in exhaustion.

"I can delay our departure for a few days if you are willing to come with us." Their bags were already packed and his sons had been prepared to begin the journey the next day. Mirela wanted to leave that very evening, but at least he was able to dissuade her from that. "It is not good for two people who have made a commitment to each other to be away from each other so long. I know this from the months and years I spent away from Marie. Already my soul longs to join itself with yours, but I fear this may never happen if I walk away from you at this point. Come with us to Kentucky. Please."

"I can't go with you," she said in an aching voice. He did not miss the way she turned her shoulders away from his and she looked around the familiar surroundings of the street.

"Can't go, or do not wish to go?" The distinction was suddenly very important to him. She glanced back at the house.

"I am afraid that if I leave, I might never come back," she said. "I've never imagined a life anywhere except Colden. Tillie is here. I have responsibilities to my father."

He glowered at the house. For years it had been something he dreamed of and fought to obtain, and now it was something that was standing between him and the woman he loved. "Libby, I cannot make you promises that I will be able to afford to live in this town. After this afternoon, I have almost nothing left to my name, and I must find a way to provide for my family. The only thing I know for certain is that I can never permit my children to live under the same roof as your father. If you wish to live with me, you must leave your father's house. When I return, I hope you will be able to make that decision."

When she tried to look away from him, he cupped her face in his hands. "I understand your loyalty to your father will not permit you to come with us now, but you will be in my heart with every mile of the journey. I studied the map and believe I can return in a month, perhaps a little less. It is hard to know how travel over the mountains will go. Were it possible, I would send you letters every day that would spell out exactly my feelings for you, but I don't think your father would welcome reading such letters to you."

Her voice was hesitant and he had to lean closer to hear. "You could send them to Mr. Auckland," she said, and his heart soared at the words. He could barely speak because his grin was so wide.

"You would welcome my letters then?"

She glanced up at him. He could not be certain because the light was so dim, but it looked as if her cheeks were suffused with the most stunning blush he had ever seen on a woman. "Yes," she said. "I would welcome your letters."

One month was not such a long time. Perhaps it would serve as a test to see if their love was fueled by something more than the excitement of a forbidden summer romance. "Then it is decided," he said. "I will leave tomorrow and send you letters when I can. And when I return, I hope you will be ready to make your decision."

Beneath the spreading branches of the silver maple tree, he kissed her, praying this would not be the last time he held Libby in his arms. Never had he known his soul could long for a woman so badly, a combination of joy and hurt that he wanted to feel for the rest of his life. If he thought it would work, he would toss her over his shoulder and carry her with him all the way to Kentucky. Instead, he breathed deeply of the scent of her skin, imprinting it on his memory to last him through the weeks ahead.

26

It took less than twenty-four hours for Willard Sawyer to outline a plan for dismantling the chimney, removing two fireplaces, and repairing the outside of the house. Although the work did not appear to be complicated, Libby did not believe a seventy-year-old man was capable of the amount of backbreaking labor it entailed.

She believed wrong. Within a week her father had managed to bring down the bulk of the chimney, climbing ladders and working crowbars into the mortar that fastened the bricks to the side of the house. Throughout every hour, Libby worked in tandem beside him. When she climbed on the roof, she wore clothing she borrowed from the Barclay boys down the street; after the debacle in the windmill, she was not willing to risk her life over entanglement with skirts.

As the days passed, her skepticism about her father's plan eased. After the initial surge of rage on the evening when he attacked the chimney, he approached the work as logically as any engineer. She helped him dismantle the joists, cart bricks, locate tools, and prepare boards to cover the scar left after the removal of the chimney. She sanded, painted, and hauled. Her father treated her with respect, asking her opinion on how best to blend the newly constructed boards with the old. When he needed supplies, she drove the wagon into town and purchased the necessary paint, plaster, and carpentry tools.

One week after the project had begun, she stopped by the library to ask Mr. Auckland if any letters from Michael had arrived.

"Not yet," he said. He reached out and gave her a reassuring pat. "Don't look so crestfallen. I am certain he will write. The morning they left for Kentucky, Michael stopped by the library and told me himself he planned to send you letters. Sounded very emphatic about it."

She stood a little straighter. "He did?"

"Oh yes. He had all sorts of questions about Kentucky too. He wanted to know the price of land, the type of agriculture best suited for the climate of Kentucky. That sort of thing."

The breath in her lungs froze. Why would Michael need to know such things? Wasn't he only going to drop off Mirela and then turn right around and come back to Massachusetts?

She clenched her teeth. Why would that big strapping man come back for the illiterate spinster with the unstable father? She forced her tone to remain calm. "And how is the price of land in Kentucky compared to Colden?"

Mr. Auckland laughed. "No comparison. They are practically giving land away in Kentucky." He went back to reshelving some books, while all Libby could do was stand in a daze. For a cash-poor man like Michael, the allure of cheap farmland would be more tempting than Aphrodite and her entire retinue of half-naked nymphs.

Mr. Auckland turned around and must have noticed the stricken expression on her face. "Don't worry," he said kindly. "That man is carrying a torch for you, and there is no need to fret about his return. He promised to write you letters, and I am confident he will."

Over Mr. Auckland's shoulder Libby saw Sally Gallagher, eaves-dropping with wide-eyed enthrallment. Fabulous. The news of her

300

jilting by a man who preferred farmland in Kentucky to the town spinster would be splashed across the newspapers by morning. Libby met the woman's gaze and forced her tone to be gracious. "Have you overheard everything you need, or are there any questions I can answer for you, Mrs. Gallagher?"

Mrs. Gallagher stuck her nose back into a book. "Just reading up on how to replace a *massacred* rose garden," she mumbled, her stony opinion of Michael as hard as ever.

Libby remembered her own outrage at Michael's destruction of her mother's roses. It seemed like years ago, but now that she understood Mirela's history, Michael's crude actions were a classic example of his forthright sense of protectiveness. She dipped her head so Mrs. Gallagher would not see her smile. Mama would approve of Michael Dobrescu. True, he had ruined her prized roses, but given a little time, Michael would create a garden with a profusion of jasmine, orchids, and wisteria. Michael would show the same fierce protectiveness toward Libby as he did the rest of his family, and her Mama would definitely approve.

Libby's spirits lifted when a flurry of letters from Michael began pouring into Colden. Although she was enjoying her strengthening relationship with her father, each day she was racked with nervous tension as she walked to Mr. Auckland's house to see if any mail had arrived for her. After the incident in which Mrs. Gallagher overheard her conversation in the library, Mr. Auckland suggested they would have more privacy if she called on him at his home. The arrival of the letters was sporadic and sometimes they arrived out of order, but she treasured each one. It was pathetic how her entire day could be colored by a note from Michael. On days she received a letter, she felt more beautiful than Venus de Milo, more skilled with a paintbrush than Rembrandt. Her heart soared and she wanted to scale mountains. On days there was no letter, she was only the frumpy spinster wearing a paint-stained smock who deserved the dead mouse her cat laid at her feet.

Mr. Auckland read Michael's letters to her, while she committed every word to memory. She took each of them home, not because she could make any sense of them, but she found it reassuring to watch the stack of letters grow taller with each passing week. She wished she could reply to his letters, but there was nowhere for her to send them.

Some of the letters included sketches of the plants and trees Michael found interesting. Her favorites were when Luke or Andrei sent along drawings. Neither was a talented artist, but she loved the rudimentary drawings of the wagon, the buildings in New York City, the Susquehanna River in Pennsylvania.

One day she arrived to see that Michael had sent her a small package. Libby's spirit soared. No man had ever given her a present before, and her heart thudded with excitement as she tore open the wrappings. Inside were wads of crumpled newspapers to provide padding for a much smaller box. She hoped he had not wasted his scarce resources to buy her anything of value, but what on earth could it be? Michael did not seem the type to buy jewelry, and it certainly could not be a book. Art supplies? Candy?

But when she lifted the lid of the smaller box and pulled away the cloth, a smile lit her face.

Perfume!

"What a lovely bottle," Mrs. Auckland said as Libby lifted it from the box. A note was included, but she was too anxious to open the bottle to worry about what it said. The moment she lifted the stopper, the air was filled with a delicate, fresh scent that energized her spirit. Libby knew nothing about perfume, but this scent was magnificent, an impossibly beautiful fragrance that wafted through the air and enveloped her in a sense of well-being.

Mr. Auckland opened the note, and she calmed herself enough to listen to the words:

Libby,

The perfume industry in New York is thriving. Forgive me, but we dallied a full week here while I explored the possibilities. I had to sell the jasmine essence. It will not last much longer, and since I had no chance to tap the red juniper trees, I was forced to sell it. It was a disappointment, but I was able to get a good price for it.

While in New York, I hunted for essential oils that reminded me of you, and have blended them into a perfume that is a reflection of your spirit. I know you have little knowledge of perfume, so I will explain the layers of fragrance that are in the bottle.

The major scent is from an evergreen essence, because this is a deep green fragrance that reminds me of the hours we spent walking through the woods. For top notes, I used the essence of apples and blackberries. You often smell of blackberries after you make jam, and I included the apple scent because your skin has a faint scent of fresh green apples. On hot days, the entire town of Colden carries the scent of cranberries on the wind, so I have added a bit of that oil as well. All of these scents remind me of you. And of course I added a drop of my night-blooming jasmine, because it is the most beautiful fragrance known to mankind and I could not resist. I have kept a small vial of this perfume because it reminds me of you and I enjoy smelling it.

Luke is jealous and wishes me to think up a perfume for him. I explained to him it is not manly to wear perfume, but still he is jealous and pesters me for some.

My memories from our summer together are like gold to me. My perfume is only a pale imitation of what I think of you, for you are God's creation, perfectly and beautifully made.

The pale amber liquid in the bottle was vibrating, and Libby realized it was because her hands were trembling as she cradled the most precious gift she had ever been given.

"Well!" Mrs. Auckland exclaimed. "If you had any doubts about Michael, I certainly hope the bottle you are holding in your hands drives a stake through them." She cast a glance at her husband. "You never made something like that for me."

Mr. Auckland rubbed his chin. "That man has definitely raised the bar for displays of affection. This makes the gold bracelet I gave you for our thirtieth anniversary look like a piece of string."

The Aucklands continued to trade good-natured barbs, but Libby was too enchanted with her gift to pay them any mind. Even more precious than Michael's gift were his words. *"God's creation."*

It would be arrogant to think of herself as such, but it was time to stop belittling herself for a failing she would never be able to change. She might never understand why God made it impossible for her to read, but surely there was a reason. Perhaps it had served to make her more sympathetic to the difficulties of others. Or maybe it was so that she would learn to develop her talent for art. Whatever the reason, she would always be grateful to Michael for helping her to understand and accept God's will.

27

Late August was cool in the mountains of Kentucky. As their wagon jostled over the badly rutted mountain passes, it was clear to Michael why the Romanian sisters would have been attracted to this area. The terrain and forests were astonishingly reminiscent of what they would have known in the Carpathian Mountains. Despite Mirela's meticulous scrutiny of Mother Alma's letters, she knew very little about the nuns. The letters were written almost thirty years ago by a woman living in Romania and in vastly different circumstances. What had become of her? How did they earn a living in this rural wilderness? And would Mirela truly be happy living out here after the rest of the family returned to New England? With each mile, Michael grew more concerned about the distance that would separate him from Mirela.

Aside from the one-week interlude in New York, travel by train had allowed them to make good time in their journey until they reached West Virginia. There were no train routes that took them into the rural mountain area where they needed to go, so Michael bought a cart and team of horses to continue onward toward Kentucky. His children were learning to sleep under the stars, which was certainly a good manly skill to have.

Mirela was joyful. Never did she complain about sleeping

outdoors or bathing in the frigid mountain streams or the rigors of their journey. To spare the horses, all of them walked alongside the wagon. He had feared her health would not be hearty enough for the daily strain, but Mirela was thriving, her skin taking on a healthy glow and her spirits high. Each day she studied the map and tried to figure out how much farther they were on their journey. Sometimes they went days without encountering a town or farm, so it was difficult to track their progress, but Michael believed they would reach the convent early that evening. The hunter they encountered two days ago told them to travel to the top of the ridge, approximately twenty miles, and then they would see the convent nestled in the valley below.

It was hard to tell precisely when they scaled the ridge, but it seemed they had been descending for at least a mile. The dense screen of the birch and maple trees prevented them from seeing more than a mile or so ahead, but the hunter had told them to expect a break in the trees and then they would have a clear view of the valley.

As the trees thinned, Mirela sensed they were getting closer. "I can't wait any longer. I need to run ahead . . . do you want to come?" she asked him.

They had left their home in Romania fourteen months ago. After heartache, sacrifice, and the physical rigors of the past month, Mirela was finally on the verge of discovering what she had been seeking all along. Not for all the gold in the world would he miss this moment. He passed the reins of the horse to Joseph.

"Let's go," he said. Mirela was off and running before he had even finished speaking. "Don't twist an ankle!" he called ahead to her.

Mirela cast a glance over her shoulder. "Don't be a fussy old woman!" she taunted, her laughter echoing across the mountainside as she scrambled down the gently sloping land. How many years had it been since he had heard Mirela laugh like that? Sunlight broke through the canopy of leaves, creating sunny patches where wild blueberries thrived. Mirela did not stop to look, she just kept scampering down the hillside. As they rounded a great outcropping of basalt rock, the valley spread out below them. Michael caught his breath and Mirela was speechless with wonder.

It looked like Eden. The immense sweep of the valley was dotted with farms and bisected with patches of forest. A lapis-blue lake glistened in the sunlight, and tucked beside a wide stream was a cluster of buildings surrounding a small chapel. The convent they had come so far to find lay before them.

"I am home," Mirela murmured.

Michael savored the moment, hoping that Mirela would find the answer to her prayers here. It looked like paradise, the land brimming with health and abundance. Large fields under cultivation surrounded the convent, and the buildings looked well constructed and maintained.

But when he looked closer at the fields, his eyes widened in disbelief and a wall of despair crashed into him. The strength left his legs and he sank onto his knees. It was not possible this could be happening, but when he refocused on the convent, his fears were confirmed. He swallowed hard, wondering what Mirela would do when she realized what lay ahead of them; surrounding the convent, in hundreds of acres of beautifully cultivated aisles, were rose fields.

The nuns supported themselves by growing roses.

"Should we wait for the others to catch up or can we run down now?" Mirela asked, her voice trembling with excitement. She shifted in a little dance and tweaked his ear.

Was there no end to the disappointments that Mirela must suffer? If it were possible, Michael would pick her up in his arms and carry her away, shelter her from the sight of what awaited her below. He wanted to wrap her in cotton and shield her from anything that would dim the sparkle in her eyes.

"What is the matter?" She cocked her head at an odd angle. "Michael? Why are you looking like you just swallowed a frog?"

There was no way he could protect her, no way he could divert the pain that was about to come hurtling straight toward her. "Look at the fields, Mirela. Look closely."

She paused at the gravity of his tone, then turned to look down at the convent. He could tell the moment she understood what she was looking at because the color left her face and the breath left her body. She swayed a bit as she stared down at the rose fields. He stepped to her side, bracing her.

"I see," she said in a shaking breath.

He put his arm around her shoulders, hugging her tightly to his side. "What do you want to do?" he asked. She said nothing, just stared down at those rose fields as her breaths came in shallow little rasps. Despite the heat of the afternoon, her hands felt clammy. Behind them came the lumbering creaks of the wagon as it wended its way down the bumpy path. Turk and the others would be there shortly, but still Mirela stared down at the fields, her face inscrutable.

"You don't need to decide now," he said. "We can camp out for a few days while you think about things."

Mirela's stare was fixated on the rose fields, but she gave an infinitesimal shake of her head. She shrugged out of his arms and took a few steps closer to the valley, her eyes taking on a glint of determination as she stared down at the fields. When she set her jaw like that, she reminded him of their father when he looked his most imperious. She took a deep breath and raised her chin a notch.

"I am a Dobrescu," Mirela said with resolve. "For hundreds of years we have grown the finest roses in Europe. It is in every drop of my blood. Now, I am meant to help the sisters grow the best roses in America."

He caught his breath. Mirela's voice was unflinching and full of confidence, but he was haunted by the sounds of her screams shattering the night. They were over a mile away from the convent and the scent of the roses did not reach them there. He would need to watch her carefully once they drew closer.

∽◈◡

Michael didn't believe her.

Skepticism radiated from him as they descended the hill and strode toward the rose fields, but Mirela refused to slow her pace or flinch from what lay before her. What had happened in Romania was her past. This convent, with its rough-hewn walls and simple chapel and miles of rose fields, was her future.

The ringing of a bell pealed across the valley and a handful of women laboring among the roses set aside their work and returned to the convent building. It was probably suppertime. *All to the good,* Mirela thought. *It will give me a chance to walk among the roses in privacy.* Turk and the others waited in the wagon at the top of the ridge while she headed straight for the rose fields.

Each breath of air was a little more foul as she drew closer to the fields. Combined with the heat, it made her dizzy and nauseous.

"Are you sure, Mirela?" Michael asked.

She did not even break her stride to glance his way. She clenched her teeth and forced herself to breathe through her nose and experience every bit of the odor. They had reached the rich soil of the bottomland and she trekked forward.

This wasn't going to be easy.

A hedge of yew shrubs served as a windbreak along the border of the rose fields. Mirela pushed through the dense shrubbery, ignoring the scratchy leaves scraping against her skin and snagging on her clothing. She pressed forward into the fields, Michael less than a yard behind. How badly she wanted to hide behind him, to flee back through that hedge of yew shrubs and up the hill, where Turk was waiting with the wagon. She wanted to run to someplace where the air didn't stink and she could hide from every dark memory.

She strode forward, focusing on the rich vermilion shade of the blooming roses. "This is the same strain of Gallica roses we grew at home," she said in a flat voice. The scent was foul and polluted her brain. It triggered the memory of other smells, of sweat and horses and filth, but her hand was gentle as she reached out to finger one of the velvety petals. This particular variety of Gallica rose emitted a particularly strong scent that was ideal for perfume.

"Uncle Constantine probably supplied Mother Alma with the rootstock," Michael said.

"He did. She thanked him for them in one of her letters," Mirela said, proud that she was able to keep her voice from trembling. She was doing well—perhaps even well enough to fool Michael.

If only the nuns had grown a different variety of roses it might have been easier for her to cope with these awful smells, but the stench was identical to that of the fields of Vlaska. Even the cushiony layer of yew needles they used for mulch was what they had used back home.

Could she possibly live here? Or was the scent she once loved about to destroy the brightest dream she had ever had?

Her hands curled into fists. It was intolerable that she would allow three terrible days to define the rest of her life.

Mirela closed her eyes, forcing herself to breathe deeply and endure the smell. She would push past the dark memories. If this dream was going to happen, it was necessary to do this. She reached further back to the memories of the sunlit days of her childhood, when she sat atop Papa's shoulders as he strode through the rose fields. From that lofty height she could see for miles. She always felt like a princess as she rode on her father's shoulders when he surveyed his fields.

Some of Mirela's earliest memories were of playing in the rose fields with Michael. He was a young man of sixteen when she was born, but he always had time for his baby sister. When they played hide-and-seek, she thought herself so clever by sliding into the empty wooden frames that were used to dry rose petals in the barn. Even empty, the frames carried the scent of roses. When Michael came into the barn searching for her, he always wondered aloud where his baby sister was hiding. It was impossible to stay concealed when he sounded so bewildered, and when Mirela burst free of the trays, Michael always pretended great surprise. How she loved it when he praised her cleverness.

Those wonderful memories were saturated with the scent of roses, and they would be her salvation. No longer would three terrible days decide her fate. She would choose to remember what it felt like to be a princess riding on her father's shoulders. Or playing with her adoring older brother. As she learned to work with these roses, she would emulate Michael's clinical approach to fragrance as he blended his perfume. She was a Dobrescu, and it was time to start acting like one.

A fierce smile lit her face. "Let's go," she said, and hiked her skirts to rush down the wide aisle. Michael was following, growling like a worried bear, but what else was new? She was surrounded by beauty and was going to learn to love it once again.

At the end of the aisle, a rutted path bisected the field. The roses were different on the other side of the path. She stopped and stared at the dusky pink blooms. "It looks like they have Provence roses in the neighboring fields," she said to Michael.

He drew alongside her, caution still shadowing his face. "They are also good roses for perfume," he said. "The petals are densely packed, so you can get a lot of oil from them."

She ambled across the path and leaned over one of the Provence specimens and inhaled. *Clinical . . . be clinical about the fragrance*, she warned herself. *Don't allow the panic to set in.* "It has a bit of honey in the scent." She leaned closer and breathed deeper. So many layers of fragrance here. "It has a clean scent. Very bright."

"Yes. It will make for a lighter perfume," Michael said. Normally, when he spoke of blending scents, Michael was full of excitement, but for now he was scrutinizing her as if he expected her to snap at any moment. His concern was understandable, but unnecessary.

She nodded. "I suppose it makes sense to be diversified," she said. "If a pest takes root in the Gallica roses, perhaps the Provence roses will survive."

He quirked a brow. "Now you are thinking like a good farmer."

There was cautious optimism in his tone. What a lion this man had been in defending her all this time, but she could not hide behind his strength forever. He needed to know she was ready to be set free. "That is the plan, Michael."

They walked through the lush blooms for over an hour. They discovered tea roses in a neighboring field, as well as a strain Mirela had never seen before. Michael said it was a Darius rose, a cultivar originally from China. As the sun sank lower in the sky, the weight of fragrance in the air seemed to get even stronger. With each new cultivar, she sampled the fragrance and tried to dissect the layers of fragrance. She would not allow panic to intrude into these thoughts. A woman destined to grow roses needed to be as clinical and discerning as Michael. She could be happy here. There would be days when darkness would still haunt the edges of her mind, but God had given her all the tools she needed to battle those dark memories.

The early evening sun sent shadows lengthening across the fields when she cast Michael a blinding smile. "I could not be certain until I walked among these fields, but now I know. The roses will be no problem for me, and I think it is time for me to introduce myself to the sisters."

Michael could scarcely believe it, but the woman known as Mother Alma was still alive. In her eighty-sixth year, she was ill and beginning to fail, but still firmly in charge of the convent.

Turk and the others were waiting outside the gates, as Michael was not certain of the protocol for men or children inside a convent, but the nun who ushered them to this spot seemed to have no quibble with his presence. The young redheaded nun introduced herself as Sister Madeleine. She took their names, asked them to wait in the sparse foyer, and went to inform Mother Alma of their presence. She warned them that the mother was often ailing and might not be able to see them for some time.

"It is so quiet here," Mirela said. Her voice echoed against the stone floor and unadorned wood walls. They sat on a plain oak bench in the nearly empty foyer of the main building. The only ornamentation was a table with an icon of the Virgin Mary, flanked on either side by small arrangements of freshly cut roses.

They heard Sister Madeleine's return before they could see her. A rapid clatter of footsteps echoed down the halls as she came running toward them. Sister Madeleine was out of breath when she burst into the room. "Mother Alma wishes to see you right away! When I told her a Dobrescu was here to see her, she began to cry. Come quickly!"

Mirela caught her breath and grabbed his hand. He was stunned at the iron strength in her slim hand as she tugged him down the arched hallway in pursuit of Sister Madeleine. They soon came to a rough-hewn door with a tiny cross embellishing the front. Sister Madeleine gave a little tap, then opened the door.

"Your visitors are here," she said.

The room was dim except for the fading sunlight streaming through an arched window. The room was sparse, with only a single cot and a table in the corner where the light from the window illuminated stacks of papers and open books. An ancient woman sat in a chair before the table, looking at the two of them with joy shining from her face. She started to rise from the chair, but when her gaze locked on Mirela, the strength drained from the old woman and she sank back down again.

Mirela rushed to kneel at the woman's feet. "Mother, I have

brought the treasures from the holy convent with me. My uncle kept them safe for you."

The old nun was trembling as she folded Mirela's hands within her own. "You have Dobrescu eyes," she said with a wobbly voice. "I have waited so long for this moment, but I always knew you would come someday."

Michael felt dizzy as he watched the scene playing out before him. Never had he seen Mirela look so radiant as when she knelt at the woman's feet. He could sense the energy flowing between the withered hands and the smooth, unblemished skin of his sister. It was almost as though the old woman was bestowing power on Mirela. Mother Alma murmured a prayer of thanksgiving, and then a traditional Romanian welcome.

The nun's eyes were watery with tears when she turned to look at him. "And who are you?"

Suddenly, the months of traveling in the wilderness weighed down on him. He was exhausted down to his very bones and it was hard to keep standing on his own two feet, but he had accomplished what he had set out to do. He swayed a little and had to reach out for support against the wall. "I am Michael Dobrescu, and this is my sister, Mirela. Constantine was our uncle. We have come a great distance to meet you."

Despite his fatigue, Michael was filled with a profound sense of well-being. The peace of God's presence surrounded them and he knew his task had been accomplished. The mission that began more than a year ago in a tiny Romanian village was finally fulfilled.

28

All Libby needed from the general store was a single gallon of paint to complete the repair of the demolished chimney. She wanted to get the paint and hurry home, hopefully avoiding the neighborhood gossip that swirled around her like a plague of locusts whenever she stepped out of the house. Yet the moment she set foot on Main Street she was surrounded by a flurry of covert looks and whispers. Did these people have nothing more fascinating to occupy themselves with than her nonexistent love life? Still, she had to admit that Michael Dobrescu had given them plenty of ammunition. It was not everyday the illegitimate son of a Romanian duke descended into town in such a spectacular fashion, courted the local spinster, and then disappeared just as dramatically.

The store owner, Mr. Robbins, leaned across the counter. "Is that the perfume the Romanian made for you?"

Heat flushed her face. Those three ounces of perfume had been more powerful than a barrel of nitroglycerine to keep the flames of gossip burning. Oddly, it did not bother her that everyone knew of Michael's unusual gift of custom-blended perfume. Every morning, when she opened the bottle and was surrounded by the dazzling fragrance, she could not suppress a helpless grin. "Yes, it is," she acknowledged.

Rachel Spencer, the prettiest of the young girls at the local school, slid a little closer. She pretended to be inspecting the horse bridles, but Libby heard the telltale sniffing and knew exactly what the girl was doing directly behind her back. Miss Spencer's mother was not so shy. She walked right up to Libby and leaned over her.

"Well, that's a rather nice scent, isn't it?" It was disconcerting when Michael Dobrescu used to follow her about sniffing her hair and her skin, but now complete strangers were doing so as well. She expected Michael's arrival any day, for which she felt a curious sense of anticipation mixed with dread. Would he still feel the same way about her? She could hardly voice her concerns to anyone, as the entire town seemed to be waiting with bated breath for the return of the curious Mr. Dobrescu. People had begun teasingly referring to her as "the duchess," which was ridiculous, because Michael would never be a duke, and they were not even officially engaged. It was all a bit premature.

Libby nodded to Mrs. Spencer. "Thank you, ma'am." She paid for the gallon of paint and waited for her change, tapping her toe impatiently as the little bell over the front door heralded another customer. She cringed when she spotted Roger Kraft, the prodigy who'd won first place in a math contest for the entire New England region. If she could collect her change and reach the door without making eye contact with the boy, she might be able to avoid another embarrassing encounter.

But it was not to be.

"Miss Sawyer, Miss Sawyer," a breathless Roger said as he blocked her exit. "Do you know where they are? Have you heard any news?"

When school opened last week, the teacher showed the students where Kentucky was on the map. He made a great game of charging the older students with graphing out a potential route for the Dobrescu clan, estimating the mileage and the rate of speed, and predicting where the travelers would be on any given day. He even declared that a barrel of cranberry candies was going to the winning team. In the classroom, they hung a map upon which each team moved their tacks to mark where they believed the Dobrescus were. One team estimated that the Dobrescus should have easily completed a roundtrip by now, but Roger insisted they had at least another few days of travel time. She took comfort in Roger's superior mathematical abilities and prayed he was correct in his assessment that Michael was not yet overdue.

"I'm sorry, Roger. It has been a while since I have had a letter, so I can't really tell you where they might be."

Mr. Auckland had warned her that Michael's letters would get very sporadic as he got farther west. There were no train tracks laid through the Appalachian territory he would be traveling over, and mail delivery would slow to a crawl. Still, it had been almost two weeks since she had heard anything, and it was worrisome.

Roger looked a bit deflated. "Oh. You'll tell me if you hear anything, won't you?"

"You'll be the first to know," she said wryly.

"Thanks!" He reached inside a glass jar for a string of licorice and put a penny on the counter. "Nice perfume, by the way," he said as he scampered out the door.

"We are in desperate need of help," Mother Alma said. "The roses are healthy, but we are overwhelmed during the harvest. Every year a third of our crop is wasted because we can't get the petals distilled fast enough."

They were sitting on the terrace of the convent's main building overlooking a panoramic view of the rose fields. Michael pondered the problem as he scanned the terrain. Rose petals should enter the distilling process within hours of being picked, and this required a carefully choreographed deployment of laborers. There was no room for error. In Romania, he operated the stills around the clock until the oil had been successfully extracted.

"Constantine taught me how to lay out the fields for the most efficient use of irrigation," Mother Alma said from her chair on the terrace. "He provided us with cultivars and recipes for fertilizer. The roses are flourishing, but I don't have enough hands to get the work done. The sisters have other responsibilities that prevent us from making full use of our labor. Last year there was an influenza outbreak during the harvest, and the sisters were busy tending to the sick. We lost more than half the crop. All Constantine could advise for orchestrating the harvest was to have double the normal workforce. In Romania I could do so, but I have never been able to accomplish it here."

In the previous days, Michael and Mirela learned of the long history between Uncle Constantine and Mother Alma. The elderly nun told them how, in 1835, an earthquake destroyed the buildings of her convent in Romania. The same disaster also ruined their distillation equipment that extracted the rose oil. For centuries, the nuns had supported themselves by selling rose oil, but Alma had no training in engineering, so when their equipment was destroyed, she was helpless to build a new system. Constantine Dobrescu heard of the nuns' dilemma and traveled to their remote convent in the Carpathian Mountains to help them rebuild their distillery. He brought rootstock from the famous Vlaska rose fields to ensure the sisters would have a diversified crop.

"Constantine was a great leader," Mother Alma said as she sat beside Michael on the terrace. "He taught me how to set goals and inspire others to follow. It is because of him I was able to make this convent thrive." She nodded to the rose fields, where Sister Madeleine was showing Mirela how the irrigation system worked. Mirela was wearing the simple frock all the sisters wore, and she wore a broad-brimmed straw hat on her head to shield her face from the sun. They had been there for three days, and Mirela had yet to display any anxiety around the roses.

"We have provided free education to hundreds of children,"

Mother Alma continued. "We tend the ill and try to inspire the people of this land to live a godly life. My only failure has been that I have not found a woman who has the natural aptitude to lead this convent after I die. I believe your sister has the qualities I have been searching for."

Michael stood and rested his arms on the railing as he looked at Mirela in the fields. It was true that Mirela was a born leader. She made decisions quickly and decisively. She valued tradition, but was not afraid of change. Never had he seen her so happy as she had been these past few days, but there were other factors to be considered.

"Mirela has an illness," he said. "I do not know how long she will live after you are gone."

Mother Alma nodded. "She told me of this. She told me everything that happened to her in Romania and what the doctor has advised her. I do not see any hindrance to her joining us. The course of Mirela's illness is in God's hands. If she is meant to lead the convent, I believe He will make it happen."

Looking at the bounty of the land before him, it was easy to believe that Mother Alma had been guided by divine providence when she established this convent. This order of holy sisters had been founded by a medieval woman who turned her back on her aristocratic life of privilege. Perhaps it was fitting that a similar woman would follow the same path seven hundred years later to carry on her mission in a new corner of the world. Saint Katerina, Mother Alma, Uncle Constantine . . . and now Mirela Dobrescu. Michael's heart felt like it was swelling inside his chest. How proud he was to have played even a small part in this heritage.

Mirela sensed him looking at her. With one hand bracing the straw hat, she lifted her other arm and sent him a sunny wave, faint traces of her laughter carried on the breeze. Could it be possible that his beautiful sister, who had been raised in a palace and danced with princes in Europe, was destined to live out her remaining years in this secluded convent? It had taken him over a month to get there. Depending on the course of her illness, he might never see her again after he left to return to New England.

And he needed to go back soon. He had promised Libby he would return for her, and already he had been gone longer than planned. Since they began crossing the mountains, only twice had he found a town where he could post a letter to her, and given the sporadic mail system, he could not even be certain those had reached her. He thought of her constantly. When he saw a wild flower, he thought of her. When he smelled wild blackberries in the wind, he remembered her kindness to his boys. He longed to hold her and share the joy of his journey with her.

But when he looked out at the rose fields, so intensely reminiscent of Romania, his soul longed for the familiarity of home. Mother Alma was practically begging him to stay and help her solve the problems with rose oil production. His boys had already made friends with the children of a cheese maker in the nearby town. Turk had informed him that he intended to stay in Kentucky and serve Mirela in whatever capacity she needed.

Most importantly, Enric was no longer a threat to Mirela. Safe behind convent walls, with Mother Alma to vouch for her, no American court would order Mirela back to a sanitarium in Romania.

And that meant Michael was finally free to sell his estate in Romania. The proceeds would be more than enough to buy equipment for making perfume. He could form an alliance with Mother Alma to turn her plain rose oil into magnificent perfume. This land was familiar to his boys, and they would thrive here with other children who did not find their rural ways so strange. If he stayed, he could help Mirela as she transitioned into this completely new way of life.

It would be so easy to stay in this bucolic paradise. Really, there was nothing to stop him.

29

"Modern ventilation!" Libby's father declared with pride. "Now that we have one less fireplace, we will need to design the house to take advantage of the heat from the kitchen." Her father proceeded to outline his plan for piping heat away from the kitchen and into the upstairs bedrooms during the frigid New England winters.

Libby sketched as he described his vision. "Will we do the labor ourselves again?" she asked. Strangely, she hoped he would want to. Never had the two of them gotten along so well as during their work tearing down the chimney and repairing the house.

"Of course!" her father said, and Libby breathed a sigh of relief. It would give her something to distract her from thoughts of Michael, whose letters had stopped coming and, even by the most generous accounting, was more than a month overdue. Getting a decent heating system installed into the house was enough of a challenge to keep her brain diverted. Besides, it was September and getting chilly at night.

Was Michael sleeping outside under the stars? Wouldn't that be terribly cold for the children? She ought to quit worrying about them. If there was one thing for which Michael Dobrescu could be counted on, it was that he would provide for his family. Perhaps that was where his dependability ended, but she need not fear that Luke or Andrei would be suffering in the cold.

Libby heard a knock on the door, and her heart surged. Her father moved to stand, but she beat him to it. "I'll get it," she said, proud of how she kept the excitement from her voice. It could be anyone, but they were not expecting visitors and it would be like Michael to show up with no warning. She tidied a strand of hair and adjusted the line of her vest. She wished she was wearing anything other than her "man's suit." Something a little more feminine, which was what Michael seemed to appreciate, but it would have to do.

She flung open the door to see Jasper. "Oh, it's you."

"Good afternoon, Libby," he said with remarkable grace, given her disappointed greeting. There was no sign of Regina, for Father was still likely to go into a rage when he saw his treacherous daughter-in-law. "I brought you a treat," Jasper said, just as Tillie jumped out from where she had been hiding behind a potted juniper bush.

"It's me!" Tillie said with her arms flung wide, offering herself up like a little morsel of ambrosia. Libby scooped up Tillie and hugged her tightly. "A treat indeed," Libby murmured.

Jasper looked mildly uncomfortable as he stepped into the foyer and adjusted his tie. "I brought more paperwork for Father to sign," he said quietly.

For several weeks, Jasper had been gathering together all the licenses Regina had sold and was making arrangements to redirect the revenue into Professor Sawyer's name. Regina had been clever in diverting the money into various accounts, so reconstructing exactly how much the Professor's inventions had earned was impossible. They would never recover the massive amount of money Regina had already spent on her lavish way of living, but Libby believed Jasper was genuine in his desire to correct the fraud.

More importantly, her father believed it as well.

Libby was ashamed at the sense of triumph she felt when Jasper was knocked from his pedestal in his father's esteem. Did she really believe Father would love her more if he was disappointed in Jasper? It certainly had not been the case, and she felt small and petty for handling it as roughly as she had. In any event, her father now believed that Jasper knew nothing of Regina's duplicity, and this allowed him to make peace with his son.

"Where is the cold Romanian?" Tillie asked.

Libby paused at the curious comment. "Who called him that?" Libby asked.

"Mommy. She said you wanted to marry him, but he got cold feet. He should put some shoes on."

Libby found it fascinating that such an innocent statement could bring such a grinding halt to a conversation. Libby turned her prettiest smile on Jasper, who had the decency to look embarrassed. "Just out of curiosity," she asked pleasantly, "are you ever tempted to set your wife's hair on fire?"

Jasper leaned down to kiss Tillie on the forehead to smother his laughter. "On occasion," he said as he picked up his leather case and headed to the study. Libby sat Tillie down in the parlor, where she could fashion the little girl's hair into French braids.

She wished her misery over Michael could have remained her own private torment, but it had become the season-long entertainment for the entire town. The story of medieval treasures hidden in the professor's chimney had dazzled the people of Colden, who were now eager to learn more about Michael Dobrescu and the mysterious Lady Mirela. Although they had once assumed Michael's attentions to Libby were a ploy to secure the house on Winslow Street, now they knew he was some sort of European aristocrat, and the entire population of Colden was curious to know if he would return for her as promised. It was mortifying, but people continued to call her the duchess. It was the end of September, but according to all the students in Mr. Carlyle's math class, the projected rate of speed should have had the Dobrescus back in town five weeks earlier. Roger Kraft's team had thoughtfully continued to move their tacks eastward on the classroom map. They now had Michael pegged a hundred miles into the Atlantic Ocean, somewhere south of Greenland.

She parted Tillie's hair in a straight line and began the age-old process of weaving the silky strands into a tidy braid. No matter how strong her pangs of loneliness, at least she would always have Tillie's unabashed love and devotion.

She tied a ribbon into the bottom of the first braid. "When we are finished here, how would you like to go out to the greenhouse and see the little jasmine babies?"

"Babies?" Tillie asked with delight.

"*Jasmine* babies," Libby said. "They are bright green and almost three inches tall. But these are very special jasmine plants. They have been designed to bloom at night and smell prettier than any other type of jasmine in the world." Michael had told her how many decades the old duke had worked to refine this unique cultivar, breeding and cross-pollinating the jasmine until this exquisite plant was produced. The jasmine seeds were the first thing Michael had planted after he renovated the greenhouse last summer. All summer long, Libby had been nurturing those seedlings, preparing fertilizer and adjusting the greenhouse panels to maintain a precise temperature. Over the past few months, she had carted hundreds of gallons of water to feed the thirsty seedlings. It had given her a sense of maternal satisfaction to take care of these tiny green shoots for Michael. Someday these plants would bloom and create more of the precious jasmine oil he prized so highly.

Libby's mouth thinned as she tied off Tillie's second braid. Michael might not return to Colden for her, but she was certain he would one day return for those jasmine plants.

And he would have to deal with her if he wanted them back.

30

The windmills were as magnificent as Libby remembered. As soon as their cart reached the edge of the miller's property, her father pulled the brake to let her and Tillie scramble down for a better view. Libby leaned over to ensure Tillie's cloak was properly fastened against the chilly October wind, then shaded her eyes as she looked up at her father in the driver's bench.

"Aren't you coming?" she asked softly. The whole point of bringing her father to see the windmills was to help him come to terms with the release of his technology. He was still roiling with resentment over Regina's betrayal, but Libby hoped this trip would help. If her father could learn to take pride in his accomplishments, rather than dwelling on their flaws, he would surely sleep easier at night. It was impossible to look at those powerful, majestic windmills and not stand in awe. Seeing them ought to help ease his feelings of betrayal, and if that happened, perhaps it would help mend the family rift.

Her father's face was a mass of conflicting emotions. There was pride, but it was mixed with uncertainty and anxiety. Sure enough, he was staring at the distinctive wind shaft in the center of the sail. It was his dissatisfaction with the design of that single piece of technology that had caused him to scrap the entire windmill project eight years ago. Libby knew he was castigating himself for the inadequacy of the wind shaft, frantically wishing there was something he could do to correct the tiny flaw only he could see.

"You go on ahead with Tillie," her father finally said.

Libby nodded and folded Tillie's small hand into her palm and walked toward the first windmill, whose grand sails were slowly turning in the stiff breeze. Her boots crunched on the oyster shell path as she savored the crisp air blowing from the estuary. The last time she had been there, she had walked hand-in-hand with Michael. It had been the first day he'd kissed her. For those thrilling few hours, Libby had felt like she had a companion as she walked side-by-side with a man she adored.

Michael was probably never going to come back. He was two months overdue, and his letters had stopped coming a month ago. At first she thought perhaps weather had caused a delay. Or a broken axle wheel or a washed-out bridge or maybe even inaccurate maps. But she needed to quit fooling herself. Michael was a strong and confident man who knew how to travel and how to contact her if he wanted to. Before he left Colden, Michael inquired about the price of farmland in Kentucky and Massachusetts. That really should have been her first clue about his intentions.

She had been a brief, glorious summer romance for Michael, but Libby could not hold that against him. For a few exhilarating months, she had been dazzled by a man who was every hero from a fairy tale, with a bighearted laugh that could shake the rafters. He was a man who could slay dragons as easily as he could wipe a runny nose or raise a fine crop of Gallica roses. Michael showed her what a family should be and what loyalty meant. Most importantly, he taught her that she was worthy of love, and that it was time to start demanding it from her father and maybe even from a suitor in the future.

Perhaps she was no match for fine Kentucky bottomland, but that didn't mean Libby intended to disappear into a life of miserable spinsterhood. Not anymore. Michael was gone, but she would build a brilliant life without him. She had Tillie and someday she might even have a family of her own. And as her gaze wandered over the splendid sight of the windmills, slowly creaking and turning in the breeze, Libby felt a surge of pride that not even her paintings had been able to provide.

A gust of wind lifted the flat-brimmed hat from Tillie's head and sent it sailing across the scrub grass. "Whoopsie!" Libby laughed as she hiked her skirts and chased after the straw hat. She was breathless by the time she caught it and brought it back to Tillie. She knelt down to fasten the satin ribbons beneath Tillie's chin.

"You see how strong the wind is?" she asked Tillie. "The wind makes those sails turn and moves the great big millstones inside the tower. That's how we get our flour and cornmeal. Wasn't Grandpa clever in how he designed these pretty windmills?"

Tillie craned her neck to look up at the windmill that towered over them, holding up her little arms to feel the stiff breeze. "It's like magic!" she said.

Libby gazed at the slowly turning sails, the tightly stretched fabric a stark white against the vivid blue sky. It *was* like magic. And she had played a part in helping make these windmills happen. Plenty of other artists had the skill to capture the design, but she was the one who had worked patiently alongside her difficult father, year after year, to translate his dreams into a format builders could see and implement. Long after she was dead and gone from this world, these windmills would still be there turning in the wind.

The sound of footsteps crunching on the oyster-shell path signaled her father's arrival. The expression on his face convinced her she had been right to bring him here. He was looking at the windmills with hesitant pride. "They are beautiful, Papa," she said softly.

"They are like castles!" Tillie said. Not that Tillie had ever seen a castle, but her enthusiasm coaxed a smile from the professor.

He swallowed hard and cleared his throat. "I suppose they look okay," he conceded. But his look of pleasure was unmistakable, and Libby was certain this day was the best gift she had ever given her father.

Libby got the picnic basket out of the wagon and spread a blanket on the scrub grass, far enough away from the windmills so they could admire their splendor as they turned in the wind. Tillie brought a few rocks she had found to anchor the corners of the blanket down. It was a simple meal, just some bread and cheese with a few pickled cherries and walnuts. The only delicacy was a honey cake she'd made with Tillie the day before. The secret was in beating the honey into the butter until it was as light as air. She and Tillie had taken turns until they were exhausted, but it was worth it to see the delight on Tillie's face as the mixture expanded under their labor. The little girl recounted each step of the cake-making process for the professor, who had the grace to appear suitably impressed.

"Aunt Libby can make anything," Tillie said as she laid a slice of cheese atop her bread. "Not like Mommy. When Mommy made blackberry jam, it was so bad Daddy said it tasted like cough medicine and we had to throw it away."

At the mention of blackberry jam, Libby's thoughts soared back to the summer, when she'd lavished the treat on the Dobrescu boys. With each jar she brought them, Michael had looked at her with gratitude shining in eyes that were bluer than the cloudless autumn sky.

Libby straightened and brushed away a strand of grass that had blown onto their blanket. Would there ever come a time when memories of Michael did not creep out of nowhere with a rush of bittersweet longing?

She turned her attention to Tillie. "The cranberry harvest will be in soon," she said. "Would you like to come over and we can make cranberry preserves? It is not all that different than making jam."

Tillie was enthusiastic, as Libby knew she would be. How fortunate she was to have this sweet girl in her life. Libby would do her best to count every blessing she had, rather than mourn the loss of something that would never be.

Autumn descended on Colden. The leaves turned vibrant shades of gold, scarlet, and orange. They dried, withered, and began to swirl away in the October wind. The fields surrounding Colden had been harvested of their cranberries, and throughout the town, Libby could smell the scent of simmering cranberry preserves. She finished the drawings for an improved heating system for the house and worked with her father to complete it before the New England winter. It had taken ten days to install, and now the only remaining task was to repair the roof, which had been opened to accommodate the new ventilation pipe.

Libby was proud of how perfectly she had measured, cut, and installed the flat sheets of copper flashing around her father's cleverly designed exhaust pipe, even though the installation meant she had spent the better part of two days climbing on the roof. Dressed in a sturdy pea coat and a pair of boy's trousers, she felt better about doing the installation herself rather than letting her seventy-year-old father handle the task. Ivan the Terrible generally scrambled up on the roof with her. There was no stopping the cat from clawing his way up the silver maple next to their house and springing onto the roof. It was pathetic how much she enjoyed his company. Every hour or so she took a break, nibbling from a basket of peanuts and staring up at the slow-moving clouds overhead as she lay on the roof.

The only task left was to repair the roof tiles. A dozen tiles were needed to cover the small area of exposed roofing. Each tile had a small hole drilled along the top rim, and nailing them into place would be an easy task. She was just about to begin nailing

329

the first tile into the roof deck when a commotion came from the far end of Winslow Street.

"He's coming, Libby. He's coming back!"

Libby looked down the street toward the noise, but a screen of orange and yellow maple leaves blocked her vision. Ivan froze, swiveled his head around, then scrambled down the nearest tree. The moment his paws touched the ground, he bolted like a shot down the street. That cat never liked anyone, with the possible exception of Luke Dobrescu.

Libby's breath caught, but she refused to get her hopes up. She had given up waiting for Michael's return and wasn't going to go chasing down the street like a foolish jilted woman. Mr. Carlyle's math class had given up on Michael's return and divided the cranberry candies among the entire class. "The candy will never survive if we have to wait into the next decade for the man to get here," he had joked.

Mr. Stockdale from across the street must have heard the commotion, because he came outside to see what was going on. He looked up at Libby and gestured down the street. "He's coming!" the old man said, then ambled down the street, but Libby still could not see past the screen of trees to be certain it was actually Michael.

Now she could hear the clopping of horse hooves and the rolling of wagon wheels. Could he really be coming back? She shouldn't let herself hope, but her heart was racing and it was hard to draw a full breath of air. Michael had told her he was coming back, so why had she been so foolish as to doubt him? He was the most loyal, honest man in the world.

If it was really Michael, should she climb down the ladder? Head down the street and greet him like everyone else seemed to be doing? That would make her look pathetic, ready to pounce on her man. She should not reward him for being a full two months late. She grabbed the hammer and a roof tile. Lining it flush against the neighboring tile, she placed the nail through the hole and began tapping it in. It was far better to continue going about her day as if nailing this piece of tile were the most fascinating task in the world. Like placing the final strokes of paint on the ceiling of the Sistine Chapel. The finishing touches of the Magna Carta.

The breeze carried snatches of voices and laughter. The group was too far away to decipher the words, but one voice stood out among the others. She would recognize Michael Dobrescu's booming laughter if she was blindfolded and at the bottom of the sea. If she wasn't on the top of the house, she would be jumping for joy. Instead, she carefully set the hammer down and angled her body so that she was sitting on the roof, arms resting across her bent knees as she waited for him. Couldn't he at least have written a letter to let her know he was coming back?

Pants. She would be wearing pants when Michael finally returned for her, but there was no help for it.

When the wagon finally cleared the trees and drew up in front of the house, it was swarmed by people from the neighborhood. Right away she saw him on the seat of the wagon, looking toward the house in anticipation. How could she have forgotten how magnificent he was? As always, he was in desperate need of a haircut and his clothes could use a good washing, *but those shoulders.* Ivan the Terrible was cradled in Luke's arms and Andrei was making eyes at one of the neighborhood girls. When she looked back at Michael, he was staring up at her with murder in his eyes.

"Get down from there!" he roared. He pulled the brake on the wagon and sprang to the ground, stalking across the yard like a barbarian on the march. Even from three stories up she could hear him muttering in Romanian, and whatever he was saying did not sound complimentary. He stood in the middle of the yard and yelled up at her.

"Why can't you be a normal woman and keep your feet on the ground? I have traveled nine hundred miles to get back to you, and look! Trousers!"

The man was two months late and he had the gall to criticize her wardrobe? For weeks she had been the laughingstock of the town, and now he had the audacity to criticize her in public. "The duchess" indeed.

"I suppose the women in Kentucky dress a lot nicer!" she shot back down to him. She was thrilled down to her toes to see him, but she was not going to let him ride roughshod over her.

"Yes, they do." He braced the ladder against the house and was getting ready to mount. She had to move quickly. He was only on the second rung when she nudged the top of the ladder with her foot to send it hurtling backward. Michael sprang harmlessly onto the grass as the ladder clattered to the ground. Catcalls of approval rose from the crowd. Libby noticed it was the women who cheered her, while the men were taking Michael's side. Mr. Stockdale was already helping Michael get the ladder back in place.

"Don't you dare come up here," she shouted. "Did those well-dressed women in Kentucky water your jasmine seedlings every day without fail, even when they were so mad they could spit?"

He planted his hands on his hips, his eyes narrowed as he glared up at her. "The women in Kentucky are too ladylike to spit."

"Well, I'm not!" She grabbed the basket of peanuts, took aim, and hurled them down on his arrogant head. Peanuts and cracked shells floated down harmlessly, but Sally Gallagher was thrilled. "Give it to him, Libby!"

Michael turned and gestured for Joseph, who pushed through the crowd, a three-hundred-pound force of nature. Both men carried the ladder to the house for a second attempt to storm the roof. With the ladder held solid at its base by Joseph's massive hands, she would have no prayer of pushing it over a second time. Not that she really wanted to, anyway. The ladder jostled as Michael mounted again. She slid higher back on the roof so she could be away from the blast of those eyes when he finally reached her. The angle of the roof made it impossible to see him, but she heard the pound of each footstep as he climbed higher and higher. Could this man do nothing quietly? Even his return to town had to be accompanied by throngs of onlookers who trailed after his wagon like he was the Pied Piper.

But he came back to me. Already she longed to indulge in his big, generous spirit.

His hands were the first thing she saw. Callused and blunt, they grasped the sides of the ladder as he raised himself the final few rungs. He was grinning by the time he cleared the base of the roof.

"Hello, Liberty Sawyer," he said casually.

She nodded in his direction, mimicking his nonchalant air. "Michael."

He was about to step onto the roof when he paused to sniff the air. The expression on his face was sheer masculine satisfaction. "You are wearing my perfume."

"Every day."

His grin deepened. "Good." For a big man, he was surprisingly graceful as he stepped onto the roof. With an agile twist he turned and sat beside her. "I have traveled nine hundred miles to see that smile again. It was worth every step."

Libby did her best to kill the smile. "Tell me about those beautifully dressed women in Kentucky," she said. After all, the man was two months late and she was entitled to an explanation.

"Well," he began cautiously, "there were attractive women all the way from here to Kentucky and back. But the women of Kentucky were especially beautiful."

"Were they," she said dryly. More than two dozen people were loitering near the wagon in the street, all of them staring straight up at them. They could see, but they could not hear.

"Oh yes. But none of them snort when they laugh the way you do."

Oddly, Libby knew he meant it as a compliment. "They don't?"

"No. And none of them know the difference between a red juniper and a silver maple."

"The dullards."

"Yes. This is why I had to travel all the way back to fetch you. I find I missed you more with each day."

Her heart warmed at the words, but her mind still wanted an explanation. "Does that explain the torrent of letters you flooded me with these last few weeks?"

He picked up her hand and kissed the back of it. Even from the rooftop, she could hear the murmur of approval from the crowd below. Michael shot the spectators an annoyed glance. "The townspeople don't bother me, but I can't do this in front of my boys." He stood up carefully and braced his hands on his hips. "Joseph!" he bellowed.

Joseph came lumbering forward. "Aye?"

"Take the boys to Mr. Auckland's house. The rest of you can stay if you want, but I plan on spending the rest of the afternoon up here with Libby, so you will get bored."

Joseph gave a little salute. Libby sent a broad wave down to Andrei and Luke. "Can I take the cat?" Luke's childish voice carried up to them, and Libby was pleased when Michael looked to her for permission. "Tell Luke not to feed him table scraps," she said. "He is getting fat."

Michael called down the instructions, then rejoined her as the wagon rolled away. "I hope you don't mind staying up here," he said. "I think we will have more privacy here than anywhere else. People began following our wagon the moment I reached Storybrook Lane."

How strangely natural this felt as he folded her hand within his own and they sat beneath the fragrant autumn leaves. "I had to stay much longer than I planned in Kentucky," he said. "The sisters needed help with their roses, and there is no one in the country who understands this cultivar as well as I." He explained the nonexistent mail service from that valley, and that by the time he had crossed the Appalachian Mountains, where mail delivery

334

was fast, he knew he would be able to reach her within a week or two. "I wanted to explain all this to you in person," he said. "I figured another couple of weeks without letters would not matter so much. Was I wrong?"

Libby carefully held her tongue. If ever she doubted there was a profound deficit in men's understanding of the female mind, she had just been disabused of that bit of foolishness. "A note or two to let me know you were alive might have been nice."

As Michael anticipated, after a while the onlookers eventually lost interest, as it appeared the fireworks were over and she and Michael were sitting like a boring old married couple perfectly content to hold hands on the top of a roof. Despite appearances, Libby was filled with exhilaration. Michael had come back for her and it was as if he had never left.

The afternoon grew cooler as he told her about his time in Kentucky, how he stayed to help the sisters improve their operations for harvesting and distilling rose petals. Mirela entered the novitiate process, learning the ways of the sisters in preparation for taking her vows. To her surprise, Turk insisted on remaining with Mirela. He found lodging with a nearby farming family, but promised he would help the sisters work the fields during the harvests.

Michael asked after her father, and Libby was pleased to report that they were getting along better than ever before. Her father had quit demanding perfection of her, and of himself as well. Now that his wonderful, albeit imperfect, inventions were performing useful work out in the world, he was beginning to take greater pride in his accomplishments. At times he was still surly and impatient, but she no longer feared he was slipping into dementia.

After they filled each other in on the last three months, they talked about nothing, and it was magnificent. Michael asked her if the leaves of their maple were always this brilliant shade of yellow in autumn, and she wanted to know if the boys behaved themselves on the journey. Throughout the afternoon, people kept checking on them. She saw draperies pulled aside as curious neighbors sneaked a peek, and sometimes people even strolled past their house, making a point to nod and wave up to them. Probably a third of the population of Colden came by to check out the peculiar sight, but Libby did not care.

The afternoon shadows lengthened, and Libby knew they could not linger up there forever. She drew a breath and asked the question that had been in the forefront of her mind all afternoon.

"What happens now?"

Michael's hand tightened around hers. "I would like to share my life with you," he said. "I would like to marry you and have children with you. I would like you to help teach my boys to become fine young men. I want to walk through the woods with you and fall asleep with you beside the light of a fire."

Libby's heart swelled with a surge of joy, but Michael's next words sobered her. "Libby, I would like us to move to Kentucky."

It was as she'd feared. When he spoke of the rose fields surrounding the convent, he was alive with an energy that was contagious. It was as though he had found the Holy Grail and could now rest in blessed peace. "I need to make arrangements for the sale of my estate in Romania," he continued. "Once I have that revenue, I will be able to afford the kind of land and house where I would be proud to raise a family. I would like you to be a part of that life, but if you find you cannot make this move, I will understand. I will remain in Colden if this is where you need to be."

Libby looked at the street where she'd lived for as long as she could remember. She knew the life story of every person in each house, the location of each loose cobblestone in the street. She could leave these things behind. Harder would be leaving her father, as problematic as their relationship was. Missing the weekly luncheons in Jasper and Regina's garden and saying good-bye to Mr. Auckland forever would hurt. She would miss these things, but they were all a normal part of growing up and becoming her own person. After the initial adjustment, she would be fine.

But leaving Tillie would break her heart.

From the moment that girl had been born, Tillie was like a daughter to her. That relationship had been the best thing in her world, and she did not want to imagine a life without Tillie in it.

Could she tell Michael that without sounding selfish? She traced the outline of his strong, callused thumb as she thought. In the space of two short months, she had bonded to Michael's children and looked forward to being a part of their lives, but nothing could ever replace the soul-deep bond she had with Tillie. If Michael stayed in Colden, she could have everything. Did she dare ask for it?

But if she was to marry Michael, she needed to stop thinking about what *she* wanted and do what was best for the entire family. Last summer she had slipped seamlessly into the Dobrescu clan and had savored every hour of it. She wanted more. She wanted to teach his children to paint and feed them blackberry jam until their skin was tinged indigo. She wanted to help Michael grow roses and learn how to make perfume. She wanted to listen to Michael's stories of Romania and watch him pour wine on the ground to toast Uncle Constantine. It was the Dobrescu family that mattered now. She was going to be a part of that family, and her love for Tillie was only one piece of what must be considered. Michael Dobrescu always made his decisions based on what was best for his family as a whole. Libby Dobrescu must do the same.

The thought of picking up and leaving Massachusetts was daunting. She lowered herself to lie down against the roof, feeling the sun-warmed roof tiles on her back as she stared up at the wisps of clouds in the late afternoon sky. "What do the boys think of Kentucky?" she asked.

"They loved it. It reminded them of home." Michael lay back as well, his hand still clutching hers as they lay side-by-side, staring up at the sky. "If we remain in Colden, they will learn to adjust." His voice was strong and confident as he said it. "Libby, no matter where we live, we will bloom and thrive. I find that I wish to be alongside you, but I do not know how strongly you are tied to this town."

Her answer was unequivocal. "My ties to you are stronger."

Michael's fingers tightened around hers. Kentucky made sense for them. She had never found a partner here, and the man she loved more than the sun, the moon, and the stars rolled together wanted to live in Kentucky. She would be proud to go with him.

There was a rustling of fabric as he turned on his side, resting his head in his crooked arm. How oddly intimate it felt to be lying beside him like this, but his eyes were gentle as he rested his hand across her stomach. It was so big it nearly covered her entire middle.

"I hope someday we have a daughter who has your kindness."

Yes, a daughter. A smile curved her lips as she tried to imagine how Michael would pamper and fuss over a little girl. Or would he roughhouse with a daughter as he did with his boys? It was hard to predict, but no matter what, she knew Michael would be an amazing father. And she knew she would gladly follow him to the ends of the earth, for God had blessed her with the priceless gift of a family. She would honor that gift by treating it with the reverence that it deserved, be it in Colden, or Kentucky, or on a desert island. She had found her family, and she, like a rare hybrid rose, would bloom wherever she happened to be.

Epilogue

THREE YEARS LATER

After weeks of travel, Professor Willard Sawyer's legs were shaky as he stepped down from the wagon to inspect the house the Romanian had built for his daughter. It was a fine farmhouse, no doubt about that, with a wide front porch that wrapped around the entire front and the east side as well.

"Are you sure this is the right place?" the driver he had hired to take him there asked.

"I'm sure." Who else but a crazy man would plant a hundred acres of roses? Willard had seen fields of corn interspersed among the rose fields, so at least Dobrescu was not a totally impractical man. But it wasn't roses or cornfields he came nine hundred miles to see. There was a new granddaughter to meet, and a promise he needed to fulfill. He had not been the world's best father to Libby, but at least he was a man of his word, and it was time to deliver on the promise he'd made to Michael Dobrescu three years ago. Glancing at the sprawling two-story farmhouse sitting amid a hundred acres of healthy cropland, it looked as if the man had done well by his daughter.

As he walked closer to the farmhouse, Willard noted the hammock strung between two mighty oak trees and a pink rocking horse on the front porch. If the carefully manicured patch of lawn with a series of wickets staked into the ground was any measure, it looked as if Libby was still indulging her love of croquet.

Still . . . what kind of man made perfume for a living? For the past three years, Willard had been receiving the letters his daughter had dictated to Michael, describing their partnership with the sisters at the convent to harvest and sell their rose oil to the New York perfume industry. Michael had already bought equipment to begin blending his own perfume, but needed his jasmine before he could begin the process.

The seedlings for Michael's rare strain of night-blooming jasmine could not be transported when Libby moved to Kentucky, so for the past three years Willard had been nurturing those plants. Through the hot dry summers and months of bitter cold, he had fertilized, pruned, and fussed over those plants. Following the instructions Michael had sent, he carefully raised the plants to maturity and tended the bean-like seedpods until they were ripe for cultivation.

Some men gave their children a home upon marriage. Some gave a piece of the family business or enough money to start a business of their own. In his pocket, Professor Sawyer carried the only gift his daughter and her husband desired. It was the last thing his crazy son-in-law needed before beginning to blend his own perfume in America.

A sack of rare night-blooming jasmine seeds.

Discussion Questions

1. Libby feels flawed because of her illiteracy, but learns to accept herself by the end of the book. Do you have a physical or psychological characteristic with which you struggle? Have you ever considered if there may be an upside to the problematic trait?

2. Early in the novel, Michael instructs his children not to run from a fight. Given the circumstances, was this the right thing to do? Would his advice have been different if he had daughters rather than sons?

3. The townspeople were sympathetic to Professor Sawyer's claim to the house and proceeded to shun Michael and his family. It was a peaceful, nonviolent way to support Professor Sawyer, but do you think there may have been a better way?

4. A big theme in this book is how to treat people who are different from us, be it a different culture, level of intelligence, gender, or even outward demeanor. Why do people tend to distrust those who are different?

5. Libby's father is a frustrated and difficult man, yet she feels an instinctive loyalty to him. Does there ever come a point

at which a Christian *should* disengage from a parent or a problematic relative?

6. Understanding his father's need for perfection, Jasper knew the professor would never file patents on any of his inventions. Jasper believed he was protecting his father when he secretly submitted the paperwork to patent the inventions. Was he right to do so?

7. For much of the novel, Libby felt limited by her illiteracy and Mirela felt defined by her brutal rape. Have you ever felt defined by a tragic life event? How were you able to overcome it?

8. Does Mirela have a happy ending or is she making the best of her circumstances? Girls are often raised to view marriage as the culmination of their ambitions, but can a celibate life be a truly fulfilling option?

9. Michael's first marriage was brokered between two sets of parents. Arranged marriages are still common in many parts of the world, and often work well. Why is that? Have you ever known anyone who was part of an arranged marriage?

Elizabeth Camden, author of *The Lady of Bolton Hill*, received a master's in history from the University of Virginia and a master's in library science from Indiana University. She is a research librarian by day and scribbles away on her next novel by night. Elizabeth lives with her husband in Florida.

More From Elizabeth Camden

◊ BETHANYHOUSE